FICTION   Mathews,
MAT

Menopause man.

DATE			

DISCARD

BY THE SAME AUTHOR:

LeRoi

SamSara

Menopause Man

MEL MATHEWS

FISHER KING PRESS

This is a work of fiction. Names, characters, places, and incidents either are the product of the author's imagination or are used fictitiously, and any resemblance to actual persons, living or dead, business establishments, events or locales is entirely coincidental.

Fisher King Press
P.O. Box 222321
Carmel, CA 93922
www.fisherkingpress.com
1-800-228-9316

Menopause Man

ISBN-13: 978-0-9776076-1-7
ISBN-10: 0-9776076-1-5
LCCN: 2005937567

Suffering isn't noble:
It's humanity's birthright.

Chapter 1

He punched the button of the electronic opener, watched the door rise and let the MG coast into the garage. Malcolm lived in a studio apartment below the home of his landlady, Mrs. Shams. She and her husband had purchased the house in nineteen sixty, thirty-nine years ago, the same year that Malcolm was born. Her husband had been dead for nineteen years, and she now inhabited the home alone.

Mrs. Shams was a feisty eighty-year-old weighing in at a whopping eighty-six pounds, but with the attitude of a heavyweight. Her hair was white and her eyes a crisp, clear blue. She went to yoga at least three times a week. When she talked, her head bounced around on her shoulders like one of those fake Chihuahua dogs that you occasionally spot in the rear window of an automobile.

A friend had told Malcolm that the studio was soon to become available, and he called immediately after receiving the tip. In Carmel, nice little studios like this one were hard to find even at seven hundred dollars a month; this one went for three-fifty. It was such a bargain, he figured there had to be a catch.

"What do you expect from me?" Malcolm asked, figuring that he might have to take out her trash or do some work around the yard.

"Well, we're not going to be chums or anything like that," she answered cautiously, and that was fine with him, because he hated yard work, and befriending a grumpy little old lady certainly wasn't anywhere to be found on his to-do list, not in this lifetime anyway. More than anything, or so it appeared, Mrs. Shams just wanted a token man around the place so she'd feel a little more secure at night.

The home had been built on a hillside that provided a panoramic view of the area. The studio was part of the lower foundational structure that supported Mrs. Shams's living quarters above. It had a separate entrance on the downhill side of the house. The small apartment was completely self-contained. Malcolm found out later that her son had lived in the lower apartment as a teenager and used the kitchen as his darkroom.

As time passed, Malcolm found out quite a few other things as well. Some of what he learned she volunteered; other things he learned from a quiet, distant observation. In the year and a half that he'd been living there, he had yet to witness a visit from her son. Actually Mrs. Shams had only mentioned him twice to Malcolm, and one of the times was when she asked him to fax her son a copy of his birth certificate because he had lost his passport.

"It's beautiful," Kate said, admiring the yard as she walked out of the garage onto the driveway.

"Wait 'til you get around to the other side," Malcolm answered, as he finished unloading the trunk and set the last bags on the ground behind the car. After everything was unloaded, he closed the trunk, grabbed a couple of bags, and started walking along the stepping-stone path. It led down and around to the opposite side of the house, into a gardened courtyard, the entryway to the studio. Kate hesitated, looking first at the car and then at Malcolm.

"Don't worry about that black bag. I'll come back after it in a bit," he said, pulling up the strap from the duffle that had slipped from his shoulder.

Kate picked up her overnight bag and purse and followed behind Malcolm.

"Careful of this loose stone," he said, teetering back and forth on it so she could witness its instability. A root had grown up under it, and the gardener hadn't found the time or the necessity to dig it out. It had been that way since he'd moved in.

"Thanks, I see what you mean," Kate answered, taking her turn on the concrete teeter-totter. "Wow, look at that!" she added, taking in the view of the mouth of Carmel Valley. She stared down at Carmel River Beach to her right and then swept left taking in the grassy green mountains that rose a thousand feet above the Highlands before she dropped her gaze. "What's down there?" she asked, pointing to the area where Highway 1 and Rio Road intersected.

"Crossroads."

"I mean the buildings."

"It's the Crossroads shopping area, and over there's the Barnyard," Malcolm answered, pointing to the left of the Crossroads. "It's all shops and restaurants," he added.

"And you live up here above it all."

Malcolm nodded with a cocky smile.

"I love it."

"I bet you do," Malcolm said grinning, reflecting on his good fortune. "Wait 'til I take you back there," he added, pointing east toward the valley.

"What's back there?"

"Carmel Valley."

"Where's Big Sur?"

"South of here about thirty miles."

"What's *it* like?"

"I'd tell you, but words don't do it justice," Malcolm answered, dropping his handful of bags on the brick patio just outside the apartment door. He pulled open the wood framed screen door and wedged the doormat under it to hold it open. He slid the key into the door lock, jiggled it as if whispering a secret password, and before taking another breath the door swung open, granting passage into the secret hide-away. Malcolm held the door and let Kate cross the threshold before him.

"How about a tour?" he joked, making light of the small apartment.

"Please," she cordially insisted while standing just inside the front door.

"Directly in front of you is the closet," Malcolm announced, standing right behind Kate and pointing to the west wall of the apartment. "The door to the right is my kitchen," he explained, ignoring the dresser on the north wall. A framed poem: *The Definitive Journey* by Juan Ramon Jimenez hung over a replica of a dresser that Malcolm had as a young boy.

She went towards the kitchen and stepped in. "You've got to be kidding."

"It's all I need," he smiled. It was simply a closet under the stairway that led up to Mrs. Shams's home. It had a sink to the left. Above the sink was a shelf that supported a microwave and a coffee pot. Below the sink, an old bookshelf was used for a few plates, and cooking utensils. There were also a couple of dusty canned goods that Malcolm had purchased at the grocery store a year earlier, remnants of a few other good intentions that had been discarded shortly after he had discovered Tillie Gort's and the Pink House in Pacific Grove, both restaurants that the locals frequented.

"Come on, let me show you the rest of my palace," Malcolm offered, walking around Kate and pulling her by the elbow from the kitchen. On the opposite side of the clothes closet was a desk.

"That's a great looking computer," she said, looking directly at a lime colored iMac as she stepped from the kitchen.

She ignored the painting that hung on the wall over the computer; the "Trickster" was Malcolm's favorite. It had the silhouette of a human-like coyote shadowed onto the sidewalk in front of a city café. Red and blue mountains rose up behind the city. The setting sun was reflected from an infinite string of golden stratiform clouds that appeared to have no beginning or end. The painting had something magical about it, like it wouldn't be difficult to fall into, getting lost in another world.

"It's an odd looking thing, huh," Malcolm answered, just to confirm her reaction to the iMac. "I've been thinking about getting a bigger place, one with a little more space and a real kitchen," he added, drawing out one of Kate's beautiful smiles. "This is the living room," he explained, pulling her three steps from where she was standing.

With the exception of a small casement in the bathroom, the east wall had the only window, but it looked down and out into the mouth of Carmel Valley. Beneath this picture window was an imported Italian black leather Natuzzi couch. The couch was fifteen years old; it was the first nice piece of furniture he had ever purchased. In spite of its history, the leather couch appeared to be in the same condition as the day it had been newly delivered.

Against the south wall were a queen-size bed and two small wooden bookshelves that held several classical novels, books on myth, and the works of several authors that had enticed Malcolm with archetypal symbolism and their analytical interpretations of the human condition, not that any of this literature had actually delivered him from evil.

Above the bed was a large, black-framed painting of Sydney Australia. It was done on brown paper that had been painted completely black. The artist had scratched off the black paint to reveal a light brown silhouette of the Sydney skyline including the famed Opera House. The painting was finished with highlights of bright colors emanating as reflections from the city's towering skyscrapers above and water from the bay below. Malcolm had purchased the painting in Sydney several years earlier. He was told that the artist was an imprisoned petty thief who was allowed to paint and sell his work for the benefit of charity. It was one hell of a claim to fame or a sleazy gimmick to sell some deadbeat's work.

The west wall had a door that led into the bathroom. To the left of the bathroom door was an original painting by one of Malcolm's good friends. It was of two dancing coyotes, one black and one white, opposing each other in a dance, face to face, both playing a flute or horn in front of the crimson sunset background that melted into a blue sea.

To the right of the bathroom door was a honey-finished pine armoire that contained a seldom-watched television and an abundantly played Sony carousel CD with an Aiwa stereo receiver. On top of the armoire were speakers and a glass picture frame with a photo of a naked old man riding a horse.

"Who's that on the horse?" Kate asked, gazing at the old man making sure that what she saw was real.

"My grandpa," Malcolm lied. The picture had actually come in the frame and he had failed to replace it with one of meaning. The naked old man had drawn so much attention over the years that Malcolm decided to leave him as a conversation piece.

"Your grandpa?"

"Yeah, he was a crazy old fart," he answered, continuing the innocent deception. "The bathroom's here," he said, pointing to the door to the left of the armoire.

"Excuse me," she said, and walked toward the restroom.

"Make yourself at home," he replied, as she pulled the towel that hung over the door top so that she could close it behind her. "I'll get the rest of our stuff," Malcolm volunteered, as the door closed.

The bathroom had a full size tub and a showerhead. Pale

green tile covered the floor as well as the bottom half of the walls. What wasn't tiled was painted the same color as the rest of the apartment, a creamy off-white. The sink and toilet were a pale yellow. A mirrored medicine cabinet that was beginning to rust from the inside out was mounted over the sink.

There was a screened, crank-type window on the south wall that was always left cracked open for ventilation. In the windowsill were a few boxes of stick matches that Malcolm collected from the local restaurants to use as an air freshener or to light a candle in the event of losing electricity in a winter storm. A bottle of Windex glass cleaner and Tilex mildew remover hung on a rail between the sink and toilet.

Malcolm heard the toilet flush from the bathroom window as he teetered on the loose stepping-stone on his way back down to the studio. The bath water was running. He threw the bags down on the floor, lay down on the bed and closed his eyes. A few minutes later, the bathroom door creaked open a couple of inches.

"I need a towel," she said in a soft tone.

"They're on the wooden stand in the corner."

"How about some soap?"

"Below the towels."

"I think I need your help," Kate said, having slipped an arm through the cracked door, beckoning Malcolm with her index finger rolling open and closed.

He hopped up like an expectant puppy dog being awakened from a nap by his master's voice promising some cuddling attention. Her long brown hair hung down over her breasts, the ends dangled over her nipples. Two clean towels had already been folded over the edge of the sink. A half bar of soap was in the tub's dish. He looked into her blue-green eyes, followed her hair down to her breasts, dropped his gaze further down to her bush, and finished the downward trend admiring her thighs, calves, feet, and toes. There was nothing on her petite, yet solid, young body that he didn't want to gobble up.

Eighty pounds heavier, he leaned in to kiss her and she supported him effortlessly. Their love affair was still new and she was always ready to receive him. Kate never needed to be warmed up; their coming together lacked any awkwardness.

When Malcolm kissed her, she was all there, completely present. It was like the whole world stopped and all of its energy flowed back and forth between the couple.

Kate pulled the sweaty blue T-shirt over Malcolm's head and arms, and when his head popped out, he leaned forward trying to mouth one of her nipples. She pulled away and dropped down to help him out of his jeans and boxers. She stood up, reached for his hand, turned, and started to step into the bath. He reached around her, grabbed her breast and pulled her back. Teasingly she pressed her ass cheeks up into his groin, and he tried to slide into her from behind, but she quickly evaded him and stepped into the bathtub. She turned to face him with her melting smile. Like a loyal pup, he followed her into the tub of warm water.

Chapter 2

It had been a week since Kate last phoned. Her father had died, an unexpected heart attack. He was in his early fifties and had no history of heart trouble. She'd flown back east for the service. Malcolm had offered to accompany Kate but their relationship was too new. She felt it was better for her to go alone so that she could give full attention to herself and her family. It made perfectly good sense; he wouldn't know anyone there and his being fifteen years older than Kate might have only added to the family's grief. Bringing an older man home to mom at a time like this would have been more than just a little inappropriate, especially considering the unstable history of Kate and her father's relationship.

Against her father's wishes, Kate had moved away to school. His overprotection and her rebellion had proven a bad combination. The two probably wouldn't even have been on speaking terms if her mother hadn't been acting as a mediator. Anyway, Kate's rebellion had brought her to California, and Malcolm was damn happy about it in spite of her father's indignation.

Malcolm first met Kate while she was working at a coffee house that also served soup, sandwiches, and salads. The place looked more like a bar than a coffee house. It was where Malcolm would meet his buddies Lewis and Devin for a late afternoon bullshit session over an iced tea. Lewis's wife had nicknamed them the TWA's - short for Time Wasting Assholes. They were still trying to figure out the reason for this tag.

Kate worked afternoons at the local watering hole and had to tolerate the TWA's. Her then-current boyfriend would occasionally stop by to visit. Malcolm called him Pretty Boy: a blonde, blue-eyed twenty-three-year-old punk who believed his destiny was to be a movie star. She never appeared to care all that much for the guy. It seemed that something other than love and admiration kept the two together. At first, Malcolm thought it was jealousy on his part. He thought he had dreamed up the story about Kate and Pretty Boy just to believe he stood a real shot at her, but his initial take of the situation eventually proved to be right.

It had taken Malcolm a while to trust his instincts, but it took him even longer to learn patience, not to over-react, and to let fate run its course and be realized instead of becoming just another dashed dream. Fortunately, the wait-and-see method had worked with Kate. Had he pursued her like his body and senses demanded, she'd have probably ended up married to that little blue-eyed queer.

It was odd how he eventually reconnected with Kate. It was late January, over a year since Malcolm had moved to the coast. All the women with whom he'd been involved back in the Central Valley had moved on. Malcolm had walked to the Pine Inn in downtown Carmel for his morning coffee. It was the AT&T classic and he was pissed about the crowds. Actually, he was pissed off about everything.

He'd been up reading and watching television the night before until three in the morning. He was restless about what to do with his life, uncertain of how he could support a woman and at the same time honor his call to freedom. He didn't know exactly what he wanted at this stage of his life, and... well, he was afraid of becoming a failure, afraid that he wouldn't find his next calling, and afraid of spending all the savings he'd acquired over the years.

He thought of how much easier it would have been just to go back to tractors. The problem was he'd be selling his soul in this return. Then again, maybe he really didn't have a choice. Perhaps his soul was really running the show, and had been all along. All the stuff in the outside world, the call to conventional duty, was just a distraction. Anyway, that's what was going on in Malcolm's mind.

On his way back to the studio from coffee, he decided to sell his airplane. He'd considered selling off this piece of himself in the past, but it had only been a fleeting thought. Walking back to the studio that morning, he finally resolved to let go of this particular attachment, too. He'd left that old dream a year earlier but had held on to N1MC like Kate's father had clung to her.

He was actually selling the airplane for three reasons. It no longer served him economically, and the proceeds from the sale would earn enough interest to more than pay the rent. He was also finished with the identity that went along with owning and flying the Beechcraft, but the most profound reason for selling the airplane was that he'd become frightened of it, afraid beyond a healthy respect.

Bonanza's had years ago been nicknamed Forked-Tailed-Doctor-Killers because they were fast slippery airplanes that took low-time pilots, like inexperienced doctors who could afford the airplanes, to an early and untimely death. He was also aware of how many men in the midst of a mid-life crisis cracked up airplanes or killed themselves in some other stylish fashion. They weren't intentional suicides, but the men couldn't grow up internally. For some reason, they were unable to make the transition into adulthood and eventually their short-looped psyches got the best of them. Consciously, their deaths appeared to be an accident; unconsciously it was suicide.

Two weeks later, he pre-flighted N1MC, pulled her out of the hangar, and departed from the Carmel Valley airport on runway three-zero with full power. After gaining altitude, he turned crosswind and then downwind before adjusting the propeller and manifold pressure to twenty-three inches square and then proceeded to call Monterey approach to pick up flight following.

"Monterey approach, this is Bonanza One Mike Charlie."

"November One Mike Charlie, remain clear of class C airspace until advised."

Malcolm was at twelve hundred feet and at fifteen hundred feet he'd enter class C airspace. He leveled the plane at fourteen hundred and flew a couple of three-sixties hoping to gain clearance to transit the protected airspace, but after making two more unsuccessful attempts at contacting air traffic control, he gave up on the buzzards.

It was a clear day, so he flew east through the valley at fourteen hundred feet until out of protected airspace and then climbed to seventy-five hundred and leveled off. After leaning the fuel to air mixture, he switched on the autopilot, set the heading bug to zero-one-eight, and let the Bonanza guide his final flight home.

The man who took care of N1MC was based in the Central Valley. Malcolm had decided to have Ryder look after the plane. Ryder had one of the most reputable Beechcraft shops in the Western U.S. and often received calls from people looking for a well-kept Bonanza. It would also be handy for any routine maintenance that the plane might need before it sold.

After making one of the smoothest landings in his flying career, Malcolm taxied up to the gas pump to top off the airplane. He leaned out the mixture to shut down the engine, turned the key off, pulled it from the ignition switch and then climbed out of N1MC to chock and ground the aircraft before refueling. While topping off the fuel tanks, Ryder walked up and told Malcolm to leave the plane where she was and that he'd put her in a hangar before the day's end.

When Malcolm retrieved his bag and cellular phone from the Bonanza, he discovered a voice message his mother had left. He returned her call.

"I'm alive," he announced when she answered the phone.

"Why don't you hire someone to fly you home if you're nervous?" his mother suggested, knowing that he had been anxious about his final voyage.

"I'm already here," he announced. Fear or no fear, he wouldn't have let someone else pilot him home; that would have been a defeat.

"Where are you?"

"Airport."

"So then you haven't heard?"

"Heard what?"

"A plane just went down," she said in a sad, yet relieved tone. "Three people died and a fourth is in the burn unit."

"No, it wasn't me," he said in a choked up voice as a few tears came. He had no power to create what had happened, but the timing of the plane crash was enough to validate the decision he'd made to end his flying career. He'd had a lot of fun in N1MC, had flown places and done things most people only dream of doing in a lifetime, but now it was over.

Lewis drove up a few minutes later. After locking the Bonanza's doors, they headed for lunch.

"Hey, whatever happened to Kate?" Lewis asked, after they'd

been on the road for about ten minutes.

"I don't know. I called her several months ago, but she never called me back," Malcolm answered. "I've got her number programmed into my cellular phone. I'll call her right now," he announced and keyed up her number. Her voice mail answered. "Kate, this is Malcolm. I called you a few months back, but you never called me back. Call me. I really want to know what's been happening with you," he said in a direct authoritative tone. "Well, we'll see if that works," he said, laying the cellular phone down on the seat.

"Man, I sure hope you can tap into some of that shit," Lewis encouraged. Lewis was married with two children. He was always hoping that Malcolm could tap into some of whatever he couldn't.

After lunch, Lewis brought Malcolm back to the airport to get his car. The MG was stored at the airport in the Central Valley. Malcolm kept a Chevy Tahoe in Carmel and the MG in the Valley. That way, when he flew back and forth between the two destinations, he always had a set of wheels waiting for him once he touched down.

Several months had passed since he'd last started the MG, and she was a bit stubborn. After a few prayers, and cranking on the little red mid-life-crisis-bucket-of-bolts until the battery was nearly dead, the stubborn Brit fired on one cylinder. She choked and coughed until eventually all four were firing.

He had just left the airport when his cell phone rang. It was Kate and the call threw Malcolm at first because he'd forgotten that he'd left her a message. She apologized for not getting back to him a few months earlier. They visited a bit and then he thought that he'd test her with an invitation for a coffee. She couldn't because she had plans that evening, so he offered to take her to lunch the following day and she accepted.

At lunch, Malcolm learned that Kate was still seeing Pretty Boy off and on. They were still doing the same break-up-get-back-together routine that they'd been doing when she worked at the coffee house. Over the next several months Kate and Malcolm stayed in contact by e-mail. Whenever he returned to the Valley, he'd phone ahead to make a date with her for lunch or dinner. He didn't push anything with her, mostly just listened.

Then one day, Kate phoned to say she had dumped old blue eyes a month earlier, and that this time it was for good. Malcolm kept in contact with her, but figured it best to sit back and let her seesaw for a while longer. The following month, he did another Valley run. It was a Friday afternoon, and he phoned her on his drive over. She wanted to get together that evening for dinner. That was the first night Malcolm didn't leave when he took Kate home. Actually, he didn't leave until the following Monday morning.

Kate and Malcolm had only been seeing each other for about a month when her father passed away. She was employed by the county as a social worker for child protective services and still had her apartment in the Valley. They'd spend weekends together. Things felt good between them, but it wasn't time to be living together, not yet anyway. But now Kate was back east burying her father, and Malcolm was slumming around Carmel, living alone in his three-hundred and fifty dollar a month studio, pretending that he was a retired millionaire like the rest of the people there, and wishing the hell that he wasn't feeling lonely and missing Kate.

When she last phoned, Kate told Malcolm she planned to stay with her mother for a while. He understood, but was alone and wasn't so fond of the idea. He wanted to ask her how long she planned to be away but didn't want to burden her with the demands of his trivial narcissistic tendencies. He'd been alone for a long time. Having Kate come into his life had raised a hope that his life as a single man had come to an end.

* * * * *

Bored and lonely, Malcolm set off to seek solace from a good friend. Unfortunately, no one was home. Malcolm let himself in with a spare key, poured himself an iced tea, and turned on the television in hope that someone would soon return. Named after his maternal grandfather, Judas Turner despised his birthright, and at an early age chose to be called by his surname. Turner was a few months younger than Malcolm. They'd been friends since the summer before their freshman year at high School.

Turner was a few inches shorter and twenty pounds lighter than Malcolm's six feet, one hundred and ninety-five pound frame. They both had very fine sandy-brownish-blonde hair. Turner had blue eyes; Malcolm's were green. Malcolm had been Turner's best man twice, and Turner had been Malcolm's once. If Malcolm was ever foolish enough to do it again, it would be Turner standing next to him whispering into his ear, reminding him of what a stupid ass he was, and singing a little tune that would be something like: "I do, I do, I do. I don't know why I do, but I do."

Cassandra was ten years younger than Turner. She was from the South. They had met when Cassi was visiting her grandparents in California. After her initial two-week visit she returned home and that's when Turner showed up on Malcolm's doorstep. Hell, he hadn't seen Turner in months, so something was up.

"I met this girl a few weeks ago," Turner said, as he settled into the black leather sofa in the den of Malcolm's home, having found the last beer in the refrigerator and a non-alcoholic beer at that.

"What's she like?" Malcolm asked, reaching to put his iced tea down on a coaster next to the couch.

"She's cuter than hell," Turner said, before taking a swig of the O'Doul's.

"What's her story?"

"Lives in Memphis."

"Memphis? Where the hell 'd you meet her?"

"At a party here in town. She was out visiting her grandparents."

"You going to Memphis?"

"No, Memphis is coming here. I've been on the phone with her every night since she got home. You ought to hear her voice. She just drives me wild," he said, eyes all glazed over.

Turner was… well hell he was gone. He was so mesmerized, that he didn't even bother telling Malcolm what Cassi looked like. He was like a wagged-tail puppy close to peeing himself every time he started mimicking her cute southern "hi y'all." Cassi moved out to California a few weeks later. More than ten years had gone by, and now they were a happily-ever-after story with two little boys, four and two, and a third kid in the hopper and ready to pop out of the chute anytime.

They were married a year later and not long after, moved to Memphis to try life in the south. They returned to California six months later. Turner's old company rehired him and transferred him to Salinas to run a facility that had been failing because of poor management. Malcolm was divorced by then and had no woman in his life, so he started visiting Turner and Cassi on the occasional weekend. One Christmas, Malcolm had come over to celebrate the holiday with them and the following day he drove Cassi to the Del Monte shopping center in Monterey to exchange some gifts. Turner hated shopping; Malcolm didn't care for it much either, but he still had a woman to cross off his list.

So, Cassi set off on her gift-exchanging mission, and Malcolm bought a cup of coffee before settling into one of the heavy cast iron chairs that were scattered around outside of Starbucks. He sat and sipped his coffee and watched the legs that were attached to the ass ends of all the women scurrying about in a frenzy as if it was the last shopping day on earth.

It was Malcolm's birthday. He turned thirty-six that day, the day after Christmas; it was Boxer's day in Canada and St. Stephen's day in other parts of the world, or so he'd been told.

Gleaning for remnants of bagels and scones, a black bird landed on the cast iron table less than a foot from Malcolm. He watched the bird bob its head a few times and then fly off drawing his attention up to the coastal mountain range. Malcolm felt a bit odd, took a deep breath, and then it hit him. He was thirty-six, single, no kids and had been living his entire life back in the San Joaquin Valley. It wasn't a bad life by any standard, but he'd become a prisoner of his identity. In other words, all that Malcolm had become and acquired was running him instead of him running it.

A sweet southern "hi there," woke him from his trance.

"Oh, hi Cassi. You done?"

"No, but we better go before I spend what we don't have," Cassi answered, smiling her smile.

When they arrived back at their apartment, Malcolm picked up the newspaper and found the classifieds. In the new-today section, he found a studio apartment for rent in Carmel. He phoned and asked to see it and was invited to come and have a look right away. Two hours later, he was writing a check to rent the studio for the month of January.

Malcolm returned to the Central Valley and told his manager what he'd done and of his plans to take off the next month. After putting his business in order, he returned the following week for a month long sabbatical that would hopefully cure him of the same discontentment that three years later he was still trying to escape. Turner and Cassi eventually purchased a home in Monterey, about a month before Malcolm had quit his job and moved into his studio below Mrs. Shams. And now, that's where Malcolm was, sitting in their new house, sipping an iced tea, watching television and waiting for Turner, Cassi, and the boys to return home.

Chapter 3

It was just after one in the afternoon when he left the studio. As usual, he had skipped breakfast, was running on a pot of coffee, had low blood sugar, and was in one of his trance-like states where he couldn't decide on what to do for lunch. He stopped at the frozen yogurt shop at the Crossroads for a chocolate to boost his blood sugar and then drove east on Carmel Valley Road. He made it to the Mid-Valley shopping center before turning around and driving back toward what he'd just run from. Just after making the u-turn, Devin, one of the TWA's, rang his mobile.

"Hey Malcolm, how's it going?"

"I'm in one of those fucked up places, you know," Malcolm confessed. Devin had made the mistake of asking. Besides, he was so damned in love he could afford to relieve Malcolm of a little of his self-pity. So, driving towards Pacific Grove, Malcolm pissed and moaned in Devin's ear for a while.

"Well, hang in there friend," Devin coached, as Malcolm turned around halfway to Pacific Grove and motored back towards Carmel, having in his mind settled on Paolina's for lunch.

"Always do, don't I?"

"Heard from Kate?"

"Yeah."

"When's she coming home?"

"Don't know, man. How's your lucky lady doing?" Malcolm asked, not wanting to fall farther into the pit.

He parked outside Paolina's, visited for a few more minutes and then said goodbye to Devin. He ate lunch at Paolina's occasionally. It was a small self-service restaurant where the patrons ordered and paid at the register. They'd call you by name when your order was ready. It was in the Doud Court in downtown Carmel. He watched as some European family struggled over the decision of their lunch order. Bypassing the indecisive family, Malcolm ordered the special: Pasta Carbonara with mushrooms. He didn't eat pasta at Paolina's often, but when this Carbonara dish was on special, he usually indulged.

After ordering, Malcolm sat down and watched the European teenage boy try to get comfortable inside of himself. He was with his parents and younger sister. The boy was wearing a dark blue beret that matched the rest of his attire, with the exception of a tan overcoat that the kid fooled with while his parents and younger sister were at the counter ordering. First he dragged a chair from another table to drape his coat over, making certain that it didn't touch the floor. The next time Malcolm looked, the kid had folded the coat and set it next to him on the bench where he was seated. Once his dinner arrived he stood up to drape his best friend over the spare chair again.

An old Asian, a Mongolian looking woman who had to be eighty-plus-years-old was eating with her fifty-year-old daughter. They were sharing dishes; the daughter was anyway. The daughter was a big woman; she just kept shoveling it in like there was no tomorrow. The mother sat quietly, slowly eating her meal.

At first they appeared to be enjoying each other's company, but it soon became clear that the mother was a burden to her daughter, but only because the daughter was making her a burden, not because of anything the old woman was doing. The daughter kept raking food from her mother's plate and then in return would offer her mother a fork-full of whatever she'd grown tired of eating. The mother would refuse for a bit. Then, more from duty than desire, she would eat what was being forced upon her. It almost seemed that the mother was choking down a forced feeding of her daughter's guilt.

The kid with the trench coat dropped his fork and jumped up to get a clean one, bumping a table and pinching the old lady's arm as he whisked by on his way to the counter. The boy's father noticed what had happened and tried to get the kid to apologize, but the boy was clueless. The old lady shook her hand at the teenager when he returned to his seat, swatting at him. The kid looked at the old lady oddly, not understanding her reprimand until his father explained to the boy what he had done in his self-absorbed haste.

Soon after the table pinching incident, the mother and daughter team began to argue about staying or leaving. Still in the process of eating her meal, the mother wasn't ready to leave, but the daughter had emptied her plate and was ready to vacate. The mother rebelliously dug in for a few minutes, but the daughter finally won out. As they got up to leave, the Mongolian daughter made some nice comment about the teenage boy's little sister's sandwich to compensate for her mother's swatting at the boy, but she was really admiring the sandwich, her appetite still unsatisfied.

Malcolm had nearly finished his pasta when three women and two men sat down at the table next to him. There was an entire dining room of empty tables, but they had to pick the one right next to Malcolm. They started flapping on in a boisterous conversation as he finished his last few bites. He then stood up, his ass to their faces as he slid out between the tables. His melancholic condition put its arm around Malcolm and walked him to the MG.

He drove back to the studio, still consumed by discontent. He didn't feel like being around anyone, but at the same time could hardly stand to be by himself. Malcolm normally savored his solitude, but his mood, coupled with the quietness of the day, had evoked a sort of terror disguised as boredom and uncertainty. He decided to drive to Turner's to see if he could aggravate Cassi and wind up the boys.

Malcolm and Turner had been friends for so long that he never bothered to call ahead before a visit. Cassi's suburban was in the driveway, but Turner's work truck was gone. Malcolm parked, walked to the door and knocked, but no one answered. He knocked again, but to no avail. He could hear voices inside and he had a key, so he unlocked the door and showed himself in.

Cassi was walking down the stairs. "Hey you," she said, greeting him first with a smile and then a hug.

Cassi was as beautiful as the first day Turner had introduced her to Malcolm. She had sandy-blonde hair that was a little beyond shoulder length. Her bluish-green round eyes sparkled with or without her genuinely warm smile. She was just an inch or two over five feet and, between babies, kept herself fit and trim. When Malcolm stopped off to see them that day, she was nearly full term with her third child.

"Turner should be home anytime," she said, as Malcolm followed her into the kitchen. "Mom and Aunt Cindy are here," she continued, as both women walked in from the back yard. Karen, Cassi's mother, had been outside dragging on a cigarette, trying to satisfy a nicotine fit or calm some other unresolved psychological complex.

"Hi Karen. Hi Aunt Cindy," Malcolm said, in a polite, yet smart-ass fashion, never before having met Aunt Cindy.

"Hi Malcolm," Karen said, in her southern way, before hugging him.

"Nice to meet you, Cindy," Malcolm said, shaking her hand to appease his initial flippant introduction.

"Nice to meet you," she courteously responded, still uncertain of Malcolm.

"You stayin' for dinner?" Karen asked.

"Well, I didn't come for dinner. I just stopped by to..."

"Yes, he's staying for dinner," Cassi interrupted. "Why else do you think he's visiting at this time of the day," she added, with her head in the cupboard looking for something to pacify her youngest son's restlessness.

"I..." Malcolm stopped. She had him pegged, and he knew better than to argue. He damn sure wasn't going to argue over a home cooked meal, and a free one at that.

"How you feeling Cassi?"

"I'm ready for this kid to be out!"

"I bet you are," Malcolm smiled, as she danced around the kitchen as if she was at ballet rehearsal. If Malcolm ever married again, the woman would have to be a whole lot like Cassi for the marriage to survive; she could put up with a lot of shit.

"Why don't you call your mom and ask her what I can do to hurry this along," Cassi suggested.

Malcolm's mother had been a nurse for the past thirty years. Turner's sister trained as a student nurse with Malcolm's mother. That's how Turner and Malcolm first met, back when they were just fifteen. Cassi handed Malcolm the portable phone, and he dialed the direct line to his mother's ward.

"Hi mom!"

"Hi... Malcolm?" she asked hesitating a moment before guessing which of her four boys was calling.

"Hey, mom, I'm at Turner and Cassi's. She's ready to pop, but the baby isn't. She wants to ask you something," he said, handing Cassi the phone before his mother could respond.

Malcolm's mother and Cassi babbled awhile, while Karen and Aunt Cindy cooked dinner. Turner got home and ran up to shower. Malcolm slid into the love seat that was in the dining area of the kitchen and watched television. Carson, the four year old ran in and jumped into his lap. Carson picked up the remote and tuned in to Scooby Doo. Carson then stood with his feet on Malcolm's knees, put his arms around Malcolm's neck, and pulled their heads together until they were nose to nose. "I love Scooby Do. I just get so wound up when Scooby comes on," Carson screamed into Malcolm's face, danced a little jig on his knees and then turned a flip onto the vacant side of the love seat landing right side up next to Malcolm. He put his arm around Carson to pull him to his side and they watched Scooby together.

Carson soon grew restless and walked to the television to turn up the volume. Malcolm had the remote hidden under his calf and as soon as Carson turned up the volume, Malcolm would change the channel. Carson would change the channel back to Scooby and Malcolm would lower the volume with the remote. Unaware of Malcolm's influence, this went on for about five minutes with Carson trying to figure out why the television was acting so oddly. Aunt Cindy looked on without letting out a peep as Malcolm tortured the boy. His father walked in and Carson finally began to throw a fit.

"Dad, something's wrong with this TV! I turn it up and the channel changes," he whined.

"Where's the remote?" Turner asked, looking at Malcolm and swapping smiles.

"Uncle Malcolm!" Carson screamed.

"What?" Malcolm asked, handing him the remote.

Turner walked over and sat with them to watch the rest of Scooby. Dinner was ready shortly after they had all settled into the love seat.

"Malcolm, Turner, come on, fix a plate so you two can go in the other room and talk," Karen offered. She'd been there for a couple weeks and had really taken a load off Turner and

Cassi, cooking and caring for the kids. Aunt Cindy had been there for five days in anticipation of Cassi delivering on her visit. Cassi had two more days to fulfill her aunt's wish before Cindy's return ticket to Birmingham expired. There's nothing like putting pressure on a pregnant lady.

Cassi carried her plate in and joined Turner and Malcolm at the dinner table in the formal dinning room. "Have you ever met any of my Mom's sisters before?" she asked, opening up the dinner topic.

"No, but I met Morgan's brothers I think," Malcolm answered, acting dumb.

Morgan was Karen's husband, Cassi's stepfather. Turner's move to Memphis had supposedly been on a promise from Morgan to bring Turner in as a partner in the restaurant business. A couple months later and two thousand miles from home, Turner figured out that he'd been suckered. The slightest reference to Morgan always sent Turner into a spiral.

"Which one?" Turner asked.

"I don't know. It was that time I flew out to Memphis to see you on the Fourth of July. You called him Shovel Head. I think he was a preacher."

"Jerry, that shovel-headed goofball, thought he was a faith healer," Turner said, rolling his eyes.

"You met his brother Henry, too," Cassi added, trying to shift away from Shovel Head.

"Henry was pretty cool, but old Shovel Head was something else. He tried to heal me. Remember that Cassi?" Turner asked, turning to see her reaction.

Cassi shook her head slightly to acknowledge her husband and then kept on eating dinner. She was trying to keep him from a sudden outburst, just like she did with her two little boys.

"He tried to heal my hernia," Turner continued.

"One of them, huh?" Malcolm asked, helping to fuel the fire.

"It worked," Turner claimed, and then paused briefly before adding: "For ten whole seconds!"

"Was it a hands-on experience?" Malcolm asked, egging Turner on.

Cassi choked another bite of her food down. "How's Kate?" she asked, trying to shift the topic. They'd met Kate a few weeks after she and Malcolm had started seeing each other. Cassi and Kate had hit it off from the start.

"Well, fine, considering, but her mom is really taking things hard."

"He said that it didn't work because I didn't believe," Turner interrupted, with a give-me-a-break-dumb-ass look.

"Was it a hands-on thing?" Malcolm asked again.

"Turner! Mom's right in the other room," Cassi scolded with a scowl on her face. Then she turned to Malcolm with the same look and shook her index finger at him: "You too!" She was used to Malcolm's provocations, and he was used to being reprimanded for it. Like the rest of her boys, Malcolm savored the attention.

"Oh yeah, sorry, Jerry, that's not my hernia. Or better yet, hey, Jerry, how about getting your thumb out of my ass?" Turner joked. "And it didn't work just because I didn't believe. I could just hear them after I left. Dumb Californian just didn't believe." Turner continued his banter and by then, he had Cassi and Malcolm both choking in tears of laughter.

After dinner, Cassi seemed restless and went upstairs; a while later, she poked her head over the rail and asked Turner to come on up. Malcolm took this as his cue to leave, so he thanked them all for dinner and said his goodbyes.

The phone rang shortly before midnight.

"Malcolm, I have a new baby girl," Turner announced.

"Everyone alright?"

"Everyone's fine."

"What's her name?"

"Mallory Catherine."

Chapter 4

He'd spent most of the day studying for an anthropology test. After quitting his job and moving to the Peninsula, Malcolm decided he needed to take classes for sanity's sake. He took at least two night classes a semester at the community college. After having worked for so many years, he was afraid he'd go silly without having something like school to keep him grounded.

He took the test early that evening, and after class, headed over to Tillie Gort's for a cup of tea, hoping to run into Carly. Tillie's was celebrating their thirtieth year of business catering to the health conscious natives as well as a few straggling tourists who were looking for something other than fish and chips, or who were avoiding the upscale chic restaurants scattered throughout Pacific Grove, Carmel, Pebble Beach, and Monterey.

Tillie Gort's was very casual and stayed open later than most other restaurants. Malcolm had made friends with most of the wait staff at Tillie's and attended a good many of their off-duty birthday celebrations. He knew the menu by heart. Years ago, he'd substituted his alcoholic binges with sugar, so, needless to say, he had become intimately acquainted with Tillie's dessert selection.

A huge photograph hung over the swinging doors that lead back into the kitchen. It was a picture of Tillie's staff and a few locals who were hanging out there thirty years earlier. The staff photo shoot had become an annual event and along the wall in one corner of the adjoining dining room hung smaller framed photos taken in later years.

He parked, walked in to the coffee counter, and said hello to Chloe and Kristi, two of the waitresses who were on duty. Things appeared slow and they were both sitting at the counter.

"I sure like your Tahoe," Kristi commented.

"Thanks, me too…"

"Hi there," Carly said, surprising Malcolm as she popped up behind the counter.

"Hi Carly. You're a pleasant surprise." Carly was always a

pleasant surprise. Malcolm had met her in a psychology class during his first semester at college. She was a twenty-four-year-old half Panamanian and half something else, a natural beauty with long brown hair. Her brown eyes and slightly crooked nose were just part of her natural beauty. She had a very slender body that carried, at least, a set of thirty-six D cups. She had very narrow hips and an ass with an average tilt but with very little meat. In Malcolm's mind, her backside would age gracefully. She spoke fluent Spanish and it threw Malcolm every time she engaged her native tongue to speak with the cooks in the kitchen. It just didn't seem right having the fluency of another language part the lips of a young woman who seemed so American.

"So, whatcha been up to Malcolm?" Carly asked.

Chloe and Kristi sat a couple seats away in their own little world.

"Oh, this weekend I went back to the Central Valley and had lunch with my fishing buddy, Rob."

Carly listened intently as the other two girls still remained wrapped up in their own thing.

"After lunch, I headed over to visit friends and bring their three-year-old son the John Deere peddle tractor I had bought for him last December but failed to get to him for Christmas. His baby brother was born just a few months ago, and, being the firstborn son that lost his mother to a younger brother, I knew that the John Deere would be a welcome arrival for a youngster who might be feeling a little neglected."

"How thoughtful of you!"

"It was a timely opportunity to redeem myself," Malcolm added, not wanting to appear too overly empathetic and compassionate.

"After that I headed over to my parents' house and spent the night. We barbecued Sunday afternoon. Then I went on to an ex-client's daughter's birthday party."

"That sounds like fun."

"I got to see several people that I haven't seen since quitting the tractors. It was really nice. They were a huge part of my life for many years. I kind of just chopped them off."

"Yeah, that must be kind of hard," Carly answered, validating the fact that she was actually listening to Malcolm's long-winded account of his weekend.

"I planned on leaving the party by nine, because of the two-hour drive back to Carmel from Tranquillity, but I didn't get out of there until eleven."

"Where's Tranquillity? It sounds like a really neat place."

"It sounds a hell of a lot neater than it really is. The name's about all it has going for it."

"Really?"

"That's not entirely true. Some very fine people live there. It's a small farming community on the west side of the Central Valley."

"What's it like?"

"The farmers meet for coffee at the hardware store when it opens at eight in the morning. I used to arrive there every day between eight and eight-thirty. Sold a hell of a lot of tractors there. There's also a grocery store, drive-in hamburger-burrito joint, a Chevrolet dealership where everybody buys their Chevy extended cab four-wheel-drive pickups, and a card-lock gas station where all the Chevy trucks can get fueled twenty-four hours a day. There're also a few other small businesses and about a hundred homes that make up the remainder of the town. Oh, I almost forgot the Catholic Church, the Presbyterian Church, the Methodist Church, and the United States Post Office where the mail is almost always out by ten-thirty. People start arriving around ten-fifteen checking their boxes and complaining about having to wait. I had a box there, too. More than anything else, it was an excuse to meet up with clients."

"Why'd you need an excuse?"

"I guess excuse isn't the right word; it was convenient. I sold a lot of tractors and cotton pickers outside on the front steps of that Post Office, too. I used to get teased about conducting business on federal property. My comeback was that it was the only way I could recoup a small portion of the tax money that Uncle Sam so willingly collected from me."

Carly probably wished she had never asked what Malcolm had been up to, and the boring tale was certainly not the topic that would tempt Chloe and Kristi away from their own little rumor-mill. He started to tell Carly of the entangled relationships he had built out in Tranquillity.

"Being an outsider gave most of my clients some sense of security. They told me things they'd never dream of sharing with their neighbors. With me they had a captive audience. I had to keep my mouth shut because if I didn't, I'd lose their trust and three million dollars a year in machinery sales."

"Wow!"

"I'd just shut up and listen, never peeping a word to another person. Many of them lived lonely, reclusive lives. They trusted me, and I could have become an outcast just as easily as I'd been accepted into their community, had I not kept my mouth shut."

"Sounds like a movie script or something."

"It's a drama for sure, but a boring one. Nobody would waste the time or money on the theatrics of Tranquillity's inflated dramas. Anyway, enough about Tranquillity."

Tillie's was slow that night, or Malcolm would never have had so much of Carly's undivided attention. Normally at that time of the evening, she'd wait on the local Alcoholics Anonymous members who came for coffee after their twelve-step meetings. A younger couple in their twenties came in, and after Carly seated them, she came back up to the counter where Malcolm was sitting.

"When did you get back to Monterey?" Carly asked, carrying on their conversation.

"One this morning."

"Got any plans for the summer?" she asked, wanting to tell Malcolm about some plans of her own.

"Sleep 'til I wake."

"Sounds perfect."

"Going fishing in July with Rob. Steelhead fishing on the North Umpqua in Oregon," Malcolm answered quickly, an unconscious attempt to stay focused on himself instead of allowing Carly to tell what her summer plans might be.

"That sounds like fun."

"What'll be even more fun is missing my twenty-year high school class reunion because of being knee deep in the North Umpqua, flinging flies at steelhead. I hate the goddamn things."

"Steelhead?"

"I wouldn't know. I've yet to catch one," Malcolm laughed. "I hate class reunions. Can't stand the phoniness, the masks people hide behind. I don't like the keeping-up-with-the-Joneses crap either. I hate getting all wrapped up in that sense of being superior to some and a sense of shame for having accomplished so much less than what many of the others have achieved in their lives."

"Aren't there people you'd like to see?"

"I still see the ones I want to see. Don't need a class reunion to do that. If I went, what would I say when we started talking about wives and children? I'd really be batting zero. I haven't got either of them to brag or cuss about."

"Sounds like you've been to one before."

"I went to my five-year reunion. I was still drinking then but was fighting it and at the same time trying to resurrect a lost faith in my Calvinist heritage. I was scheduled to publicly make a profession of faith with my good friend Samuel the following evening in front of the entire congregation. Thank God it was scheduled for the evening service instead of the morning one. I think the preacher knew I was a drunk anyway. So, after arriving and shuffling through the crowd of former classmates, I ended up having a few whiskeys," he explained, as Carly's smile grew bigger. "Generously poured whiskies, too. Crown Royal on the rocks, and after a few Crowns, I was publicly professing my religious faith to the whole goddamn class. Telling people that I could only have a couple, and that I had to stop because of my renewed faith in God and the commitment I was about to make in church the following evening."

"This sounds pretty interesting. I'm getting to see a whole different side of Malcolm," Carly said, continuing with her big smile.

"If you've got the time, I've got loads of bullshit," Malcolm teased.

"Come on, what happened next?"

"After a few more Crowns, I really began to publicly profess my faith. I was tangled up with Kathleen, an old classmate, lip-locked back in the corner of the bar. I mean we were all over each other."

Malcolm's story about making out with Kathleen in the

back of the bar was enough to stop Chloe and Kristi dead in the tracks of their own little rapture. Malcolm followed Carly's eyes over to the two gals and found them both mesmerized with dropped jaws, fully engulfed in the recap of his five-year reunion. Up until that night, they probably thought Malcolm was some boring, lonely old man who came in late to Tillie's for dinner and companionship. At least now he had their attention, even if their prior suspicions held a much greater truth.

"I woke the next morning and realized that I would never need to go to another class reunion for as long as I lived."

"Oh, I almost forgot about that couple. I'll be right back," Carly said, as she trotted off to take an order.

Earlier in life, Malcolm had become what he now most disdained, a Bible thumper and an alchy. As far as he was concerned, reformed alcoholics and religious fanatics were cut from the same cloth. Both usually wanted to make everyone else into what they were, just to justify their own conversions. He was still carrying the shame and embarrassment of having made such an ass of himself that reunion night, and he damn sure didn't want to have to rehash that evening with any of his fellow classmates ever again. He could see himself with his future wife, bragging about one of his life's accomplishments when someone would interrupt: "Hey, Malcolm, remember that reunion when you were high on Jesus, drunker than hell on whiskey, and lip locked with Kathleen back in the corner of the bar?"

Malcolm reached for the newspaper that was lying on the coffee counter and started going over the classifieds, picking over the jobs that looked interesting, when Carly's man, Leonard, walked in. That was reason enough to shit-can the whole work-idea. Leonard was in his early thirties. He was short with a slight build. Probably didn't weigh a hundred and fifty pounds. He had shoulder-length, thin brown hair with a receding hairline. Malcolm thought he was a real wiener and a complete mismatch for Carly.

"Hey Leonard, how's it going?"

"I'm beat."

There he went again. Last time he came into Tillie's, Leonard started telling Malcolm about all the projects he had going, complaining of how he was overworked. Then, when he began to get the idea that Malcolm might be interested in his girlfriend, he started telling Malcolm all about how much he and Carly did together. No matter where the conversation went, Leonard kept bringing Carly into the topic. "Carly and I did this. Carly and I did that," he reasoned, intuitively sensing that Malcolm wanted a mess of what was wrapped up in his girlfriend's thirty-six D cups. He was right, and he was pathetic, and it was time for Malcolm to leave.

"Gotta go Leonard," he said, as he slid out of the stool.

"You take care, huh?"

"Yeah, you do the same. I'll catch you later," Malcolm said, patting him on the back as he walked away before having to listen to anymore of Leonard's problems. Malcolm was only interested in Carly, not her wiener boyfriend or any of his trifles. So he left Leonard alone to wallow in his own self-doubt and to bear the misery of his own insecurities. Well, Carly most likely had to bear a chunk of Leonard's load, too. Malcolm was also a little concerned that if he didn't leave, Leonard might soon stake claim to his territory by hiking his leg and pissing all over the coffee counter.

Chapter 5

He talked to Kate a few times over the next few weeks. She never mentioned anything about returning to California. She mostly spoke of how worried she was about her mother, and Malcolm took it as a sign not to push her, even if he did miss her. The new dimension of their relationship never really had the chance to develop or not develop. I suppose you could say that it was in some sort of purgatorial holding pattern.

His days consisted of waking up late after having studied and written until at least two in the morning. He'd walk Mission Trails or Carmel Beach for cardiovascular, and on returning to the studio he'd lift a few weights and do a hundred and fifty crunches. By the time he showered, it was well beyond noon.

Malcolm had started frequenting the Pink House, a local hangout in Pacific Grove. He would take his cellular phone, the manuscript from the book he'd written, and his homework and camp out on the Pink House porch. That way, he could alternate between editing the book and completing his homework. The phone came in handy for a timely bullshit session with Lewis when he needed a break. Logistics didn't allow them to meet for coffee in person much anymore, but they were still good at wasting time, and if Malcolm wasn't wasting time shooting the shit with Lewis, Jake, a man who helped out at the Pink House, filled the slot.

Jake was in his mid-fifties and when he looked at you, his eyes went out in opposite directions. He stood six feet plus and weighed a good two-forty. He wore a multi-colored stocking cap that his mother had knitted for him. She'd actually knitted several of them. Every year, when he'd return to Brooklyn for her birthday, which always fell a few days before Halloween, he'd get another cap, and always with a warning that this was his last.

Malcolm was on the phone talking with Lewis when he pulled into the parking lot across the street from the Pink House. They were in the middle of a pretty good bullshit session, so after parking, Malcolm carried on the phone conversation walking towards the coffee house.

"Hey Jake," Malcolm said, acknowledging him as he walked up the steps into the Pink House, still on the phone.

"Don't tell me, Malcolm. Yeah, Malcolm, how's it going?" he said, touching his temples, proud of himself that he'd remembered Malcolm's name.

Malcolm nodded to him, showed him the cellular phone and smiled, making sure that Jake knew that his lack of response was because of the phone call. Then he finished the call, set the binder and cell phone on the porch ledge to save his place before walking in to order his, one-in-the-afternoon, morning cup of coffee.

The Pink House was an old Victorian home that had been converted into a coffeehouse/bistro-type hangout where many of the locals gathered for coffee in the mornings as well as for lunch and dinner every day of the week except Thursdays. At one time, they were closed all day on Thursdays, but the locals had made enough noise that they started opening on Thursday morning to cater to their addiction to the Pink House secret blend of coffee. Every cup was fresh; it was served Americano style.

When he walked out with his coffee, Jake was bullshitting some guy, a gardener who had stopped in for lunch. Jake loved to talk and he was talking his way into this guy's afternoon work schedule. The gardener was trying to get back to work, but Jake was still talking to him when finally the guy just walked off right in the middle of their conversation. People walking off mid-conversation never seemed to bother Jake. It almost seemed like a game for him; the more people tried to excuse themselves, the more Jake reeled them in. As the gardener walked away, Jake turned around with a handful of dirty plates, and, with the same breath, shifted his conversation to Malcolm.

"Malcolm, how's it going?"

"Pretty good Jake. How 'bout you?"

"Good, good," he repeated, setting down the dirty dishes on the porch ledge and walking down the steps to clear the two tables on the sidewalk. Jake had blue eyes and graying, bushy brown eyebrows that were mostly gray. His face was full. If a person hadn't been around him much, he might appear to be meaner than hell, but Jake was two hundred and forty pounds of compassion. He loved dogs and babies. Hell, Jake seemed to love everything. Well, everything that didn't appear to want something from him. He worked at the Pink House a couple of days a week but wouldn't take a paycheck. He didn't give a shit about the money and didn't want anyone thinking they owned him.

"It sure is a beautiful day," Malcolm said, as Jake walked up the steps with another handful of dirty dishes.

"Yeah it is; typical Pacific Grove weather. Hey, I talked to my friend in Brooklyn this morning," he said, setting a few more dirty dishes down on the porch ledge to add to the collection.

"How was that?"

"Good, good. He phoned, but I missed him, so I called back." Jake loved to reminisce on Brooklyn. He moved to Pacific Grove, PG to the locals, twenty-five years ago, but most of what he talked about was of being a kid and going to school in Brooklyn.

"This guy used to live here in PG in the early seventies."

"Why'd he leave?" Malcolm asked, already knowing the answer. He had become accustomed to listening to Jake's nostalgia, much of it he'd already committed to memory from overhearing Jake tell the same stories to many of the others who frequented the Pink House.

"Ah, some business deal or job."

"So he left Brooklyn for Pacific Grove and then went back?"

"Yeah, man. Every time I talk to him he says that he's got to get out of there though."

"Why doesn't he?"

"He says his rent's so cheap that he doesn't want to give up his apartment."

"Is that really it?" Malcolm asked, sensing a hesitation in his voice.

"He's been saying that for fifteen years. He ain't leaving; if you're leaving, you leave."

"Don't matter how much rent is," Malcolm confirmed.

"That's right. I told him you aren't getting any younger man, but he ain't leaving," Jake said, shaking his head as his lower lip protruded. He stacked the dirty dishes into three piles and carried one stack inside.

Malcolm opened the binder with the manuscript and started proofing. Jake came back for another handful of dishes and honored the silence that Malcolm's task demanded. Actually, if Malcolm had engaged Jake in conversation, he could have continued editing while nodding his head up and down acting as if he was actually listening. Jake would have carried on as if he had Malcolm's undivided attention, never knowing that Malcolm hadn't heard one of his words, but instead, Malcolm chose silence that afternoon.

He was still sitting outside on the porch at the Pink House with the red binder open when the dog jumped up on the bench and sat down next to him. He instinctively reached over and started to pet the pooch, even if his ex-wife was a dog lover. Ever since divorcing her, Malcolm had developed a taste aversion to canines. He didn't even know if 'It', was a he or a she, and he didn't know 'Its' name. But he did know that 'It' had one hot looking master whose attention he'd been trying to arouse off and on for the past few months. Malcolm looked up, and 'Its' master was walking towards him.

"Wonderful dog," Malcolm said, continuing to pet the pup.

"Isn't she sweet?"

"Yeah, there's just something about her," he answered, wondering what the hell he was doing loving on 'It'.

"Oh, I know it," she said in a soft, sweet, sexy voice.

"She's so lovable," Malcolm said, and she was, too.

"She's nicer than most people I know."

"What's her name?" Malcolm asked, taken by her comment about people. His guess was that she had recently been screwed over by some guy.

"Diana."

"Nice to meet you Diana," Malcolm said, rubbing Diana's head without pushing the master for her name.

"Come on, Diana."

She carried Diana back to where she had been sitting, which was on the opposite side of the stairs that led up into the house. They sat where an iron rail fence had a shelf attached to its backside. A couple of old wooden stools were parked below the shelf. This formed a perch to eat, drink, and watch people from as they walked by on the sidewalk five steps below. When the bench on the porch was occupied, Malcolm would occasionally sit at the perch, catching a peek at the femmes passing by down below.

Within a few minutes, Diana came back over, and this time jumped up into Malcolm's lap. Not long after that, the master realized her pup had wandered off, and she came to retrieve her.

"Come on, Diana," she said, trying to get the pup to come to her. "She really likes you."

"She's okay. You can let her hang out here."

"Are you sure? She's not bothering you?"

"Not one bit. Go ahead and eat. Enjoy your lunch," Malcolm answered, flashing back to his hostage held days of marriage, longing to grasp the fleeting attention of his wife between the feedings of her five dogs, two parrots, one cat, and however many strays she might have picked up on her way home from work on any given day.

Diana's boss stared at Malcolm and the pup for a minute, as if she was trying to size up the situation and get a feel for this stranger who was befriending her best friend.

"Really, she's fine," Malcolm reassured her, before she returned to her lunch.

Diana was a small dog, a mix of some sort, but she had those fall-in-love-with-me Cocker Spaniel eyes. She didn't weigh more than eight pounds. Her soft, short, fine coat was black with white and caramel colored spots. She was extremely clean and smelled more like a little kid who had just finished an evening bath than a dog. Malcolm wondered if Diana's hygienic disposition was in any way a reflection of her master's personal habits. After she finished with lunch, the master walked back to fetch the pup.

"What breed is she?"

"I'm not sure, but I think she's English toy spaniel and Lhasa apso."

"Yeah… now that you mention it, she does resemble some English toy spaniels I know."

"Oh, you know someone who has an English toy spaniel?"

"Two of them. They're great dogs, too. The guy takes them to work with him almost every day."

"Around here?"

"No, he's a farmer in the Central Valley. They're a little bigger than Diana though."

"Well, she's part Lhasa apso, too."

"Yeah, that must be it."

"Come on Diana, time to go," she said, scooping up the pup and clasping the leash to her collar.

"See you later Diana," Malcolm said, as the two walked down the steps.

Diana's master was in her late twenties or early thirties, a tall blonde with green eyes. She was beautiful. You could sit across a dinner table from that face and fall in love with her over and over again. She was the type of woman who could have a man drifting off into a fantasy not hearing a damn thing she was saying. The rest of her body was pretty hot, too. She wasn't overly busty but had long legs and plenty of ass to grab hold of if the opportunity ever presented itself.

Malcolm looked across the street to see the master smiling and holding onto Diana's front paw, waving it up and down as if to say good-bye.

Chapter 6

About a week after Malcolm's encounter with Diana, he showed up at the Pink House for coffee with Sheila and Lance. Sheila was a twenty-three-year-old brunette who was in love with her newfound, pot-growing, dope-smoking, bohemian boyfriend who lived in Big Sur.

Realizing they had a whole lot in common, Sheila and Malcolm had developed a very real and open friendship. They both went through lovers like candy, never quite able to find their favorite piece. Actually, that isn't exactly the truth. Sheila wasn't anywhere near as bad off as Malcolm; he just wanted to believe she was in order to make himself feel better. There was still hope for Sheila finding love. Malcolm, on the other hand, had an extra sixteen years of pole-position starts and last place finishes.

He had heard about Sheila several months before ever meeting her. She once worked with Carly at Tillie's, before Malcolm had moved to the Peninsula. Carly had mentioned Sheila occasionally, but Sheila had quit working at Tillie's before Malcolm had become a regular. All that he knew about her was from Carly's occasional reference about her hooking up with Sheila after psychology class.

In need of some extra cash, Sheila had returned to Tillie's to pick up a few shifts. After one of Malcolm's night classes, he walked into the back room at Tillie's and seated himself at an empty table. An unfamiliar brunette waitress with long brown hair whisked passed him. She was short, maybe five-two with brown eyes. She wasn't too busty, but damn, this gal had an ass-end that was muscled like a quarter horse. I'm not talking about the size of a quarter horse, just sculpted like one. When she flew past Malcolm's table, it was as if she'd just broken free from a chute. He could really sense her presence as she whisked by to deliver an order to an awaiting guest. On her return trip, she dropped off a menu, and he asked her how her day had been.

"Let me get caught up, and I'll come back and tell you all about it," she said in an animated tone and then hustled away to take care of business. She surprised the hell out of Malcolm; he was used to getting some pacifying answer that eloquently brushed him off, but still left the waitress eligible for a decent tip. She set a glass of water in front of him and made a few more laps around the track. The next thing Malcolm knew, Sheila was back at his table pulling out the empty chair and sitting down as if she was joining him for dinner.

"My day, huh? Well, I've had better. I went with my boyfriend to Sacramento this weekend and my damn car broke down there. We had to have it towed back here, and now it's at the mechanics. It's a flippin' mess. Going to be almost a thousand bucks," she explained, without as much as offering to take his order or introducing herself. Not that it mattered; after all, he asked how her day had been.

Malcolm asked her a few more questions about the actual details of the repairs being made on her car. She explained what she could, which wasn't much, because she knew next to nothing about auto mechanics. He was asking just to make conversation. She could have been telling him about her mother, and it would have been just fine with him. Having her attention was all he really gave a damn about anyway. She eventually took his order and continued to buzz around the place making sure her tables were attended to properly.

A few days later while walking down Cannery Row, Malcolm spotted Sheila pulling into a parking place in front of the Driftwood Cellars. She was delivering lunch to one of the ladies who worked at the Tasting Room. Malcolm yelled a, "hey you," to Sheila, and she sent a smile and a, "hey there," back to him. She was double-parked and didn't have time to shoot the breeze, but, for some reason, he still felt acknowledged. She had something besides a quarter horse ass-end that was calling to him. The next time he was at Tillie's, Sheila told him she was quitting and going to work at the Tasting Room and invited him to stop by some time. Anyway, that's how it all started with Sheila. They never did formally introduce themselves. He knew she was Sheila, and she knew he was Malcolm, because that's what everyone else called them.

A month or so later, after several visits to Driftwood Cellars, Malcolm helped Sheila move out of her boyfriend's apartment and into her friend Vanessa's place. He never did get into her pants, though. She started dating another guy and telling him all about it. Occasionally she talked about setting Malcolm up, but when she did come up with a prospect, it was always a woman who was considerably older. Deep down, Sheila knew Malcolm wouldn't be interested in any of the women she was rounding up for him. It was as if she didn't want him as a lover but also didn't want him with another woman. It was more like Malcolm was to be her big brother or father, and that was fine with him.

Don't get me wrong, at first he'd have liked it to be something else, but it wasn't and for some reason it didn't matter. Something more was happening between the two of them. It had to do with her presence, how she listened and received him. He loved her. He wasn't *in* love with her, but he loved her, and told her so whenever he felt it.

Lance was another story. He was in his mid-twenties, about five-eight, with short brown hair. He wore a relatively thick pair of wire-rimmed eyeglasses; they weren't coke bottle bottom thick, but they weren't your everyday over-the-counter reading glasses either.

Lance lived next door to Sheila in her apartment complex on Alice Street. The complex had been nicknamed the Alice Palace by Vanessa, Sheila's roommate. Vanessa loved playing with words. She was always nicknaming people and things. She nicknamed the apartments the Alice Palace because most of the inhabitants of the complex were friends and they all liked to party. When they threw a gig, it was a four-alarm sort of thing. In other words all four apartments on the upper deck participated, and that's how Malcolm had met Lance.

Lance had this innocent naïve little-boy way of living life. He was either high most of the time or had a genuine sense of awe and wonder for life and the people he encountered; it was hard to tell. The girl who lived next to him, Chloe from Tillie's, said he was theatrical as hell, too, and that she'd often catch him alone in his apartment talking to himself out loud, like he was rehearsing lines for an upcoming play.

Lance had just lost his job as a pastry chef at one of the local resorts on the Peninsula. He was from North Carolina, and after attending culinary school in Maine, showed up on the Peninsula looking for work. He was hauled in for drunk driving his first week in Monterey, and after a few unrewarding stints at the local resort restaurants he'd had his fill of the Peninsula. He had accepted a job in Boston and was leaving the next morning. Sheila and Malcolm had taken him for a burger and were now at the Pink House for coffee.

Diana and her master were perched on the same stools as the day Diana had plopped herself onto Malcolm's lap. Malcolm smiled at them as they walked up, but they didn't acknowledge him, and the three of them went inside to order coffee. It was a beautiful sunny day, so after getting their drinks, they decided to sit outside at one of the tables on the sidewalk below the perch but on the opposite side of the steps. There were only two seats, so Malcolm sat on a step next to the table while Lance and Sheila took the chairs. They sipped their coffees and continued the bullshit session they'd started over their burgers.

"What time you leaving tomorrow?" Malcolm asked Lance.

"Probably around nine."

"Have you got your route lined out?" he asked, curious about the direction Lance had plotted for his cross-country trek back to Boston.

"Yeah, I sure do. This is really going to be an adventure," he answered with that boyish sparkle in his eyes.

"What way you going?"

"The southern route. I came over from the north. I want to check out this other direction on my way back. I bought a new tent, and I'm going to camp out in the national parks along the way."

"Sounds fun," Malcolm confirmed.

"Yeah, I've got the tent set up on the deck in front of the apartment. You ought to check it out when we get back."

"Remind me when we get there," Malcolm said, feeling something nosing him in the back. He turned around to find Diana with her leash still tied to her collar but no master holding the other end. "Hey there Diana," he said, petting her as Lance looked on. Sheila was engaged in conversation with someone she knew who was walking by on the sidewalk. Malcolm looked up and found Diana's master looking around for her companion.

"Over here," he announced, holding up her leash.

"Come on Diana," she said, walking over to retrieve the dog. Malcolm kept petting Diana to keep her from running off. He wanted to make sure Lance got a good crack at the master, not to mention that he desired the same for himself.

"Hi there," Malcolm greeted the master as she reached for the leash.

"Oh, hi there," she answered in a soft, listless-like tone.

"How are you?" Malcolm asked to hold her up for a few more seconds.

"Fine thanks. Come on Diana," she said, smiling half-heartedly as she led Diana away.

"See you later," Malcolm said, as the couple walked towards the parking lot across the way. "What do you think of Diana?" he asked, looking up at Lance with a big grin after dog and master had crossed the street.

"How do you know Diana's name?" Sheila asked, as her friend walked off.

"It's my job," Malcolm quipped.

"Yeah, right! Your job," Sheila said.

"She's got the most potential of any woman I've met around here, yet."

"She is pretty damn cute," Sheila conceded.

"Cute. Hell, she's hot!" Lance chimed in.

"I'm partial to the dog, myself," Malcolm smiled.

"You *are* a dog," Sheila snapped. "I know what you're really after," she added, punching Malcolm's shoulder.

"What's her name?" Lance asked.

"Diana," Malcolm answered with a smart-ass grin. "Weren't you listening?"

"Not the dog, the woman?"

"I don't know."

"But you know her dog's name?" Sheila asked in a give-me-a-break tone.

"Yeah, she came and jumped up onto my lap one day."

"Right," Sheila said, shaking her head

"The girl or the dog?" Lance asked grinning.

"Really," Malcolm said, holding back his laughter to Lance's question. "I was sitting right up there on that bench," Malcolm said, pointing to the porch. "The pup just trotted right up those steps and hopped up into my lap."

"How do you know her name's Diana?" Lance asked.

"I asked."

"But you don't know the woman's name?" Sheila chimed in.

"I didn't ask," Malcolm answered in an impatient tone.

"Why not?" Lance asked.

"She wasn't ready to tell me."

"How do you know?" Sheila asked.

"I just know, all right? I can sense these things, you know."

"You just think you can," Sheila said teasing.

"Yeah, whatever you say Sheila," Malcolm said, getting in the last jab.

They hung out for a while longer and laughed a lot. It was just one of those days when everything was funny. Sheila had become a good enough friend to give Malcolm all the shit in the world, and he loved her enough to let her. One of the nice things about Sheila was that Malcolm could be a boy around her. She seemed to like it, and that was exactly how Lance and Malcolm were acting that morning. They were sitting around, carrying on, making more noise than they should have been, but not really giving a damn, when Sheila smart-assed Malcolm about something.

"Yeah, but you've all but moved to Big Sur," Malcolm said in retaliation, testing a hunch he had about her moving down the coast to be with her new dope-smoking boyfriend. "It wouldn't surprise me if you're moved within a couple of weeks," he added.

"You little shit…" Sheila started, and then hesitated.

"That's what I thought," Malcolm said smiling.

"We'll see," she said, with a not-right-now look. She had yet to tell Vanessa of her plans and didn't want it getting back to her from Lance during his going away party at the Alice Palace that night. Actually, she ended up telling Vanessa a couple of days after Lance had left. She gave her a month's notice and before long, Sheila had moved to Big Sur.

* * * * *

That evening Malcolm went to Turner and Cassi's. It was their youngest son, Connor's second birthday party. It was all women and kids when Malcolm walked in. The kids started calling him some goofy uncle so-and-so name. They had whistles and were sounding them off in the same room where their mothers were clucking about whatever mothers clucked about when they gathered. He heard a "Hey, Malcolm!" and looked up. Turner was walking down the stairs in a clown suit with a painted face and wearing a finely ratted multi-colored wig.

"Hey there, Bozo," Malcolm teased.

Turner ignored Malcolm and started entertaining the kids. Malcolm spotted the cake but no ice cream.

"Where's the ice cream?" he asked Cassi quietly. The house was already a mess and the cake had already been served. He didn't want to start round two, giving them all a reason to stick around for another treat and two more hours of whistle blowing.

"Oh, yeah," Cassi said with an embarrassed look on her face. "Forgot it," she whispered, not wanting to fool with it or appear to be a bad host.

"Don't worry," Malcolm said, quietly.

"Thanks," she said with a relieved look. "Get some if you want," she whispered and then carried on, shifting her attention back to her guests.

Malcolm spotted one of the mothers coming down the stairs. She was a pigeon-toed, blue-eyed blonde who had her hair pulled into a ponytail. She had a huge set of knockers that looked like they were going to pop right out of her low cut top.

"Hi, I'm Malcolm," he said, and adding unconsciously in silence: *and I'm an alcoholic.*

"Oh, hi, I'm Chrissie."

"You live here in the neighborhood?"

"Yeah, but I'm originally from Hollywood... but we are really blessed to be here," she added, as a disclaimer. "How about you?"

"I've been friends with Turner since high school."

"Do you live in the area?"

"Yep. Little studio in Carmel. Quit my job and moved here

last year," Malcolm answered, watching her bend over to pick up a toy or a stray piece of birthday cake. She was wearing a pair of black leather pants, a leopard-print Danskin top with long sleeves, and silver high-heeled sandals. As she straightened back up, she caught him looking at her boobs.

"Have you seen a curly blonde boy running through here?" she asked, preparing to exit the imaginary corner that Malcolm was backing her into.

"No, sure haven't," he answered, looking her in the eyes and smiling.

"He's probably upstairs," she said, starting to return from where she'd just come.

"Yeah, probably so," Malcolm answered, watching the black leather pant legs ascend the stairway.

Turner had been washing off his make-up and changing out of his clown suit. He passed Chrissie in the middle of the staircase and caught Malcolm checking her backside. Turner just slyly raised his eyebrows, smiled, and went on past Malcolm into the kitchen; Malcolm followed.

Malcolm cut a piece of cake and put it into a bowl. Then he walked to the freezer in the garage for the ice cream and returned to the kitchen. He piled it onto the piece of lemon birthday cake that had a fluffy white marshmallow frosting. He sat down on the love seat next to Turner who was watching Sean Connery in *Medicine Man*. Turner put his arm around Malcolm, pulled him close and kissed him on the top of the head as his mother-in-law, Karen, walked in from the backyard after having a smoke.

"Strawberry ice cream on lemon cake?" Karen asked, with her nose curled up.

"It's great!" he answered, feeling gratified with her reaction. She already considered Malcolm somewhat of an oddball, and this only confirmed her suspicion. "Who whipped up this flavor combination in the first place?" Malcolm asked, knowing that she was the responsible party.

Karen left the room.

"That was easy," Turner said in a thankful tone, continuing to gaze at the television. "Heard from Kate?"

"Yeah, she's still at her mother's. I don't know if that whole damn thing with her can work anyway," Malcolm answered in a disgusted and a not-wanting-to-get-his-hopes-up tone.

"You just never know," Turner replied.

Malcolm turned to Turner and found what he expected: a squinted, Jack Nicholson, gotcha-smart-ass grin. After finishing the cake, Malcolm stood up and reached for the Cheese Nips that were on the counter and sat back down next to Turner. They watched the movie for a while and soon found themselves surrounded by little boys who'd grown tired of blowing whistles and listening to their mothers' cackling out in the living room. After settling a few boyish territorial battles over the bag of Cheese Nips, Malcolm decided that he had breathed in all the fumes of domestication that a single man could stand for one day.

"Turner, I'm going," he announced, putting his right arm around his back and pulling Turner to him in a shoulder hug.

"Thanks for coming over," Turner said, continuing his stare into the television.

Malcolm left and went into the living room to say good-bye to the skirts.

"Hey, Malcolm!" Turner yelled from the kitchen.

"Hey, what?" Malcolm asked, walking back to find Turner still lounging in the love seat.

"What you need is a wife and three kids," he said, smiling with a take-me-with-you look in his eyes.

"I love you, Turner."

"I love you, too," Turner answered. He loved his wife and kids as well and had no desire to change anything in his life, yet at times, Malcolm's free lifestyle was inviting.

Chapter 7

Waylen had seen Malcolm hanging around the Pink House for the past couple of months, but they never spoke, didn't even acknowledge each other. Waylen, as well as most the other people who frequented the Pink House were locals, and Malcolm wasn't, not yet anyway and he wasn't sure if he ever wanted such status. Being a local meant being a part of the dramas, fabricated and real, of any small town community.

Fortunately, or unfortunately, Malcolm had a knack for getting drawn into these things just because he liked to hang out at places like the Pink House. He didn't go to talk, as much as just be around people; their presence was all that he was seeking, but it seemed that his silence was often what attracted people to him. It's that whole thing about people making other people into what they need them to be, and it's damn easy to do this to someone who doesn't have a voice.

When Malcolm was at the Pink House a few months back, he ran into Chloe and she introduced him to Luke, and it was Luke who later introduced him to Waylen. Luke was a tall, thin man in his late twenties, probably of European descent, with wavy, thin, brown hair, brown eyes, thin face, and a pointed nose. He had that California-coastal-artsy look, like he could be a writer or a painter of some sort. Luke moved very slowly. It seemed that he was half asleep, although, after visiting with Luke a few times, it became obvious to Malcolm that his mind worked nothing like he appeared to be moving through life.

Waylen, on the other hand, was quite different. The next time Malcolm ran into Waylen at the Pink House, the time just after having been introduced to him by Luke, it was like Malcolm was one of Waylen's long-lost childhood friends. Waylen was a body builder, not a fanatical one, but he had his own gym and made his living as a personal trainer. He was also a partner of Luke in some sort of failing business venture.

Waylen was a few inches shy of six feet, had a dark complexion, and hazel eyes. His brown hair was a little kinky with hints of a golden tone. It was cut very short on the sides up over his ears and an inch and a half layer of an almost afro-like, pompadour hairdo sat on the top of his head. He had a small mouth, nose, and ears, but his eyes were wide and round. Waylen talked with his eyes; his eyebrows moved like a mouth.

Malcolm was sitting on the bench out on the front porch late in the morning when Waylen walked up, greeted him like he'd known him for years and sat down at his side. A mid-nineteen-eighties vintage, orange, two door BMW convertible pulled into the parking lot across the street while they were still talking about the weather, or some other insignificant phenomena that Malcolm liked to use as a shield until he could find the comfort of common ground with any stranger.

"Check this shit out," he said, nodding toward the BMW and raising his eyebrows.

Legs, long legs, stepped out of the Beamer, and attached to the legs was a thin body with a long neck. She had the look of a thoroughbred racehorse. The only thing that wasn't long and lean on her was her short brunette haircut. She walked right past Waylen and Malcolm as if they didn't even exist, Waylen gawking at her and Malcolm following his lead but not wanting to be too obvious.

She came out a few minutes later.

"Hey there!" Waylen called to her as she descended the front steps.

She turned around knowing exactly who had called out to her. "Oh, hi. I forgot my wallet in the car. Be right back," she said, and then continued on to the BMW.

"Check this out when she walks back up here," he said, his eyebrows hopping around on his forehead.

She came long-legging it up the steps a minute or two later, and Waylen was standing at the top of the stairs in the doorway waiting for her. "Come here," he said, before he closed his eyes, puckered his lips, and stuck them out to her as she came toward him. She gave Waylen a big old smooch and he then turned to look at Malcolm with his eyes rolling around like he'd just had the blowjob of his life.

"Malcolm, this is Danette," he announced, with his forehead all wrinkled, his eyebrows locked in a raised position, and his eyes still somersaulting in their sockets. His tongue was sticking out of the side of his mouth. If someone had just walked up and hadn't been watching all of this, they'd have taken Waylen for a drunk.

She greeted Malcolm and then went back in for her order.

"Danette's kinda my girlfriend, but I won't let her call me her man, because I'm not going to let her have that kinda power over me," Waylen explained, settling back on the bench next to Malcolm after Danette had walked away.

Malcolm didn't have a chance to respond, but he did wonder why Waylen hadn't offered to pay for her coffee. Danette came back out, sat down on the porch rail in front of the two men, draped one of those long legs out and rested her foot on the bench between Waylen's knees. He goo-goo gaa-gaad over her like a little boy who was in love with his kindergarten teacher while they made dinner plans for his thirty-fifth birthday that was to take place the following weekend. Shortly after their skit, he kissed her goodbye and she was off to work.

"Where does she work?" Malcolm asked, as Danette drove off.

"Restaurant in Carmel. She's a hostess and does something with wine."

"I see. She a local, too?" Malcolm asked, noticing that Waylen was coming back to where he'd been before she showed up.

"She's from Southern California, but she won't take me to meet her parents," he answered. His face had lost a considerable amount of expression and his tone had shifted to disgust.

"Why?"

"Malcolm, I don't know if you noticed, but my dad's black," he said, looking out towards the parking lot.

"I can't tell. Not that it matters, but you just don't look black to me."

"Thanks, man," he said, sincerely. "Her parents hate niggers, so she won't take me home to meet them."

"My Grama's like that. She says it's in the Bible that a black man can't be with a white woman," Malcolm explained, as they both looked out into the parking lot.

"It does not!"

"I know," Malcolm agreed. "So I said to her: 'I suppose that it's written in the book of Lettie.'"

"Book of Lettie?" Waylen asked, looking at Malcolm confused.

"Yeah, that's her name, Lettie. She writes her own passages to serve her own needs."

"I hate that power thing. That's why I won't let her say I'm her man." Waylen might not have let Danette call him her man, but it made no difference. She still had him by the short hairs.

"Just fuck 'em anyway. You know they're that way, so just fuck 'em until a better one comes along. Grudge fuck 'em and let 'em think they have the power over you," Malcolm encouraged. "I got one right now that loves having the power over me. Pisses me off, but I'm still getting that shit, so who's winning?" Malcolm lied, trying to compensate for his own lost sense of power.

"One called me that's getting divorced and moving back here," Waylen said, appearing to be regaining some animation.

"The one I'm doing is getting divorced."

"She's still married and you slept with her? What about her husband?"

"They're split, so what? If I didn't do that shit, someone else would have."

"I can't do that man. I've got morals. I'm a Christian."

"Then what are you gonna do with the one who's moving back?" Malcolm asked.

"What do you mean, what am I gonna do?"

"You might as well just do her if she'll let you," Malcolm said, ignoring Waylen's morality comment. Malcolm knew that a fresh she, and a stiff dick had a way of overriding any sense of morality and religion.

"She says she needs time to heal. I'm gonna wait for her to be divorced and healed up."

"You're gonna do her, and you might as well accept the fact that after you do, she's probably gonna end up with some other guy," Malcolm replied, turning to him and looking for his reaction.

"That's exactly why I'm not gonna sleep with her. I'm gonna let her heal. I'm tired of the games," he answered.

Who's he trying to fool, me or himself? Malcolm thought.

"Danette's just using me to get into the community. I'm a local and it worked. Figure that one out, man," Waylen explained in a pissed-at-himself, victimized tone.

Instigated by the hotties who danced up the steps for their morning latte, Waylen and Malcolm slung a little more of their bravado around on the porch and then Waylen shifted back to the conversation about his moral obligations and how they prohibited him from sleeping with married women until another hotty walked by and reeled him out of his pious trance. Malcolm glanced up to the clock tower in the center of town. When he looked down, Diana was leading the master through the parking lot.

"Wow, it's almost one," Malcolm said, surprised that time had passed so quickly, but not making any reference to Waylen about the approaching couple. After several months of crossing each other's path, Waylen and Malcolm finally had a chance to visit, and it was quite a visit at that. Malcolm couldn't help liking Waylen, and on top of that, he was big entertainment.

"Oh, man, I've got a client at one," Waylen said, raising his eyebrows as if he was really surprised. "Got to go. Catch you later, brother," he said running down the steps as Diana and her master walked up. She tied Diana up at the perch and walked inside to place her order.

"Hi there, Diana," Malcolm said, reaching down to pet the pup while her master was still away.

"Hello there," the master said standing over Malcolm from behind, plate and drink in hand. He was blocking her path to the perch.

"Haven't seen you around," Malcolm said, stepping out of her way. "How are you?"

"Pretty good. I've been in San Diego."

"Business?"

"No. My niece's birthday."

"Spend the week there?"

"No, just the weekend."

"Long trip for just a weekend."

She just smiled.

"You fly out of Monterey or San Jose?"

"Monterey."

"I haven't been on a jet for a few years. I'm a pilot and fly myself if I'm going anywhere," Malcolm bragged. "Well, short hops anyway. The long ones I leave to the airliners, but I haven't had to hop an airliner since I quit my job."

"What did you do?"

"Sold tractors," he answered, realizing that he had been neglecting Diana. He knelt down and petted her, not wanting to appear as if he'd lost interest in what was closest to her master's heart.

"Are you married?"

"Divorced. I started spending time here a few years ago. I was house-sitting for a man here in Pacific Grove and woke from some dream saying 'disease.' That's when I knew I had to quit."

"Why?"

"Because I knew that I'd die if I didn't."

"So you quit."

"I decided to quit that day. The next day a friend called to tell me about a studio apartment that was opening up in Carmel. I rented it and went back to spend Christmas with my family. Then I quit and moved here a week later."

"That's a wonderful story. You listened to yourself. Where did you live?"

"Central Valley. You from around here?"

"No, Southern California," she answered in her soft voice.

"How long you been here?"

"Ten, no eleven years."

"Quite a while then."

"Yeah," she answered softly, almost as if she was drifting off somewhere.

"Are your parents still down South?"

"No… my father lives in Klamath."

"Klamath Falls, in Oregon?

"Yeah, have you been there?"

"Oh, yeah, it's farming country, I've been up that way on business a time or two. I go fishing up there on the Williamson River sometimes, too."

"I've only been there a couple of times myself."

"Don't blame you. Not a whole lot to do."

"My dad comes here to visit every once in a while."

"PG's a nice place to come to visit someone. What do you do?"

"I'm a physical therapist."

"So your office must be right around here," Malcolm said, finally understanding why she frequented the Pink House so often.

"Just down a few blocks," she said, pointing south.

"Well, I'd better get going," Malcolm said, not wanting to wear out his welcome and also to leave some mystery floating in the air.

"So you don't have a family of your own?" she asked, testing Malcolm's status.

"Nope, I'm divorced. I've got my parents and brothers, though," Malcolm answered, trying to make it look like he had some sort of a stable background. He reached down and petted Diana. "Nice talking to you," he said, as he backed away. "Oh, yeah, I'm Malcolm," he said looking at her, but not extending his hand.

"I'm Jenny."

"I'll see you around Jenny."

Jenny smiled with a look of uncertainty.

Chapter 8

"Hi Malcolm," she said in her soft tone. She had a quiet demeanor, reminded him of a deer who would spook at the slightest sign of an unfamiliar noise or scent.

"Hi. How's it going?"

"Pretty good," she answered. She might have been doing pretty good, but the sigh that accompanied her reply threw him. Jenny was a hard one to read. She was a beautiful woman, but something seemed to be missing. Something that Malcolm couldn't quite put his finger on.

She walked inside to order, and Malcolm took a seat at the perch thinking that she might join him. She walked out and down the steps and then looked up to him from the sidewalk and smiled.

"Where's Diana?" he asked, the question just an excuse to make conversation.

"My girlfriend took her to the beach."

Malcolm responded with a nod and a smile.

"I'm in a hurry to get back. I snuck over between patients."

"Hey, Jenny," Malcolm said to catch her attention as she began to walk away. She stopped and turned to see what he wanted. "Let me know if you want to have dinner some time," he said, reaching over the perch to hand her a card with his phone number.

"I'll see you later," she said, as she walked off. Malcolm believed that most women would open the door if they were interested. It was usually subtle, but they'd at least throw a hint his way.

Then, out of the blue that same evening, she phoned him wanting to meet for dinner. An hour later they met at one of the nicer restaurants on the Peninsula. There was an empty corner table that Jenny spotted when they walked in, and Malcolm requested it. They were seated within a couple of minutes and ordering drinks. Jenny ordered a glass of wine, and Malcolm ordered one of those expensive bottles of Italian water.

"You don't care for a glass of wine?" she asked.

"No, I don't drink," he answered, his neck muscles tensing up when he confessed to her. It wasn't clear if he felt ashamed of the fact that he couldn't drink or just vulnerable for so quickly having to expose a side of himself which he would have preferred left alone, at least on a first date.

"Never?" she asked in her sweet, but emotionally detached tone.

"Never. I'm an alchy, but don't like telling people that because I'm not an alchy."

"Oh, I have so much respect for twelve-step programs."

"They can be a life saver, but you can also get lost in them. That's why I said I'm an alchy, but I'm not."

The waitress delivered the drink order. She set Jenny's glass down on a napkin in front of her and then opened the green water bottle and filled Malcolm's glass. They ordered, and as the waitress walked away, Malcolm raised his glass to Jenny. She followed suit and joined in a silent toast.

"What do you mean by getting lost?" Jenny asked in reference to his comment about twelve-step programs.

"I mean that I needed the twelve-step meetings to give me structure and support while I was getting sober, but they also have a way of 'pathologizing' the whole process. Part of it is the medical system. They've had to 'pathologize' it in order to collect from the insurance companies. By labeling it a disease and giving it medical terminology it becomes profitable. Then people are labeled and end up living out their lives believing that they are inherently ill. It shifts them from one belief system to another, and they never really learn to trust themselves to live their own lives."

Jenny listened.

"So that's why I'm an alchy, but I'm not. I'm an alchy because I know what happens when I drink. I'm not an alchy because I refuse to be labeled and diagnosed as having an incurable disease. I refuse to live in that realm."

"I see. It would be like patients coming to me with an injury who have been told that the injury will never heal or they'll never be the same again. They'd just give up hope."

"How can anyone heal if they don't believe they can in the first place?"

"Oh, I agree. I see it happen all the time. I can help a person recover, but I can only do so much. Most of it is up to them."

"But they don't know that. We live in a world where we look outside of ourselves for answers. Got pain: go to the doctor and get a pain pill."

"Just like depression and anxiety. There are pills for that, too."

"Yeah, and so we don't listen to what our bodies are trying to tell us. We don't treat the pain, depression, or anxiety as a signal, something that is trying to get our attention and possibly asking us to make a change in our lives."

"Instead, we pop a pill and make it all go away," Jenny said, as the waitress served their dinners.

"You know what I'm talking about," Malcolm said, feeling refreshed that she understood him. He reached for the green water bottle, filled his glass, and offered some to Jenny, but she declined. They talked a little about their family backgrounds over dinner.

"Well, so far you seem like a nice guy," Jenny said, after having finished their meal.

Malcolm could sense that she was tired, but what was the thing about him seeming to be a nice guy so far? He didn't respond to her comment, but instead suggested that they call it an evening. He paid for dinner and walked Jenny to her car, not because he was expecting anything from her, but because it was nine-thirty at night and it was a gentlemanly thing to do. They had parked in the same parking lot. He stopped at the front of her car while she continued to the door. She unlocked the door and then looked up, surprised to find him still standing in front of her car. She had expected him to be standing right over her waiting for something else, like a kiss or a hug. It might have been nice, but he really didn't even know the woman. She put her purse into the car and walked back to hug him quickly and say goodnight

Malcolm didn't ask Jenny for her phone number. He figured that if she wanted him to have it, she'd volunteer. She called him a few days later and left her number on his message machine. He returned the call and she told him how much she enjoyed their time together at dinner, said something about how it was like having a brother, but even better. Well, Malcolm didn't know exactly what she meant by that, but he did ask her to join him for lunch the following week and she accepted.

After lunch the next week, they went for a walk on Asilomar Beach - Jenny, Diana, and Malcolm that is. During the walk, Jenny began to speak about one of her girlfriends. She had met a nice guy who really treated her like she deserved to be treated.

"What do you mean by nice guy?" Malcolm asked.

"Well, usually she gets involved in these destructive relationships where she isn't treated with respect or valued. They certainly aren't boring by any standards, but they're very unfulfilling in the long run. They never last."

"I see," Malcolm said, trying to understand her definition of nice guy. "So a nice guy is a man who respects a woman?"

"Well, in the women's magazines, guys are usually divided into three categories," she started explaining. "A nice guy is kind of like the boy next door. The bad boy usually appears to be nice, but he's really sleeping around on the woman. The assholes are just assholes. I really don't know any other way of describing them."

"Wow, that's really interesting."

"Yeah, I usually go out with the boy next door type," Jenny explained.

"That scares the hell out of me," Malcolm answered.

"That I go out with nice guys?"

"No, that you actually have us categorized and labeled. I mean… well I'd like to reserve the right to be all three: a nice guy, bad boy, and an asshole. Actually I'd hate to think that I was limited to just those few possibilities."

Jenny looked at Malcolm kind of funny, but he didn't care. Yeah, she was a beautiful woman, but, beautiful or not, he had no interest in taking on any of the roles that the women's magazines were handing out. He'd be damned to live within the confines of that nonsense. He just wanted to be clear about where he stood, even if it did run her off. He had either spooked her properly, or she needed to get back to work. Whatever it was, they hugged and said good-bye.

Chapter 9

"Hey, Waylen."

"What's going on?"

"Relaxing. Thought I was tired, but then I decided I was just feeling relaxed," Malcolm explained, as he sipped his late morning coffee on the porch at the Pink House.

"Yeah, think I'll go home and take a nap," Waylen said, in a tired, bummed out tone.

"What's been going on with you, man?"

"Got my car impounded."

"Why?"

"Registration's been due for the last six months."

"So now you've got to pay it anyway."

"That, the ticket, and another seventy-five bucks just to get it out of impound. It's my fault, but it's still a bunch of crap."

"Why didn't you just pay the registration in the first place?"

"I don't know, man. I…" Waylen started to give a reason, but stopped as Jenny walked up.

"Hi Malcolm, I'm sorry to interrupt you guys, but we're throwing together a last minute birthday party for one of my girlfriends tonight, and you're invited."

"Where is it?" Malcolm asked, caught off guard. Going to a party with a bunch of people he didn't know wasn't his idea of fun.

"It's at seven tonight at the beach by Lover's Point, but you can come to my place and we can go together."

"Do I need to bring anything?"

"No, just yourself."

"Okay, I'll see you a little before seven then."

"Okay, I need to get back to work. Sorry to interrupt," Jenny said, before she walked away. She didn't order anything, so she must have just come to find Malcolm.

"Hey, you've been hanging out with the nurse quite a bit lately. What's her name?" Waylen asked playing dumb.

"Jenny? She's a physical therapist," Malcolm answered.

Waylen already knew her name.

"Oh, yeah, that's right. How's that coming along?"

"Just hanging out."

"Just hanging out, huh?"

"Don't worry, if it was more than just hanging out, I'd be bragging to you about it right now," Malcolm chuckled.

"She seems like she'd be a tough nut to crack. Think it'll go anywhere?"

"Hell, I don't know. Guess if I wanted to hang in there long enough it could. But I don't even know that for certain. Waylen, I'm a thirty-nine year old divorced man who has been through a ton of women. They want commitment, and I just wanna fuck. I know how I am, and I don't have much hope of ever changing."

"If they'd just give a little of it up once in a while."

"And I am not willing to pay for it."

"What?"

"I've sold my soul for that shit before, and I'm not doing it anymore."

"They love to have that power. As soon as you marry them they can cut you off," said Waylen.

"That's why I'm not marrying one," Malcolm answered.

"It's all about power."

"But they cover it up with that love and commitment shit."

"Just so they can run your ass."

"I can tell you one thing, though."

"What's that?" Waylen asked.

"I've never been fucked by a woman who didn't want to fuck me first."

"You know I'm half black, and I'm not into playing that nigger thing," Waylen said, shifting back to his ethnic hang-up.

"Waylen, you don't have to be black to be a nigger."

"You think I don't know that, but it's that whole thing about them taking and not giving, wanting us to be their niggers."

"Waylen, they all want something."

"Hell, mine's on Prozac. Her head's spinning so bad they upped her dosage."

"That shit scares me. Why doesn't she find out what the depression's about?"

"I know; she's just masking it."

"I think she ought to quit the Prozac and start fucking more," Malcolm teased. "You know, get those endorphins kicking in," he added, smacking his right fist into his open left hand.

"Yeah! Baby," Waylen yelled, smacking his right fist into his left hand, eyebrows dancing on his forehead. "I love it!"

"I'm serious though."

"I know you are, brother. Hey, did you know that when they take Prozac they can't have an orgasm?" Waylen asked.

"I believe it. Had a girlfriend on Paxal once, same thing."

"Paxal?"

"Yeah, for anxiety. She got off that shit though."

"Mine just lays there staring at the ceiling while I go to town."

"Why don't you get her to roll over so you don't have to watch her zone out?"

"Hee, hee, ha! That's a good one, brother. What happened with the girl on Paxal?"

"I told her straight up that I was in the midst of a mid-life crisis and that I just might spin off the earth at anytime. Told her right up front that she couldn't expect anything from me."

"Oh, you're one of those hard-nosed fuckers."

"No, but we're talking man to man, so I'm roughing it up some. You know, just to make it sound better."

"Oh yeah. So you told her all that and she fucked you anyway?"

"No, she fucked me first and then I told her. Like I said, I've never fucked a woman who didn't want to fuck me first."

"Yeah, and then you dump your lost-in-life crisis on them."

"Hell, she came to me. When they come to you, it's their fault if they get it. They really want it in the first place anyway. It's afterwards that they want to doll it up with love and make us into assholes for being the men that we were born to be."

"You know what? You're right about Danette dumping that Prozac. I know she'd feel a lot better if she'd start fucking me on a regular basis."

"Not a doubt in my mind," Malcolm answered, grinning.

"Hey man, I've got to run. Got to meet a client in fifteen minutes."

"Alright man. I'll catch you later, huh."

"Yeah you will, brother," Waylen said, as he turned around on the steps and gave Malcolm a thumbs-up.

* * * * *

Malcolm stopped off at the liquor store and picked up a six-pack of non-alcoholic beer and arrived at Jenny's a little before seven. He wasn't all that enthused about going to the party, but went anyway. He was being invited into the community of locals and figured that if nothing ever happened with Jenny, it still might set the stage for meeting another woman down the line. The plotting salesman in him would never die. For most of his life Malcolm had been putting deals together, deals that often started months if not years in advance.

When they arrived at the beach, Ellen, the birthday girl, ran up, hugged Jenny, and then turned to the mystery man. "You must be Malcolm. Thank you so much for being so kind to Jenny," she said, in a theatrical tone, before hugging him and kissing his cheek.

Malcolm wasn't quite sure what Jenny had told her, but he certainly hadn't gone out of his way to be kind to anyone. It was exactly the small town community shit that he was always afraid of getting dragged into. It seemed that, in spite of himself, he was taking on the girly magazine image of a 'nice guy.' Nice guy, or not, Jenny's hugs were going to have to take on a whole new dimension if he was going to be the nice guy that she was making him out to be.

They went over to the fire where the other partygoers were gathered. Malcolm was introduced to several of Jenny's women friends. They were a group of women who, over the past few months, had befriended one another. Ellen had just fallen in love with a man named Stanley, a local attorney, and, with the exception of Jenny and Ellen, the rest of the women were all married. Not necessarily happily married, but married just the same. Jenny had mentioned them to Malcolm, but he had yet to meet any of them until that evening at the birthday party. He also had the pleasure of meeting their spouses and children and a few other people as well.

They roasted hotdogs and marshmallows, even made S'mores with graham crackers, chunks of chocolate and roasted marshmallows. To top all that off, there were two birthday cakes, to boot. The couples with children left first. Ellen and Stanley wandered off down the beach in the dark for some type of one-on-one encounter. Shortly after they walked away, a dark shadow approached the fire from the opposite direction. It was Laura, the hot, petite reddish-blonde who frequented the Pink House. Malcolm had had his eye on Laura before he started hanging around Jenny. But hell, with Kate gone, Malcolm had his eye just about everywhere.

Laura was alone, but he never introduced himself to her. She appeared quiet and seemed to shield herself by engaging in conversation with another local who Malcolm had yet to formally meet. He wanted to introduce himself, but didn't want to look like an asshole to Jenny. Besides, he'd learn more about Laura by not asking. Not being a local meant that he had to be patient. If he was to learn more about this hot, petite, reddish-blonde shadow, it would be on the locals' terms, similar to how he'd been invited to Ellen's party.

The party fizzled to just a few couples, and Malcolm was more than ready to leave when Jenny suggested that they call it an evening. He found the whole damn thing boring anyway. He was ready to get back to his studio to shower and scrub off his nice-guy mask.

Chapter 10

A few weeks had passed since Ellen's beach birthday party. Kate was still back east, and Malcolm was still hanging out on Jenny's doorstep. He was at the Pink House almost every day. Jenny had volunteered to work on his sciatica pain free of charge, so twice a week Malcolm met with Jenny in her office for physical therapy. The three of them also met for lunch now and then: Jenny, Malcolm, and Diana. He'd be at the Pink House editing or studying, and a few minutes after the clock struck twelve noon, Jenny and Diana would make their way to the old Victorian home.

Their thing had been going on for well over a month and they hadn't even kissed. There was an awkwardness between them. Malcolm didn't know if it was his resistance to Jenny and her sensing it, or if it was Jenny's resistance to Malcolm and him sensing it. One evening after dinner, they walked out of the restaurant in a satisfied mood, and he hugged her. It was the first hug in which he actually felt received by her. After their embrace, she told him that he'd have to shave off his beard if he ever expected to be kissed by her. He belly laughed for two blocks as they walked back to the Tahoe.

Anyway, Jenny and Diana came trotting up to the Pink House, and as usual, Malcolm was waiting for them.

"You two hungry?" he asked.

"Yes, but I need to go to Kinko's to have some copies made."

"Want me to drive?"

"Sure," she answered, nodding. She loved to be chauffeured around, and Malcolm didn't mind. It was his way of doing something for her since she was helping him with his low back problems. He had injured his back several years earlier, a disc bulge most likely the result of his manhandling some huge piece of iron while in the tractor business. He was around thirty-five when it happened, but his mind believed that he was still an invincible seventeen. The mind can be tricked; the body isn't as naive. So, Jenny worked on his back, and he bought her lunch and drove her around town to run errands during her break.

They walked to the Tahoe, and he opened the door for Jenny. Diana hopped in first, and Malcolm stared at Jenny's backside as she slid in behind her dog. He was dying to get his hands on her ass, and dying even more to get behind it. They ended up stopping at Tillie's for a salad before driving to Kinko's.

"Well, it ends up that Ellen went too fast with Stanley, after all. Now she's having to back off," Jenny explained, as they headed for Kinko's.

"And recant on that sixty-nine page love letter she wrote him?" Malcolm asked in a disgusted tone.

"Well, no, she wants all that stuff. She only went too fast."

"She just doesn't know how to have it."

"I don't know."

"I do."

"How..."

"Well..."

"When you've never had it yourself?" she finished asking the question that Malcolm had interrupted."

"What I mean is that she just can't expect anything from him."

"Well, yeah, it could be a lot of different things like that. But I'm talking about what she wrote in the letter," Jenny explained, as she got out of the Tahoe to make her copies.

"Me, too," Malcolm answered, just before she closed the car door. He didn't even know what was in the letter Ellen had written Stanley, except for a few faint concepts that lingered from Jenny's recap of what it had contained. She told him about it when their love affair had just lifted off the runway only a few weeks before Jenny and Malcolm started running around together.

Malcolm didn't care about what was in the letter. All he knew was that the guy left his girlfriend for Ellen after she wrote him this long love letter telling him all about everything she wanted to have with him. Now that she had justified her fucking him with falling in love, it was all right to change her mind and reevaluate her relationship with this man. When guys do it they're insensitive assholes, but for some reason, when women do it, it's always justified somehow. This was the way Malcolm saw it and it was getting under his skin.

He really didn't give a shit about the two of them anyway. He was tunnel visioned on getting under Jenny's skirt. He wasn't arguing for Stanley or Ellen. He was just trying to throw a chink into Jenny's justification for not sleeping with him because Ellen had done Stanley too soon.

Malcolm watched Jenny shake her ass into Kinko's. He hit the lever on the side of his seat and reclined back before closing his eyes to plot. Diana climbed up onto his chest and started licking his face.

"Diana, I need a big favor," Malcolm said, getting her to stop kissing him. "I need you to have a little talk with your master. Lick her ear or something, and see if you can get her horny enough to fuck me." Diana yawned a great big sigh of dog breath onto Malcolm's face. "What do you think, girl? It's bound to do all of us some good. I mean, hell, there's a case of premium dog biscuits in it for you. I'll even let you pick 'em out, girl." Diana just nuzzled her head between Malcolm's chin and chest.

Jenny walked out and found Diana planted on Malcolm's chest. He was hoping that her mutt would give Jenny a few pointers.

"Where to now?" Malcolm asked eager as a pleasing pup waiting to be pitched a treat.

"Well, I need to go to the vet next to Tillie's."

"Okay," Malcolm answered, returning his seat to its upright position. It beat the hell out of him why she couldn't have gone there after they had finished lunch.

He pulled out into traffic, and a few minutes later pulled up in front of the Veterinary Hospital.

"We'll be right here waiting for you," he told her, Diana still in his lap.

A few minutes later Jenny came walking out of the vet. "Okay, a blow job, Diana. Tell her I'll settle for a blow job," Malcolm whispered to the dog just before Jenny opened the Tahoe door.

"What did you get?" Malcolm asked, as Jenny buckled her seat belt.

"Advantage."

"Flea killer, huh: get some for me, too?" He asked grinning.

"No, but I got some for Kira." Kira was her cat. "They make you buy four applications at a time and tell you to use it once a month. Actually, it really works for about four months," she answered, dancing around his smart-ass question.

"Where to now?" Malcolm asked, hoping for another shot at one of her good behavior snacks.

"How about the bank on Fountain Street?"

"You mean the credit union?"

"Yeah, the credit union."

He drove to the credit union and waited with Diana while Jenny ran her last errand. It only took a minute and she was back in the Tahoe.

"Where now?"

"I have a new patient scheduled at four. Oh, I need to go home to feed the kittens I'm sitting."

"Okay," Malcolm answered, driving to her house, which was only a few blocks away. "Oh yeah, I wanted to tell you while it was fresh in my mind," he added, turning the corner. "Just in case you get this irresistible, overwhelming desire to be with me tonight or tomorrow and decide that you can no longer deny yourself the longing, I'll be around. All you have to do is call."

Jenny smiled real big and then started laughing.

"You've been running errands, and I've been dreaming up smooth lines to use on you," he said, before joining in the laughter.

"I've got a copy of my book if you'd like to read it," he volunteered. He was really giving it to her to read with the hope that she'd no longer be able to resist him, once she'd finished. At the very least, she'd know what an asshole he really was. Then, if she still slept with him, it would be her own damn fault.

"Okay," was her only response; she didn't even seem excited.

When he dropped her off in the parking lot, he gave her a copy of the manuscript and then they embraced in another listless, lifeless hug.

* * * * *

After class that evening, Malcolm went back to Tillie's for a late dinner. He was already sitting at the counter when some fifty-something-year-old guy walked into the place. He wore a beige and brown plaid wool jacket and made just enough noise to announce his arrival to the rest of Tillie's patrons. He went through to the back dining room and returned a few minutes later. Malcolm hoped that it was just a newspaper and not the seat next to him that the dude was after; it was the seat. Malcolm turned in his chair a little to the right with his back partially toward the newcomer and ignored him. Malcolm was busy trying to make time with Lisa, the hotty manager, who was in her late twenties.

Lisa was raising a couple of kids on her own and had some religious blood of some sort pumping through her veins. Malcolm was certain it could be converted into the hottest passionate love affair his imagination could dream up, if only he could just set her off on the toot of having to save his soul from eternal damnation. Women like Lisa were always a challenge to Malcolm. The challenge wasn't getting them into bed; it was not having to go to church with them afterwards.

The guy in the plaid jacket got up and walked into the back dining room for an art appreciation session, ogling at the photography of a local artist whose work was currently being displayed at Tillie's. With all of his oohs and awes, he was drawing twice the attention to himself than he was giving to the photos. He walked back to the counter, sat down next to Malcolm again, and picked up the drink that had been set out for him.

"Now that's a work of art," he applauded, reaching for his warm drink and swigging down a third of it in one swallow.

"What is it?" Malcolm asked.

"Mellow Elixir. It's great on a cold night like tonight. Beats a coffee," he answered, with whipped cream still dangling from his mustache.

"Looks good," Malcolm said, having just had one himself but not confessing they had something in common. The Mellow Elixir was steamed milk with vanilla and spices and topped with whipped cream. Malcolm tried to ignore the guy so that he could eat his meal in peace.

"You a regular here?" he asked.

"I'm irregular, but I guess you could call me a regular. Been coming here for about a year," Malcolm answered.

"So you just moved to the area, huh?"

"'Bout a year ago," Malcolm repeated, with a half chewed mouthful of his chicken sandwich, stuffing in a few corn chips to hold back more of the forced conversation.

"They took that picture up there thirty years ago and the only reason that I'm not in it is because I was a couple of blocks from here, down on Cannery Row," he explained, pointing to the huge employee photo that hung over the swinging double doors that led back into the kitchen.

"Quite something that after thirty years you can still come back to the same place," Malcolm said, realizing that he was helping the ol' boy interrupt his dinner.

"Hell, we didn't think..."

"You'd see the next day?" Malcolm finished his sentence.

"Yeah, guess you're right about that, but I was going to say how I never thought they'd be here in this century," he said with a chuckle.

Malcolm took a swig of water without responding to him.

"I've been eating Jive Turkey sandwiches and drinking Mellow Elixirs for thirty years."

"No Kidding," Malcolm said, thinking how boring, yet appreciating the fact that someone could actually have been downing Jive Turkeys and Mellow Elixirs for that damn long.

"Amazing thing is that most of the people in that picture are still running around here. Carol there in the middle, the cute young girl with long brown hair works at the aquarium. She feeds the otters. She takes care of the babies, the orphans."

"What do you do?" Malcolm asked.

"I'm an entrepreneur," he answered. "Do a lot of different things."

"Seems to be a lot of those around here," Malcolm answered.

"You got that right. I do electrical repairs on antiques and other things. Got an antique warehouse. I'm a jack of all trades and a master of a few, I hope."

Malcolm listened. Chloe, the other waitress on duty walked up to refill Malcolm's water and offered Talkie a refill as well.

"Yeah, I had to bring my buddy to work. He works at the Seven Gables Inn. I worked on that remodel five years ago. Had to fix a pipe there the other day. Someone put a brass fitting on a galvanized pipe and it finally gave."

Malcolm nodded, taking another bite of sandwich.

"My buddy sleeps over at the Inn five nights a week. He does other things there, too. Stays at my place the other couple of nights a week when he's off. He's got a dog."

"Yeah?" Malcolm muttered.

"Yeah, I like the dog better than my friend. He knows it, too. You've probably seen the dog," he said, waiting for Malcolm to ask what the dog looked like.

"What kind of dog?" Malcolm conceded.

"Just a mutt."

"Big or small?"

"He's got Dalmatian in him. He's smarter than hell. You can talk to him just like a human being. He understands, really."

"I thought that Dalmatians weren't all that smart," said Chloe, who was standing behind the counter listening to Talkie's flow of bullshit.

"He's only part Dalmatian. His brain is another breed," Malcolm said, winking to Chloe as she tried to hold back a giggle.

"He stands about this high," Talkie said, holding his hand about eighteen inches above the counter. "His name is Zero. He's all white, but has a big black spot over his right eye."

Malcolm nodded, finishing the last of his corn chips.

"Can I get you guys anything else?" Chloe asked.

"None for me," Talkie answered.

"I'm done, too. Thanks," Malcolm answered, contemplating his capacity to stomach dessert while having to listen to his newfound, long-lost friend.

"I stay up late. A night owl," Talkie said, pitching out some fresh bait.

"That's how it should be. Stay up 'til you fall asleep and wake when you're rested," Malcolm answered, nodding. "That's how I do it, too."

"I was born at ten-seventeen at night. I was born a night owl."

"I was born at six-nineteen in the morning, and I keep the same hours as you do," Malcolm said.

"Guess that shoots that theory all to hell," he said chuckling.

"Maybe not. I've been rebelling since the moment I was born," Malcolm answered, joining his laughter.

"I lived in Pacific Grove for twenty years. Now I'm living in Carmel. Got a good deal though," Talkie said, shifting from his shit-canned theory.

"Yeah?"

"Yeah, my friends own a home there, but they're up in Oregon running a bed and breakfast. Only come down twice a year. So I've got cheap rent, and I keep their room open for them."

"Sounds like a good deal."

"Yep, just take care of the place for them. Well, I pay rent, but it's a hell of a deal," he repeated.

"You're lucky."

"You should see the stars there in Carmel. There aren't any street lights, you know."

"No kidding," Malcolm said, not mentioning that they might well be neighbors.

"Yeah, the illumination in Pacific Grove from the street lights makes a big difference. Most people don't pay attention to things like that, you know." Talkie explained, as if he was one up on society.

"Yeah, I guess you're right about that," Malcolm answered, thinking about how much some people miss because they never shut up long enough to listen to what might be going on around them.

"Moved here thirty years ago."

"Where from?"

"Chicago. Too cold for me."

"The Windy City, huh?"

"Man, when that wind comes off Lake Michigan, it gets cold. I lived there before there was wind-chill, you know," he said, as if wind-chill had been invented in his lifetime.

Malcolm didn't bother responding.

"People here walk around in cotton T-shirts in fifty degree weather," Talkie added. "That's why everyone around here has a cold all the time."

Chloe walked up with their bills. Malcolm gave her his credit card, and Talkie gave her a twenty. Chloe ran the credit card through and brought Talkie his change. She walked back to the register and waited for the charge receipt to print.

Picking up the ten-dollar bill that Chloe had set in front of him, holding it between his thumb and index finger and letting it dangle in the air, Talkie said: "I'm going to need some change."

Chloe was still waiting for Malcolm's credit card receipt and didn't hear Talkie's request. She returned with the credit card voucher for Malcolm to sign and left to tend to a table in the back dining room. Malcolm signed the voucher and stuffed the card back into his leather business cardholder that doubled as a money clip.

Talkie stood and walked to the till. "Can I trade you this ten for a five and some singles," he asked, as Chloe returned to the cash register.

"Sure thing," Chloe said, changing the ten.

Talkie set down a dollar and some change on the ledge next to the register. He turned to Malcolm as he was putting the rest of the money into his pocket.

"It was nice talking to you," Talkie said.

"It was a pleasure to meet you," Malcolm said, extending his hand to Talkie.

"I'm Alan."

"No kidding. I'm Alan, too," Malcolm answered, as they shook hands.

Chapter 11

Curious about her reaction, Malcolm stopped by Jenny's a few days after giving her the book. She was nearly finished, only had four chapters to go. She seemed lost that day, in a daze. She and Diana joined Malcolm for a long walk on the beach. They talked some, but she was somewhere else. Malcolm often wondered if she was really alive. Physically she was, but he wondered if she was really living with the rest of the humans who inhabited the planet.

He invited her to dinner at Tillie's, but she wasn't up to it, said she was happy just lying around napping, listening to music, reading, and watching television. Diana and Kira filled her need for companionship. Malcolm had different needs. The companionship he was looking for was with a woman who could be present with him. The napping and music thing was right up his ally, but so was curling up and rolling around together.

He walked into Tillie's around eight that evening for dinner. Some guy was sitting at the counter. His overcoat was draped across the seat next to him with a book placed face down on top of the coat. He was in his mid to late forties with partially receding, brown, collar length hair that was feathered and parted in the middle. He had a bushy brown mustache and wore wire-rimmed glasses with thick lenses. A miniature loop earring hung from his pierced left ear lobe and two silver bracelets draped his left wrist. He wore a light blue, striped, cotton, short-sleeve shirt, blue jeans, and pointed cowboy boots.

"Is my jacket in your way?" he asked, as Malcolm passed the coat-covered empty seat next to the man.

"No, not to worry," Malcolm answered, as he sat in the stool on the opposite side of the jacket. *The perfect buffer zone*, he thought.

"What can I get you?" Lisa asked, having just walked up to take Malcolm's order.

"I don't know yet."

"Water?"

"Yes, please."

"My daughter just got this CD," Lisa said, talking about the song that was playing on the radio.

"Who is it?" Malcolm asked.

"Santana," she answered, as she set his water down on the counter.

"I thought so. I like it."

"It's driving me crazy," Lisa said. "She plays it over and over again."

"I just bought a John Cougar Mellencamp CD last night. It's a remake of some of his older stuff. It's great," Malcolm said, as Lisa left to check on her tables. The guy two seats down shifted in his chair.

"I saw him lead off a ZZ Top concert years ago," the guy said. "He was pissed off because things weren't right on stage and he started kicking shit all over the place."

"Really?" Malcolm asked, as Lisa walked back up to take his order.

"What's it going to be?" Lisa asked.

"I don't know yet, but I am going to have carrot cake after dinner," Malcolm announced. "Give me another minute. No, give me the Blue Bird," he said, as if he had just had an epiphany.

"You got it."

"Does that come with potato chips?"

"Sure does."

"Can I get corn chips instead?"

"You bet." Lisa said, scribbling down the corn chip side bar before walking away to place the order.

"Sorry about that. We were talking about Mellencamp," Malcolm said.

"Yeah, I've got a few of his albums. Got tired of him though. He never seems to come out with anything new. Same stuff, over and over again."

"Have you listened to his *Mr. Happy Go Lucky* album?"

"Yeah," he nodded, with an unimpressed expression.

"That's some hellacious writing man."

"It's all right."

"How 'bout John Haitt?" Malcolm asked.

"Got four of his albums."

"I watched him on TV one night and then went out and bought one of his CD's, but I can't ever remember the name of it."

"He's pretty good. Wasn't until he wrote something for Bonnie Raitt and played on one of her albums before he got any money and started to make it though."

Malcolm didn't respond, as he reflected on how many experts graced the counter at Tillie's. The man then picked up the book on the counter in front of his jacket. It was a C.S. Lewis book, but Malcolm couldn't make out the title.

"Which Lewis book you got there?"

"*The Great Divorce*," he answered, holding up the book to show its cover and as he did, Malcolm noticed a ring of flames tattooed around his left bicep. "My sister's married to a preacher. She mails me stuff to read all the time. I'm just starting on a new pack she sent. She's prejudiced though."

"What do you mean?"

"I send her stuff, but she just throws it away."

"Because it challenges her beliefs?"

"Yeah, exactly. Has to fit into her set of rules," he said. "I still say it how I see it, though. Even if she can't handle it."

"That's how it should be," Malcolm encouraged.

"You're damn right about that."

Lisa set Malcolm's Blue Bird down in front of him: a turkey burger with melted blue cheese.

"Catsup or mustard?" Lisa asked.

"Yes, please."

"Regular mustard or spicy?"

"Regular, and more water, please."

Lisa set the catsup and mustard bottles on the counter and went to get the water.

"I'm going on three hours of sleep today," the man announced. Chloe walked by while he was making his confession. Malcolm had been hanging around Tillie's long enough for Chloe to catch on to his instigating antics, even though he was always complaining about people and acting like he'd rather be left alone.

"Last time I went on three hours of sleep it was damn well worth it," Malcolm needled. Chloe looked at Malcolm and began to shake her head and smile. Malcolm started drifting back to the last all-night encounter he had with a guilt-ridden, sexually repressed, divorcing girlfriend who hadn't gotten it proper for months, if not years. For some reason, Malcolm was the safe one, the lucky man who was present at the resurrection of her lost passion and newfound proclamation of sexual liberation. He'd bedded a lot of women who were in this slot. For some reason, he was always the one who seemed safe to them; who was he to shatter their illusions? They were going to make him into what they needed him to be, regardless of what he said or did.

"I stayed up all night last New Year's, too," the cowboy bragged, not wanting to tell Malcolm that his sleepless night had nothing to do with sex. "I went to a party on New Year's Eve, and ended up in the guest house. I was watching Kung Fu when the sun came up."

Malcolm wanted to ask him what she was really like, but didn't have a chance or the heart.

"It was the original Kung Fu movie. I just sat there in the guesthouse watching television while the sun came up. I can still do it. Didn't think that I could, but I can," the cowboy announced in a proud of himself tone.

Malcolm still wanted to ask him what she was like, but by then he knew that the guy must have been alone. Any other man would have been bragging about having her under the covers as he watched the sun coming up, and here this guy was watching the grasshopper snatch pebbles from the master's hand.

"I've been coming here for sixteen years," he announced. This guy wouldn't stop. The quieter Malcolm was, the more the cowboy volunteered.

"I met a guy here the other night. He's been eating Jive Turkeys and drinking Mello Elixirs for thirty years," Malcolm said.

"I bet I know him."

"Alan?"

"Yeah, that's him. He's probably in that picture up there," he said, pointing to the thirty-year-old photo above the kitchen door.

"No, he was two blocks down on Cannery row when they

took that picture."

"That guy has all kinds of guns. He repairs and collects them."

"He told me that he was into antiques and repairing electrical things, an entrepreneur he said."

"Yeah, he does a lot of things, but I remember when he moved from PG to Carmel. You should have seen all the shit he had."

"Told me that he lived in Pacific Grove for twenty years."

"He did. I don't say much to him though. I mean, he's a cool guy, but if you tell him anything, he tells everybody else."

"No kidding," Malcolm said, wondering if the cowboy might be guilty of the same crime.

"Well, like if I said that I was interested in renting a place or something like that, he'd leave and go tell the people that I was interested in it."

"I'm not following you."

"Like take a woman for example. I might say that I like her *dress* and he'd go tell her that I was interested in *her*."

Malcolm laughed, glad that he hadn't said much to Talkie the evening he ran into him.

"Are you taking classes next semester?" Chloe asked Malcolm from the other end of the coffee counter.

"Yeah, but I don't know what," he answered.

"I went to Monterey Peninsula College to get my associates degree. Went back after twenty years," the cowboy announced.

"That's what I'm doing," Malcolm said. Chloe looked at him and rolled her eyes.

"I took statistics. I couldn't get a counselor to sign me off to take the class, because I didn't have any prior math, so I signed myself off. They never checked, and when the teacher found out, I told him it was my forty-nine bucks and that I was taking the class anyway."

"He didn't care?" Malcolm asked, thinking about how he still needed to take all his math.

"He was cool."

"Sounds like something I need to look into."

"I took the psychology of women, too. There were thirty-eight of them, and me, the only man in the class."

"Did you take it to figure women out?"

"Hell, no, I took it to fix an 'F' I got in an earlier psyche class. My buddies all have these stories about how tough it is with women, and then I tell them all about how I took the psychology of women, alone, with thirty-eight of them, so top that!"

"I'm gonna do just what you did in statistics," Malcolm announced. He liked the idea and had actually considered something of the sort before he ever ran into this cowboy.

"I remember there was this really hot looking Asian woman in my statistics class. I got her to help me. She was smart *and* good-looking. I mean, *really* good-looking. The two guys sitting next to her flunked."

"Dumb fucks were probably staring at her all the time instead of her papers," Malcolm said laughing.

"And she smelled just like kimchi, too. Hell, I didn't mind. I like the smell of kimchi," the cowboy said, laughing along with Malcolm.

"You ready for your carrot cake?" Lisa asked, interrupting the shit-slinging session.

"Sure," Malcolm answered, and half-a-minute later he was forking into a fresh slice of cake as the cowboy carried on.

"I went with a buddy to eat one night on Alvarado Street and ordered three pieces of cake. The waitress got smart-ass with me and asked if I wanted them served one at a time. I told her: 'Hell no, I want them all three lined up right here in front of me along with three glasses of milk.' I fixed her ass," the cowboy said in a defiant tone.

"Sounds like you wanted to have your cake and eat it, too," Malcolm teased, and then started belly laughing all over again. Chloe was standing behind the dessert case busted up laughing, too, and for a moment, the cowboy seemed clueless that the laughter was about him.

"You're damn right about that one," cowboy said, before joining the laughter, and then announced: "Man, I've got to go take a leak. I had five cups of coffee since I got here."

The cowboy took off to the bathroom, and Chloe walked over to refill Malcolm's glass. "You're awful," she said, shaking her head and giggling.

"Yeah, but you love it," Malcolm answered, grinning one of his smart-ass grins.

The cowboy was back at the counter a few minutes later and picked up where he'd left off.

"In seventy-three I was going to LSU, majoring in drugs and women. After three weeks, the dean called me in and told me not to bother going to class anymore. Told me that I could stay in the dorm and use my meal card for the semester, but I might just as well skip class, because I wasn't going to pass them anyway. Guess I must have been disrupting things somehow," cowboy said, with a go-figure look.

"Where you from?" Malcolm asked.

"Texas; my dad was a special investigator. Got shipped out there on the JFK case. He was a mean son-of-a-bitch. Fucker loved to ask questions. After hounding me about something for a dozen times, I'd just look at him and tell him that it was none of his goddamn business."

"What did he do?"

"Slapped the shit out of me. I was already in trouble, and he was going to do it anyway. I just got tired of all his goddamn questions. He was real sweet to be around, if you know what I mean? He'd be in jail for child abuse these days."

"Sounds like it," Malcolm answered.

"My mom was meaner than hell, too. I mean, her whippin's were more than a punishment," he said, in a serious tone, then looking around almost like he was checking to see if his mother had overheard his betrayal of her.

"Sounds like she was in a rage." Malcolm suggested.

"She'd break my fucking fingers. Just grab them and bend them right on back. Then on the way to the hospital, she'd tell me to say that I fell out of my little red wagon. I'd go in and they'd jerk my finger back into place, put a splint on it and send me on my way. They never asked how it happened."

"Where in Texas did you live?" Malcolm asked

"Anywhere you can think of."

"It's a damn big state."

"I lived in New Orleans, too. Used to go out fishing with the Cajun. Did you know that a seagull can breathe in but not out?"

"No, I sure didn't."

"Air goes in, but it can't come out."

"What do they do, fart to exhale?"

"Not always," cowboy explained. "When we were out fishing, these Cajuns would start chumming the seagulls by pitching baitfish out to them and then they'd grab Alka-Seltzer tablets and start pitching that shit. Those poor seagulls would gulp down the Alka-Seltzer, and a few minutes later they'd literally blow up. Those goddamn Cajuns got the biggest kick out of blowing up seagulls," cowboy said, shaking his head.

"My brothers and I used to fish. Every now and then we'd catch a seagull in our line when we'd cast out."

"Hell, I caught some other kind of bird fishing one day down at the wharf. I had just baited up and cast out, and the next thing I knew, my rod started doubling up like nobody's business. I had these Japanese tourists watching me. Filming me with their video camera," cowboy explained, as a big smile grew on his face. "They thought I had one hell of a fish on. You should have seen them when I pulled that goddamn bird out of the water."

"I bet they really got a kick out of that bird biting the shit out of you when you had to take the hook from its bill."

"Yeah, hell, I had one of those Japanese guys hold my pole while I took the hook out. I know those goddamn Japs went home with their film telling their buddies how us crazy fucking Americans are fishing for birds now," cowboy said, grinning from ear to ear, proud of himself for having added some more confusion to an already spinning-out-of-control world.

Chapter 12

He had a late morning therapy session with Jenny, and when they were finished, he offered to buy lunch. Diana guided them on the walk to Tillie Gort's. Jenny tied Diana up outside the restaurant, and Malcolm went ahead to snatch the window seat that had a view out to where Diana was being tethered. Jenny had just finished reading Malcolm's book, and it was understood he didn't want any feedback from her. He had given it to her so she would get to know him better. The real motive was, of course, so he would get to know *her* better, that is to say, every square inch of her body.

They ordered and then made small talk. Somehow, Malcolm got on the subject of his many failed love affairs. Feeling somewhat ashamed and vulnerable, he caught himself and backtracked because he didn't want her to think he'd fucked half the women in California. He hadn't slept with that many women, although it wasn't because of a waning libido, just a lack of opportunity. What he was trying to tell her was that he'd been through a few women and that they had been lovers, just not in love.

"It's not like I had a new woman every other week or anything like that. It was more my need to have an outlet," he tried to explain, but somehow it didn't come out right. It was the truth, though. Malcolm pretty much had the same girlfriends for months if not years. He was just the typical bad boy who had more than one at a time. He didn't lie to any of them, just didn't volunteer things. He had even been faithful to his wife in his marriage, just not to himself.

"Oh, come on. You know you're a slut," Jenny jabbed, as she spread mustard on her veggie mushroom burger.

"It isn't like I've gone through that many women," Malcolm defended, "and I didn't sleep with all of them," he added, as her dog started in on one of her yipping fits.

She stood up and walked outside to quiet Diana, and after giving the pooch some attention, Jenny returned to finish her lunch, but as soon as she sat down, Diana started in again.

The barking was working on Malcolm's nerves. He couldn't command the situation, and Jenny wasn't paying attention as he tried to justify his past. She had yet to invite him back to her place for a mid-afternoon roll in the hay, and he seemed to be powerless over this dilemma as well. So, needless to say, at that moment Diana and Jenny were both a royal pain in Malcolm's ass.

It was a bad day to be expecting anything. Malcolm should have stayed at home, but it was too late for that. But, he could damn well return to his studio and that's exactly what he did after walking Jenny and her little yipper back to their office.

He seldom took a nap but did that afternoon. He wasn't tired as much as he just needed to escape. At times, being with Jenny threw him into a funk. The problem was, she was so damn beautiful and captivating that he was often unaware of the affect she had on him. He was a lot like a little boy who worshiped his mother.

* * * * *

It was Turner's birthday that evening, and Cassi had called to invite Malcolm over for cake and ice cream. When he drove up to their home, there was no sign of any other cars, so Malcolm thought he might be the only visitor, but as he approached the front door, he heard the laughter and cheer. Cassi had invited several of the neighbors over to help celebrate.

Turner had a way with people. He had a way of being honest with words, which held a subtle shock factor, yet he was harmless. In other words, he'd joke about life and the nuances of relationships in a way that would instantly connect him to whoever it was he was engaging. It was that persona that allowed Turner to be liked by most people, and, at the same time, it allowed him to maintain a certain distance. So Turner's neighbors loved him, and they had all gathered together to celebrate him and his persona.

Malcolm, and a few others close to him, related to Turner in a much deeper, more honest way. Malcolm and Turner really knew each other, knew what was behind the mask they wore that allowed them to dance around the dogmas of society.

Turner looked up at Malcolm when he walked into the hallway leading to the kitchen; a smile of relief lit up his face. Malcolm could tell he was happy to have someone around who really knew and understood him, not that Cassi didn't, but Turner and Malcolm had a history that went back twenty-five years.

Turner left the kitchen where everyone had gathered and joined Malcolm in the hallway where he had waited. They embraced. It was Turner's thirty-ninth birthday, his third child had just been born, his first daughter; Turner was living his life to the fullest and loving every minute of it.

"How's Kate?" Turner asked, as he let go of their hug.

"She's fine, and still five thousand miles away."

"Come on. Let's go have some cake," he said, dragging Malcolm into the crowd-infested kitchen.

Cassi's mom was still there, helping out with the newborn. Karen was a hell of a cook. She had baked Turner a birthday cake from scratch. It was white cake with chocolate frosting. She had also whipped up some homemade banana ice cream. Once again, Karen had out-done herself.

Someone handed Malcolm a bowl of cake and ice cream, and he settled into the crowd and greeted the neighbors. Their kids played and went to school together; most of them went to the same church. They'd all been working at the same jobs for years, their lives peaceful and stable; nothing much ever seemed to change. Malcolm had met most of them on previous occasions over the last couple of years. Many were curious about his so-called free and adventurous lifestyle and all the joy it supposedly brought him. Malcolm was Turner's crazy friend who had quit his job, moved to the coast, was going to the community college studying general education trying to get an AA degree for reasons only God knew, and writing books for reasons even God didn't know.

Malcolm was the mystery man. He stood for everything they weren't and they wanted to know all about it. He downplayed everything. There really wasn't anything to play up. His life was just as mundane if not less fulfilling than their own, but it seemed as if he'd become their symbol of freedom and hope. Then again, maybe he wasn't. Maybe Malcolm just needed to believe that they were all living vicariously through him, just to make himself feel more justified in his actions and comfortable in his chaos.

"Come on," Turner said, leading Malcolm into the garage and out the side door into his backyard. There was a fire smoldering in a terra cotta clay firepot Cassi had bought a year earlier at some garage sale. Turner threw a few pieces of wood on the fire, squeezed some lighter fluid on it and watched it flare up. They pulled a couple of chairs up to the fire and sat down.

"Still messing with that physical therapist?" he asked, knowing that Malcolm wasn't too happy about not having Kate around.

"Messing's a good word for it, but it's more like she's messing with me. Hell, she's got me so confused I don't even know what it is to be a man anymore."

"Why you messing with her then?"

"Because I don't have anything better to do."

"Maybe."

"All right. Cut the shit. Let's have it."

"I think you're messing with her 'cause she won't sleep with you."

"That's all the more reason for me not to be messing with her."

"For you, that's all the more reason to be chasing that shit."

"I don't even know what I'd do if she did turn my way."

"Yeah, and what about Kate?"

"What about her?"

"Well, hell! Did you haul her all the way across the country to fuck around and cheat on her?"

"I didn't haul her out here. She came here to go to school."

"Yeah, but now that her dad's dead, you might be the only reason she stays."

"I never really thought about that. Hell, for all I know, she might not come back at all."

"Then what the hell are we even talking about this for?"

"You brought it up," Malcolm answered, trying to throw things back Turner's way.

"Maybe you care about Kate a lot more than you'd like to admit."

"Yeah, but caring about her and having her are two different things," Malcolm answered. "Turner, I'm tired of being a bachelor."

"If you really want her, you'll have to make a stand for her, but give her a little time and space right now. She's dealing with some heavy shit and she's got to get clear with herself."

"I am."

"Yeah you are, but you're trying to fuck that physical therapist, too."

"So?"

"So, hell…"

"What?"

"Don't give me that what shit."

"You're a grumpy old fucker tonight, aren't you?"

"It's my goddamn birthday; I can be as grumpy as I damn well please."

"Yeah, go on."

"Malcolm, you've been single way too long, and I don't think there's any hope for you to change that."

"You mean with Kate?"

"I mean with you."

"Why with me?"

"You know what? You and I have been friends for the last twenty-five years."

"Almost twenty-six."

"And we've been through a lot of times together: good and bad."

"You're my best friend Turner."

"And you're mine, but if you fuck that little Kate around I'm going to kick your ass."

"What do you mean?"

"I mean, I've seen you go through women like they were cotton candy, and most of them did need to disappear. But Kate doesn't deserve to be treated like a carnival ride that you can hop off of when you get bored."

"She's not even here. What that hell am I supposed to do with her, Turner?"

"You are going to treat her like she's… like she's God."

"How the hell am I going to do that?"

"With some Goddamn respect! That's how! She isn't fucking throw away material!"

"Shit, Turner, you don't have to get so mad about it," Malcolm said, knowing that no matter what happened between Kate and Malcolm, Turner would still be standing next to him. He didn't have a choice, they knew too much about each other not to be friends.

"Mad's the only thing that penetrates that thick skull of yours."

"Hey Turner."

"Hey what?"

"Fuck you!"

"You're not my type you queer fucker. Come on lets go see if there's anymore ice cream."

Chapter 13

Jenny had purchased tickets to an event in Santa Cruz. The Fat Fry was a concert series that a local radio station and several other Santa Cruz area businesses hosted. John Hiatt was the headliner. The concert took place in a park-like amphitheater setting. In front of the stage it was all grass, so if you wanted a seat, you brought your own.

Jenny had phoned Malcolm earlier and was running late. They hadn't set a time, but knew that Hiatt would be performing at five-thirty, although there were several other big name acts that would be on stage the entire afternoon before Hiatt's gig. Malcolm wanted to arrive early but, instead of pushing things, went with the flow.

He finally picked Jenny up around two that afternoon. She was wearing a sundress. She had put some lotion on her face that had little luminescent sparkles that dried on her skin. Malcolm thought it was cute, kind of a flower-girlish retro look.

Their first stop was at the market to purchase some food for the outing. Next, they went to a variety-like drug store to buy some lawn chairs and at last were ready to take the forty-five minute drive to Santa Cruz. They merged smoothly onto the freeway.

About twenty minutes north of Monterey, traffic was backing up where Highway 156 merged into Highway 1. Malcolm already felt that he was missing out on things, so he turned off the highway hoping to find the back way he'd taken on his way late one evening from Santa Cruz while trying to avoid road construction at Moss Landing.

He wound through the hills on the back roads without having a clue where they were, but to Malcolm it felt right. He'd traveled this way for years. He knew they were heading in the general direction of their destination. The route he chose might have taken longer than if they had waited for the traffic jam to clear up, but at least they were moving. Malcolm was the type of person who would rather drive around in circles and go nowhere than be stuck in traffic.

They couldn't find a parking place once they finally did arrive, but there was an open field behind the designated parking area, so Malcolm hopped the curb and parked in the weeds. It was four-thirty by the time they were inside the park and found a place to set up the chairs. Bruce Cockburn was on stage. Jenny saw some guy she knew so she wandered off to go visit him. Malcolm kicked back and soaked up all the Cockburn that he could. A while later, Jenny came back and sat down next to Malcolm. She seemed restless or uninterested in the music.

"I'm going to look for Nial," Jenny announced. "He's supposed to be here with his wife," she added, and then, before getting up, kissed Malcolm on the cheek. He almost fell out of his chair. It was the first time she'd actually taken the initiative to show any type of affection towards him since they'd met.

Hiatt was great. They actually walked down to be close to the stage when the show kicked off. The music and the crowd, it was all one great big vibration. A vibration that Malcolm hoped would open Jenny to him. After the first few songs, they walked back to their spot on the grass to take in the rest of his act in a more relaxed setting. When the concert was over, they folded up their blanket and chairs. While waiting for the departing crowd to disperse, Malcolm hugged Jenny, but the vibration hadn't penetrated her like he had hoped. If it had, it certainly hadn't changed the quality of her listless hugs. He wanted to be all excited about her, but she wasn't helping him out one bit. *Did she really kiss me earlier or was that something that I carried back from dreamland last night?* Malcolm asked himself, as they walked out with the herd to the Tahoe. After the traffic had thinned, Malcolm hopped the curb and started making their way out of Aptos.

"You haven't said anything about my sparkles," Jenny said, as Malcolm turned onto the freeway for the drive back to Pacific Grove.

"No, but I noticed them as soon as I picked you up."

"Do you like them?"

"They look delectable."

"Oh, you pervert!"

At a loss for words, Malcolm tried to figure out how in the twinkling of one of her sparkles, he'd become a pervert; even if he did want to lick every last one of those shining little stars off her Milky Way until there was nothing left but a black hole. He tried to roll with the punch. After merging into traffic, he started a new conversation. They talked some on the drive back, even held hands a little bit, but the hand holding thing was about as awkward as her hugs, lifeless and empty. The only real problem was Malcolm not being able to accept the fact that nothing was going right in their relationship, at least from his point of view.

If they were to spend anymore time together that day, Jenny would have had to make an about face and lay a lip lock on Malcolm that dropped him to his knees, and she wasn't showing any signs of enlisting into the infantry of his fantasies or desires.

He dropped her off at home and made his way back to the studio. He found a message from Jenny requesting him to call because she needed to ask him something. He returned her call right away.

"Hello, it's me. What's going on?" Malcolm asked.

"I just felt like you checked out somewhere on our drive home. I wanted to check that out with you. Is everything alright?"

"I don't know," he hesitated. The pervert thing flashed to Malcolm, but he considered it trivial and tried to follow himself to see if something else surfaced, but nothing came to him. "I think it was that pervert comment you made. Yeah, that's it. I mean, I guess I wonder if you really see me that way."

"Oh, no. I was just teasing you."

"Well, it just went in. I mean, it stung, and I just couldn't figure what I might have said or done that would make me out to be a pervert to you."

"I'm sorry if I hurt your feelings. You haven't done anything to make me think that about you. You've been the perfect gentleman to me. I mean, I'd have you here in bed with me right now, but something just isn't quite right about it."

"It's an awkwardness," Malcolm said. "It was there when I hugged you at the concert."

"You hugged me?" she asked, forgetting that they'd actually made physical contact. It was so seldom that they did embrace.

Malcolm figured that when they did come together it meant something.

"Yeah, when the concert was over."

"Oh," was her only reply, and then after a moment of silence asked: "So you don't think we should be sleeping together?"

"Hell, I don't even feel comfortable hugging you. How in the hell could I be sleeping with you?"

"Oh, I feel so relieved," Jenny answered and then sighed.

"I never push a woman," Malcolm confirmed. "Well, I've pushed a woman before, but it wasn't about sex. I was already involved with her, and I wanted to be closer to her. It was my own insecurity though, but I never push a woman about sex," he added.

"Oh, I'm so glad that we can talk about this."

"The woman always comes to the man. I mean, hell, look how we're physically put together. Woman is the receiver. She's the one who has to open to the man. As far as I'm concerned, if a woman doesn't open herself up, nothing can really happen; nothing of any real meaning anyway."

"Well, it doesn't feel right to me. Not that it might not be different someday. I mean, it's possible that it might be the right thing for us someday, but there's no need for me to have to decide right now, right? I mean, I don't have anything else happening with me right now, and you don't have anything else going on with you right now that would make me have to choose, right?"

"Uh huh," Malcolm answered, caught up with her comment and wishing that he did have something going with another woman.

"So there's nothing we need to do right now?" she asked.

"You know, Jenny, normally, I would have left a woman like you a long time ago, but for some reason I haven't," Malcolm confessed, clinging to the idea that they'd come together for a reason, and he was sticking around to find out what the reason was, even if Jenny had achieved about the highest rank in the pain-in-the-ass section of Malcolm's little black book.

* * * * *

Lewis phoned later that evening. He was making a run to the store for milk or diapers. He often called Malcolm in the evening from his cellular phone when he was running errands, having escaped for a short time from the demands of his wife and kids.

"Hey man, what's going on?"

"She's fucking driving me nuts, man!"

"Who?"

"Jenny."

"The physical therapist?" he asked, laughing. Lewis had been with Malcolm through so many women that it was a lot easier for him to relate to them by their professions as opposed to their names. Sometimes he even made up nicknames for the women because of some story Malcolm had told him. It was kind of funny even if it did have a way of depersonalizing the women.

"Yeah, the physical therapist," Malcolm confirmed, joining his laughter.

"What's she doing?"

"I've been hanging with her for couple months now and she's yet to even kiss me on the lips."

"You're letting her do it."

"Every time I get pissed off and back away from her, she calls and seems to let herself get a little bit closer."

"And then she's got you panting for her all over again."

"She bought tickets for us to go to see John Hiatt in Santa Cruz today."

"You go?"

"Yeah!"

"So what happened?"

"First of all, she called yesterday and wanted to hang out, so we did for most of the day. I even cuddled up with her for the first time. I think it was more about her needing a nap, though. Nothing happened, not even a kiss. Then we go to the concert today and pretty much had a great time. I hugged her after the concert, thinking that she might be opening up to me a little."

"Why don't you just kiss her, or kiss her goodbye."

"I'm waiting for a sign. You know when a woman's open to you."

"And this one isn't! So leave her alone."

"She feels like a limp noodle when I hug her. Like she's not really there."

"Maybe she's not. Maybe she's already got some guy taking care of her."

"I don't think so."

"Don't be so sure of it."

"Okay, check this out. We're leaving the concert, driving home. I make some comment on her looking delectable and she comes back calling me a pervert. It went in like an arrow. I mean fuck! I've treated her like the Queen of fucking Sheba. Haven't laid a hand on her!"

"You sure she wasn't just teasing?"

"She was, but it still threw me. I was lost on the drive home. I mean we talked, but I wasn't there. I dropped her off, and when I get home, I already had a message from her. I phone back and she says she's feeling insecure about how things ended. Wanted to know if I knew anything about it."

"Yeah?"

"So I asked her if she viewed me as a pervert. She said that she was only teasing. That's when we really got honest. She said that she's feeling more affection toward me lately, but that something was still not right or she'd have already gone to bed with me."

"She's jerking you off!"

"I don't think she knows how, but you know what, she's right. It does feel awkward; something's missing for me, too."

"She's a challenge for you, that's all."

"Lewis, you know me too well. Part of me is just hanging in there to get a return on my investment. Another part of me wants to cut the loss and move on."

"With as many women that you've been through over the last few years, you can damn sure afford to take a loss. Cut her loose, Malcolm. She's robbing you of a shit-load of energy, and besides that, you're not getting laid."

"How?"

"What do you mean how? Turn asshole on her if you have to."

"Well, I like her. I don't want to be mean."

"What about that NLP shit you used to always tell me about. You know, some people are visual, some auditory, and some kinesthetic..."

"And I figure out what she is, and start communicating in a different way," Malcolm interrupted, finishing Lewis's sentence. "I'm going to have to talk to you more often."

"Now, go have a beer and forget about this honey," Lewis suggested.

"But what if . . ."

"Just go drink an O'Doul's and forget about her. She's fucking history. We've got more important things to worry about."

"Like what?"

"Like where your next piece of ass is coming from. Hell, you're keeping me married. I can't afford to have you fall in love and out of crisis."

"What the hell you talking about?"

"Malcolm, you can't stop now. I got a wife, two kids, and a mortgage up the ass. I can't afford to leave. You got to live this shit out for both of us, man."

"Like you don't like being married."

"Just remember my wife and kids next time you start thinking about settling down," Lewis answered.

"You've got a great wife and kids," Malcolm told him.

"Exactly! So don't make me fuck them all up by having to go out and do what you're doing. You're doing it for both of us, man. Actually, if the truth were told, I'd say you're doing it for all mankind."

Chapter 14

Over the next few weeks, Malcolm fell into the same routine, Jenny worked on his back, and he edited and studied at the Pink House where he was available for her to track him down and enlist his companionship. His evenings were either spent at school or at home correcting in the computer what he had edited earlier in the day.

Midweek, Malcolm spoke with Kate. She sounded over-burdened and depressed. He wanted to ask her to come back to California, but didn't. He didn't want to push her; he knew better. Now that her father was gone, he didn't want to become the object of her rebellion.

On the weekend there was a celebration of some sort going on in Pacific Grove. It was called the Feast of Lanterns. Other than the fact that they had a fireworks-show in the evening, he was unsure of what the whole event was about. Jenny asked Malcolm to come over to her place that Saturday afternoon. She wanted to take a walk and then in the evening go for a bite to eat before taking in the fireworks. Malcolm went along with the whole damn thing, thinking that they might have their own little fireworks-session after the smoke from the real one had settled.

He arrived at Jenny's mid-afternoon. It was sunny when they left for their walk. Diana led them along the recreation trail from Pacific Grove towards Monterey.

"I'm having a hard time being around them," Jenny said, referring to a girlfriend and her husband.

"Why's that?" Malcolm asked.

"It's really just a negative thing. The harder he tries, the more difficult she gets."

"I don't think she wants to be married to him," Malcolm suggested.

"Yeah, but she wants her children to have a family."

"Like I said, I don't think she wants to be with him."

"He hauled all these things down to the beach the other night and cooked this wonderful meal for her while she was huddled up with the women bitching about how worthless he was. He even fixed her plate and brought it to her, but she said that she couldn't eat it."

"When?"

"There was another party at the beach when you were out of town. He carried the barbecue and everything else down to the beach and cooked dinner for her."

"And then she decided that she wasn't hungry?" Malcolm asked.

"She found some other reason to be pissed off. She was talking to us about him when he walked up. We had to change the subject real fast."

"What was she saying?" Malcolm asked as they strolled up to Lovers Point.

"I can't even remember right now, but it wasn't anything good."

"Jenny, I've got to get something to eat," Malcolm announced, as they approached the snack bar. He was starving. His habit of sleeping late and drinking coffee without eating breakfast was catching up to him. He should have had lunch earlier, but for some reason it wasn't high on his priority list that day.

Malcolm walked up to the order window at the snack bar. The woman who ran the joint was at the grill, so he asked her to throw on another hamburger patty. She did so, and then formally took his order and his money. In addition to a cheeseburger, he ordered a Coke and a blueberry muffin that was wrapped in cellophane and sitting right inside the order window. Between the muffin and the Coke, his blood sugar would stabilize and provide a cushion for the grease-bomb burger when it hit the bottom of his belly.

"This tastes so damn good that it has to be bad for me," Malcolm said, knowing what a health nut Jenny was.

When Jenny wasn't looking, he'd drop pieces of the muffin onto the ground for Diana to vacuum up. She hated it when he fed Diana his junk food. He liked treating the pup, but more importantly, he liked getting away with something taboo. After finishing the burger, Malcolm stood up, and without saying a word Jenny followed his cue. They continued their walk towards

Cannery Row.

"I remember that time you told me how he had done all these things for her, trying to bring the romance back into their lives," Malcolm said, picking up the conversation where it had been cut off when Malcolm's belly interrupted. "That's when I knew they were in trouble."

"Oh, yeah, that's right. She had been gone for a few days, and when she got home, he had all these flowers and things, almost like a shrine set up for her when she walked into the house."

"I thought it was in the bedroom?"

"Yeah, that's right. It was," Jenny confirmed.

"You know what I think?"

"What?"

"He's a dumb ass."

"So he's a dumb ass?" she asked laughing.

"Hell, yeah. He ought to tell her to fuck off. Might jerk her back to her senses."

"I don't know," she said, staring out into the distance across the bay.

"He won't keep putting up with that shit."

"You don't think so?" she asked, continuing her distant stare.

"I used to do shit like that with my ex-wife. She always threatened to leave. I'd end up buying into the whole damn drama begging her not to go."

"Did she finally leave?" Jenny asked, as she let go of Diana's leash. They were on the part of the trail that was far enough away from the road that Diana wouldn't stray off and get hit.

"No, but I wished the hell she would have. She wasn't going anywhere. She was just manipulating me."

"Why did you guys split up?"

"I had my belly full of her cooking," Malcolm answered, as he picked up a stray tennis ball and threw it for Diana to chase. Malcolm's ex never cooked a single meal the entire time they were together.

"So *you* left?" Jenny continued to question him. It was her opportunity to see a side of Malcolm that he seldom revealed to her. He was a little concerned that he might spook her, but, with the direction that they'd been going, he didn't really give a shit if it did scare her off.

"No, she went to stay with her sister for the weekend, and I had the locks changed."

"You can do that?"

"No, but I did. I had already been to this woman attorney a few weeks earlier and found out how bad she was going to screw me in the divorce."

"Why a woman attorney?"

"Because I knew that this woman attorney had it out for men," Malcolm explained. He stopped walking and waited for Diana to bring back the ball. Jenny put her back on the leash when Diana dropped the ball for Malcolm to pick up. They were getting close to Cannery Row and the street.

"So why'd you go to this woman attorney?"

"To find out her strategy."

"Was she your wife's attorney?" Jenny asked, as Malcolm ditched the tennis ball under a bush so that he could have it for Diana when they returned.

"No, but that was the other reason I went to her, so my wife couldn't hire her. I went to her because she was a woman, and I needed to know how she thought, so I could set myself up to fight like a woman. I mean, after all, that's who was going to be fighting me."

"You what?"

"Emotional warfare," Malcolm said grinning. "I knew I better be prepared, so I learned how a woman would fight a legal battle in divorce court."

"So you learned it from a woman who neither of you knew?"

"Yeah, and it was an initial counseling session so it didn't cost me a dime," Malcolm grinned his sly, smart-ass grin.

"Then I suppose you went and hired another woman attorney."

"No, I hired a man attorney who had a real bitch of a paralegal working for him. This gal was happily married and had three little boys. She also had three older brothers who she loved and adored."

"How did you know all of this?"

"I used to get drunk with her brothers in high school. She hated all her brother's girlfriends. She was always hanging out with the guys."

"She didn't hang out with *any* girls?" she asked, in an unbelieving tone.

"Well, maybe a few, but she really liked being with the guys."

"You're full of it."

"Maybe, but it worked."

"How?"

"I'll tell you about it sometime when you got a couple of days and no other dramas going on in your life," Malcolm answered, as they stepped from the trail onto the cement sidewalk. Cannery Row looked like it had been bombed by an atomic syrupy snow cone. The weekend tourists were crawling around it like ants. They hiked along the sidewalk for a few blocks and then turned around in an attempt to escape what Jenny despised: tourists who invaded her home, her space.

"So you think he's going to leave her?" Jenny asked, as they stepped back onto the dirt trail.

"I think he's a stupid ass if he doesn't, but he will. One day, he'll have his fill of her bullshit, and he'll walk."

"She'll cross way over the line, huh?"

"She might only have to cross it by an inch. That's all it'll take if he's had his fill," Malcolm answered, as he reached under the bush retrieving Diana's fun. "And that'll be it. Her honey-pies will be all used up," Malcolm added, as he stood there with the tennis ball.

"Guys are like that," Jenny said, as she dropped Diana's leash.

"Like what?" Malcolm asked, throwing the ball.

"A woman can go on like that forever. We can say it's over but change our minds later and carry on like nothing's happened. But it seems like once a man slams the window shut, there aren't any second chances."

"All I know is that I don't like being taken for granted."

"I don't think anyone does."

"When that shit starts happening to me, I turn real cold, real quick."

"And then you slam it shut."

"They think that you can't live without them. Hell, I've lived most of my life alone, and I can do it quite well," Malcolm said in a harsh tone.

"Yeah, me too."

* * * * *

After their walk, they lounged around Jenny's place for a couple of hours before walking down town to Pepper's, a Mexican restaurant in PG. Pepper's was packed, so they sat at the bar. Gene, the bartender, who also worked part time at Tillie's, took their order. Jenny had a glass of wine, and Malcolm had a fake beer. They ordered some nachos and fish tacos. Jenny excused herself and went to the bathroom, and as soon as she was around the corner, Gene cornered Malcolm.

"So, inquiring minds would like to know," Gene said, raising his eyebrows looking for some gossip to spread around the community.

"Just walking the dog, Gene."

"Just walking the dog, huh?" Gene asked, with his elbows up on the bar, his hands resting below his ears with his palms holding his head up, waiting for Malcolm to begin his confession.

"Just walking the dog," Malcolm reassured. "You got anymore of them fake beers back there, Geno?"

"For a thirsty dog walker, you bet," Gene answered, realizing that he'd gotten all that he was going to get out of Malcolm.

Jenny came back up to the bar and sat down, and soon after, Gene brought out their food and poured Jenny another glass of wine. By the time they finished their meal, it was approaching detonation time on the fireworks front. Hoping to loosen Jenny up, Malcolm tried unsuccessfully to have Gene pour her a glass of wine in a paper cup for takeaway. Pepper's wasn't an off-sale establishment, and Gene wasn't willing to risk his job over one glass of wine, so they left empty-handed.

As soon as they stepped out of the restaurant, the first boom sounded. They were a couple of blocks from Lover's Point where the crowd had gathered for the show, but it was overcast. Malcolm thought it was kind of cool watching the fog turn colors, but Jenny was bummed, she wanted the full effect. After the show, they walked back to her place, but the private fireworks show Malcolm had hoped for turned out to be a dud, too.

Chapter 15

He hadn't seen Sheila since she moved to Big Sur several weeks earlier. She had called, but Malcolm had lost the paper he had penciled her new number on. Instead, he decided to drive down the coast, hoping to stumble into her. Malcolm needed a new perspective. The Jenny thing just wasn't happening, and he needed to get out of the rut he'd fallen into with her and the whole Pink House scene.

He left his studio, drove to the post office and then to the ATM at the bank for a hundred dollar's worth of cash. Forty-five minutes later, he turned off Highway 1 into a parking lot below the Nepenthe Restaurant. The parking lot was full, so he drove down to the employee's housing site. He spotted Sheila's car parked in front of a cabin, got out and walked up to the door. It was open; Sheila saw him approaching.

"What's up Malcolm, the Malcolm who never returned my phone call?"

"I did, too. I called the restaurant and tried to leave a message, but they were too busy," he lied. "You guys get your phone hooked up yet?" The number she left him on her previous call was the number of the restaurant.

"A couple of days ago," she answered, walking up to hug him.

"It's great to see you."

"You too, Malcolm," she answered, taking his hand and leading him into her cabin. "Have a seat," she offered, patting the vacant spot next to her on the love seat. "How's Kate?" she asked, as Malcolm sat down next to her.

"Okay, I guess. Haven't talked to her for about a week."

"So what's going on then?"

"Hanging out with that gal some."

"What gal?"

"You know, the one with the dog. Nothing's really happening, though," Malcolm answered, not wanting to go into the whole Jenny scene.

"How about the book?" she asked excitedly.

"Oh yeah, the book," he answered, not really having anything new to report. "Hey Sheila, I'm hungry. Do you have time to go down to the Coast Gallery? I think Travis might be working. That way I can say hi to him and catch up with you there," Malcolm suggested. Travis was a waiter from Tillie's who had quit and taken a job at Big Sur's Coast Gallery. Travis was really a musician but worked at the restaurant to make enough change to get by on until his music career took off.

"Yeah, that sounds great. I just have to be back around three to get ready for work, because I'm on at four. Let me put on some shoes," Sheila said, walking into the closet. It was actually a little bedroom that she and her roommate had named the community dressing room. They had made the loft above the dressing room into their sleeping quarters. A ladder led up from the dressing room into the center of the loft; a perfect line of demarcation. They had twelve feet of space between their mattresses. Several nice pieces of linen and cloth hung from the pine ceiling to serve as a makeshift privacy barrier.

"I figured you'd be at Andy's."

"I just got back. Been there for a couple of days."

"I called there, but the machine answered."

"Oh, that was you," she said. "We just got finished and neither of us wanted to move."

Sheila had a habit of vaguely teasing Malcolm with leading comments about her sex life. She wasn't graphic nor did she carry on long, but she seemed to be proud of her sexuality and enjoyed bragging about it some. She may also have been confessing out of some hidden sense of guilt or shame, or perhaps it was just a way to keep Malcolm at bay. He was jealous at first, because he had seen himself in the role of her next lover, before Andy popped into her life. But, after she had hooked up with Andy, his lust for her seemed to subside. They remained good friends, but his physical desire for her disappeared, or at least got pointed in another direction.

"I see," Malcolm answered, not knowing how else to respond. His jealousy had shifted. It had nothing to do with Malcolm not making it with Sheila; it was now about how she was getting it on a regular basis, and he wasn't.

"I got in a fight with him before I left," she said, tying her second shoe.

"Why?"

"Because I'm on the rag. Cramping that's why! You got a problem with that?" she growled, smiling at the same time.

"Hell, I've been hanging out with a goddamn woman for over two months who doesn't seem the least bit interested in sleeping with me. If I can put up with her shit, you better believe I can hang with you, baby. Rag on," Malcolm reassured her, feeling like a gay dude who was hanging out with one of his fag hags.

They drove a couple of miles south to the Coast Gallery. Travis had only been working at the Gallery Café for two weeks. He was still on the schedule at Tillie's. He had given notice and had only three or four more shifts to go before he left that part of his life behind.

Travis was a restless, thirty-year-old songwriter/singer who played the guitar. Travis's band was slowly coming together but had roller-coasted along for some time. He'd waited tables at Tillie's for the last five years to support himself. In the hopes of derailing from the same old set of tracks he'd been chugging up, down, and around on over the last few years, he took the job down in Big Sur and was planning a trip to Europe in a couple of months. Travis was of Italian descent, tall, thin, and brown eyed. He had shaved his head, but now most of his black hair had grown back several inches. He usually wore a pair of baggy corduroy pants and a white T-shirt.

When Malcolm first met Travis, he felt a little uncomfortable around him; thought that he might be gay because of his warm greetings whenever he walked into Tillie's. Travis always looked deep into Malcolm's eyes, smiled, and followed it up with a meaningful, "hello." After hanging around him for a while, Malcolm realized that Travis was just very present and full of energy, and it had nothing to do with his sexual orientation. He was a 'She' lover just like Malcolm, and also a single man just like Malcolm. They were both on a 'Her' search, and they were both pursuing 'Her' on the material plane in hopes of satisfying an ethereal longing.

After parking, Sheila and Malcolm made their way through the gallery and up the stairs to the café.

"What's up guys?" Travis asked, greeting them with one of his genuinely charged smiles. He walked up, gave them both a hug and went back behind the counter to take a patron's order.

"Malcolm drove down and surprised me, so I thought we'd surprise you," Sheila said, as she walked toward a table in the dining room, Malcolm a few steps behind her.

"Are you here for lunch?" Travis asked.

"Please," Malcolm answered, as they sat down at a table.

"Okay, I'll be with you guys in a minute."

After helping the people at the counter, Travis came over to take their order. "We're out of all meat, except ham," he said, setting menus down on the table.

"I just want a salad," Sheila said, without even looking at the menu. She was shifting around on the stool, full of energy like she normally was.

"How 'bout you, Malcolm?" Travis asked.

"No tuna?"

"Just ham. It's good ham, though."

"I'll have this vegetarian burrito wrap thing," Malcolm said, pointing to the menu, his heart still set on a tuna sandwich. He rarely had ham, maybe twice a year, during the holiday season.

"How 'bout drinks?"

"Iced tea," Malcolm answered.

"Yeah, me too," Sheila agreed.

Travis scribbled down the order and made his way back to the kitchen to get it started.

"So what's up with the book, Malcolm?" Sheila asked.

"You know, Sheila, I was all upset over the book, and then got over it."

"What were you upset about?"

"About doing anything with it. About having to publish it, about it having to be a best seller. You know, as in making money. Then I went and had a sit with myself," Malcolm explained. Travis walked up with their iced teas, and Malcolm hesitated in his conversation with Sheila. It wasn't that he didn't trust Travis or really even care if he heard what they were talking about. It was just a habit Malcolm had; he was paranoid that someone might be eavesdropping like he did on everyone else.

"Yeah," Sheila said, to let Malcolm know she was still listening as Travis returned to the kitchen.

"And I finally figured out that I was doing it all for the wrong reasons and putting undue pressure on myself."

"You were making your fun into work," she said, summing up Malcolm's story-telling production into a few nice and concise words.

"Yep. I was making it about money, and as soon as I started doing that, I started editing."

"You've got to edit."

"Yeah, but I was editing before the words ever came out."

"I thought you finished the book."

"I did, but I'm talking about new stuff. I was all over my own back, afraid to write a fucking cuss-word. I was afraid to be real and say whatever I felt and needed to say," Malcolm explained, feeling a twinge of anger, having fallen into the censor's trap. He'd been censoring his whole life and was good and tired of it.

"So what are you doing with the book you finished?" Sheila asked, patiently waiting for his answer, as Malcolm danced around her question with one of his bullshit side stories.

Deep down he still had a lot of salesman's blood pumping through him. Most of the tractors he'd ever sold were sold in silence. He always tweaked the curiosity of a potential client. When the client wanted to know more about the special deal Malcolm had subtly suggested, he'd start talking about something else: speeding tickets, women, current events, how his ex-wife was trying to fuck him over, the client's children, whatever was closest to their hearts. He'd dance around the tractor for as long as he could until they pinned him down wanting the details. When he got them that far, they'd all but written the check. So anyway, Malcolm may have left the tractor business, but the salesman in him was always at work. He was always selling himself, even with Sheila.

"So what about the first book you wrote?" Sheila asked again.

"Shelving it for awhile. Just going to focus on new stuff for now."

"Good," Sheila answered supportively. Sheila was great for

that, but she wasn't phony and just going along with Malcolm to be nice. She wasn't shy about speaking her piece when she didn't agree with him.

Travis brought their lunch, topped off their iced teas, and asked: "Can I bring you two anything else?"

"Not for me," Malcolm answered.

"Me neither, but thanks, Travis," Sheila answered.

"Okay guys, I'm kind of busy, so yell if you need anything," Travis said, before he walked off to help another party. Travis was a one-man band that day.

"This has got to be a great place to work," Malcolm said, looking outside and breathing in the view before taking his first bite.

Sheila was already chewing and didn't respond to his excitement over being in one of the most beautiful places on earth. Living there didn't take away from the beauty, but a person could grow so accustomed to their surroundings that it could easily have been taken for granted. Living in Big Sur, or anywhere for that matter, didn't insure against one's suffering from discontentment. Malcolm had his doubts about Sheila's period being the sole source of her suffering.

"How's your lunch?" Sheila asked

"Okay," Malcolm answered. The burrito tasted like crap. The view had the food beat hands down.

"Just okay, huh?" Sheila asked again, knowing him well enough to read between the lines.

"Shoulda had the ham," he smiled.

"What's up with Jenny?"

"Just friends."

"Any kissy action yet?"

"She actually told me that if I ever wanted her to kiss me, I'd have to shave off my beard," Malcolm said, laughing off the whole idea.

"She what?" Sheila asked, knowing clearly what he'd just told her.

"So, I shaved it off."

"Did it work?"

"Nope. Waited two weeks and nothing happened, so I grew it back. Fuck her!"

"There's something wrong with her."

"Then I told her that I was pissed off because she wasn't fucking me," Malcolm explained, before taking another swig of tea, trying to wash down the pasty vegetarian burrito.

"You did not."

"In those very words. Then she told me that she's never fucked a guy unless she's known him for at least a year."

"That's fucked up," Sheila said, with a funny look on her face. "I mean, two months is a long time if you ask me, but a year."

"I don't get it either. I think she's lying."

"Why are you still messing with her?" Sheila asked, after munching another bite of her salad. "Have some," she added motioning with her fork in response to Malcolm eying her plate.

"Something else is happening. I mean we're good friends. We're both Capricorns. We get along real good, really seem to understand each other, almost like we can guess what the other is about to say."

"And she's not sleeping with you," Sheila added, trying to jerk him from his denial.

"Guess we're just going to be good friends is all. But something special is happening between us, Sheila. It might not be a love affair, but something's happening inside me, something's changing."

"Like what?"

"I can't put my finger on it. Don't even know if I'm supposed to, but something's happening."

"Well, that's cool then. At least you're getting something from the relationship," she said, as Travis came back to check on them.

"Can I get you guys anything else?" Travis asked.

"Yeah, a cappuccino," Sheila said, standing up.

"How 'bout you Malcolm?"

"Just more tea," he answered, handing Travis the empty glass. "Ice, too," he added, as Travis left.

They both followed Travis to the counter and waited for their drinks. Malcolm looked into the dessert case and saw some prefab burritos wrapped up in cellophane. Then he knew why the damn things tasted like crap. He turned to look outside and decided to drink his tea on the deck.

"I'll be out here, Sheila," Malcolm said, pointing toward the deck as Travis handed him the refill.

"Okay…" she answered, as her face took on an awkward and disgusted look.

"What?" he asked.

"I'm leaking," she whispered, staring at Malcolm like a helpless little girl, obvious that she wanted to kick and scream. "Can you tell?" she asked, turning for Malcolm to look over her backside.

"Doesn't look bad to me," he answered, after giving her the quick up-and-down once over.

"I can't get back into your truck this way," she said, frustrated with her untimely inconvenience. "Do you have any shorts?"

"No," Malcolm answered. He did have a pair of sweats, but he didn't want her to bleed in them in case he wanted to wear them later.

Travis finished making Sheila's cappuccino and set it on the counter.

"Travis, do you have any shorts I can borrow?"

"Shorts?" Travis asked with a dumbfounded look.

"I'm leeeeakiiiing," Sheila screamed quietly through her teeth, her nose wrinkled up in disgust.

"I got some in my van. I'll run down and get them when I have a break here in a minute," Travis volunteered.

"Thanks," she said.

"I'll be outside," Malcolm announced again, already halfway to the patio door. Sheila followed him. Malcolm walked to the corner of the deck and looked down the coastline, dreaming of having his own cabin and living there full time. "This would be a wonderful place to write another book. I could find some good-looking young hippy chick who liked to fuck and make me coffee. Her being hippy and making me coffee could actually be negotiable," Malcolm conceded teasingly.

"And what about Kate?" Sheila asked.

"What about her?" Malcolm asked, as they hung out on the deck waiting for Travis to go on his mission of mercy. "Man, I love it here, Sheila. I want to stay."

"Sarina's going out of town tonight; you can stay at my place."

"She won't mind?"

"Hell, her whole damn family's been there for the last four days. Who cares if she minds," Sheila answered, in a righteous tone.

Malcolm looked over the deck and spotted Travis running across Highway 1, waving a pair of denim shorts over his head like a flag, like he was surrendering to the enemy.

"Check that out, Sheila," Malcolm said, pointing to Travis. "This is going into the next book," he teased. "It's perfect. Travis rescues Sheila from a runaway train," Malcolm laughed.

"Just shut up, okay," she said, elbowing Malcolm with a big smile.

Travis walked in huffing and puffing from his run and handed Sheila the shorts. She went into the bathroom, changed, and walked out with her pants rolled up in a bundle.

"Travis, do you have a plastic bag?" she asked, again wrinkling her nose up in disgust.

He bent down behind the counter, and half a minute later stood honoring her request with a plastic Safeway bag in hand.

"Okay, we've got to go," Sheila said. "I have to get ready for work."

Malcolm settled up with Travis at the register, and then said goodbye. In less than ten minutes, they were coasting down the drive to Sheila's cabin.

I've got to hurry," Sheila said, opening the door before Malcolm had come to a complete stop. "I've only got half-an-hour to get ready," she said as she stepped out of the Tahoe, and ran up to the cabin. After jostling the lock on the front door, she rushed in.

He waited outside on the cabin deck while Sheila showered and changed for work. About twenty minutes later, she came bouncing out onto the deck, all polished up and ready to go.

"Sheila, I'm not going to stay tonight. I feel like getting back to town," he said. It was beautiful and he felt so at peace that he seriously thought about spending the night, but for some reason felt a tug to return to the darkroom.

"Okay, no problem. Just as long as you know you're welcome

anytime," she said, walking up to give Malcolm a hug. "I have to go; I'm on in five minutes."

"Okay, have fun," he said as she approached the gate. "Hey Sheila! Thanks. I love you," he hollered loud enough to be heard as she started to run up the hill.

She turned around, smiled and continued towards Nepenthe.

Chapter 16

The next time Malcolm ran into Jenny, she was at the Pink House sitting outside on the front porch reading the newspaper. She loved reading the classified section. She was always in search of a different place to live. Malcolm wasn't sure if she didn't like her home and genuinely wanted to move or if she was just suffering one of life's normal existential discontents.

Malcolm was in one of his pissers, not knowing what to do with his own life, torn between returning to the selling world and writing. In the first of the two alternatives he was a master, the second was just an unproven dream, and he had a hard time banking on a dream. His savings account reflected the reality that he wanted to escape. It was one of those days when he was hypercritical of anyone and everything. In other words, anyone who crossed his path he found to be a mindless dumb fuck.

After getting a coffee, he joined Jenny and Diana on the porch. There was a woman in her late twenties sitting at a table below them. A man in his mid to late thirties came bouncing up the stairs to this young woman's table. She stood to greet him, and he tried to kiss her cheek. Teasingly, she hesitantly pulled away but then allowed the man to complete his affectionate gesture. He sat down across the table from her, reached for her hand, and sat there stroking it as he gazed into her eyes and drooled all over himself.

"Look at that goofball," Malcolm said, as Jenny continued surfing the classifieds.

"What?" she asked, looking up.

"He's all goo-goo gaa-gaa over her," Malcolm said, nodding his head and looking towards the lovers.

"So?"

"So, he just bugs me."

"What bugs you?"

"He's a phony bastard," Malcolm answered in a disgusted tone.

"Because he's in love with her and feels good about it?"

"Because he's a fucking goofball. Look at him," Malcolm

said, wanting to go kick his chair out from under him.

"Maybe you're jealous."

"Of what?" Malcolm asked, continuing to gaze at the love-struck fellow who was floating on cloud nine.

"Him being in love and her response to him." Jenny answered in her standard, unexcitable tone.

"Maybe."

"Well, I'm not jealous," she announced.

"No, I don't feel jealous. It's something else," Malcolm answered, feeling jealous, but unwilling to let her know that she had him pegged.

Malcolm wanted Jenny to respond to him the same way that this woman was responding to the goofball. Malcolm wanted to be goofy in love like this guy was, but cynically he believed love to be just an illusion, a stage that these two people were going through, a rapture soon to be swept away by a cool breeze. He wanted to be in love that way again, but something had robbed him of his naïveté. If he was ever to fall again, it would have to sneak up and capture him in a way that was completely unknown.

"I have to go," Jenny announced in an unanimated tone. "I've got a nail appointment."

"Where?" Malcolm asked, not really giving a damn. "Want me to watch Diana?" he quickly added, saying what he had really meant to say and not giving her a chance to answer his first question.

"Oh, that would be great," Jenny announced. "Now I don't have to take her home and leave her all by herself."

"How long will you be?"

"Probably an hour or so."

"Think I'll take her to the beach," Malcolm tested. "How about I bring Diana by the house when we get done walking."

"Oh, that would be perfect."

"Okay, have fun. We'll see you after a while." Malcolm said, happy to get another "oh" out of her.

"Oh," meant that she was excited. Malcolm had actually been blessed with two of her "ohs" in less than a minute. Eliciting an "oh" from Jenny meant that he'd really moved her. In the entire time they'd been hanging out, he might have gotten a couple dozen or so "ohs" out of her. He figured that sex for her were "ohs," or at least the closest thing to an orgasm that he'd ever provoke from Jenny.

"That must be it," Malcolm said to Diana, "I've been having my brains fucked out for the last month and failed to recognize it." Diana lay beside Malcolm as he finished his coffee, and then they left the lovebirds to wallow in their bliss.

The beach was normally crowded on weekends, and that particular day was no exception. The crowd didn't stop them, though. Diana chased birds, and Malcolm checked out the bikini tops and bottoms. A couple of hours later he took Diana back home to the master.

When the two returned, Jenny was lying on the futon in her living room listening to some new age digital music from the cable channel. Malcolm went and sat on the futon next to her.

"Oh, I have a short video I wanted to show you," she announced, as she stood up and walked to the armoire. Another "oh." Jenny was really having a wild Saturday. Malcolm was hoping for something X-rated but knew that his imagination had gotten the best of him.

The video was a short scientific clip about vibrations and how a certain tone would create a certain vibration. It proved that an identical tone created an identical vibration every time by using sand on something like a pizza pan. A tuning fork was used to create the vibration and the sand on the tray would take on a certain form. The form was mandala-like. A different tone meant a different mandala, but the same tone created the same mandala time and time again. Anyway, that's what she wanted him to see.

When Jenny got up to take the video out of the VCR, Malcolm grabbed her and pulled her onto his lap. She sat there listlessly for less than a minute as he hugged her and then she pulled away from him and finished retrieving the tape. He hung out for a while longer in spite of her unresponsiveness, mostly to be polite, and then announced his departure. Jenny followed him to the door. He'd already opened it and stepped outside. He turned around to say goodbye and found her standing in the doorway.

"You want to do something later?" he asked just to be saying something. He was tired of how they weren't coming together, and he couldn't imagine that another evening with her would prove to be anymore fruitful than the afternoon session he was walking away from, but for some illogical reason he asked anyway.

"Not tonight," she answered, as he looked past her over towards the armoire.

"What are you looking at?" she asked, catching his drifting gaze.

"I'm looking at you," he lied. "Why?"

"It just seemed like you were looking behind me."

"No, I was looking right into your eyes, at your beautiful face..."

* * * * *

He felt drained when he arrived back at the studio. He fell onto the bed and drifted away. Not long after dozing off, he woke to the phone ringing. It was Lewis. He had run to the hardware store for something and was driving back home so he had time for a quick bullshit session.

"What's going on?" Lewis asked.

"I was taking a nap," Malcolm answered in a groggy tone.

"That physical therapist keep you up all night?"

"In my dreams," he answered in a disgusted tone. "I was at her house today and she put on this video."

"Was it a fuck flick?"

"Fuck, no! It was this video about sound and vibrations. There was sand on this flat surface and then they'd make a tone or vibration with something like a tuning fork and the sand would take on some shape according to the vibration. Different vibration, different shape. Same vibration, same shape, time and time again."

"What was that all about?"

"Hell, I don't know. It was six minutes of that horseshit, and then it was over without any explanation."

"That's weird."

"That's not as weird as what happened next. She walked over to take the video out, and I pulled her down onto my lap and tried to love on her. But for some reason, I couldn't bring myself to kiss her."

"Just do it and get it over with," Lewis said, in a frustrated tone.

"I'm waiting for her to be more open to me. You know, they'll help you kiss them the first time."

"If it's there, that is."

"Well, that's the problem. It's not there, and I've been hanging around waiting for her to turn my way. Actually, I've wanted to give up on the whole damn thing, but something's keeping me from making a clean break."

"It's there, or it isn't. Simple as that."

"No shit, so I get up to leave. I hugged her, and asked her if she wanted to do something later. She told me that she was busy, while I just stared passed her. Then she asked me what I was looking at, and I said her. She said it looked like I was looking away from her. I told her that I was looking at her eyes and her face. She said okay, but it seemed as if I was looking away from her at something."

"So you left without kissing her."

"Hell, I've left fifty times without kissing her."

"She's weird."

"That's what I thought until I started driving off. I was half a block away when it hit me."

"What?"

"I didn't want to kiss her."

"I thought you had the hots for her."

"I thought so, too. I said it out loud to myself, 'Oh, I don't want to kiss her,' and that's when I knew I didn't. I mean, it felt right. I felt relieved after I said it."

"You're the weirdo."

"Maybe, but it's the truth."

"Now let me get this straight. She didn't want to kiss you, but it was really you not wanting to kiss her?"

"Yeah, and think about what she said, about me not looking at her, as if I was looking away."

"So?"

"And the video."

"I don't get it?"

"I didn't either at first, but I went by there to be clear."

"I think you went by there hoping she'd answer the door naked."

"That's why I went there, but I really went there so I wouldn't have to keep going back to where I wasn't supposed to be."

"So you wanted to be with her, but you really weren't supposed to be seeing her?"

"I thought I wanted her, but the vibration, it just isn't there, man."

"Oh, she doesn't have it for you and she was trying to tell you with the video?"

"I don't think that's why she played it, but it started to make a lot of sense to me after I left. And think about it, when I looked at her to say goodbye, she thought I was looking away from her, and I was. I was looking for something that's just not there."

"You mean her."

"I mean the feelings that I've been trying to find for her."

They analyzed Malcolm's drama for a while longer and then shifted to something Lewis had going on. Then Lewis told Malcolm he had to go because he was sitting in his driveway and his wife had just walked outside and busted him talking on the phone.

* * * * *

Later that evening a restless Malcolm phoned Turner. Cassi answered and invited him over for dinner. Turner was family and Malcolm needed some family. The call was just a formality. Malcolm was just checking to see if they were home.

He drove the MG, winding up and down the hills through the back roads to Turner's place. Carson greeted Malcolm with his great big smile as an excited look of wonderment glowed from his bright blue eyes. Malcolm picked Carson up and hugged him. Like Malcolm, Carson, was the firstborn.

Cassi was walking down the stairs with their new baby girl. "Hey there," she said, greeting Malcolm with the same warm smile that Carson had inherited from her.

Malcolm set Carson down and went over to Cassi. He put

his arm around her and pulled her to his side. It was the closest thing to a hug he could give her while she held Mallory. Connor, the middle child came around the corner with a Match Box car. He threw the car at Malcolm and then started laughing as he ran to hide.

Malcolm chased Connor into the kitchen. Connor ran to hide in the pantry and shut the door. Malcolm pounded the door without really trying to open it. A few seconds later, Connor peaked out smiling and holding a big bag of animal crackers. His mouth was full of the baked critters. Cassi had followed them into the kitchen, and Malcolm looked up to see if she saw Connor. She did and shook her head in loving motherly amazement while Malcolm belly laughed.

"You got a way of bringing out the best in my kids, Malcolm," she teased and laughed. "Turner's out back," she added, as Malcolm turned towards the refrigerator.

Malcolm had a habit of winding the kids up, and Cassi was trying to direct him out of the line of fire for sanity's sake. Malcolm still had a lot of little boy running through him, and Connor and Carson had a way of tapping into Malcolm's youthfulness and vice versa.

"I just made some iced tea," Cassi suggested as Malcolm opened the refrigerator.

"Thanks," he answered, and then poured himself a glass before going out to the backyard. Turner was standing in front of the barbecue smoking a cigar. He finished flipping the steaks, put the lid down, took the cigar between the fingers of his left hand, and hugged Malcolm with his right.

"What's going on daddy-o?" Malcolm asked, needling Turner about his life sentence of paternity.

"Yeah, go ahead and laugh it up," Turner said, putting on a funny grin and taking a puff of his cigar. "What's going on with you?"

"Same old stuff," Malcolm answered, unconvincingly.

"Yeah, right," Turner said in a don't-give-me-that-shit tone. "Hey, would you do me a favor?"

"Sure, what?" Malcolm asked.

"Tell Cassi that these steaks are almost done."

When Malcolm reached the kitchen to tell Cassi, he could

hear her in the bathroom muttering something while she was probably wiping Connor's ass. Mallory Catherine was in her rocker screaming a newborn baby scream.

Malcolm opened the cupboard and pulled down some plates so he could set the table, which was what Turner wanted to have done when he sent Malcolm in to summon Cassi. After finding the napkins and getting the clean silverware out of the dishwasher, he finished the chore. Cassi walked out of the bathroom and picked up Mallory.

"Thanks, Malcolm," she said in a sincere tone, as she comforted her newborn.

"Where's Carson?" Malcolm asked, having lost track of him after having chased Connor into the pantry.

"He's across the street at his friend Jonah's," Cassi answered, as Connor walked up to her and started hanging on her leg.

Malcolm went back into the kitchen to get the steamed rice and green beans that Cassi had prepared to go along with the steaks. There was French bread on the counter. Malcolm sliced half the loaf, wrapped it in a cloth napkin, and set it into a breadbasket. The last thing he brought to the table was the butter, salt, and pepper. Malcolm looked out of the kitchen window. Turner was walking toward the sliding door, steaks in one hand, as he puffed his cigar one last time before pitching it out into the flowerbed.

No one bothered calling Carson home for dinner; Cassi would heat something up for him later. With three kids under the age of five, the youngest still an infant, they took every break they could get.

Turner cut some steak into little bite size pieces for Connor to snub. All that interested him were the green beans, which he ate as finger food. His belly was still full of animal crackers. Cassi had set Mallory down in her rocker, and she was sleeping peacefully. Dinner was spent mostly gossiping about people back home. They talked about people who had died, people who were getting divorced, and people who they thought might have been closet queers.

"So what's really been going on," Turner asked as he pushed his empty plate away.

"That all depends on what day you're asking about,"

Malcolm smiled a fake grin. "One day I'm going back to selling. The next day I'm chucking it all and moving to Big Sur to write another book," Malcolm answered, as Mallory started to fuss.

Connor had excused himself and was playing with the toys in the garage. "I'm going to give these two a bath," Cassi announced, as she stood up from the table.

Cassi called Connor, and he walked inside the house, whining about having to come in. "Come on Connor. Help me give your sister a bath," Cassi suggested, as the disappointed look on his face turned into one of purpose. Connor loyally followed his mother upstairs.

"What do you wanna do, Malcolm?" Turner asked, after he knew that Cassi was out of listening range. It wasn't so much that they didn't want Cassi to hear the conversation. They were just in the habit of having their privacy, and Cassi respected the long history of their friendship.

"Fuck, I don't know... yeah, I do know. I want to feel secure."

"Yeah, don't we all," Turner said, "Actually, I'd settle for not being scared," he added.

"What do you mean?"

"I mean, I don't want to feel scared," he said, shaking his head and looking at Malcolm like he should understand his fear. Malcolm understood fear, but he was just unclear of the fear Turner was trying to describe.

"What are you afraid of?"

"Everything, losing my wife, kids, and the job I have to keep in order to support them."

"You don't even have a choice, do you?" Malcolm asked, as he got up and started gathering the dirty dishes.

"Oh, I got choices, but they're different than yours. My choices affect more than just me," Turner answered, as Malcolm joined him in the domestic chores.

"That's what I mean. You just can't do what you want to do."

"Neither can you."

"How do you figure?" Malcolm asked.

"It's life," Turner answered, as Malcolm started rinsing.

"What's that got to do with choices?" Malcolm asked, as he

began to unload the clean dishes from the dishwasher.

"We make choices every day. Right now, I choose to be married and to stay with my family," Turner answered, as he started loading the dirty dishes. "Tomorrow, I might wake up and change my mind."

"Change your mind about having a wife and a family?"

"I choose to stay or leave every day. It's that simple."

"It's not that simple."

"Maybe not for you, but it is for me."

"That's why I said, you just can't do what you want to do."

"I can, too. I make the choice everyday, actually every minute of the day," Turner emphasized. "I think your problem's in the choosing. That's how you complicate everything and get all fucked up," he explained.

"How do you figure?" Malcolm asked, walking around to the bar stool on the other side of the counter.

"You're afraid to choose, because you're afraid of having to pay the price."

"No, I'm not."

"The hell you're not. You're greedy. You want it all, and you don't want to take a risk. That's why you can't choose," he said, as he stuffed the last dish into the dishwasher.

"Bullshit!" Malcolm shot back at him, even if Turner did have him pegged, and after knowing him for twenty-five years, chances were pretty damn good that he did.

"Then why you messing with that Jenny chick?" Turner asked, pouring detergent into the soap slot before latching the dishwasher door.

"You'd be fucking her too if you could."

"If the opportunity presented itself, then I'd have a choice to make," Turner answered, as he turned on the dishwasher.

"You'd slip it in her the first chance she gave you."

"No, you would."

"Fuck you Turner."

"I'll pass."

"It's a good thing you're a man, Turner," Malcolm teased.

"I don't think I had much of a choice," he said grinning.

"Yeah, if you were a woman we'd have done it years ago. We wouldn't even be here talking to each other right now."

"Maybe we'd be married," he said, as Malcolm's stomach churned.

"You're a sick-o," Malcolm said, almost puking at the thought of two hairy old men getting it on.

"You're a faggot anyway," Turner answered, acting as if he was trying to kiss Malcolm on the lips.

"I'm going to Jenny's," Malcolm joked, as he turned to the door.

"You're going home to beat off, Sweetie Pie," Turner said, in his feminine queer-boy voice.

"Jealous?" Malcolm asked, just before walking out to the MG.

Turner opened the front door when Malcolm was about halfway to the car. "Want to make a bet on who gets laid tonight?" he yelled, loud enough for his neighbors to hear.

Malcolm turned around. Turner was grinning and flipping him the bird. Malcolm conceded the round to Turner, but got one last "fuck off" in before he fired up the MG and backed out of the driveway.

Chapter 17

Sheila phoned one evening saying she needed to bring her car to the mechanic in Monterey to have the brakes and shocks replaced. She wanted to know if Malcolm could pick her up at the garage and drive her back to Big Sur. The Jenny thing was going south, and besides, there wasn't much Malcolm wouldn't do for Sheila. He picked her up at the garage the next day. They drove to the Loose Noodle in Monterey, one of their favorite places to have Italian food. After lunch, with full bellies and high spirits, they set off on their trek back down the coast to Big Sur. Planning to stay the night, Malcolm had packed a bag before leaving late that morning.

"I've got to hurry, or I'll be late for work," Sheila said, hopping out of the Tahoe and running to her cabin.

Once parked, Malcolm walked up the hill from the cabin and phoned home to check for any messages on the answering machine. He had a hard time picking up a cellular signal down at Sheila's cabin, so he hiked up the hill, just below the Nepenthe's parking lot, to place a call. The only message was from Jenny, which he didn't bother returning. Once back down the hill, he grabbed his bag and a book before locking the door of the Chevy.

Once inside, he dropped the bag next to a footstool. The cabin smelled of incense. He took a good look at the articles lying around on the bookshelves and hanging from the walls in the great room. The last time he was there, the girls were still moving in and, with the exception of the loft, hadn't decorated the place. Cats were one theme, certainly Sarina's doing. Malcolm didn't recall Sheila having an affinity with felines.

He opened the French doors of the cabin that led out from the great room onto a wooden deck and found a green cast iron patio table and two chairs. Over a dozen flower pots with a variety of plants and flowers lined the deck railing. He sat down and opened his book. He had to pee, but Sheila had taken over the bathroom. He thought about whizzing off the deck, but had second thoughts. There were too many other cabins nearby and he wasn't ready to be run out of Big Sur, not yet anyway.

"Make yourself at home," Sheila said, as she walked outside. "I'm going to work." She had the evening shift and was due on at four.

"What's your roommate's name again?" Malcolm asked, setting the book down on the cast iron table.

"Sarina, for the fourth time!"

Malcolm pretty much knew Sarina's name but wanted to make sure he didn't call her Sabrina when he did actually meet her.

It was almost four o'clock and there was still a sliver of sun beaming down through the pines. Malcolm had positioned his chair in the sunlight and teetered on the two back legs; the railing that ran around the deck supported his balancing act.

"You'll tell her I'm here so she doesn't freak out when she gets off work and finds me camped out on your deck, right?" Malcolm said as a reminder.

"Yeah, she's cool."

"You sure she doesn't mind me staying?"

"She's leaving anyway."

"Okay, thanks. I'll be up for dinner later," Malcolm answered. Sheila was late, and Malcolm was keeping her with his questions.

"Okay, I gotta go," she said, walking to the gate.

"I'll probably be up around eight-thirty or nine," he shouted, as she ran up the hill toward Nepenthe.

Nepenthe was one of Big Sur's premier dining attractions. It was built out on a point, a cliff overlooking the Pacific Ocean, and at thirteen bucks a burger you could breathe in the dramatics of the mountains rising and descending along the Big Sur coastline. The high price was really only justified if your timing was right, because then you could revel in one of the most beautiful sunsets imaginable.

Sheila and Sarina were both waitresses at Nepenthe. The restaurant provided living quarters for their employees at very reasonable rents. As remote as Big Sur was, they had to offer housing to keep good help. It was hard to get an employee to drive eighty miles round trip just to pick up a wait shift, especially with the abundance of restaurants in Monterey and

Carmel.

Malcolm had relieved himself and once again sat teetered back in the green cast iron chair. He was reading a perspective on the mythological Lilith when a Ford Ranger pickup drove up to the cabin. He heard a couple of women talking and a few minutes later a blonde, with her hair braided in several strands and pinned up with a variety of clips, came swinging through the front gate.

"Hey Malcolm! It's been awhile," she said, in a rather loud and raspy voice.

Malcolm hesitated and then answered: "Hello," as he tried to erase the image of Medusa that was flashing through his mind.

"I'm only kidding," she laughed. "Hi, I'm Sarina," she added, as she walked up to him. She dropped a net laundry bag down on the deck next to his chair and they shook hands. Sarina was about five feet four and a hundred and fifteen pounds. She had brown eyes and, looking at the roots of her hair, it appeared she wasn't a true blonde. The way she had colored her hair didn't make her in any way unattractive, but it certainly was noticeable. She was wearing black pants, a black top and white tennis shoes. A minute or so later, the driver of the Ford Ranger, a brunette, came through the gate.

"Hi, I'm Talli," she said in a listless tone, as she walked onto the deck.

"Hi Talli, Malcolm," he said, as she passed through the French doors into the cabin without stopping for the introduction.

Talli was a good four inches taller than Sarina and thirty pounds heavier, too. She was an attractive woman, also with brown eyes. She was wearing a sarong with a white, short-sleeved cotton top. Her hips were big and she had a bit of a belly. She wasn't bad, but she wasn't held together as tightly as Sarina, nor did she appear to have Sarina's type of energy bounding through her. They were like a sports car and a touring sedan parked next to each other.

Next, a small, red import drove up and parked on the far side of the Ranger; it was of Japanese descent. The driver, on the other hand, had South American blood coursing through her veins. She was a tall, brown-eyed girl, with long, straight brunette hair pulled back into a ponytail. She wore a yellow floral-print skirt that was cut below the knees and a solid-white, cotton blouse. She was just as hippy as Talli, but her ass was flatter and her stomach wasn't as paunchy.

"Hi, she said, without introducing herself before walking into the house to join the other two. Malcolm later learned that her name was Gina.

He continued to read about Lilith when a black cat brushed up against his leg trying to seduce him into petting her. He occasionally reached down and scratched her on the top of the head. She had a wet spot on her neck and back. Malcolm figured she was in heat and had been out rolling around somewhere, pleasuring herself and stirring up a fight among the stray tomcats.

The scent of incense flowed from the cabin, and Malcolm kept hearing a clicking sound. One of them started talking shit about some guy who took her out to dinner but had failed to bathe before he came a-calling.

"I mean that fucker could have at least taken a bath. Like, it's one thing if he has bad breath from eating onions, but he had B.O."

"They don't have a clue," one of the women chimed in.

"I mean, it's not like I just wanted to fuck him. We were going to dinner. If I'm going to be with a man, he's at least got to clean up for me, hell!" the first voice said and that's when Malcolm realized that the coven was having this discussion on behalf of their audience of one who was sitting out on the porch in the green cast iron chair.

"I can't believe that he didn't even bother taking a shower after working all day," one of the three little witches added, stirring the pot.

"And he still had bad breath," number one hissed.

"It's a sign," Malcolm yelled.

Sarina walked out onto the deck while number one was still dissin' the guy.

"It's a sign, I'm telling you."

"Yeah, did you hear that? Malcolm says it's a sign," Sarina said, reaching for her laundry bag and giving Malcolm a good shot of her ass. She knew she had it going on, too. She had the tilt, as in pelvic tilt. Her ass end sloped off the small of her back like a finely groomed ski slope. It wasn't big and wide nor was it flat; she was competition run material, and Malcolm was trying to remember where he'd last left his bar of Sex brand ski wax.

"Looks like this cat's been out getting a little," he teased.

"Don't be talking about Maya like that. That's from the flea medicine I just put on her neck," Sarina defended with a smile.

"Oh, that's what it's from," he said, grinning, as he put the book down on the table.

Gina got up and was pacing inside the cabin, occasionally coming to view through the French doors. She was flicking a Bic lighter and reciting some hip-hop rap poetry that she'd committed to memory. After Sarina loved on Maya, she walked back in to join the two brunettes. All three of them were hip-hoppin', trying to outdo each other in their own little poetry slam. That's when Malcolm realized the incense was just a cover-up for the Big Sur-grown tobacco they'd been puffing.

Ten minutes later the girls walked out to their cars, and Sarina came for Maya. I'll see you after awhile, Malcolm. I'm leaving Maya with a friend for the weekend while I'm gone," she said, as she picked up the cat.

"Oh, that's right. Over at your ex-boyfriend's," Malcolm answered, tossing it out to see if he could stump her. She hesitated for a minute. It worked: he got her back for the 'Hey Malcolm! It's-been-awhile' thing she had thrown at him when she first came in. "Sheila told me, but now we're even," he smiled. "Where you going this weekend?" he asked, helping her out of her silence.

"L.A.," she answered, as she hurried through the gate. "I'll be back in awhile," she yelled, before climbing into Gina's rice burner.

Malcolm finished the Lilith book, went over to the Tahoe and threw it in the back seat on top of the mail he'd picked up at the post office earlier in the day. Sarina came bouncing back into her cabin about thirty minutes later. She was still dressed in her work clothes. Now that Maya was in the hands of her ex, all that Sarina had left to do was change and take care of some last minute packing. Malcolm had moved into the cabin and was sitting on the black imitation-leather love seat that had a sheepskin throw draped over it.

"I wasn't sure if you were coming back or leaving after you dropped off Maya."

"Oh, no man, I just had to get Maya over there, and Gina was my only ride," she said in a soft, stoned tone.

"Your car broke down?"

"Wrecked it. Need to get another one. I want one with a big, long, front end on it for protection," she said, laughing nervously as she walked into the bathroom. She started to run a bath and left the door open so she could continue visiting with Malcolm. She rolled up her pant legs, stepped in, sat on the edge of the tub, and started washing her feet.

"When'd you wreck?"

"Valentines day," she answered, looking up and turning her head to the right to look at Malcolm. "I've got some money saved, but I don't know what I want to get yet."

"Hell, it can't be that hard to buy a car."

"I've kinda been stuck down here. Too busy to really deal with it," she answered, swinging her feet out of the tub and landing them on a towel.

"I'm sure you'll figure it out," Malcolm said, thinking that if she really wanted to buy a car it would have already been bought.

"I just now got my computer set up," Sarina said, changing the subject.

"You on-line?" Malcolm asked

"No, have to get another line in here first."

"You don't need a separate line."

"It's an old computer. I want to get a new one, so I can do more things with it," she said, ignoring what Malcolm was trying to tell her about her phone line.

"Like what?"

"Well, I sell clothes. I have a shop down the road where I sell things, and I want to be able to use my digital camera."

"What else you gonna use it for?"

"I have this comic strip that I want to do. I've been into it for several years. Anyway, I want to take my drawings and incorporate them into a magazine. I'm into erotica," she explained, crossing the great room and into the dressing room.

"Then you want a Mac."

"Why a Mac?"

"If you want to do desktop publishing, you don't want anything but a Mac."

"What's the difference?"

"If you're going to be in corporate America, you might get a PC, but I worked for a magazine that did the local travel guides for a few months and everyone in the publishing world uses a Mac; at least all those I met."

"I still need it to do business."

"That's no problem," Malcolm reassured her. "All I've ever owned are Macs, and I've done all kinds of business on them."

"Websites?" Sarina asked, walking out of the dressing room, and looking really hot. She was wearing a pair of black Dickeys that molded her bottom half, and a silky olive green bra-less top with spaghetti straps that kept her top from rolling down over her nice firm C-cups and exposing her perky nipples. They weren't huge, but damn, they fit her just fine. To Malcolm, her tits were perfect. Besides, he was more interested in what she was toting around on her hind side.

"No problem," Malcolm answered, staring at her breasts, imagining himself being straddled by her as he pulled the straps down over her arms and continuing with her top until he had her nipples in his mouth. "But get a PowerBook."

"That way I can take it with me, huh?" she said, as she sat down on the step that led from the dressing room to the great room.

"You got it. And when you got stuff pouring out of you, you can capture and record it right then and there."

"I've got a tape recorder that I use for that."

"So do I, but writing it when it is coming up out of you is a hell of a lot more effective than speaking it in a few words and trying to make it flow again later. Once you've lost the feeling, it's hard to put words to it later."

"Yeah, I know what you mean. Sheila told me that you're a writer. She said you wrote a book."

"Yeah," Malcolm answered, trying to keep his head.

"What kind of book?"

"Fiction."

"Are you publishing it?"

"You know, I got all fucked up over that a few weeks ago. Having to be published and make money. I'm not even trying. When I start worrying about that shit, I get all messed up."

"What do you mean?"

"I mean it's pressure, and then all my energy goes into worrying about that instead of writing. Then I lose the freedom to write whatever it is that wants to come up out of me."

"I don't get it."

"In other words, I edit when I start writing for money or fame. I quit saying what's true for me. What really wants to come out of me gets distorted or doesn't come at all," Malcolm reasoned, starting to get agitated because it was a state that he was just overcoming, finding his way back to free expression.

"Okay, okay, okay, I got you," she said. "But what if you have a best-seller?"

"That's what I'm afraid of."

"A best-seller?"

"Of accidentally writing one and then not being able to produce another because of the expectations and pressure that comes from having to top the first one. So I just write. I'm writing two more right now. When those are done, then I might try to find an agent, but I'm not ready yet. I mean, hell, I'm just a damn tractor salesman. I don't even know the difference between a verb and an adjective."

"That's what's so great about it!" Sarina said, walking into the bathroom, this time closing the door for privacy.

"I don't really fucking want to know either!" Malcolm yelled rebelliously as he moved back out to the deck and sat down in one of the green cast iron chairs. He just wanted freedom to do it his way, without being burdened with the imagined ruler-induced bruised knuckles from the psychic imprints that had been burned into him from his puritanical heritage, as well as all the other socially imposed dogmas of his day. His bravado was a front he used while trying to build an inner conviction to support his rebellious transition from the world of commerce to living the life of an artist.

He was struggling inside. He wanted to be a writer and give

up the security and enslavement that went with having a real job. Malcolm wrestled with exploiting the hard-earned resources that he had stashed away and saved up for the time in his life when he was ready to accomplish his desires.

He wanted to have the freedom to sleep as late into the morning as he damn-well pleased and stay up and write into the wee hours of the morning if he felt like it, and he was doing just that, but not without a fight.

His problem was the inner voice that woke him every morning and kicked his ass out of bed with: *Here we go, wasted another day, you worthless little fucker. Who do you think you're fooling? One of these days, you're going to be broke again and then you'll go back to work and wish you had never set off on this foolish, unrewarding stint of yours. Your retirement will be gone, you won't have a damn cent to your name and no woman in the world will have anything to do with you.*

Malcolm had become all too familiar with his morning ritual of self-castigation. He was treating himself like a parent would a rebellious teenager. Funny thing was, his parents never treated him that way when he was a kid. They didn't even treat him that way when he was strung out on the dope and booze; they loved him enough to give him the space and freedom to figure things out and decide what was right for him on his own. So why did he wake up to this voice of inner condemnation every morning?

Why couldn't he give himself the same time and space his parents had allowed for his chaos to take form? Knowing that his writing would sell might rob him of his creative edge and provide him with yet another false sense of security. It would be just another lie, like the lies he told himself about selling just one more tractor or one more cotton picker, about how that would put the finishing touches on fulfilling that insatiable sense of insecurity that an already abundant and productive year of selling had yet to provide. It meant more bucks in his pocket and a higher sales volume report to bolster his ego. It was always the elusive one-more-thing that he had to attain in order to bring solace to the existential anxiety he suffered.

Sarina walked out on the deck and sat down at the table in the other chair. She had a pipe in her hand.

"You smoke?" she asked, as she offered Malcolm the pipe.

"Na, I'm an alchy," he answered.

"You need a drink?" she asked, laughing.

"No, thanks. I'm a non-drinking alchy," he answered, laughing along with her.

"Oh, cool. My brother's in recovery. I stopped smoking for two months one time, but I don't have a problem with it."

"I usually don't tell people I don't drink, because I really don't give a shit if a person does or doesn't."

"You mean like if they really do have a problem?" she asked, having just taken a toke off her pipe and trying not to let the smoke out when she spoke.

"I just don't like people to justify themselves to me, is all. Who the hell am I, anyway? Problem, or no problem, it's their own, and I don't really care to hear about it. I got a lot of friends who still drink or smoke. If I feel like having a pop, I just ask them to have one for me."

"Oh, hey, I'll be right back," Sarina said, hopping up and running inside. She returned a minute later with a bottle of black finger nail polish. "Forgot to do my toes," she said, pulling her knee up to her chest and resting her left foot on the seat of the green chair.

She was painting her toes and telling Malcolm about some hiking trails that were nearby when Travis came up to the gate with a guitar case in hand.

"Hey Travis," Malcolm said, greeting him. "You two know each other?" he asked, looking at Sarina and back to Travis.

"Oh, yeah. Hi. We met last week," Sarina said, as she put the finishing touches on her toes.

"Mind if I hang with you guys for awhile?" Travis asked, with his great big, happier-than-hell-to-be-alive smile.

No one answered. Sarina just handed him her pipe. Travis took a hit and handed it back to her. He clapped his hands and started rubbing them together, grinned really big, and then started bouncing up and down in place like he always did when he was excited. Travis literally jumped for joy.

After a few more tokes, Travis sat down on the wooden deck, pulled off his shoes and socks, and folded his legs and sat like he was doing yoga or meditating. Sarina went to put away her nail polish, and Travis reached for his guitar.

"Mind if I play you guys some music?" he asked, opening the guitar case.

It was a Baby Taylor, a smaller scale version of the normal sized guitar. A guy who hung around the Pink House had a Baby Taylor. He used to brag about it to Malcolm because it was small; he could strap it on his back and take it with him when he went on his occasional motorcycle runs. The guy at the Pink House could really make his Taylor sing, just like the big ones.

Travis started playing and Sarina came out with the sheepskin throw from the back of the couch and set it down in the doorway. She lay down on her stomach on top of the sheepskin, her chin resting in the palms of her hands and her legs bent, leaving her calves dangling freely in the air allowing her toes to dry. Travis sang some songs that he'd recently written, and all this out on the deck, in the forest, under the Big Sur sky.

A couple of songs into their private concert, Sarina disappeared inside of the cabin and returned shortly after with a wooden flute. She joined Travis impromptu. She was pretty good. They played one more song together and then stopped.

"Okay, okay, okay, I want to do my poem," Sarina said excitedly. She seemed a little nervous, but something was moving her. She started this rap-like hip-hoppin' poem that nearly knocked Malcolm over. He was mesmerized. The words, the rhythm, and the speed in which it flowed from her dropped his jaw. This young woman had talent, and now she really had Malcolm's attention. It wasn't just her ass end that was teasingly calling to him.

After Sarina finished her rhythm, she sat back down on the throw. She and Travis both took a few more puffs, and started talking about the effects of smoking pot.

"The reason I smoke is because I have so much energy; it helps me take the edge off," Sarina attempted to justify herself.

"Maybe that edge is where all your creativity lies," Malcolm suggested. "Just think of what you could create if you weren't smoking. You might be throwing away the best part of yourself."

"You know, I've been through all this stuff," Travis chimed in. "I don't really believe that it makes a difference," he added.

Then Travis started playing another song. Sarina lay back down on the sheepskin. Malcolm sat next to her in the doorway and rubbed a tight muscle in the wing of his back by leaning into the edge of the door jam.

"I've been thinking about what you said a few minutes ago, about what I could really be creating if I wasn't smoking," Sarina said, after Travis had finished his tune. "That really made me think," she said, looking to Malcolm with a serious look.

"You're the only one who knows what's best for you," he said, looking at Sarina. "You'll figure it out," he added. He wasn't there to sell her sobriety or religion. Malcolm hated preachers; he was just there.

"I just can't see where it's had any impact on me," Travis said, trying to rescue her from her doubt and his own denial.

"You could always stop for a while. See what it does," Malcolm suggested. "If it helps, great! If you don't like it, you can always start smoking again," he added, wondering what she was trying to smoke away.

Malcolm had been through the whole recovery scene and knew that it, too, could rob a person of his own uniqueness just as easily as any drug could. He didn't believe that a person with a drug habit, or any habit for that matter, needed to be told that they were wrong and that it was a black and white choice they had to make.

As a matter of fact, he didn't think anyone should be called an addict, alcoholic, codependent, or any other of the pathologized clinical diagnosis that propelled a person into yet another lie. He believed that people needed options. Options to explore so they could find themselves, find a way of being in a world that celebrated their own uniqueness. What he despised and feared most was getting strapped to some formal set of rules that would crush his spirit and take him farther away from himself again.

"You know what Sarina, it doesn't matter. Everything I wrote in my twenties doesn't compare to what I'm writing at present, now that I'm in my thirties," Travis said, stepping on her.

Malcolm shut up. He could see that Travis had his guitar in hand and wanted the stage. Hell, he had just turned thirty, two months earlier and he was still singing songs that he'd written in his twenties. On top of that, he was singing those old tunes like he had sold a million copies. That bothered Malcolm. He hated to hear someone plant the seed of doubt in the mind of someone with so much potential. He didn't argue with Travis, because he could stomp out his bullshit later, when Sarina wasn't high and when Travis wasn't around to defend himself.

"Guys, I'm going to dinner. You're both welcome to join me if you're up to it," Malcolm announced.

"Let me call my cousin to see when he left," Sarina answered. Sarina's cousin had yet to arrive, and it was eight-thirty. He was driving down from somewhere in Northern California to pick her up. They were going to a family reunion in Southern California.

Sarina learned that it would be a couple of hours before her cousin arrived. Travis put his Baby Taylor away while Sarina called Nepenthe to have them set up a table for three in Sheila's section.

Chapter 18

It was close to nine by the time Sarina, Travis, and Malcolm were seated under the star-studded Big Sur sky on Nepenthe's patio.

"What are you guys drinking?" Sheila asked, wanting to get them started. She had a long night behind her and wasn't in the best of moods.

"I'll have a whiskey," Malcolm announced, adding to the confusion. He loved saying *whiskey*. It was a powerful word, had an edge to it, kind of frontier-like. It made him feel like a cowboy who was bellying up to the bar after a hard day's work of herding cattle and running off bad guys.

"No you won't!" Sheila and Sarina shouted in unison.

"Water's fine," he conceded, pleased to know that people were looking out for him.

"I'd like to have a beer, but I'm driving," Travis announced.

"Just stay the night," Malcolm invited, even though it wasn't up to him to offer hospitality.

"Look, you guys make up your mind. I'll be back," Sheila said in an impatient tone, before walking off to check on her other tables.

"If I'm staying, I need to call my mom," Travis announced.

"How old are you?" Sarina asked.

"It's a respect thing," Malcolm said, answering for Travis. "I mean, he's living with her, and she's expecting him home."

"I'm running down to get my cell phone," Travis said, as he got up. He started walking away, but then stopped before going down the stairs and turned around. "Order me a beer," he yelled.

"What kind?" Malcolm yelled back.

"Any kind," Travis hollered, shrugging his shoulders and raising his arms as he started down the steps.

Malcolm nodded to confirm, but Travis was already on his way down to the parking lot.

"What's wrong with Sheila?" Sarina asked, looking at Malcolm.

"She's raggin'," he answered

Sarina didn't respond, except with an odd look of doubt. She was surprised by Malcolm's quick answer and doubted that he'd know something so intimate about Sheila.

"Really, she's raggin?" Sarina finally asked in a doubtful tone.

"You think I just made that up?"

"Well, hell, that fucking makes two of us, then, if you're really all that interested," Sarina growled.

"You guys know what you want yet?" Sheila asked, having returned to take the drink order, or any order for that matter.

"I'll have a merlot," Sarina requested.

"Which one?" Sheila asked.

"Sheila, you know wine much better than I do," Sarina answered, as Sheila scribbled something down.

"How about you Malcolm?"

"Just water; Travis wants a beer, though."

"What kind?"

"He said any kind," Malcolm answered, expecting the same response from Sheila as Sarina received about choosing her wine.

"Well, that just won't get it," Sheila announced in a pissed off tone and walked away.

Sheila brought the water and wine before Travis returned. When he got back to the table they were talking and sipping their drinks.

"Where's my beer, Sarina?" he asked, as if she was responsible for him not having a drink.

Sarina started to make an excuse, and Malcolm interrupted. "I asked Sheila to bring you a beer, but she wouldn't because she didn't know what you liked. I told her any kind, just like you said, but she wouldn't go for it."

"Sarina, I'm just disappointed you didn't have a beer sitting here waiting for me when I got back. I was really looking forward to having you choose something for me," Travis whined.

"Just lie to him," Malcolm said jokingly to Sarina. "Just make something up," he laughed, knowing something like that was easier to joke away than to fight. Malcolm thought Travis was being ridiculous blaming Sarina for his disappointment. Travis had a look of betrayal after Malcolm's response, but Malcolm didn't like the horseshit he had started down on the deck when he was trying to squash Sarina's spirit. For some reason, Travis was trying to bring the same crap up to the dinner table, and Malcolm wasn't in the mood for any more of it.

Sheila returned and Travis ordered his beer. He pissed a little to Sheila about her not making a selection for him, but she just tough-lucked him, and that was the end of the beer drama. They ordered some appetizers: goat cheese with crushed pecans, smoked trout and roasted garlic.

"I wonder if Augie will try to call?" Sarina asked.

"Who's Augie?" Travis asked.

"My cousin," Sarina answered. "He's only eighteen, but he's so good looking. Ever have a cousin you thought about doing?" she asked, as a shock factor.

"Hell, yeah. I've wanted to do her for the last twenty years. Just haven't figured out how to get away with it," Malcolm answered, swatting at Sarina's bait.

Sheila returned with Travis's beer. He was quiet before the beer came. Maybe he was catching on.

"I was in the market the other day with my girlfriend, and we stole some lip gloss," Sarina confessed. "I mean, we just did it to see if we could get away with it. Like we wanted to do something bad, but not real bad, but still illegal."

"Lip gloss! Is that all?" Malcolm teased. "I like giving people wrong directions."

"What do you mean?" she asked as Travis quietly sipped his beer.

"I used to hang out at this welding shop. It was in a remote farming community, way out in the middle of nowhere. I'd go there to meet my farmer friends. People would often come through lost, wanting to know how to get to such and such a place, and I'd send them ten miles in the wrong direction," Malcolm smiled, proud of himself.

"That's rotten," Sarina said, but she liked it, even if she was having a hard time learning how to take Malcolm. There he was, some straight-arrowed recovered alchy who still took great pleasure in deceiving people.

"They shouldn't have asked me in the first place. That's the biggest problem in the world: everybody wants someone else to solve their problems for them," Malcolm said, looking to Travis. "And the damn people are usually looking for answers from someone they don't even know," Malcolm justified.

"I'm going to have to watch you," Sarina said, as Sheila brought the appetizers.

"Just don't ask me any questions and you'll be fine," Malcolm teased.

"Thanks a lot, guys. See you later," Sheila hollered to a couple that was leaving.

"Who's that?" Sarina asked.

"That's your ex and his new woman," Sheila answered. The same ex who was taking care of Maya while Sarina was away at her family reunion.

"Oh, hi guys. See you later," Sarina yelled. Then she turned to everyone at the table and whispered, "Thanks a lot for taking care of my pussy." They all burst into laughter, even Sheila.

"Sarina, you've officially made the next book," Malcolm announced, and the laughter roared again.

"You better get that down on your note pad then," she advised.

"Don't worry. That shits locked away in the hard drive," Malcolm answered, pointing to his head.

Sheila went to close out while the other three finished their appetizers. When she returned, she had three baked potatoes and some filets of sesame-coated, seared Ahi tuna for the three freeloaders. Sheila set their meal down and returned a few minutes later with a salad and a glass of wine for herself. She was finally off and able to join the bullshit session.

Sheila and Malcolm started taking turns telling about how Travis made the book several months ago.

"That was the night when Travis, Lance, and Chloe were shroomin'. Sheila and I ran into them and we all ended up having dinner at Peppers," Malcolm explained.

"Let me see if I have this right," Sarina interrupted. "You don't drink or smoke, but you'll take acid?"

"No, hell no. Sheila and I were straight. We just met up with Travis and the gang and ended up having dinner with them," Malcolm explained.

"Yeah, and after dinner we all walked down to Lover's Point," Sheila continued, taking over the story. Travis sat quietly, smiling and occasionally laughing, clapping his hands and rubbing them together as the others tattled on him.

"They were cooking pretty good by then," Malcolm interrupted. "Travis started doing his jumping for joy up and down thing on a rock and rubbing his hands together real fast and then announced that Jiminy Cricket was his role model."

"Yeah, well, my father despised Jiminy Cricket because of the whole lack of work ethic theme. He used to say Jiminy was responsible for destroying the future of America's youth," Travis explained.

A man who worked at Nepenthe stuck his head out of the dinning room door and announced that Sarina had a phone call.

"Must be my cousin."

"You said you're doin' your cousin?" the guy teased. Sarina and Malcolm looked at each other and burst out laughing.

"Are you the cousin?" the guy asked, looking at Malcolm.

"He wishes," Sheila cut in.

Sarina walked inside to take the phone call and came right back out. "It was Augie. He's down the road at Loma Vista. I told him I'd meet him down at the cabin in a few minutes."

They settled the bill and all four walked back to the cabin. Sheila, Sarina, and Travis smoked a joint on the way down, and Malcolm lingered behind a few steps.

Within fifteen minutes, Augie, Sarina's eighteen-year-old cousin showed up on the doorstep. He walked in with a two-and-a-half-foot-long bong sticking out of the flap of his backpack. He was short, five-six at the most. He had long, blonde hair, was pimple faced, and wore thick glasses. He appeared to have quite a heavy buzz going, and I'm not sure if it was the bong that had tipped everyone off to his lost condition or if it was the way his eyes were spinning around behind his coke-bottle-bottomed lenses. He sat down and unpacked the bong and asked in a cool stoner tone: "Anyone wanna smoke some killer Humboldt weed, maaannnnnn?"

"You guys still call it weed?" Malcolm asked, thinking that they called it herb.

"It's 'erb," a couple of them answered.

"Herb," Malcolm repeated.

"'Erb, not herb," Sarina shouted a little louder.

"Okay, okay, 'erb. I got it."

The whole cabin was filled with smoke. Augie passed the bong to Malcolm, and he handed it over to the next person without taking his turn. "You don't smoke?" Augie asked.

"No, thanks, but Jiminy here will take a hit for me," Malcolm answered, smiling at Travis. They all laughed except for Augie. They were all too high to explain, and Malcolm wasn't going into the Jiminy thing all over again.

At Midnight, higher than the Milky Way, Sarina and Augie climbed into his car and headed south on Highway 1 along the Big Sur coastline for L.A.

After Sarina and Augie had made their exit, the others listened to some music for twenty minutes or so. Then Sheila announced that it was bedtime for her and the music was off. Travis went to his van to get his sleeping bag. Malcolm had already brought his bag in on the walk back down to the cabin from the restaurant.

Malcolm followed Sheila up the ladder into the loft. On reaching the top, he glanced at Sheila scratching around in her nest, and then crawled to Sarina's side. He unrolled his bag on top of the made bed. Travis came back into the cabin a few minutes later and started to make his bed downstairs. He chose the floor because the loveseat was, at the very least, two feet shy of accommodating Travis's lengthy body.

Travis was all fired up and wanted to keep on talking, but Sheila wanted to sleep. Malcolm was enjoying the comfort of Sarina's bed, wondering if he'd ever end up there again, with her. Travis asked some silly question and Sheila answered in a tired, go-to-sleep tone. It was quiet for a bit and then Travis would fire off something else that had been rolling around in his head. Sheila was close to telling him to pack it.

There was an "ouch!" and then a slap.

"What's going on?" Malcolm asked.

"Something bit me," Travis answered.

"A flea," Sheila mumbled.

"A flea?" Malcolm asked.

"Yeah, Maya gave us fleas. We've got to bomb this place."
Travis slapped and "ouched" for a while longer before he made his final announcement: "I can't take these fleas anymore. I'm going out to my van."

"Okay, we'll see you in the morning," Malcolm answered.

Sheila didn't acknowledge Travis's departure. The front door shut and a few seconds later the gate latch caught.

"I knew those fleas would be good for something," Sheila mumbled, as she shuffled around in her nest.

Chapter 19

"Hey Malcolm! You awake? It's me, Sheila," she hesitated before hanging up on his answering machine, knowing that he screened all his calls. She also knew that he got pissed if she phoned before ten; it was a few minutes after. It had been over a week since Malcolm had spent the evening with Sheila, Sarina, and Travis down in Big Sur.

He rolled out of bed and picked up the receiver. "Hey Sheila, what's up?" he asked in his morning voice, which usually lasted into the early afternoon, about the time he finished his coffee.

"What's up sleepy head?" Sheila teased. For a woman who he'd never slept with, she knew his sleeping habits quite well, but that wasn't saying much, because Malcolm didn't keep most of his women around long enough to become familiar with any of his habits.

"What are you doing?" Malcolm asked, still too sleepy to think.

"Getting ready to leave for Reggae on the River. You still gonna house-sit for us?"

"Sure," he answered, waking up a notch. "When?" he asked, having forgotten that he'd volunteered. They were going to Humboldt for some annual Reggae concert pilgrimage they took every year.

"I'm leaving tomorrow morning and Sarina is leaving Friday after she gets off work."

"Unless I get someone to cover for me Thursday," Sarina shouted in the background.

"Guess I could be there Friday sometime," Malcolm answered, trying to think if he had plans that would conflict.

"Friday," Sheila repeated, more for Sarina's benefit than Malcolm's.

"Tell him to come tomorrow. He can help me get hooked up to the Internet," Sarina shouted.

"You hear that?" Sheila asked.

"Yeah, I'll be there tomorrow. Later in the afternoon, though," Malcolm answered, fantasizing about having Sarina all to himself that evening.

"Okay, tomorrow afternoon. Stop by Sarina's shop on your way down. She'll have a key for you."

"Alright, tell her I'll be there tomorrow."

"I'll leave you a note about watering all the plants. Hope you have a great day sleepy head," she said in a bubbly tone.

"Sheila..." Malcolm hesitated. "Have fun, and be careful," he said, not wanting to sound like a parent, but wanting to let her know that he cared about her.

He hung up and then remembered that he had promised to drive his Mrs. Shams to her masseuse the following afternoon. He picked up the phone and called Sheila.

"Hey, it's Malcolm."

"What's up?"

"Won't be there tomorrow until five or five-thirty."

"Five or five-thirty."

"Good. He can give me a ride home from the shop," Sarina shouted in the background.

* * * * *

After his morning walk and shower, Malcolm drove to the Pink House for coffee. Jake was out bussing tables, waiting for an ear.

"Morning Jake."

"Morning Malcolm," he said, as Malcolm walked up the steps of the old Victorian, anxious for his cup of joe.

A few minutes later, he was on the porch occupying the prized bench that was seldom free. Jake was standing one step up from the sidewalk talking to a local whom Malcolm had yet the pleasure of meeting. Jake had a handful of dirty dishes he'd just bussed. He shuffled his feet in place on the step as he talked to this guy.

"Hey, Bobby! Don't let it get wet," Jake yelled at another local who was riding by on a bicycle headed down toward the beach. The other local whom Jake had trapped in conversation used the distraction as an opportunity for his escape.

"We used to always say that when I lived in the Caribbean. St. Bart's, you know," Jake said, as he stepped onto the porch.

He looked a little embarrassed over his spontaneous outburst to his buddy, Bobby.

"Yeah, I remember you were telling me about that last week," Malcolm answered, appearing not to have been put off by his behavior.

"Did I ever tell you about how I got out of the war?"

"No."

"It was in sixty-eight. I went to the doctor, and asked him to find something wrong with me," Jake explained, as he set the dirty dishes down on the porch ledge.

"What did he find?"

"Nothing, but when I was leaving he told me that I needed to see the psychiatrist and winked."

"So he did help you?"

"You bet he did," Jake said, as he repositioned the baseball cap on his head.

"Whadja do?"

"Put on a World War One officer's jacket and a black stocking cap that I pulled down to my eyebrows," he said, crossing his arms. He was standing to Malcolm's left and started doing the same shuffle he had been dancing a few minutes earlier on the step below.

"Yeah," Malcolm encouraged.

"Yeah, and I went to the draft board. And when I was standing in line, I fell down on the floor and started crying out: 'Take me home! Take me home!'"

"Did they?"

"Hell no. They thought I was faking it!"

"Well, you were."

"The MP's came to get me. Tried to make me shape up, you know?"

"What happened?"

"I kept repeating: 'Take me home! Take me home!' They didn't know what to do."

"So what *did* they do?"

"Took me upstairs to the shrink's office. Everybody else in line was cussing me."

"Yeah, no shit?"

"They thought I was full of it, but I just kept on saying: 'Take me home! Take me home!'" he answered, waiting for Malcolm to catch on.

"Yeah."

"Yeah, I used to work with autistic children. You know what that is?"

"A little."

"They check out of reality. Keep repeating things. So that's what I did."

"So, whadja do once you got in the shrink's office?"

"Kept on repeating: 'Take me home! Take me home!' But I never looked any of them in the eye."

"No?"

"If I had, they'd have figured me out. I had to pretend that I was lost in my own world. If I had acknowledged them, they'da had me."

"So it worked?"

"Yeah, I scared the shit out of those people," Jake said, grinning and shaking his head. "They didn't know how to handle me. I had one of those MP's really spooked. He wouldn't get close to me; let the other officers escort me out. The guys in line were still all cussing me when they showed me to the door."

Malcolm sipped his coffee and listened.

"I made that one MP touch me before I left, though," Jake said, wearing a nostalgic grin, looking across the street into the parking lot as if he saw something.

"How?"

"Right before I was out the door, I stopped and asked him for a cigarette and he gave me one. You know, just to be getting rid of me. Then I asked him for a light, so he handed me his lighter."

"Yeah," Malcolm smiled.

"I put the cigarette in my mouth and tried to light it, but acted like I was shaking too bad. Then I dropped his lighter. He picked it up, sparked a flame, and held it up to the cigarette that I had bouncing around in my lips. I grabbed his hands to steady myself and pulled the lighter to the smoke. I made sure I touched that son of a bitch. Made sure I touched everyone of 'em there before I left. He was the last one," Jake said, slowly nodding his head up and down.

"They couldn't wait to get rid of you."

"Yeah, but I made sure that I touched everyone of 'em before I got out of that place. I didn't want none of 'em forgetting about me," Jake explained, continuing his nod.

"And that was the end of it?"

"That was it. I went home to my mother, and she asked me what happened."

"You tell her?"

"Nah, I just told her that I got off because I couldn't hear well. She was in the Russian army, you know?"

"That's one hell of a crazy story, Jake."

"Hell, that's no story. It's the truth," he said, as he reached for the dirty dishes he had set down before he had started his tale. Malcolm picked up his cup of coffee and took another swig, and Jake walked inside with the stack of dirty dishes.

Malcolm looked out and across the street to the parking lot and saw a cop writing parking tickets. The officer walked past Jenny's car because she had a local's parking permit that granted her amnesty. He had continued to see Jenny on a professional level after the vibration video, but the only other time they spent together was limited to short friendly exchanges when their paths crossed at the Pink House. He liked her, but he'd become frustrated and found himself withdrawing.

Jake walked out onto the porch and leaned against the supporting column that rose from the ledge up to the ceiling.

"So, your mother was in the Russian army?" Malcolm asked.

"Yeah, she got out because she couldn't hear good. They barked some orders to her one day and she walked off like she didn't hear 'em."

"So your mother is Russian?"

"Yeah, and my father, may he rest in peace, was a Jew."

"How'd he meet your mother?"

"It was the Warsaw thing. He met her in Russia and they ended up in Poland. That's where I was born. In forty-six."

"I thought you were born in Brooklyn."

"No. I can still remember running all around that boat."

"Boat?"

"The boat that brought us to the States from Germany. I was born in Poland then we went to Czechoslovakia. From there we went to Austria and then to Germany."

A really hot woman got out of her car and was walking through the parking lot across from the Pink House. Jake and Malcolm were both goggling.

"Not too shabby, huh?" Malcolm asked, testing Jake's reaction.

"She'd hurt you."

"Well, I'm ready to be hurt. Nothing wrong with being hurt every once in a while."

"Yeah, every once in a while's all right; just as long as you don't get caught."

"Caught?"

"I've had a lot of fun, but never married."

"I was once," Malcolm said. "Married, that is."

"I remember the Sugar Lady."

"The Sugar Lady?"

"Her real name was Patricia, but I called her the Sugar Lady."

"Patricia the Sugar Lady, huh?"

"I was twenty-one and she was thirty-three. She worked for some brokerage firm."

"Older woman, huh?"

"I couldn't get it up," Jake confessed.

"Must not have been the right scene for you."

"She was married."

"Where was her husband?"

"Flying jets over Nam."

"And you were afraid that he might fly one of those jets right up your alley and dive bomb the living shit out of you."

"Damn right I was. She called one day: 'Hurry up! Hurry up! He just left and won't be back until tomorrow!'"

"You go?"

"Yeah, but something wasn't right. In twenty-two seconds she was all over me. Had my pants down around my ankles, but then I said, hey, wait a minute, something's not right here. So, I pulled up my pants, and ten seconds after I had them all buckled up, her husband walked through the door. Wouldn't be back, hell. I knew something wasn't right."

"You listened to yourself."

"She called me after I moved to California. She got divorced and moved out here. Moved to San Francisco and called my mom back in Brooklyn to track me down."

Malcolm listened.

"I went to see her one time. She wanted me to do her just as soon as I got there."

"Did you?"

"No. She started telling me about how she was having to masturbate."

"She was horny."

"Maybe. But I didn't need to know that stuff. I mean, that's fine, but just don't make it any of my business," he said, holding his hands up, palms open and fingers extended as if he was holding something away from himself. "Then, the next thing I knew she wanted me to eat her quiche," Jake explained, shaking his head with a disgusted look on his face.

"Whadja do?"

"I left."

"And that was the end of it?"

"No, she started calling my father's house looking for me. Let it ring twenty-five times, so my father, may he rest in peace, finally answered the phone thinking that there might have been a tragedy in the family. When I got home, my father, may he rest in peace, asked me what the deal was with this woman. My father didn't need to be worrying about stuff like that. Him and my mother split up years ago, you know. She stayed in Brooklyn, but my father, may he rest in peace, moved out here."

"So what did you ever do about the Sugar Lady?" Malcolm asked, as Jake was about to go back to work.

"I called her and told her that I needed to see her," Jake answered. "Let's just say that I took care of it, okay," he explained, as he straightened his hat and started to walk away. "The phone calls, that is," Jake said, loud enough for Malcolm to hear as he made his way down the hallway towards the kitchen.

Chapter 20

"Chickens lay eggs. People lie down."

Malcolm didn't respond. Then she said something about his misuse of prepositional phrases. He still didn't respond.

"Don't you remember that from your English classes?" she asked, trying to incite a riot.

He just smiled, having expected this type of reaction from her.

"And, you should never end a sentence with an adverb," the old Mockingbird lectured, holding up her right hand and pointing with her index finger at the windshield like it was a blackboard.

"I don't even know what an adverb is," Malcolm answered, finally breaking his silence.

"Well, maybe it's time that you learn if you want to be a writer," she answered.

"I'm not a writer. I'm a tractor salesman who wrote a book," Malcolm defended, as he drove Mrs. Shams to her masseuse.

She said that they weren't going to be chums, and for the first year it was pretty much that way, but then things changed. Ever since Malcolm had cleaned out her garage and hosed down her patio, she began to warm up to him some. Then one day she asked him to go for Sunday brunch to celebrate the millennium, and that's when he told her that he was writing a book.

Mrs. Shams seemed to be a lonely lady even though she did have friends and went to yoga three times a week. She was suffering from macular degeneration and after having had some sort of ocular surgery, had to return to San Francisco for a check-up. It was supposed to be a one-day trip. She had hired a driver to take her to the city, but they ended up running some test on her that required her to stay overnight. Her driver couldn't stay because he had another job the following morning, so Malcolm had to pick her up the following day. A few weeks later she smashed into the rear end of a car, ending her driving career. So, after the millennium brunch and Malcolm retrieving her from the city, she recanted on them not being chums.

The old girl's eyesight might have been going, but her hearing was as keen as a bat. It got to the point that Malcolm would quietly lock up his studio so that she wouldn't hear him leave and catch him at the garage when he was getting into the Tahoe. When she did catch him, she'd inquire about the progress of his book, and other events in his life, like school and women. She caught Malcolm taking the trash out one day, and asked if he'd finished the book and, mistakenly, he confessed its completion but didn't offer the manuscript for her to review.

After a few months passed, curiosity finally got the best of her, and she asked to read it. Malcolm danced around the subject quite well for the next few months. He even told her that he was afraid that she might not be able to handle the profanity and that he needed to do another round of editing before he'd let her have it. He never could quite shake her comment about cussing: "I always say that profanity is the sign of an undeveloped vocabulary." The ol' Mockingbird loved repeating things that she'd heard from her husband.

One evening she took Malcolm to dinner as a reward for doing something around the house, and, in a weak moment, he finally granted her privilege to the manuscript. He knew he messed up just as soon as he conceded, knew things would never be the same.

She was an eighty-year-old woman. Her husband had been her only lover. He'd been dead for twenty years, but she had immortalized him and still secretly loved this man as if she woke next to him every morning. She had no business reading about the exploits of a single man caught up in the throes of a midlife crisis, and Malcolm had no business giving her the manuscript in the first place.

He never should have told her or anyone else that he was writing a book. Once again, his ego's need for an identity, self-importance, and admiration had backfired on him. He was young enough to be her grandson. If she'd led a life of denial for this long, who was Malcolm to rob her of her illusion? Oh, well, in one way or another, we all have illusions shattered almost everyday of our lives.

"I'd like to comment on the subject matter, but don't think you want to hear what I have to say," she said, breaking the silence that crept into the Chevy after having delivered her brief English lesson en route to her massage.

"Please, I'd like to hear," Malcolm encouraged. "It can only help me," he added. He wasn't so interested in perfecting his grammar, not that it didn't need a good deal of help; it was her reaction that he was really interested in. She'd read it in two days, so something had snagged her and held her interest.

"I just wish my husband was alive so he could sit you down and..." she hesitated. "Well, I just think you'd take it better coming from a man," she said, shuffling in her seat while her head bobbed around on her shoulders in an uncontrollable fit-like reaction.

She was still gathering steam for the delivery of her impending sermon. Malcolm didn't respond, knowing that shit was about to hit the fan anyway.

"I don't want to sound like Flo, but..." she hinted, and then caught herself.

Malcolm laughed to himself. Flo was a character in the book, a meddling motherly-type who had a habit of sticking her nose into things that weren't her business.

"We all have bodily functions," the Mockingbird said, finally getting down to saying what she wished her husband had been around to say. "We don't need to hear about this sort of thing. I mean, the greatest love story I've ever read left the love-making scenes to the reader's imagination," she screeched.

"Well, I got the opposite feedback in the book evaluation I received from my editor last week," Malcolm defended. "Actually, she suggested I make the sex scenes more graphic. Said I needed to make the reader feel as if they were actually in bed making love to the characters," Malcolm continued. He liked the scenes just as they had been written. They were descriptive enough to draw the reader in, and the rest was left to the imagination. He might not have been a writer, but he was a salesman. He knew how to lead people by saying just enough. He knew that too few words wouldn't whet an appetite and with too many words, he could actually talk himself right out of a sale.

She shrugged her shoulders to the comment about the sex scene. "Honestly, do you really think you could be with just one woman? I mean... it is quite obvious that you have a highly developed libido." Mrs. Shams's relief valve had finally given way and she started spewing as her head danced an excited little jig on her shoulders. "With all the experience you've had, I don't think that you could ever be satisfied with just one woman."

"That's probably why I didn't stay married," Malcolm answered, feeling obligated to defend himself. He was losing ground. Her relentless attack was undermining his initial detachment towards her ridicule.

"Well, yes!" she said excitedly, needing to justify her reaction to the book and how she had literally translated Malcolm the writer into Malcolm as the book's main character.

"That's what the book is all about," he answered. "My battle with Flo is really a battle with the dark mother who resides within me," he explained. "Flo acts like she wants me to grow up to be my own man, but she's really a greedy and jealous old hag who wants to hold me captive. She wants me to stay the dependent little boy so she can control and manipulate me. That way she can continue to run my life. By going back for Sarah and rescuing her from Flo, I stood up to the critical devouring mother in my own psyche. The story's about me slaying the dragon of my own mother complex and rescuing the princess, Sarah, my inner feminine, who has been waiting for me to come for her so that she can breathe new life into me, animate me, and give me new meaning. Sarah is me. By rescuing her, I'm rescuing myself. That way I don't have to continue seeking the ethereal in physical woman."

Mrs. Shams looked at Malcolm in an odd way. She hadn't read the book the way he wrote it. He was glad in one way because this was how he expected most people to read it, simply as the literal story. He had expected more from Mrs. Shams though, and that was why he was disappointed. He thought that she'd read beyond the dramas and the simpleton characters in the book and understand the metaphoric story that was being told.

"Well, what about that comment you made about possessing a woman? Malcolm, nobody wants to be possessed. We all need our freedom."

"You're exactly right. If I wasn't conscious of this tendency, it really would be a problem," Malcolm answered, defending his own freedom. "What we know doesn't run us; it's what we don't know."

"Who do you think your audience will be?" the Mockingbird screeched, continuing her attack on Malcolm's first real attempt at self-expression.

"I may never do anything with this book. I wrote it more for myself than I did for anyone else," he answered, realizing that she couldn't understand what he was trying to tell her. He regretted having shared his writing with the old lady. He knew better; it had instigated the very response he'd anticipated.

"To me, it's something I'd expect to find on a rack in the airport," she said, as Malcolm drove into the parking lot across the street from her masseuse. It was the same parking lot that he used when frequenting the Pink House.

Part of Malcolm took her response as an insult, and part of him took it as a real compliment. "If I'm not here in my truck, I'll be sitting over at the Pink House," he told the old crow, as she started to open her door.

"All right," she answered in a kinder tone. It was a forced tone though, and behind it still hid the disapproving critic that had embodied her for most of the drive to Pacific Grove, actually that had probably possessed her for most of her life. She looked at Malcolm before opening the door and said: "That Francis... well, remember how I was saying he had too much time on his hands?" She was referring to a man who had been her neighbor for the last fifteen years. Francis was in his fifties. He'd inherited money and never worked a day in his life. She was always telling Malcolm about how he'd never get social security because he'd never paid into it.

"Yeah, I remember Francis."

"Well, maybe you have the same problem," she said, nodding her head in agreement with herself as she slid out of the seat before closing the door. Malcolm had really worked this old girl into a lather. The virginal dream image that she once had of him was gone. She had been raped and robbed of her naïveté, and was trying to pretend it hadn't happened. She was trying to be gracious and not react, but she couldn't contain herself.

She had been an active woman all of her life, but never had to work. Her dead husband had left her a house that had been paid for in full, a home that sat up on a hill overlooking the Carmel Mission, along with all the other resources that would allow her to live comfortably without further concerns.

Malcolm, on the other hand, had busted his ass for eighteen years sucking up peoples shit just to be able to afford her cheap little studio apartment. He was taking a much needed and justified sabbatical in hope of recapturing his lost soul. He had desperately retreated to Carmel to rest and to recreate himself. Things were becoming a lot clearer about why the Mockingbird's only son never returned to the nest.

Malcolm felt liberated, yet ashamed. He wanted to move away, out of Hephaistos' forge where he had retreated to for the last year and a half. The dirty work of bringing things up from the bowels for that particular book had been completed; it was still in the rough, and most certainly needed to be refined into a finished piece, but the story had been written. It was now time for filing, buffing and polishing.

Mrs. Shams had become Flo incarnate. She'd come back to haunt Malcolm and had inflicted him with his own critical arrows of self-doubt. It was time to leave Flo and the forge behind. Malcolm was tired of being the nice guy that the Mockingbird, or anyone else for that matter, needed and expected him to be. He was also tired of being the shackled prisoner of the almighty dollar, and the bargain, three hundred and fifty dollar a month studio for which he'd sold his soul. The place had been good to him, served its purpose, but the leftovers had become stale.

He left the parking lot and crossed the street to the Pink House to have a late lunch while Mrs. Shams got rubbed down. All he had to do was get her back home, and then he'd be off to Big Sur to house-sit and out of the little old lady's line of fire for at least a few days. He was stepping onto the sidewalk when a car tooted its horn. Malcolm turned to find Waylen driving Danette's orange BMW, the same Danette whom he'd sworn off a week earlier.

Malcolm walked in and ordered lunch while the BMW parked. A couple of minutes later Waylen bounced in as Malcolm was paying for his bowl of potato leek soup. He bought Waylen's coffee and they walked out front. They settled at the round table on the patio, below the front porch, to soak up the sun.

"I see you're driving the Beamer again, huh?" Malcolm teased.

"Had to take her to the airport."

"Where's she going?"

"Catalina. Her sister's getting married. Three hundred fifty nine dollars for a ticket."

"From here to Catalina?"

"Just to L.A. She could have got it for two hundred. I told her to keep her legs closed, too."

"You what?" Malcolm asked sounding a lot more surprised than he actually was.

"When I was driving her to the airport, I told her that she needed to keep her damn legs shut and not be giving that shit up all over the place," Waylen said in an agitated tone. "Not like I'm even getting any of it," he added, shaking his head in disgust.

A week earlier he wanted nothing to do with her, and now he was her airport shuttle driver who was telling her not to be screwing anybody on her weekend festival in Catalina.

"It's just a bunch of single people looking to get laid," Waylen said, referring to Catalina.

Malcolm ate his soup and listened.

"So, I drive a few more blocks, and then she tells me not to be sleeping with anyone else either. I told her that that means she must still have some feelings going on for me."

"Well, at least you've got a nice car to drive around for a few days," Malcolm teased, trying to lighten things up. Having the car was nice for Waylen, but it damn sure wasn't going to help him get laid. If anything, it was a leash to keep his mind tethered to Danette's image. Better yet, it was a corset.

"A few days. Hell, she won't be back until next Tuesday," Waylen moaned. It was only Wednesday afternoon.

"I think you ought to get a date and use her car," Malcolm suggested.

"Don't think I haven't thought about that, brother."

"Hell, better yet, get a date and take her home to Danette's house," Malcolm laughed. "If your date asks whose place it is, tell her it's your sister's," he added, with a sneaky grin, raising his eyebrows like Waylen always did.

"Oh brother, you are bad."

"Yeah, and?"

"You know that's not a bad idea," he answered, and then they both laughed like two sneaky little boys who were getting away with dealing a dirty deed. Malcolm stood up and reached for his empty water glass and, without words, excused himself to walk inside for a refill. A minute later he returned and sat back down at the table, front and center ready for round two.

"I was at her house the other day, and I got on her computer. Got into her e-mail," Waylen confessed, still reveling in his sneakiness. "No wonder all her friends can't stand me," he laughed nervously.

"Alright! You got into her e-mail?"

"Yeah, brother, she wrote to one of her friends about the psycho who broke into her house and took her chair. Hell, brother, I didn't break into that house, and it was my flippin' chair. I just went there and got it back, is all," he said, defensively. Waylen had put his elbows down on the table and his forearms were sticking up in the air. His head was leaning forward in front of his hands as he excitedly explained all of this to Malcolm. "Now, I'm the psycho. No wonder none of them like me," he said, rolling his eyes and shaking his head.

"Well, next time you call Danette and have to leave a message just say: 'Hey, Danette, it's me, the psycho,' and then hang up."

"Yeah, I like that one, brother. Hey, check this one out over here," Waylen said, referring to a hotty blonde who was walking across the parking lot.

"Easy, boy. Don't go psycho on us now," Malcolm teased.

"Really, you know me. I'm not that way," Waylen said in a serious tone. "Not anymore anyway," he joked.

"Hi, I'm Waylen, and I'm a recovering psycho," Malcolm laughed.

"Oh, brother, don't even go there with that shit."

"I only have one question for you, Waylen," Malcolm said, leaning back in his chair.

"What's that?"

"If you're the psycho, why's she popping the Prozac?" he asked, robbing Waylen of the self-doubt that was hanging over him like a fog.

"Right on! Thank you for that brother," Waylen shouted, slapping Malcolm a high five.

"Why didn't Danette drive to L.A.?" Malcolm asked. "Driving only takes a couple hours more, and then she'd have her car to get around in once she got there."

"She has this condition. Gets really tired."

"Is it that Epstein-Bar syndrome thing?"

"I don't know what it's called."

"It's depression."

"Yeah, but we already know she's tweaking that way, brother," Waylen said, leaning back into his chair.

Malcolm didn't respond.

"Says she made a new friend. A guy friend. I found his number when I was snooping around her house."

"What's up with that shit?" Malcolm asked.

"She says she's not attracted to him that way, but the woman lies, so I called the guy myself."

"You called this guy? What the hell'dja do that for?"

"Find out if she was lying to me," Waylen said, cocking his head back. "I told him that I was the guy Danette's been seeing for the last four years. I asked him… you know how I am. I asked him straight up if he was trying to facilitate something with Danette."

"Like he'd tell you if he was."

"I know, but I told him that I didn't care what he was up to. I just told him that Danette lies all the time, and I just wanted to get the story straight. Now he thinks she's a liar. At least I got that fixed up anyway."

"Hi, I'm Waylen and I'm a recovering psycho."

"Oh, brother," he said frowning and shaking his head. "She said she wasn't attracted to him anyway."

"So then why'd you call him?"

"It's just like I told Danette. You're not attracted to him, hell. A couple of those other guys you slept with weren't very attractive either," he said laughing and slapping Malcolm another fiver.

"Well, at least you've got her car for the next week."

"Yeah, this one woman who I'm training saw me with

Danette before I took her to the airport."

"Screw up something that you might have going with her?"

"No, brother, she just asked me about it. I mean it's a small town. Everyone knows everything around here."

"Yeah, no shit," Malcolm answered, thinking about how Waylen had made their relationship a public record. Waylen was like the town crier who sat on the porch of the Pink House pouring out all of his and Danette's intimate secrets. "So this woman you're training knows all about your thing with Danette?"

"Oh, yeah. She says I got to stop that shit."

"You were just taking her to the airport," Malcolm reminded him, knowing that it was a hell of a lot more than a friendly ride to the airport.

"She said that I got to stop being there for Danette. Danette's never there for me, so why should I be there for her? She's right, you know."

"You're there because you got nothing better going on," Malcolm reminded him.

"You're right about that. It's that time of the month when she's…"

"It's the moon," Malcolm interrupted.

"That cycle shit," Waylen added. "You know, the two or three days in a woman's cycle when they actually like having a man around."

"You sound like an experienced man," Malcolm teased.

"Hey, how's that thing going with your girlfriend, Jenny?" he asked, wanting to shift the topic.

"Well, for starters, I don't think we can call her my girlfriend," Malcolm answered.

"Has she got an attitude or what?" Waylen asked.

"Yes, but not like you think."

"Does she think she's better than?" Waylen asked. "Danette sure does," he added before Malcolm had a chance to answer his question.

"No, she doesn't think she's better than. She comes across that way, but she's not," Malcolm defended. "She's just quiet. But, she does have an attitude," Malcolm added, without going into it any further.

"So nothing's happening there, huh brother?" he asked, sensing that Malcolm didn't want to go into Jenny's personality. He really only wanted to know if Malcolm was getting any.

"Don't worry, if anything was happening with Jenny, I'd be telling you all about it right now," Malcolm lied. He'd be bragging somewhere, but not to Waylen, or any other local for that matter. It would probably be to Lewis. Not only did Lewis live two hundred miles east of Malcolm, he could also keep his mouth shut.

"Just hanging then, huh?" Waylen asked again, as if Malcolm was holding back on him.

"You know..."

"Yeah, I know," he interrupted. "You haven't ever fucked a woman who didn't want to fuck you first," he finished.

Malcolm just smiled and took a swig of his water.

Chapter 21

He drove the Mockingbird home after her massage and then made his way down the coast. By the time Malcolm pulled into the parking lot of Sarina's shop, it was a little after five. The building was a greenhouse that had been converted into a small shop that sold the works of local artists. The building was rectangular with windows running the length of the structure on the side that faced Highway 1. The entrance had doors that swung open like a barn. The roof consisted of white corrugated fiberglass strips to let the sun shine through to heat and light the place.

Sarina had a partner, Regina, not the Gina that worked at Café Kevah. Regina was responsible for the artwork and jewelry that had been crafted by local artists, and Sarina ran the clothing section. There were several articles of nice second-hand clothing in the shop, as well as a limited line of new, younger women's clothing. Sarina loved clothes, so if anything came in that caught her eye and was her size, it never hit the sales rack.

Sarina's step-grandmother was sitting down on an old covered chair in the back of the shop visiting with Sarina while she priced a shipment of inventory that had just arrived. Sarina introduced Malcolm to Laine, the grandmother, and shortly after the introduction, Laine said goodbye, leaving Sarina to finish her pricing chore.

"I'm going to be awhile. I'll give you a key if you want to go up to the cabin."

"That's fine. I'm not in a hurry."

"I've still got to pack when we get back, then I'll cook you dinner," she volunteered. "Are you hungry? I've got a bunch of stuff in the refrigerator we need to use before it goes bad."

"Sounds good to me," Malcolm answered, impressed and grateful for her willingness.

Malcolm looked around the shop, occasionally asking questions about different articles that sparked his curiosity, but soon grew tired of groping all the goods and sat down in the seat that Laine was sitting in when he arrived. He shifted his inquisitiveness to Sarina, admiring her enterprising nature. She had fire, and it wasn't just about making money, it was about living a life: a life in which her heart was invested. She drew, was a poet, and worked in her own shop selling the creations of others. Sarina was an artist who had carved out her niche, and Malcolm found that very appealing.

By the time they closed the shop, set the alarm, and padlocked the place, it was seven o'clock. Five minutes later, they drove down the private drive and pulled up to the girls' cabin. Sarina helped Malcolm carry in a few necessities that he brought along to accommodate his passing the time during the house-sitting chore.

Malcolm walked inside behind Sarina, threw his goods in a corner, and then relieved Sarina of what she had carried in. The place was cluttered with half-packed bags and there were branches of eucalyptus leaves scattered all over the place. Sarina walked back into the dressing room, while Malcolm remained standing in the living room trying to get a feel for the place.

"What are all of these eucalyptus branches doing in here?"

"For the fleas," she answered, not bothering to stick her head out to look Malcolm in the eye.

"Thought you guys were going to bomb this place last weekend," he reminded her. Actually, it was Sheila who was supposed to take care of ridding them of the fleas while Sarina was away at her family reunion. Sheila had failed to tell Malcolm about not taking care of their infestation problem when she called requesting his services. It reminded him of how his mother worked. For that matter, it reminded him of how a lot of women worked. They never lied because of the devastating moral injustices it caused. Instead of lying, they just accidentally forgot to tell about the important stuff.

"Why don't you come in here while I pack," Sarina suggested.

Malcolm walked into the dressing room.

"You can sit down on that," she said, pointing to a wicker stool.

He pulled the stool out from under the ladder that led up to the loft and sat down. She started sorting through pants and tops.

"Check these out," she said, holding up a dress and a couple of different tops all with some sort of red rose floral print. "It's for my new image," she said smiling. "I'm changing my name to Rrrosa," she announced, rolling her "Rrr's." "In honor of my Spanish heritage," she added.

Sarina was Spanish and Hungarian, and Malcolm was still trying to figure out just exactly what you got when you crossed a Spaniard with a Hungarian. It could possibly have been a life long study before he came up with an answer. One thing was for certain though: Rrrosa was high energy. She had hot blood pumping through her body.

She continued packing while they visited. They talked about their families, about art, life, living it all as one. He watched her sort through her panty drawer and uninhibitedly toss into a pile what she planned on packing. She put on a leopard print cowboy hat that someone had given to her for her twenty-fourth birthday. The fire in her eyes seemed to cast a spell on Malcolm, that and the feline-like attitude that oozed out of every pore of her being.

Malcolm was there on a house-sitting invitation. Sarina liked him he was sure, but he was Sheila's buddy. He wasn't Sheila's lover, though, and he was riding on that one little glimmer of hope that… well, just maybe. He walked out into the great room and sat down on the love seat. Pussycat still emanating from her soul, Sarina walked towards the bathroom.

"You want to go out for a bite instead of cooking?" Malcolm asked, testing her response when the bathroom doors swung back open.

"That's okay, I'll cook us something," she answered, but still entertaining the possibility of his invitation.

"Well, it's almost eight and you still have more to pack," he added.

"Are you real hungry?"

"Yeah, but finish what you're doing and we'll go out. You can cook something for me another time," Malcolm answered, testing her reaction.

"What are you hungry for?" she asked.

Malcolm held back with a smart-ass answer. After all, she was fifteen years younger than he was. He could spook her real fast regardless of her already lost naïveté.

"I'll trust you to figure that out. I've only eaten at Nepenthe and the Coast Gallery…"

"I don't want Nepenthe," she said, almost interrupting him before he had finished. "We could go get a pizza at Loma Vista," she suggested, calculating the cost of a meal in her head.

"Where else?" Malcolm asked, "I'm not worried about the money," he added, giving her mind permission to run away with his credit card.

"We could go to Post Ranch or Ventana."

"You pick."

"I'll see if we can get a reservation at Post Ranch," she said, picking up the phone and dialing the number from memory. "Hi, this is Rrrosa from down the street. I'd like to make a reservation for tonight… Nine-fifteen," she said, looking at Malcolm. He nodded. "Okay, nine-fifteen, and put the reservation under Rrrosa… okay, thanks." She hung up, and Malcolm breathed in a little more of the wild red Rrrosa bouquet.

He put on a clean shirt while Sarina finished packing. By eight-thirty she had changed her clothes and sat on the leopard print beanbag chair that was across from the love seat and next to a suitcase lying on the floor that doubled as a coffee table.

"I'm going to smoke," she announced, picking up her glass pipe from the suitcase.

Malcolm sat there without responding.

"I always smoke before dinner, and I…"

"You don't have to justify it to me," he interrupted.

"Well, I…"

"Look, you don't have to explain," he said, stopping her again. It bothered him that she was wasting her life smoking the shit, but a part of him wanted to join her, too. He wouldn't; he'd quit it, the booze and a load of other chemicals fifteen years earlier, and he wasn't about to start again. But he always allowed himself the possibility of doing so, just so he didn't have to climb back on that merry-go-round.

Rrrosa had soon smoked her fiery personality away, and it was work for Malcolm to carry on a conversation with her. She was way out of it, her mind wandering, unable to concentrate on any type of meaningful conversation.

Post Ranch was only five minutes from the cabin. Sarina strutted like a peacock as she ushered Malcolm into the restaurant. She wasn't the same woman he had been with earlier in the day. It was almost as if she was compensating for an inferiority complex of some sort.

"Hi, I called a while ago to make a reservation."

"What was the name?" the host asked with an odd expression after looking over the reservation book.

"Rrrosa."

"Oh, okay, here we go," the man said, with a confused look on his face. The host, as well as most of the staff, knew Sarina; they just didn't know her as Rrrosa.

A friend of Sarina's mother walked past and greeted her. Sarina acknowledged the woman and then turned to Malcolm. "It's a small community. People like to gossip," she said, suffering a paranoia high.

"Great! That's right up my alley," Malcolm answered.

"No, you don't understand..."

"I understand better than you think," he answered, flashing back on the small communities that he'd been a part of in his past life. "Let's have some fun."

"What do you mean?" Sarina asked.

"Nobody knows me around here. Make me into a celebrity or something."

"I don't want to be part of something dishonest," she answered. It bothered her that Malcolm was willing to tell a lie. She was qualifying him, but he didn't give a shit. Just because she didn't trust him, didn't mean she wouldn't sleep with him.

"Just for fun. It's innocent, and no one gets hurt," Malcolm encouraged. "I never lie if it's going to hurt anyone," he added to redeem himself, wanting to be a bad boy whom she could trust.

"How 'bout a screenwriter?" she asked, joining in on the fun.

"No, then they'll want to know what I've written."

"I got it. You're a rock band promoter."

"That'll work," he grinned.

Dinner was superb. It was a prix fixe menu, eighty bucks a pop, with several choices for each course served. They decided to order different menu selections and share.

They started off with oysters on the half shell and figs as appetizers, then green salad and tomato soup. Malcolm's main entree was black cod with a wasabi sauce and a cucumber salad with shitake mushrooms. Sarina's entree was a green pea fritter that was accompanied with a variety of tomatoes and mushrooms.

The waiter returned with a chocolate soufflé and a mango sorbet in raspberry soup and Sarina jumped at the chance to stir things up a bit: "Jason, this is Malcolm."

"Pleasure to meet you, Jason," Malcolm responded, extending his hand.

"Nice to meet you as well..."

"You know the rock band Cake? Malcolm's their promoter," Sarina interrupted.

Joining in, Malcolm turned to Sarina, and shook his head in disapproval as if he didn't want her revealing his celebrity status.

"I understand," Jason said. "We'll keep things low key," he added.

"Thank you, Jason," Malcolm answered, nodding graciously. "Well, that ought to give them something to scurry around about," Malcolm whispered to Sarina after Jason had left to attend to the needy egos of other demanding patrons.

"Why didn't you say anything?" she asked, as if Malcolm should have responded differently.

"Didn't need to; people make us into what they need us to be anyway. The less you say, the more they can dream up," he answered confidently, having successfully let this philosophy serve him over the years.

Sarina stared at Malcolm with a can-I-trust-this-guy look, as Jason returned to check on the fibbing duo, distracting Sarina from her doubt. Jason offered to bring them an after-dinner drink, so Sarina ordered a port on the rocks, and Malcolm had coffee.

Now that she had the locals guessing, Sarina was really enjoying herself. She wasn't pretentious nor did she seem to revel in the acquisition of the material, but dinner at one of Big Sur's finest restaurants with an older man who was doubling as a celebrity was feeding her. It was almost as if she believed her own lie, basking in the spotlight of attention that was shining on her.

Sarina was a damn sharp twenty-four year old woman. Nothing had been handed to her. What Sarina had, she earned, but she'd suffered to get her smarts. Behind her I-don't-need-anyone tough-girl act, hid a wounded little girl trying to smoke away an old pain.

Other than her buzz that caused a slow start between the two of them, the whole experience at Post Ranch was memorable. It was almost midnight when they returned to the cabin. Malcolm took the loveseat and Rrrosa sat on her leopard print beanbag chair. She stood up right after sitting down, remembering that she needed to pack an additional item. The Reggae on the River thing was one of Rrrosa's highlights of the year.

Sarina was a hopper. She kept remembering things that she forgot to pack earlier. She'd hop up to go find what she'd forgotten. Malcolm liked how her mind worked; it was a lot like his. She'd start talking about something, think about something else, and hop to that new topic. Then before you knew it, she was back talking about what she'd hopped away from five minutes earlier. Sarina packed her bags the same way, so they hopped around in conversation as she hopped around the cabin packing more things.

The next thing Malcolm knew, Sarina hopped out of the dressing room with a big fat baggy full of buds. It was dreamlike, like stepping back in time, into the life he'd once lived. When he'd stepped out of that dream, he had left the people who lived in that world behind as well. His illusion was that when he quit, the whole world had followed suit.

She grabbed a rolling tray and started breaking up some buds. "This was a birthday gift," she said, looking up to Malcolm.

"What are you doing?"

"I'm rolling some up for the road tomorrow."

"Mind if I help? I mean, I'm sure I can still do it."

"Sure."

"The worst that can happen is that I'll have to tear it apart and start over," he reasoned, giving himself permission to play. They rolled eight joints and she put them in a brass cigarette holder. For Malcolm, it was kind of weird, handling the stuff, feeling the stickiness as he pulled the buds apart with his fingers and sniffing the pungent skunkweed aroma. It was tempting.

After a while, Sarina announced she was going to bed. Then she stuffed a bud into her glass pipe and puffed it a few times before getting up. Malcolm pulled the sweats from his bag and stepped into the bathroom. After he finished, she took over the bathroom, and Malcolm climbed the ladder up into the loft. He unrolled the sleeping bag on top of Sheila's bed and took off his T-shirt before sliding into the bag. A few minutes later, Sarina hopped up into the loft wearing her flannel pajamas.

"Oh, thanks again for dinner," she said, hopping into bed.

Chapter 22

Returning from the bathroom, Sarina woke Malcolm as she crawled back up into the loft.

"What time is it?" he asked, staring up at the pine ceiling. He was happy to wake to her presence, even if she was crawling back into her own bed.

"Eight-thirty," she answered. "I'm laying here until nine, though."

"Easing into the day, huh?" Malcolm asked, turning his head towards her.

"Always," she said, rolling over on her tummy. She was still dressed in her flannels. She reached over for something on the shelf next to her bed.

"Not me. I usually sleep until ten and then jump out of bed," Malcolm answered, rolling over onto his right side.

"Why?"

"I'm hardly ever in bed before one or two," he answered.

"I mean why do you jump out of bed?"

"Oh, 'cause I got this voice that says: 'Come on you worthless piece of shit, get up and do something with your life.' It cries out to me every morning like a goddamn Mockingbird."

"That's screwed," she said, rolling onto her back, her knees bent and her feet flat on the mattress.

"Yeah, guess I'm kinda still caught up in that rat race that I supposedly left last year. Hey, how was your trip to L.A. anyway?" Malcolm asked, wanting to shift away from the topic. "Your family reunion?"

"A mess, I don't even know why I bothered going. My family's all fucked up," she answered in a discouraged tone.

"How are they fucked up?" Malcolm asked. Sarina was a different woman when she wasn't high.

"Well, my brother, the one who went to rehab," she said checking to see if she needed to tell Malcolm the story all over again.

"Yeah, I remember."

"Okay, well, my aunt down in L.A. has a business, and she

lent him the five thousand to go through rehab. Now he's down there working for her to pay her back."

"What's wrong with that?"

"He's down there out of obligation. And, he's getting all caught up in that rat race thing you're talking about."

"He's probably feeling obligated to your aunt and to himself," Malcolm suggested, remembering what it had been like to get sober and become responsible. "Sounds like he's making up for lost time," he suggested, recalling all that came along with his newfound sobriety. "How old is he, anyway?"

"Twenty-nine. The only reason I went down there was to see him, but now he's got a girlfriend who's trying to run his life, too."

"So you probably didn't even get to visit with him much?"

"No, and my aunt just takes off for a pedicure and doesn't even bother to invite me. I mean, she can give him five thousand fucking dollars, but she won't even treat me to a pedicure. She thought she could just send me down to that big ol' cat litter box of a beach to hang out with all the turds for the afternoon."

"Your brother still sober?" he asked, not wanting to go to the litter box with her.

"That's the other thing. He's drinking and smoking again," she said, stretching her knees to one side. "And my aunt doesn't say a damn thing about it."

"She wants him that way. As long as he's still fucked up, he's dependent on her. Keeps him under her thumb that way," he answered, as if he actually knew the people he was analyzing.

Sarina listened intently without responding.

"What's his girlfriend say about his habits?" he asked.

"She just bitches at him," she answered, looking up to the ceiling.

"Bitches, but she needs him to stay that way just like your aunt."

"You really think so?"

"They don't do it because they're bad people. They do it because it's all they know," Malcolm answered, finding it nice to be talking to Sarina about real things, talking to her while she was all the way awake, sharp, and not high. He wanted to crawl into bed with her, but he knew that he'd never have his way with her if he didn't let her make the first move.

"Want some tea?" she asked, as she rolled out of bed, rescuing Malcolm from the trouble his hard-on was provoking.

"Sure."

"I have English Breakfast in the morning," she announced, making her way down the ladder.

"Sounds good to me." Malcolm rolled out of the bed, slipped his T-shirt on, and followed her.

After their morning tea, Sarina took her shower, preparing for the lunch shift she was scheduled to work. The cabin's bathroom had double doors that pulled together in the middle, a design similar to the shop's entrance, only much smaller. From the loveseat, Malcolm looked through the gap that was left after she'd latched the doors but shifted his stare back into the book that he was reading, fearing she'd catch him and write him off as just another dirty old man. He didn't mind being one, just didn't want anyone else thinking that he was.

A few minutes after the shower stopped, the doors swung open, and Sarina waltzed out with a towel wrapped around her head and another wrapped around her middle that covered her from breast down to ass-cheeks. Malcolm kept on reading, acting as if he was ignoring her, but sneaking in as many rapid peaks that he could fit in as she walked from the bathroom to the dressing room. She was about to step up into the dressing room but hesitated and went over to the CD player to put on some music.

Sarina was prancing about shaking that twenty-four year old power thing in front of Malcolm just to remind him and herself that she was still in charge. As teenagers they're curious, in their twenties they think they have the magic box, by thirty they don't have anything left to prove and can finally settle down to enjoy and feel good about sharing themselves with a man. Malcolm's problem was that he was still trying to recapture his youth, unwilling to give up young, hot, hard, twenty-something-year-old bodies.

He turned the page as Rrrosa stepped into the dressing room and continued reading. It was Henry Miller's *Tropic of Cancer*. Malcolm thought himself to be a bit on the raw side until he'd started reading Miller. After Miller, he considered himself a saint.

Pants on, bare back exposed, holding the towel over her breast, hopped the fiery hip-hopper from out of the dressing room. She needed to get something she'd packed. Malcolm's ass! It was her last chance to rub it in his face before she ran off to work, leaving him and his imagination all alone in her cabin. One thing was certain though: he had inspiration for the day, and it wasn't even noon.

The next time she came out of the dressing room she was fully clothed, so Malcolm put the book down, and it was a good thing because if he read much more of Miller, he might have raped Rrrosa right then and there.

"Damn, I forgot to charge the battery for my video camera, and it's at the shop," Sarina said, as she plopped down in the beanbag chair and loaded her glass pipe. "I'll call Regina and ask her to charge it for me."

Malcolm started telling Sarina about a friend of his who was going through a hard time in his marriage and leaned on him quite a bit more than he cared to be leaned on.

"He'd call wanting to know how I was doing, but he really wanted to tell me about his problems," Malcolm explained, as she took a hit off of her pipe.

"They show up like they want to help, but really they're the ones looking for help," she said, after exhaling.

"Yeah, I had this friend who I met years ago when I got sober. He quit drinking a few years before I did and we became friends; fishing buddies. He was going through a lot of crap with his wife. He needed to get a divorce, but couldn't because of money and being tied up in that rat race thing."

"You mean he was afraid."

"Yeah, and he was living his life through me instead of doing what he needed to do for himself."

"What do you mean?"

"Instead of doing what he needed to do, he latched onto me. Said that he didn't have friends and that he was grateful that I had befriended him. He'd call damn near every other night pissing and moaning about the same old thing over and over again. Then he started telling me how brave I was for walking away from a career without having anything else lined up. It took me a few months, but I finally caught on to what his gracious applause for me was really all about."

"He set you up."

"Yeah, because he needed me. He made me into what he needed me to be, because he couldn't do it himself. He was empty and robbed me of all the energy he could find. Hell, I wasn't even getting laid for it."

"You what?" she asked, sitting up, eyes growing wider.

"I'd normally have to be getting my lights fucked out by a pretty hot woman to be putting up with that kind of shit. I mean real hot."

"That's just like that fucker I was with two years ago. I was getting laid, but he was sucking up all of my energy. He had no fucking balls when it came to getting something done. I managed his business. I initiated everything and then he'd step in to take all the credit."

"That's what this guy was doing. He tried to take credit for me staying sober. That's when I finally woke up to what was happening. I told him that he was full of shit if he thought I was sober because of him. He finally backed down. That's when I realized that I had been getting robbed, and that I didn't need people like him in my life."

"Same reason why I got out of the mess I was in. One good thing did happen, though. I ended up with my own business, but he still calls whining about how he's in love with me. He's not in love with me. Just thinks he is."

"His love's a disguise. He's in love with what you gave him, and I'm not talking about sex. You have it and he doesn't. He'd be back in a heartbeat to rob you some more if you'd let him."

"That's why he still calls here whining all the time," she said, looking at the clock up on the window sill. "Shit, I've got to go."

Malcolm walked her to the door.

"I only have this one key, so if you leave while I'm at work, drop it off, so I can get in to get my stuff later," she said, handing Malcolm the key before walking out the door.

"I'll be around," he reassured her, wanting to hug her and maybe even more, but afraid of her smoking habit. If she could stop, she'd do something big someday.

The phone rang. Malcolm let the machine answer. It was

a call reminding Sarina that she was scheduled to work in five minutes. He looked up and saw her at the top of the hill. She'd be there by the time her shift started. He put on his baseball cap and walked up to Café Kevah for a coffee and a story.

The Kevah was an exorbitantly priced snack bar that was built out on a lower deck below Nepenthe. Gina, Sarina's hip-hop buddy, poured Malcolm's coffee. He found a sunny seat on the deck and sipped the dark brew while soaking up the rays and thinking about everything that happened since he'd arrived the day before.

He looked over to the Kevah's counter and saw Gina taking another tourist's breakfast order. Malcolm remembered how Gina walked up to Travis and himself a week or so earlier while they were having coffee at the Kevah one morning. It was before he had ever met Gina. She knew Travis and, while she was out wiping down tables, she walked over to them and announced that she had forgotten to brush her teeth and spit over the side of the patio wall as if she was trying to get the morning taste out of her mouth. Then she rubbed her right boob saying that she was a little sore and hoped she didn't have breast cancer.

When Malcolm looked up from his daydream, Gina had walked out to bus a few tables. She was wearing khaki pants and some three-inch platform shoes. She had on a lapis blue sweatshirt that was unzipped, so he couldn't make out the words.

"What's your sweatshirt say?" Malcolm asked, as she came to wipe off the table directly in front of him.

"Planet Earth, ha, ha, ha," she cackled. "It's a skateboard company," she added, before walking back to her post at the Kevah.

After finishing his first cup, Malcolm returned to the counter for a refill and stood in line behind a man who was ordering breakfast. He wanted his coffee in a doubled paper cup. They offered him a Java jacket, but he wanted it in a doubled cup to keep it hot. They ended up offering him a ceramic mug while he ate, and told him he could get a refill in a paper cup when he was ready to go. He seemed happier than hell, but Malcolm couldn't figure out why, because coffee always seemed to cool much faster in an open ceramic cup as opposed to a paper cup with a lid, especially a doubled paper cup.

"You worked here last night?" Double-cup said to Gina.

"What's that?" Gina asked, actually having heard his question.

"You were on duty last night when I was here," he repeated.

"You mean yesterday morning when your wife ordered huevos rancheros for breakfast," Gina answered, sharp as a tack.

"Maybe it was in the morning," he answered, not smart enough to quit being friendly to someone who didn't want his friendship.

"Are we having a senior moment?" Gina quipped. "I'm just kidding," she quickly added to ease some of the sting from her venomous bite. It was enough to send him sailing.

Double-cup's white Reebok tennies walked his tail-tucked self to his table. He had on a purple, cotton, button-up-the-front shirt and a faggy pair of teal colored shorts that had been out of style for... hell, I don't think they had ever been in style. His wife, who sat waiting for him, was dressed in the same color coordinated matching apparel that her queer husband was wearing.

After getting his refill, Malcolm looked up from the Kevah's patio to Nepenthe's deck. He spotted Sarina running around playing waitress. He sat back down, took a deep breath, a sip of coffee, and looked around the patio.

Double-cup was rolling breadcrumbs into little balls and throwing them over the side of the deck. The Blue Jays and Ravens started flocking to the rail in front of him. He went over to the rail, causing the birds to scatter and started throwing more scraps over the side and down into the forested area below. Malcolm imagined going over and pitching Double-cup's queer ass over the side but refrained in deference to the birds, not wanting to pollute their living space.

Looking up, Malcolm spotted Sarina again. There was something magical about her. He was breaking up. It had taken thirty-nine and a half years, but Malcolm's iceberg soul had finally caught a current that had taken him into the tropics. His Big Sur visit and encounter with Sarina was melting him.

He was beginning to feel a freedom to be and express himself as never before.

After coffee at the Kevah, Malcolm returned to the cabin and showered. It was close to one by the time he settled down to his writing. He found an extension cord in the dressing room, plugged it into an electrical outlet, and ran the cord through a window so he could use his Power Book outside on the deck. He sat down in the green cast iron chair, scooted up to the table, and went to work.

Chapter 23

It was three-forty. He was still out on the deck punching away on the keyboard of the PowerBook when the phone rang. He listened to a long-winded hip-hop purring pussycat greeting that Sarina had recorded on her message machine. Then he heard her voice hollering for him to pick up, but he didn't get to the phone in time. A few minutes later Sarina came running down the hill towards the cabin.

"I forgot my rent check," she shouted, as she bolted through the gate. The check, along with a couple hundred dollars of cash, was lying on top of the pile of her packed bags. She ran in, grabbed the loot, and then, rent in hand like she had just robbed a liquor store, ran out the door and started back up the hill. "I'll be back down in a little while," she hollered halfway up the grade.

Thirty minutes later a dark blue midsize pickup with a camper shell backed up to the gate. Rrrosa hopped out of the passenger side before the truck had stopped moving and bounced through the gate like she was a kid just getting to an amusement park and wanting to be first in line. The driver of the truck, a woman, calmly stepped out and walked around to the back of the pickup, raised the camper shell door and dropped the tailgate. A carpeted camper conversion kit had been installed in the bed of the truck. It was already half packed.

"Hi, I'm Angie," the driver said, as she walked onto the deck. "You must be Malcolm."

"That's right," he answered, smiling and shaking her hand. Sarina had mentioned Angie as being one of her good friends. Angie was a few inches taller than Sarina. She had auburn hair, rosy cheeks, long legs and arms. She was wearing a pair of black stretch leggings and a light-blue, short-sleeve cotton top. Sarina had also mentioned that Angie worked with her at Nepenthe. She must have gotten off work at the same time as Sarina. Angie took over the bathroom announcing that she would use the shower to freshen up.

Sarina ran around in circles trying to remember what she

might have forgotten. Malcolm sat out on the deck, out of her way. Gina and a blonde haired dude in his twenties came through the gate. A black Labrador retriever followed. Gina walked inside without acknowledging Malcolm, and the blonde headed dude stepped onto the deck, the dog at his side.

"Hi, I'm Cliff," he said, extending his hand.

"Hi Cliff, I'm Malcolm. Nice to meet you," Malcolm answered, shaking his hand. "This your dog?"

"Yeah, this is Sadie," Cliff answered, looking down at Sadie scratching a flea.

"How old is she?" Malcolm asked, watching Sadie transition from scratching to biting the little bastard that was munching on her back thigh.

"Almost a year," he answered. Sadie tried to walk inside, but Cliff caught her and held her back.

"Don't let her in there. They got fleas," Malcolm teased.

"Yeah, I know. They're blaming Sadie for it," he said, raising his eyebrows in disbelief and then looking directly at Malcolm with one of those give-me-a-break expressions.

"You can get that Advantage stuff you put on the back of their necks. Supposed to work for a couple of months," Malcolm suggested, looking at Sadie working on another flea and thinking about Jenny and Diana.

"Yeah, I know. Maybe when she's older," Cliff answered. "I hate poisoning her that way," he added.

It was the day and age of organics. Where Malcolm came from, everything was fertilized and sprayed with synthetic pesticides. He had been familiar with organically grown produce for years, but had never become part of its culture until moving to the Peninsula. Fear seemed to be everywhere, not to say that all of it was unwarranted, but it oozed through society's psyche like the plague.

Fear of dying; fear of living and not living; fear of not getting what we want, and fear of getting what we don't need. Hell, even fear of getting what we do want. Malcolm had moved out of his old Central Valley life trying to escape the fear, but found it in another form. Maybe we are poisoning ourselves with what and how we produce and consume, but I can't help believing that the most potent carcinogenic is fear itself. If it doesn't show physically, it can still turn the soul into a mushy, blighted heap that all the chemotherapy in the world can't cure.

Malcolm had started to eat healthier food with everyone else on the Peninsula. He continued to choke down his fear with every bite of organic food that made its way into the local markets. Fear sold more than life insurance.

Cliff went inside to get high, and Sadie lay down on the deck next to Malcolm. Two deer wandered into the meadow a hundred feet below. Malcolm watched them raise their wet noses, watched their bodies react to what they heard, smelled, and sensed in any other fashion. One bolted across the meadow, the other backed up the hill closer towards the deck. Something had moved them, but each of them had reacted differently. They roamed together, but moved independently, according to their own impulsive and individual instincts, not to the prophetic words of a fumbling society.

What moved the rebel within Malcolm? Perhaps it was simply for the sake of having a fight? Maybe the fight gave him purpose, even if he didn't know what the purpose was. Or, perhaps he was rebelling against his life, his very existence, rebelling against God, divination, his fate?

He looked inside and saw Cliff passing a small blue ceramic pipe to Gina. Sadie was still lying next to Malcolm on the deck, soaking up the sun, lost in a dream. Sarina was still running around in circles just to be doing what was familiar to her. Angie walked through the bathroom's double doors with just a bra covering her topside. She was still wearing her stretchies over her bottom half.

Gina went over to a wooden table just inside the French doors. There was a candy dish on the table with a condom stashed between the caramel toffees and the red and white individually wrapped mints that were probably defectors of Nepenthe's after dinner selection.

Gina reached down and picked up the condom. She looked around, didn't see anyone, and then put it in her pocket. She looked out to the deck and realized that Malcolm had been watching her.

"A condom, ha, ha, ha," she cackled. It was the same laugh she used when she told him what was printed on her sweatshirt earlier in the day at the Kevah. She started to walk away.

"That's probably the one that has the hole poked in it," Malcolm needled, wondering if picking things out of a candy dish was a reflection of how she lived her life.

"Whadja say?" she asked, turning back to the doorway, trying to hide her embarrassment, yet unable to ignore him as she usually did. She heard him the first time but had to confirm the doubt he had just created.

"I said that's probably the one that's been pinpricked," he answered, beaming a second round of doubt her way. There, now Gina had some more fear to add to her bag of tricks.

After catching their afternoon buzz, Gina, Cliff, and the flea-bitten Sadie started their trek back up the hill towards Nepenthe. Angie had her top back on, and Sarina started carrying her luggage to the truck, so Malcolm got up to help.

Sarina was inside the camper arranging things when Malcolm brought a couple more of her bags. "Did you get your batteries charged?" he asked, referring to her camera battery.

"Regina charged them for me at the shop. I'm going to stop by and pick them up on my way out," she answered, already five miles up the road in her mind.

"Good, wouldn't want you leaving without a fully charged set to keep you happy." Malcolm smiled behind her back, testing to see if she was paying attention.

"Unfortunately, it takes more than that to satisfy me," she said, as she slid out from under the shell grinning.

It took them each three trips back to the cabin for the rest of Rrrosa's goods, but then the girls were officially packed and ready for their annual journey to Reggae on the River. Malcolm was at the truck to see them off. He shook hands with Angie, and Sarina gave him a hug.

"We'll be back on Tuesday," Sarina announced, as she opened the truck's passenger side door.

"Okay, have fun," Malcolm answered, "But I guess I don't need to tell you that, now do I?" he added, realizing that he was talking to the red hot Rrrosa. He got one more beaming smile from her before the two girls drove away.

Malcolm was finally on his own. He went back into the cabin, walked around in a few lost-like-Sarina circles, and decided to get the pizza Rrrosa spoke of before they ended up at Post Ranch, before Malcolm had become a celebrity.

He drove to the café at Loma Vista. After taking the steps up to the restaurant, he looked down onto the parking lot. Sarina was at the gas pumps. They had stopped to top off the gas tank.

"Hey Rrrosa!" Malcolm yelled from the entrance to the café. She looked up surprised that someone had already discovered her wish to celebrate her Spanish heritage. She smiled big as life when she saw Malcolm and yelled something to him, but he couldn't make it out because of the traffic that was zooming by on Highway 1. He waved to her and then went inside the café. He ordered a prosciutto and arugula pizza. While waiting for his order, Angie passed by just outside the window. He tapped it to catch her attention. She smiled and waved. A few minutes later their pickup pulled onto the highway northbound.

It was dark and quiet when he returned to the cabin. There was no television, but even if there had been, he probably wouldn't have turned it on. Instead, he fired up the PowerBook. The phone rang around ten that evening. Rrrosa's voice echoed from the answering machine. She was calling for Malcolm. Well, calling for something.

"Hello," Malcolm said, having picked up the receiver early enough this time to stop the recorder.

"Hey, I need a favor," Sarina said in an excited tone.

"What's up?"

"I forgot to write down the phone number for the people we're staying with tonight."

"And now I suppose you want me to go snooping through your drawers to find it."

"No, my drawers are with me here in San Francisco," she said, playing along with him.

"Damn, just my luck," he answered. "So now what?"

"Go over to the bookcase by the door."

"Okay, I'm here," he answered, only three steps from her request.

"Do you see a black organizer down on the bottom shelf?"

"Yeah, I got it."

"It's in the index part under B."

"Okay, it's in your black, unorganized, organizer under B. I'm there," Malcolm said, opening to the B index.

"'Bout halfway down the page there should be the name Eric without a last name."

"Okay, I got it. Ready to write?" Malcolm asked, and then read her the number twice to make sure she copied it correctly.

"How was your pizza?" she asked.

"It was good, even got the locals' discount because they saw me shouting at you when I walked in."

"Cool."

"Hey, not only have you got a house-sitter, now you've got your own personal secretary to look up phone numbers for you, to boot," Malcolm teased.

"Thanks! I'll bring you a present back," she answered in a sexy tone.

"Alright, goodbye," he said, not even wanting to think about her drawers that were a hundred and fifty miles north of him. Out of reach was out of reach; it didn't matter if it was only an inch or an entire lifespan. She wished him pleasant dreams and hung up.

Malcolm wrote past midnight, until he couldn't anymore. Then he turned off the lights, climbed the loft, and slipped into his sleeping bag, wishing that he was slipping into the red hot Rrrosa.

Less than a minute had passed before the first flea bit his neck.

Chapter 24

He woke to another fleabite and a piss hard-on. Funny how Malcolm hadn't suffered even one bite until after Sarina had left. He stepped down the ladder and stumbled into the bathroom. His next stop was the kitchen to fire up the stove to boil tea water. It was Saturday, and he'd be damned if he was going to join the weekend tourists for coffee at the Kevah. When he had gone to bed the night before, he had entertained the possibility of falling in love. Something about Sarina had really fired him, even if she was a little pothead. But when he woke, he wasn't so much in love with her; perhaps the fleas had sucked the lust out of him.

His illusion of her becoming sober had also gone by the wayside. Besides, what would he do with a wounded little girl trapped in the beautiful body of a stoned twenty-four year old woman? Sarina was trying to smoke her way out of the same body that he dreamed of slipping into. It was just another one of Malcolm's many futile attempts of marrying matter and spirit.

Waiting for the water to boil, he made himself an organic peanut butter and blackberry jam sandwich. He was trying to play the role of the broke starving artist who he secretly longed to be. There was a part of him that just wanted to be shitting in the gutter, without the worry of having to cling to any assets or anything else that would rob him of following his dream.

There was also a part of him that wanted to be slurping up spaghetti and meatballs every chance he got. It didn't have to be a filet mignon, just a flippin' meatball plopped on top of some sauced noodles. It didn't much matter if it was peanut butter, meatballs, or a filet mignon because it seemed that anything he tried to choke down was sauced in fear. He couldn't enjoy a meal without having that inner voice of doom tap dancing around in his noggin, and it was dancing him damn dizzy.

The other ailment that Malcolm suffered was a conscience that he swore he must have picked up from some queer asshole that had sneezed on him out in public somewhere. This contagious disease no longer let him sleep with mixed-up women under the age of twenty-five. On top of that, the women who were over twenty-five, for some unknown reason, seemed to have his bullshit figured out even if they were mixed-up.

So, Malcolm was a mixed-up soul. He couldn't enjoy eating, and he couldn't enjoy sex. He felt like a run-out racehorse that had been put out into a weedy field only to be teased by the young fillies across the fence where they inhabited all the freshly seeded and irrigated green pastures at the ranch next door. The teapot started whistling; it was an Earl Grey morning. It was going to take another good four hours before he really woke up.

He turned on his mobile phone. There was a voice message, so he put on a pair of shorts, sandals, and a hat before climbing the hill to pick up a cellular signal. Gerald had called. They'd been playing telephone tag. He phoned a few days earlier to check on Malcolm, but when Malcolm returned the call, Gerald's voice mail answered. He left Gerald a message about being taken hostage by a hot, young, Big Sur girl. That was right up Gerald's alley, even if it was a lie.

This time Gerald's message suggested that Malcolm come up for air. He volunteered to have any needed medical devices dispatched to Big Sur for Malcolm's resuscitation. Gerald's message had somehow helped Malcolm to feel better. Gerald actually thought Malcolm was getting a little; at least someone believed in him.

Gerald and Malcolm had become friends a few months after Malcolm had moved to Carmel. Gerald was an attorney who lived in Sacramento but had a second home in Pebble Beach. Gerald specialized in riparian water rights and represented several large farming concerns throughout the state of California. Paul, a farmer friend of Malcolm's whom he ran into at a coffee shop while vacationing in Carmel, had dragged Malcolm over to Gerald's one day telling him that he needed to meet this guy. Paul told Malcolm that when Gerald was around forty, he had a midlife crisis and went back to school to take a number of art classes.

It was true, too. Gerald had left his business for his associates to run. He started taking art classes. Said he could have had a master's degree if he had given a damn, but hell, he was already a Harvard Graduate and had nothing to prove. Instead of becoming an artist, Gerald became a collector. He was now in his early seventies. Some of Gerald's riskier investments had panned out over the years and had left him a very wealthy man.

It was on the Fourth of July, six months after Malcolm had left his work, when Paul introduced him to Gerald. It was kind of weird. Malcolm always knew that Paul was kind of trickster-like. The day when Malcolm ran into him, he had this feeling that Paul was sort of a psycho-pomp who was guiding him in some unknown fashion. Malcolm ended up drinking coffee with Paul and Gerald and before long, Gerald's wife, daughter and son-in-law showed up. After being introduced to the family and telling them how he'd walked out on his career, they all started grilling Malcolm about what he was doing or going to do with his life. Gerald's daughter had even asked if he was writing.

Anyway, that's how Malcolm met Gerald and his family. Gerald asked Malcolm for his phone number, so he gave it to him, never figuring to hear from him again. Gerald called a few months later, and they had dinner together.

Gerald was in love, and not just a little in love. It was the daughter of one of the junior partners in his firm who knew nothing of the affair. They ate at Mondo's that night, and no matter what they talked about, it all came back to Gerald's new love. Malcolm didn't mind. Actually, he loved watching this seventy-year-old boy all caught up like it was his kindergarten teacher or his first piece of ass. Hell, Malcolm hoped that he would still be falling in love like that when he was a hundred.

Malcolm wasn't sure if Gerald trusted him when he confessed of his affair or if he was just so damn excited that he had to tell someone. It might have been a little of both. Besides, the odds weren't too good of it getting back to his wife, not from Malcolm anyway. Gerald also knew that a guy like Malcolm, in the middle of a midlife crisis, similar to the one he had traversed, had to be trustworthy when it came to defending a man's honor, even if it meant lying all the way to the grave.

It was official after their first dinner; they were buddies. Next to his earlier crisis, it appeared that Gerald was in the midst of a new one, and when a man was in such a place, it was damn important to have a friend for support, someone who understood what he was going through; heaven and hell all in one breath. They became friends and got together every couple of months. Gerald was in town on the New Year, and Malcolm brought him a bottle of wine and visited his family. That's when Malcolm told him that he was writing the book. They met a few months later and Malcolm gave Gerald a rough draft of the manuscript.

Gerald read it in two days, and phoned Malcolm excited as hell to tell him that he had something. He called back a few days later and praised him all over again. Then he read it to his mistress one afternoon while she drove him from Sacramento to Southern California on a business trip. The mistress was a shrink. Anyway, he called Malcolm on his cell phone that night from Southern California ranting and raving about the book. Then he introduced his shrink sweetheart to Malcolm and put her on the line.

She said hello first, but then, without missing a breath, wanted to know why Malcolm didn't like women. Gerald was in the background hollering about something, and Malcolm chose not to get into a shitting contest with a woman shrink whom he didn't know and who thought she knew him just because she'd read the book. Malcolm kept it vague and pleasant, and then said goodnight to the two lovebirds. He could have written a report on the impending doom of the Kangaroo Rat and it would have been a best seller in Gerald's mind. Love's a trick, but Malcolm didn't care. He valued Gerald's friendship, and Malcolm's ego needed all the fans it could collect.

He tried Gerald on his cellular phone before walking back down to the cabin, but he failed to answer, and Malcolm was tired of leaving voice messages. Besides, his call wouldn't ring through while down at the cabin anyway, so he set up shop out on the deck at the green table. He wrote for a couple of hours that morning, took a short break for lunch, and then went back to writing for a few more hours. His cellular phone actually rang once before dropping the call. The caller ID indicated that it was Jenny. She had left a voice message.

Malcolm wished he could have just given her up. At the top of the hill, he picked up a cellular signal and phoned her back.

Jenny loved the Myers-Briggs personality test type indicator stuff, so Malcolm had told her about a personality type seminar that he'd seen advertised somewhere. She had just returned from the seminar and was calling to report her experience, or at least she was using that as an excuse to call. She certainly never ran out of excuses.

He invited her to join him at the cabin for the evening, but she was on this special diet, and didn't feel comfortable leaving her home, said she'd think about his invitation and call him back. He didn't bother telling her about the fleas. If she knew the place had fleas, it would have been an automatic slam-dunk no. She wasn't coming anyway.

Jenny's call threw Malcolm into a funk, drained all the energy that Sarina had pumped into him. He liked Jenny, or thought he did and wanted to remain her friend, but he wanted a lover and lovers they hadn't become. Her call had thrown Malcolm back into the waiting game that he wanted to escape. He'd been waiting for Jenny to come around long enough. He'd stray away and she seemed to grow a little more affectionate towards him. As soon as he came back her way, off she'd go in another direction. For some reason, she lacked the passion to become his lover, or he did.

A few hours later, Jenny phoned again and left another message. Malcolm walked up the hill to retrieve it. She wasn't coming for the night, planned to drive down the next day. It was fine with him; she confirmed what he already knew. He could quit waiting. He'd rather be bored than wait any day. With boredom there was hope; waiting for change, waiting for someone to transform into a new image, a new person, was torture. He didn't bother returning her call; she'd call again in the morning.

Malcolm never really could picture himself with Jenny, but for some odd reason, he was still entertaining the possibility. It wasn't Jenny so much, as it was 'Him' just wanting a 'Her.' He began to daydream about living in a cabin free of fleas and a little more spacious than the one he was sitting in. It would be an open cabin with lots of windows for light so that the splendor of Big Sur could be taken in. The forest canopy around the cabin would be open enough to see the stars at night. He had counted fifteen falling stars the night before, and he was swatting fleas, so there was no telling how many he missed, stars that is.

He missed her, and he didn't even know her. He'd been around Sarina twice and in those two encounters she'd charged him enough to write in excess of seventy pages. Sarina might not be 'Her,' but if Sarina decided she wanted him, he was all hers, too. She was a new image of woman that he was desperately in need of. She was so full of life, so different from Jenny. He didn't want to rob Sarina of anything. He just needed to project his own 'Her' onto Sarina to get beyond Jenny.

Malcolm's 'Her' was all spirit. He had yet to find 'Her' in the flesh. The only way he had ever been able to encounter his 'Her' was by borrowing the material body of someone like Sarina's for 'Her' to inhabit. It was really 'Her' he wanted living with him in the cabin.

He looked into the bathroom mirror as he walked through to the kitchen. He looked tired. He'd been on a writing jag, and a damn good one at that. He didn't have the distraction of Jenny, the Internet, or any of the other circular ruts in which he normally found himself short-looped.

He was tired. He'd been working hard, creating something new again. It made him feel good. He decided to paint that night. He'd silently used words as his medium for several days and it was time to play another way. He'd brought some acrylic paints and pieces of cardboard instead of a canvas. He wasn't a painter, didn't know the first thing about it, but painted anyway. It was his way of letting the kid come out. There was no agenda, no pressure, just fun, and fun it was. He fantasized about turning his dream cabin into an art studio where he could write, paint, and screw the living, loving lights out of the red-hot Rrrosa from then to kingdom come.

* * * * *

Jenny phoned again the following morning. "Malcolm, I don't want to drive down there today. Are you lonely?"

"Am I what?" he laughed a that-figures chuckle.

"Are you lonely?" She repeated.

"I'm not lonely, but I was expecting you," he answered, fed up with her, yet relieved.

"So you don't mind? I'm just feeling so cozy here at home, but I felt obligated."

"Not at all. I'm coming home in a few hours anyway. I've had all the flea bites that I can stand," he confessed, thinking: *Sleeping Beauty, she's fucking Sleeping Beauty and I'm not the prince.*

"Oh yeah, the fleas. I forgot about the fleas," she answered. He forgot that he'd told her about the fleas.

"They were supposed to have this damn place bombed before I got here."

"They just have to put that medicine on the cat's neck and they'll all go away."

"They did it already, plus the cat's gone. It's staying with Sarina's ex and the damn house is still full of the little parasites," Malcolm explained, wondering why he bothered. She wasn't coming anyway.

"You mean the cat's gone, and there are still fleas?"

"Yeah, they're hopping all over the goddamn place and eating the shit out of me."

"Oh, I'm so glad I didn't have to experience that."

Yeah, just like you didn't have to feel the sting of my dick last night, Malcolm thought to himself. Dicks, or at least Malcolm's dick, and fleas, both seemed to be unappealing to Sleeping Beauty.

"Well, I need to get going. I've got to water the plants and lock this place up."

"Okay, I'll be at home if you want to stop by later…"

He wasn't going to visit Jenny. He locked the place up and went home. And as much as he liked the cabin, he wasn't going back until they bombed every last one of those little bloodsuckers!

Chapter 25

He woke up at ten-thirty. Having escaped the fleas, he could have slept until noon, but another parasite was sinking its fangs into him. It was the familiar nagging inner voice accusing Malcolm of being a worthless, unproductive, piece-o'-shit of a man.

Lying in bed, he thought about the upcoming evening. He was to accompany Mrs. Shams to a potluck gathering at Roseanne's, a friend of Mrs. Shams who lived out in Carmel Valley. When Malcolm had arrived home the previous evening, Mrs. Shams cornered him in the garage and informed him, in addition to a few other meaningless trivialities, that Roseanne had asked Stewart, her younger husband, to be out of the house by the time that Roseanne returned from her trip back east.

Roseanne was now back from her trip and Stewart, hubby number two, was gone. Roseanne caught her first hubby cheating on her. It seemed that he'd had a change of heart, having turned his allegiance from snuggling up to Roseanne to snuggling up to other men, or at least one other man. So, after one failed attempt, Stewart, being a younger man, matched Roseanne's ticket stub just fine, a younger man who could keep her happy and who was still boy enough to let her run him.

Not that there's anything wrong with a younger man getting it on with an older woman, but Stewart had been a damn fool for even considering marriage to Roseanne. For the small fee of selling his soul and his gonads, Stewart, the poor bastard, had been set up in his own business. Oh well, now that she'd kicked him out, he was free to find a young filly to chase around the track from dusk to dawn, a woman who was pretty enough to enjoy waking up next to in the morning.

Malcolm knew nothing about all this, and was not to ask the whereabouts of Stewart that evening. He'd never met or much gave a damn about Stewart anyway. Malcolm was much more interested in encountering any single dishes that Roseanne might have frolicking about her household at that evening's potluck.

One of the other impertinent topics that Mrs. Shams brought

up that evening before the potluck had to do with his writing. She lectured him about proper grammar usage again, and gave him the address of a website which featured a review from the Wall Street Journal of a new book on grammar that had just become available. He had shared a book evaluation that he received from one editor with Mrs. Shams and they discussed that as well.

He also reassured the ol' Mockingbird that, in spite of the main character's proclivity toward womanizing, Malcolm was living a pious life of chastity. Mrs. Shams also suggested that he aspire to a different class of woman in his ascent from the dungeons of his past life. Malcolm decided, against his better judgment, that it was appropriate to keep his burning desire for Roseanne's young and hot twenty-two-year-old daughter a secret. As usual, Mrs. Shams got one last lick in at Malcolm before dismissing him to the studio: she wanted him to develop his ambitions and aspire to greater things in his life...

It was a damn good thing that she let him go when she did. He about had his belly full of Mockingbird pie. Malcolm had danced, and always would dance, among the fleas in the gutters as well as the socialites who had built their homes up on the hills overlooking a world filled with less fortunate souls down below. Mrs. Shams didn't have a clue that the haves and the have-nots feared becoming each other, and Malcolm desired to be neither of them. He simply wanted to be entertained and was much more interested in finding and being entertained by someone from the same talent agency that Stewart had enlisted.

Malcolm was amazed that Mrs. Shams actually thought she could change him. She had a long way to go to save her wayward tenant's soul from eternal damnation, the very man who she believed to be writing erotic stories down in her basement studio into the wee hours of the morning. If she was going to make Malcolm into what she needed him to be, in spite of who he was, she'd have to hurry. Odds weren't in her favor considering Malcolm was half the age of the eighty-year-old crow.

If he'd been sleeping with half the women she gave him credit for... hell, she'd have heard all the rumblings of his misconduct down in her basement. She knew when he farted, let alone when he quietly locked up his studio and tried to sneak away before she could catch him in the garage to impose one of her many unreasonable demands.

Malcolm was lonely, no doubt, perhaps just as lonely as Mrs. Shams. The problem was, she wanted to engage a nice young man, and he wanted to be engaged with a nice young woman, not some blue-haired old lady who was ancient enough to be his grandmother. He certainly hoped that Rosebud, as Mrs. Shams called Roseanne, had a few new blossoms for his sniffing pleasure that evening.

Malcolm rolled out of bed and into some sweats. He put on his running shoes and went for his morning walk through Mission Trails. When he returned to the studio, he finished his workout with some light weights and a hundred and fifty crunches. He was almost in the shower when the phone rang. It was Jenny. She said she'd be at the Pink House after a bit and invited him to join her.

Jenny wasn't there when he arrived, but Waylen was. He was sitting up on the porch, on the preferred bench. He'd been biking and was wearing the gear, stretch pants and all, the same garb that keeps many people from becoming bikers. Damn, that stuff looks ridiculous.

"Hey brother," Waylen said, as Malcolm stepped up onto the porch.

"Waylen," Malcolm answered, not knowing how to address him because he didn't want to get caught up with Waylen before Jenny arrived.

"What's happenin'?" Waylen asked in response to Malcolm's silence.

"I'm kinda waiting," Malcolm said, feeling ashamed to admit that waiting was exactly what he'd been doing for the last several months.

"For what?"

"You know. The dog's mama."

"Who? Oh, I got you. You mean Jenny," he answered, loud enough for the two women who were sitting at the patio table below them to hear. "You got to cut that shit out man."

"I am. I'm out of it, man."

"Right on, brother, I've watched her for a long time. She's depressed if you ask me."

"I don't know what she is, but she's been kind to me. I don't want to just quit being her friend."

"Yeah, but you're paying for it man. She's getting all her needs met, and she doesn't even have to give it up to you."

"Yeah," Malcolm answered, knowing that Waylen was right. "I've been house-sitting in Big Sur for this young little honey who pumped me full of life, though. I mean, I didn't even do anything with her, and I still had her pumping through my veins three days after she'd left. Then I got a phone call from Jenny. In the first minute of the conversation it was all gone. My energy, you know."

"That's how you're paying for it, brother. They're all fucked up anyway. They want a man to take care of them and then they just want to lay down one night a month to pay the bills, if you know what I'm talking about," Waylen said, with his eyebrows perked.

"She doesn't need a man to pay her bills. She makes good money."

"Yeah, but it's still stress on her. That's why she's depressed."

"Well, whatever she is, I'm chasing that young shit down the coast from now on."

"Right on brother," he said, slapping Malcolm a high-five.

"And as soon as I tap into that stuff, I'll be right back here telling you all about it," Malcolm said confidently, trying to convince himself of his own lie.

"And I'll be waiting," Waylen answered.

Malcolm didn't know what to make of Jenny. Waylen wanted to make her into how he viewed all women. He was helping Malcolm though. Waylen's view of women, Malcolm hated to admit, was in some ways his own.

Waylen and Malcolm continued their banter while checking out the unattended, as well as the attended, women who came after their lattes. A half hour later, Jenny and Diana finally showed up. Waylen took Jenny's arrival as his cue to leave. Malcolm found out what she wanted to drink and went to place her order while she saved the prize seat.

"I haven't talked to you for a while," Jenny said just to get the conversation going.

"I've had a lot of things come up lately," Malcolm answered, as someone inside the Pink House called out his name to let him know her tea was ready.

He went to pick up Jenny's tea, and set it down in front of her. Without asking, he went back inside to get the honey.

"Tell me when," he said, squeezing the bear a few feet over her cup.

"When," she said, as he released the pressure on the plastic bear and slowed the stream of honey to a drizzle.

Malcolm returned the honey bear to the counter inside, picked up his Americano and walked back out to the bench. Diana hopped up between them and rested her head on Malcolm's thigh.

"What are you doing today?" Jenny asked, as she set her cup down on the porch rail.

"I've got to drive Mrs. Shams out to one of her socialite potlucks."

"That sounds like fun," she teased.

"Well, one thing's for certain: I won't have to worry about being set up with one of her friend's daughters now that she's read my book and has decided that I'm not quite as sweet as she thought I was," Malcolm said, grinning at the mess he'd gotten himself into with the old broad.

They both laughed and Diana snuggled her head deeper into Malcolm's thigh. They hung out for another hour or so, and then Malcolm made his way back to the studio to change. He had to be presentable for Mrs. Shams's friends who all liked to tease her about bringing the new young guy she was *living with* along to the party.

* * * * *

They were on the road to Rosebud's when the Mockingbird started in. She just couldn't give up the need to help Malcolm leave his wayward path.

"Malcolm, I think that it is very honorable and Christian-like to be helping out those kids in Big Sur," she said, knowing that he'd been spending some time with the younger crowd down the coast.

"I didn't go down there to help anyone," he corrected her.

"Well, I just think that you should aspire for more," she said in a demeaning tone. "I really don't think you should go down there anymore," she added.

He didn't want to engage the old broad, so he didn't respond.

"You might have been successful in the business world, but you still lack confidence," she suggested, as they drove east on Carmel Valley Road.

Malcolm still didn't respond.

"My husband used to tell me that I lacked confidence. He bought me this when he knew he was going to die," she added, holding up her arm and showing Malcolm a solid gold bangle bracelet that had been engraved with the words: 'Damn I'm Good.' "I never tell anyone what it means, but he gave it to me to remind me that I lack confidence."

Malcolm wanted to tell her that just because he let her read his book didn't mean she had permission to criticize him or question the way he chose to live his life, but he didn't. He had more to learn by remaining silent and breathing in what she was really teaching him, which had nothing to do with self-confidence.

She didn't know that he was perfectly capable of pulling over, turning in his seat to face her, and telling her to go fuck herself before sending her on her way. She had no idea where he'd come from, and she had no right making her lack of confidence Malcolm's lack of confidence. But, Malcolm knew that anyone who preached such rhetoric had no capacity whatsoever to ever understand a person like himself. She'd been sheltered for the last eighty years of her life and would go to her grave as if she were being gently laid into an infant's cradle.

She was teaching Malcolm how not to treat people, how not to one-up someone and arrogantly give advice just because he might not understand them or judge them for being in what he might perceive to be a less than desirable position in life. She was that universal better-than voice who wanted to help people avoid their pitfalls, wanted to keep people on her narrow path, and guide them to aspire for "more," whatever "more" might have been; and all that just to make herself look and feel superior.

Maybe aspiring for "more" to Mrs. Shams, meant doing and acting or reacting to the demands of her own inner voice, or better yet, that of her husband's. Hell, he'd been dead for nearly twenty years and she was still wearing that goddamn bracelet. Maybe aspiring for "more" meant falling prey to the social demands and dogmas of others, a set of beliefs or an organism that sheltered her and would justify and give meaning to her very existence. Whatever aspiring for "more" meant to Mrs. Shams was only for Mrs. Shams. Malcolm had to live life on his terms, not according to anyone else's aspirations.

It was becoming quite evident why Mrs. Shams's son lived halfway across the country and never bothered to visit her, not even on the holidays. Malcolm was living in her son's dark room. It seemed that no matter where Malcolm went, that dark old bitch followed.

The potluck wasn't bad. Stewart wasn't there, and Malcolm managed to abstain from asking of his whereabouts, but it was hard for him to be nice and not stir the shit. As predicted, there was one single woman for him to preview. But she wasn't really single; she had a thing going on with Gloria Steinem. She reminded him a lot of a woman who had been scorned back in the seventies and had yet to come to terms with herself. As far as Malcolm was concerned, any woman who waited for a man to liberate her from her own skewed belief of herself would die an old maid.

Chapter 26

He was scheduled to be at Jenny's at ten-thirty. When he stepped out of the shower, the answering machine was recording a message. It was Sarina. She and Sheila were coming to town to run errands, and they wanted to treat Malcolm to lunch in return for his house-sitting duties while they were away at the concert. He agreed to meet them at eleven-thirty at the Loose Noodle. He had plans to meet with Adam and would probably need it after having lunch with those two balls of energy.

Mrs. Shams had given Malcolm a blank check the day he'd escorted her out to Rosebud's and asked him to pick up her sweater at the dry cleaners that was only a few blocks from the Pink House. He first shagged the sweater, then stopped in at the Pink for coffee before his treatment at Jenny's.

Lunch with the two ladies had turned into three. Regina, Sarina's business partner joined them. The food was great, but they could have served him cardboard and he'd have thought it was delicious. It was hard to top being the only man with three young, beautiful women, let alone having them pick up the lunch tab.

Malcolm met with Adam after lunch that afternoon and then returned to the studio. Mrs. Shams was watering her front yard when he drove the Tahoe down into the driveway. He greeted her with a smile, a friendly "hello," and her freshly cleaned sweater. She invited him to join her on the deck for a glass of iced tea. He accepted her invitation, but first ran down to the studio to check his answering machine and e-mail. There were no phone messages, and responding to e-mails could wait.

Mrs. Shams was still in her kitchen pouring tea when Malcolm arrived at the patio and took a seat. A few minutes later she backed through the screen door with a tray that had two glasses of freshly brewed sun tea and a basket of Frito Lay corn chips, the same Frito Lays corn chips that his grade-school bus driver could sniff out a mile away. Ol' Hoekstra had once gotten sick after eating the corn chips and had developed a taste aversion to Fritos. They weren't supposed to eat on the bus anyway, but Fritos were about the only thing that ol' Hoekstra could sniff out. He said they made him sick to his stomach. Malcolm didn't care for Fritos all that much, but he had fond memories of annoying the old fart.

"Well, what have you done that was productive for society today?" asked the Mockingbird, her big old white head bouncing around on top of her thin, frail body.

Malcolm hesitated, already on the defense. "Actually, quite a bit. I met with Adam and we talked about my dreams," he answered, not wanting her to know that he'd had lunch with the three Big Sur girls.

"Dreams?" she asked, cocking her head back a bit with an odd look on her face.

"Oh, yeah. That's why I'm really here."

"For dreams?"

"Haven't I told you about this before?" he asked, knowing that he hadn't.

"I've heard about Adam, but I've never met the man," she responded without answering his question. Adam's brother Frank, a retired physician, had rented the studio from Mrs. Shams before he remarried. When he moved out, Adam told Malcolm about the studio, and that was the seed that sprouted into Malcolm's now full-blown love affair with Mrs. Shams.

"How did you meet this Adam?"

"I came to the Monterey Peninsula to spend Christmas with my friend Turner and his family a few years ago. I was sitting outside of Starbucks at the Del Monte shopping center, and this little blackbird landed in front of me on the table. He did this little dance, like he was trying to get my attention and then he flew off. I watched him and then found myself gazing off towards the mountains and something really hit me. I'd been living my entire life in one place, and I wanted something different. I found a newspaper, pulled out the classified section, and discovered a studio in Carmel. I called immediately, went to see it, and rented it for a month right then and there."

"Yes," she nodded for him to continue.

"Well, I'd been there for a week by myself and was growing tired of my solitude. So I walked down into the village for a coffee one morning, and that's where I met Adam."

"And what does Adam do?" she asked.

"He plays tennis quite a bit, whenever he has the chance. And he reads a lot, too."

"Yes, but what is his profession?" she asked, her head still bobbling around over her shoulders.

"Well, he's eighty-five years-old, but first, he was in the war, then he became an editor, then he became a career counselor, and now he's... well, now I suppose he's just a wise old man," Malcolm explained. "Anyway, after I met him that January, I went back to my life in the machinery world and lost contact with him for a few months. Then I was reading Joyce's *The Portrait of an Artist as a Young Man* and it hit me. I called Adam and told him what I'd been reading, and how I realized I wasn't creating anything in my life. I was selling a lot of tractors and making good money, you know, collecting material possessions. But, I wasn't creating anything and that book helped me to see that this was missing in my life. Adam asked when I'd be back on the Peninsula so that we could discuss this, but after talking with him, I let it drift away. Then in July, my friend Charles died. We'd been friends all through high school, and then after we graduated, we worked for his father and bunked together in a house out on his family's ranch. Anyway, I eventually got sobered up, but Charles didn't. He was a diabetic, to boot, and his lifestyle finally caught up with him. He was dead at thirty-five and that shook me hard. Within two weeks, I was back here on the Peninsula looking for something. I finally caught up with Adam. He suggested that I might have to come to terms with my own mortality. He said I might be starting to look at life differently. He said that I might be searching for a new meaning. I told him that I didn't know about that, but I needed to find a new image of God and of Woman. I didn't know why I said it, but I felt it and knew it was true. He said it was time for me to start paying attention to my dreams, so that's what we began to do."

"But you lived in the Central Valley," she said, with a confused, but now curious look.

"I know. I'd send him my dreams, and then we'd talk on the phone."

"Why did you say you needed a new image of woman?"

Malcolm hesitated. It was hard for him to put words to many of his experiences. Still uncertain of how to answer, he took a breath. "My mother used to beat me," is what he breathed out, and he hated hearing himself say this because he didn't want to sound like another one of the world's countless victims, but it came out anyway. "She had me two weeks after she turned eighteen," he defended. "She was still a kid herself."

"Yes. Yes she was," Mrs. Shams nodded. "But, it's too bad she beat you."

"Yeah, it is too bad," he answered. "And it wasn't just a spanking here and there," he continued. "It was a rage that overtook her, and she took it out on me. Anyway, that, my failed marriage, and a broken heart from a love affair after my divorce is why I told Adam that I needed a new image of woman."

"And you wanted a new image of God because of what you told me about being raised in that church," she said, remembering a few references he'd made in the past. "So are you looking for a woman now?"

"No! I'm looking for a new image inside of me. That's what I do with my dreams and the dream images."

"I don't understand how your dreams can help you do that."

"Okay, take a dream and let's say somebody you know is in it. Maybe somebody you like or dislike. Then instead of interpreting the dream as having to do with the person you dreamed about, you look for the meaning within yourself. In other words, if you didn't like something about that person, that dream image, then it quite possibly could be something that you can't stand and don't want to accept about yourself."

"That's sounds like a lot of work."

"It is, but it beats the hell out of blaming my mother for her own unconscious attacks on me as a child. I mean, hell, I'm a grown man. Mom isn't beating me anymore, but the mom inside of me still is. Dreams help me to see into myself; like how I still punish myself. When I take back the blame for these internal attacks that I put onto people in the world, be it my mother, or, any other woman for that matter, I no longer have to be a prisoner of my past, and don't have to repeat it in my relationships with family, friends, or even a lover for that matter.

In other words, I can see people through different eyes, not the eyes of some wounded little boy, but the eyes of a man who doesn't have to blame others for his own discontentment."

Mrs. Shams paused and looked up at the mountains that rose above the Fish Ranch. She had told Malcolm about the Fish Ranch several months earlier on another one of their refreshment breaks up on her porch. The Fish Ranch was named after the Fish family who had owned the property for years. For Malcolm it was a mountain; for Mrs. Shams it was the Fish Ranch. Much was tied to how things used to be for Mrs. Shams.

"Well, Malcolm, you have some basic skills; however, you're lacking in academics," Mrs. Shams said, her body, like a swelling hard-on, taking on an erect posture, her neck tightening and her head losing its bouncy effect. Her forehead seemed to elongate and tilt forward, and her eyeballs appeared to rise up to the top of their sockets.

She hadn't heard a word Malcolm told her, or she'd heard it in her own way. He'd been swallowing a lot of crap in his last several encounters with this fault finding old hag, and he was getting tired of it. On their drive to Rosebud's, he lacked confidence. This time he was sub-academic. He couldn't figure out why she just wouldn't let him be, couldn't figure out why she was so dead set on changing him. He was also a bit dumbfounded about why he was allowing such ridicule.

He took a deep breath, and remained silent. Malcolm wanted to step back and look beyond the person who was delivering the message, this time Mrs. Shams. He wanted to be free of having to prove her wrong. He wanted to be able to see Mrs. Shams as she was, instead of forming a judgment and closing himself off, but he was having the damnedest time doing so with the ol' Mockingbird.

"I'm going to school," Malcolm said.

"Well, I used to tell my husband, and he agreed, that people need to take the classes that they *don't* want to take. You just can't study what interests you. Have you seen a counselor?"

"Of course I have," Malcolm answered. "It's been a year or so, but I talked with one."

"Honestly, Malcolm…"

"I'm taking general education; getting that out of the way

first. I know what I have to complete before transferring to a university," he explained, stopping her from getting farther along with her compulsive need to mother him.

She didn't respond. She took a breath and her head trembled slightly.

"Mrs. Shams, I've got a plan, but I don't go around talking about it. I've never been someone to talk about what I'm going to do. I just do it, and when it's done, well then that's fine. Nobody else needs to know except for me."

It was all he could do not to tell her to fuck off. He was a thirty-nine year old man, and a successful one, to boot. He'd survived the brainwashing as well as the emotional and psychological beatings of his domestic and religious heritage. He'd made it through the drugs and booze, he'd weathered a sick marriage and divorce, and in spite of his adversities, he'd made it in the business world as well.

He'd survived all those soul-scrunching battles. He'd more than survived them; he had turned around and faced them. He'd reclaimed a good part of his soul from many of the illegitimate bastards that haunted him from within, and he was finally becoming free to live his life, to be true to himself, as opposed to those old ghosts. He'd be damned if some know-it-all Mockingbird perched out on a tree limb was going to dictate the run of his life.

"Okay, well good," she answered, in response to his private plan. "You don't need to tell anyone else," she conceded, sensing that she had tread over the line.

"There's one more thing…" he started. He took another breath. "What I told you about my mother is private. She's a damn fine woman, and for all she did wrong, she did ten times more right."

"Oh, yes I understand," she answered, nodding her head.

"If there is one thing I can't stand, it's being a victim, and I don't want to be labeled that by you or anyone else," he emphasized.

Mrs. Shams liked to gossip with her little group of uppity socialites; the same socialites who held the gatherings that she liked dragging Malcolm off to. At their last potluck, he began to see how he was getting pulled into the middle of their uppity world where they were dreaming him into being one of those lesser-than fleas. He'd become a project for Mrs. Shams and her constituents; they were trying to influence and mold Malcolm into the likes of themselves, lifeless souls, prisoners of the gray mushy contents of their skulls, and stuck in beliefs of an era gone by.

Malcolm walked down to his studio, turned a few circles, and then took a crap - a symbolic gesture of purging himself of the ol' Bird's toxins. He then locked the place up, and drove to Big Sur. It was a full moon, and he needed to be where he could feel 'Her' influence.

Chapter 27

It was a beautiful clear night. He spent the evening outside on the Nepenthe deck watching the full moon rise and move across the sky while Sheila and Sarina ran about the place waiting on customers. After the girls were phased, they joined Malcolm on the deck, remaining there until after midnight before heading down the hill. Malcolm stopped at the Tahoe, and the girls continued on to the cabin.

He had purchased a rollaway bed mattress that fit perfectly into the back of the Tahoe when the rear seats were stowed in the cargo position. He kept a sleeping bag, a pillow, several days' worth of clean clothes, and whatever other incidentals he might need in the Chevy for one of his impromptu visits.

He woke the next morning to a knocking on the Tahoe window. It was Sheila on her way up the hill. Both girls had to attend an employee meeting at the restaurant and then Sheila had the lunch shift. She told Malcolm about a barbecue that the restaurant was putting on for the employees that afternoon and suggested that he stick around. Fifty yards below the deck of the girl's cabin was a grassy park-like area where the Nepenthe maintenance crew had already set up a volleyball net and a ping-pong table for the afternoon gathering.

Malcolm showered in the cabin while the girls were at the meeting. Sarina returned an hour later but soon left for the shop to take care of some business. That meant Malcolm had the place all to himself for a few hours. He walked up to the Kevah for a coffee to go, and returned to the deck. He ran the extension cord through the window and set up shop on the green cast iron table.

Occasionally, he'd glance down below to the picnic area to check on the set-up crew preparing for the barbecue. First the tables and chairs were unloaded from the flat bed of an old Chevy one-ton truck that looked like it should have been abandoned in some wrecking yard. A while later, two, fifty-five gallon, barrel-type barbecues were unloaded from the same truck along with several big bags of briquettes. That surprised the hell out of Malcolm; he'd have guessed the Organics would be using some of the local dried oak for their barbeque. That's what he got for guessing.

Malcolm thought about Kate quite a bit that day. It had been close to two weeks since they had last spoken to each other. The longer she was gone the more infrequent their phone calls had become. He wondered if it was a sign of the direction their relationship was going. He thought about Jenny, too, but when her image came to him, he quickly changed the channel to something more lively and impassioned.

After the lunch shift had ended, Sheila came walking down the hill to the cabin. As she came through the gate, Malcolm shut down the PowerBook.

"Hey, Malcolm! Getting some writing in, huh?" she asked in her cheerful glad-to-see-him tone. "Decided to stick around for the picnic, huh?"

"I seldom pass up a free meal," he said, smiling as he stood up to hug her. "When will they start serving?" he asked, having only had the coffee and a nectarine that he'd stumbled upon inside the cabin a little before noon while stretching from the hunched up position that he took on while hovering in deep concentration over the laptop.

"Should be anytime," she answered, walking toward the French doors that opened out onto the deck. "I'm going to change. I'll be right back."

Malcolm nodded and then turned to lean against the deck's railing. Several covered dishes had been set out on a serving table down below and one of the cooks was flipping something on the barbecue while four bystanders stood around the grill looking on with expectation. Sheila walked out onto the deck, spotted the crew below, and shouted out a sweet insult of some sort.

"Come on. Let's go down there," Sheila said an excited tone.

He followed her down the trail to the set-up below. He didn't really want to go but was too damn hungry not to. He was hungry for food, not company. Meeting new people and socializing wasn't so high on his priority list; he just wasn't in the mood for it that day. Actually, Malcolm was seldom in the mood for stuff like that. He liked people, but he was more of a one-on-one person. Years ago, when he was still drinking, or even just a few years back when he was selling machinery for that matter, it would have been fine, but something had changed, and he really had a hard time painting on a smile and making small talk with a bunch of people he didn't know. In other words, it was just his belly dragging him down the trail.

He smiled for a while and met people. They were all nice and friendly, but the food was another story; it was excellent. After he ate, the people seemed to grow easier to be around. He actually kind of liked a few of them. He felt like a freeloader, though. Hell, besides Sheila and a few others she'd introduced him to, Malcolm really didn't know anyone. It was a company party, and he felt like he was busting it. He lasted through dessert. That's when Andy, Sheila's man showed up. Malcolm visited with Andy for few minutes, snuck another lemon bar from the dessert tray and hiked back up to the cabin.

Sarina was in the bathroom, so he grabbed Miller's *Tropic of Cancer* and sat down in the beanbag chair, hoping to get a full on titty-shot when she came bouncing through the double doors. The toilet flushed and then the doors flung open; Sarina fully clothed.

"Hey, what's going on? Why aren't you down at the party?"

"I've been down there. Just needed a break. You going?"

"I'm going to work. Got the night shift," she said, faking a grin.

"I'll come see you later, maybe around nine, after things have slowed down."

"Sounds good, you going back down to the party?"

"I'm partied out. I don't do parties well. Don't mind being around a few people, but when it gets to be more than a few, I'd just as soon be alone," he answered.

"Alright," she said, seeming indifferent to his introversion. "I've got to go. I'll see you around nine then," she reminded him.

Malcolm opened up to where he'd left off in *Tropic of Cancer*. Maya climbed up onto his chest and settled in, nestling her head over his heart. Maya purred and Malcolm read. The purring had a way of calming him and the reading had a way of helping to shut out the noise from the festivities below.

Half-an-hour later people started walking in and out of the house. There was no pisser below, and the girls' cabin was the closest facility. Before long, several people had gathered inside the house and were passing around a few joints. Malcolm put the book down and, once again, painted on a smile. Maya didn't move though. She just lay there purring away like nothing had changed. For Maya, nothing really had changed.

Malcolm went out to the deck for some fresh air. Andy came out and joined him; he appeared to have a pretty good buzz. Sheila had told Malcolm that Andy was into astrology. Malcolm wasn't, but not because he condemned it. He'd just never taken the time to become familiar with the study of the stars' position and the belief that they influence human affairs. Andy started to talk about the planets and how they were all lining up to reconnect their energy. He said something about how things were drawing people together instead of pulling them apart. He was trying to connect with Malcolm, but they were worlds apart.

"So you're a writer, huh?" he asked.

"Well, I write, but I'm not a writer. I just have fun," Malcolm explained. He didn't go around calling himself a writer. He wasn't particularly interested in taking on that persona. He was just shucking the mask of being the tractor man and was afraid of what people might start to expect from him if he became something else.

"It seems like you'd have to be old and wise to really write anything good," Andy suggested. His comment reminded Malcolm of the time Travis was dissin' Sarina.

"Yeah, you've got a point there," Malcolm answered, realizing that he was talking to a thirty-seven year old man who was stoned and had been for most of his life. Kafka had died in his early forties, as well as Saint-Exupéry and Camus in his later fifties. What happened if you ended up dead before you got old? And what made age the prerequisite of wisdom? Some very young people have had the wisdom of several aged sages, and some older people have gone to their graves without having developed an ounce of wisdom in their lifetime. And how could a person become old and wise if they'd been stoned their entire life? How could a person write about something when they couldn't even remember what they'd done or forgotten to do?

Andy wasn't attacking Malcolm personally when he made the comment, so he didn't argue with him. What he said actually made Malcolm feel justified in leaving his old career behind and taking time for himself. He had hopes of someday being a wise old man but all he really had was the present. He wasn't living his life on the promise of another day, let alone old age.

Malcolm was beginning to see a pattern. Several of the locals liked to call themselves artists because they got stoned and had never gotten around to fulfilling their good intentions. Malcolm didn't know why the whole bunch of pot-growin'-wanna-be-hippies didn't just call themselves farmers. Hell, that's what many of them were, growing a crop.

Another thing that kind of pissed Malcolm off about these self-proclaimed artists was that they were just as lost as the people from the world of commerce whom they constantly were dissin'. These so called artists were quick to find fault with people who hadn't dropped out of society, but these dropouts had no problem collecting the big tips left to them by the material-chasing weekenders visiting from Silicon Valley.

Andy was no artist even though he called himself one. He might have been a craftsman, a carpenter, but he was no artist, and Sheila was too caught up in the middle of it all to know any better.

One man who had wandered out onto the deck really was an artist. His name was Ross, a tall, thin fellow around Malcolm's age. He had dark hair, brown eyes, and a receding hairline; looked like he had a lot of Italian blood pumping through his veins. He did mosaics, and you could tell he was an artist because of how impassioned he was when he spoke of his life. He didn't talk about what he was going to do; he was doing it. He was living it everyday and that's what made him a real artist.

"I was living down in Los Angeles when that Rodney King thing hit," he told Malcolm, as he leaned over the deck's railing and spit. "I was right there, up in my apartment watching the riots. I got my sketchpad and started drawing. I've got some really wild shit from there, man."

"You were catching a wave of all the violent energy that had exploded. That's what was drawing those pictures for you."

"It was fucking crazy, man. That's why I left that fucked up place. I came here and found this job. It pays the bills and I can do my art," he explained, as he pulled a cigarette from a pack and lit up.

Ross talked about his projects that were in process, about his work with mosaics. His eyes sparked when he spoke of his passion. Then as others walked out onto the deck, Ross grew quieter about his life; not long after that he went back down to the picnic while Malcolm stayed topside out on the deck.

Shortly after Ross walked off, the others who had come up to the cabin took the party back down below. Malcolm went inside to find the book he was reading and returned to the green cast iron chair and table. The party continued, and in spite of the shouting and hollering that crept up the hill like a steady breeze, he successfully read until it was too dark to read any longer. It was actually a balanced situation for him, kind of like having the television or radio playing as background noise while studying, something that tricked him into feeling and believing that he wasn't alone.

The party was still going when he walked up the hill to the restaurant. Sarina and Angie were both working. Sarina's step-grandmother, Laine, was the hostess. Laine was in her late forties, had long wavy salt-and-pepper hair and loved to dress up in exotic apparel. She was wearing turquoise colored leather pants and a silky black top that buttoned up the front where she could control the amount of cleavage she chose to display, and it was quite apparent that she had little or no desire to control or hide what God had endowed. She sported an Indian-like headdress with turquoise stones that complemented her desire to stand out.

Laine had married Sarina's grandfather a year or so earlier. He was twenty-five years her senior. Malcolm never did have the pleasure of meeting the man. He'd have liked to, though, just to see if the old boy actually measured up to being the rotten drunk and good for nothing soul that Laine and Sarina made him out to be.

Malcolm greeted Laine and then sat up at the bar. He ordered a non-alcoholic beer, having yet to understand why these fake beers without alcohol were called non-alcoholic beers. He thought that they should be called alcoholics' beer because it was mostly alchies like him who drank the damn things. He liked to call them fake beers whenever he ordered one just to check out the bartender's reaction.

It was kind of like when a person goes to Starbucks for a coffee. Every damn thing in that place is named something other than what it is. You almost need a thesaurus just to order a cup of joe. Going to Starbucks, ordering a medium cup of coffee, and waiting for the baristas scripted response was one of Malcolm's favorite battles.

"You mean a grande house roast, sir?"

"No, I'd like a medium cup of coffee," Malcolm would repeat, refusing to participate in their imposed vocabulary.

"Would you like to have a chocolate covered graham cracker to go with your order, sir?" He'd just shake his head no, refusing to answer any more questions with words. "That will be a dollar forty-five, sir. Would you like room for cream?" He'd respond by handing the cashier some money while nodding yes. Malcolm would die a rebel.

He sat at the bar sipping his fake beer and watching the servers bust their asses trying to keep up with the demands of their clientele. After a couple of drinks, a table just outside the front door opened up, and he asked Laine if he could have it before actually taking it over. Sarina brought out a cup of soup, and he ordered a couple of appetizers to hold him over until the next morning.

After dinner he walked back down to the cabin and settled into the beanbag chair with his book. Sheila had a few days off and had left with Andy after the barbecue. They'd gone out of town somewhere, probably to tend to his crop. So, Maya and Malcolm had the cabin all to themselves. Sarina came in a little after eleven and found Maya asleep on Malcolm's chest as he read. She showered, contrary to what she'd told him the week before about not liking to wash away the day, which lead Malcolm to believe that he stood a chance.

Sarina walked out with the towel wrapped around her as she made her way to the dressing room. She returned wearing a pair of sweats and an old T-shirt and lay down on the love seat across from Malcolm.

"So why aren't you off to school somewhere?" he asked, thinking that most women her age were doing the school scene.

"You know, a part of me wants to be, but another part of me wants to be here with my shop and everything else."

"I thought maybe some guy was keeping you here," he said, testing her reaction.

"I've been single for ten months," she explained, sounding as if it were an eternity.

"Is that all?"

"Is that all? Hell, that's a long time if you ask me."

"It's a while, but it's not a long time," he suggested, setting his book down, careful not to disturb Maya in her sleep.

"Long enough for me," she said, picking up her glass pipe.

"Some people can't be alone because they can't face the terror," Malcolm suggested.

Sarina looked at him without responding, as if he hadn't finished explaining himself.

"I mean without anything to remove them from their experience. People think they need hallucinogenics to have these conscious revelations. Fuck, I've done all that stuff, and it isn't shit compared to being alone in silence, away from anything and everything that wants to rescue you from yourself."

Sarina set her pipe down.

"That's the edge where you can really trip. It's where you find your core, your very own essence. It's also the source of our greatest creativity."

"I've been alone at places here on the coast when I felt that. Sometimes when I bike I feel it, too."

"Most people are afraid of it, but once you get past the fear... ah, that's where we can reconnect with ourselves. It's chaos at first, but then it comes together."

"I once read a book about the five stages of something or other. The first was regaining the feminine, second the masculine, and the third was the two coming together," she said, surprising Malcolm with her response.

"Alchemy!" he said excitedly, reflecting on one of the

paintings he'd done at her cabin when the girls were away at the Reggae concert. He had painted some bright red, orange, and yellow flowers that had sprouted from a lapis-blue colored flowerbed and set the painting in the windowsill to dry. He woke the next morning and descended the ladder. While going to the kitchen to make some tea, he glanced out of the window and the painting almost floored him, tears welled up and then streamed down his cheeks.

Then he flashed on a pastel drawing he'd done with the same blue colors. He didn't know it at the time, but the pastel piece ended up looking like a pair of blue bikini bottoms; it was as if the bikini bottoms were really a pool of water that emptied into a canyon, the sides of the canyon resembling a woman's legs. He'd had a dream of standing in the middle of a river and saw a bride and groom standing on opposite shores. Standing in the middle of the water, Malcolm was somehow mediating or joining them together, helping them to exchange a bouquet or a veil. He had rendered this pastel drawing while meditating on the feeling of being this mediator who was joining the two together.

Then he flashed back to a dream he'd had three years earlier. He was up on a lake in the high country, possibly Lake Tahoe. He was knee deep in the water and there were several bluish-green lapis-like fish nudging him. They just kept bumping into him, like they wanted his attention, wanted to be fed. The flowerbed Malcolm had painted was the same color as the fish, and new flowers, new life, had sprouted from that bluish-green lapis bed.

Anyway, the painting that morning had triggered something deep within Malcolm, deep enough to move him to tears and transport him back through his dreams and to those fish of years ago that for some reason had not gone completely back down into his unconscious. The fish actually caught his attention three years later, triggering this emotional response that had lain dormant within him. Malcolm knew, then, that he could never go back to the old life he'd left behind.

"What exactly is alchemy?" Sarina asked, waking him from his trance.

"It's referenced in quite a few of the books I've read, but

I really can't say that I understand exactly what it is," he answered, wishing that he did.

"Have you read *The Alchemist*," she asked.

"By Paulo Coehlo?"

"Yeah, that's it."

"Yes, I have the book at home. You can borrow it if you like."

"Will you bring it next time you come down this way?"

"Sure," Malcolm answered. "I wish I understood what alchemy is, but I just can't quite put my finger on it," he concluded, unsuccessfully willing himself to reach for clear understanding. "I know it has something to do with these... not chemists... but they worked with metals, melting and refining, separating and purifying and then bringing things back together. But, I think that purifying things into precious metals or the refinement of metals is really symbolic for what takes place within the soul. I'm quite sure that the lapis stone is the stone of an alchemist, the philosopher's stone, and has something to do with the masculine and feminine coming together. I read it in some book: *Mysterium Coniunctionis* or something like that. It has to do with the marriage of the inner masculine and the inner feminine."

"That's some deep shit," Sarina said. "Too deep for me, anyway."

"Maybe, but maybe not," Malcolm said, not wanting to stray from their path. "I think we dream things into our lives; people, too."

"How do we dream them into our lives?"

"Perhaps we invite the people into our lives as well as the things that happen to us. The people and relationships we encounter are all only reflections of what is really happening or has already happened within us, within our own psyches. We need something to be a certain way, and so we dream it up."

"Did I tell you about my wreck?"

"Yeah, on Valentines Day," he answered.

"Yeah," she said, appearing surprised that he remembered. "Well, the day before the wreck, I was driving down the coast with my ex. We were arguing about something. He was trying to tell me how to drive and how to act. I pulled over and had it out with him. I told him that it was my life and that I could fucking die if I wanted to. I was driving back into town the next day, and I wrecked within a mile of where I threw my fit."

"Part of you probably did die there. That's what I'm talking about. A part of you needed to die, so that a new part of you could be born."

"I became more responsible after that," she said.

"I bet you leave Big Sur. Don't take this wrong, because I already see you as a woman, but I bet you leave here and then come back even more your own woman. By leaving and stepping out of where you are, you'll get a different view of yourself."

"Other people have said something like that to me before."

"By leaving, you'll step out of your whole environment here. You'll leave your whole identity here and go reclaim who you really are."

"Like in that terror thing?"

"It's about going through it. Remember, the terror is only a smoke screen. Once you're past the smoke you can step into the fire, and that's where you get to the core of who you really are."

Sarina reached for her pipe. "Well, speaking of smoke. I'm going to be who I really am right now."

"Wait for a few minutes," Malcolm suggested.

"Why?" she asked, with a confused look on her face. For some reason she honored his strange request and lay back down on the love seat.

"Look, I'm not into getting people to smoke or not smoke, but I just thought that something might be coming up for you. Like maybe…"

A few tears rolled from the corner of her eyes. Malcolm took some deep breaths and silently hung out there with her. The tears stopped, she breathed, and then a few more tears came.

"Thank you," he said, and continued breathing.

She didn't respond. "May I sit by you?" Malcolm asked. "I don't want anything at all from you. I just want to be here with you," he added.

She didn't respond, so he sat next to her. The tears continued to slowly move through her. He massaged her temples and a frown of sadness creased her forehead. Then the tears really started to come. He caressed them, wiped them back into her hair. When they stopped, he rubbed his thumbs in circular motions above her eyebrows until a peaceful look replaced her frown.

"They get rid of toxins," she said, in a very soft tone. She was embarrassed.

"What does?" he asked, knowing what she meant but wanting her to talk about her tears.

"Tears," she answered.

"Ah, I see. Thank you," he said, and then kissed her on the forehead.

"Do you always make people cry?" she asked, slightly embarrassed and subdued.

"Maybe you dreamed me up just so you could cry," he suggested. "Maybe we both dreamed this up for some reason," he added.

"You mean this whole thing with you and me?"

"I know why I did..." Malcolm hesitated.

"Are you going to share that?"

"Because I was stuck in this rut with a woman who was dead," he answered, referring to Jenny. "Dead to living anyway. She walks around like she's lost in a trance all of the time. No passion. Fuck! I just can't hang with her anymore. That's why I drove up here to see Sheila last month. I knew that Sheila had life pumping through her. Then I met you. I mean, hell, the two of you are helping me to get some passion back into my life. Thank you!"

Sarina wasn't sure of how to respond to Malcolm. A part of him wanted to be inside of her and possibly she felt the same, but for some reason he was concerned that she might feel obligated to sleep with him, and he didn't want to confuse the experience they'd just shared. He sat with her for a few more minutes to make sure that she was going to be all right. Then he stood up and went to the bathroom. When he came out, she was standing up. He walked over and hugged her. "I'm going to bed," he announced.

"Are you going to sleep in your Tahoe?" she asked. "I mean it's late, and I don't know if you already have your bed made."

"Yeah, it's made already," Malcolm answered, considering

the exploitation of her vulnerable state, but knowing that if he fucked her then, he'd never make love to her later. Actually, they had just made love, and he didn't want to fuck it up with sex. He didn't want to fuck up the sanctuary she'd just entered, that they'd just entered.

"Thanks for the goodnight," she said.

"Thanks for being real," he answered. "Goodnight."

"I have to work lunch tomorrow. Maybe we can have breakfast before my shift starts," she suggested.

"Sounds good. I'll talk to you in the morning."

"Sweet dreams," were the last words Malcolm heard before stepping out the door.

Chapter 28

He woke to a tapping on the Tahoe's window the following morning. Sarina was on her way out for a morning walk. Malcolm rolled up the sleeping bag and stuffed it into its pouch, then gathered some clean clothes from the plastic chest where most of his life's necessities could be found. In addition to clean clothes, the items ranged from an ample supply of condoms that had passed their shelf life to a set of heavy-duty jumper cables. After bidding Maya good morning, he showered, and then watered the potted plants that lined the deck railing while waiting for Sarina to return.

"Still wanna go out for breakfast?" Sarina asked, as she joined Maya and Malcolm as they breathed in the morning.

"Ready when you are," he answered.

"Okay, lets go. I've got to be back to work the lunch shift," she announced. Sarina was different that morning. She was guarded, but he halfway expected her to be.

On the drive to Deetjen's, Sarina told Malcolm that her friend Louise and a few other people would be joining them. Louise was one of Sarina's life long friends. She was a few years older than Sarina and taught dance and movement classes at one of the local resorts. Sarina idolized her. When they arrived, the breakfast club was already seated out on the patio at a large round table. Courteously, Sarina introduced Malcolm to the group.

Louise was an attractive young woman who thought that she was a hell of a lot hotter than she actually was. She wasn't overweight, but she was a little chubby and it made her boobs look a hell of a lot bigger than they really were. She had long straight blonde hair and wore a pair of wrap-around sunglasses with yellow lenses. Louise lounged in her chair like the Queen of Sheba. She oozed arrogance, surely an overcompensation for some sort of inferiority complex.

Stu was mid to late twenties. He had short, blonde, kinky hair and blue eyes. He was in tiptop physical shape. His mental capacity seemed to match his jock image. Malcolm figured that he must have been Queen Louise's love slave but later learned that her lover lived in Seattle, which in turn confirmed his suspicion of Stu lacking much cognitive capacities. He sat upright in his chair. He was a good-looking man, and in spite of Malcolm's critical assessment, Stu appeared to be a kind and courteous gentleman.

There was a couple, Debbie and Sean. Debbie was a freckled, blue-eyed redhead who was in her early twenties. She worked as a receptionist at one of the local resorts and had nearly completed her intern hours and was about to become a licensed massage therapist, or body worker, as she preferred to be called. Debbie seemed to be comfortable with herself.

Sean was the liveliest one of the bunch. He waited tables at Nepenthe with Sarina and Sheila. Sean had short, straight hair a couple of shades darker than a sandy brown. His brown eyes had fire. He sat in his seat loosely, appearing to be without any pretenses. He was clean-shaven with the exception of his flavor-saver; a small triangle clump of hair that grew just below his lower lip. He smiled a lot and when he spoke his head moved around nodding and swaying.

They placed their orders and settled into conversation. Sarina sat on Malcolm's right and Louise sat to the right of Sarina. Debbie sat to Malcolm's left and Sean was to the left of her. Stu sat directly across the table from Malcolm, between Sean and Louise. Malcolm was making small talk with Debbie when the rest of the table started giggling about something that he'd missed.

"I don't see why we all don't just come out," Sarina said, looking at Louise. It was obvious that this was a topic that the two of them had previously discussed. Sarina received an approving nod from Louise.

"You stopped that old guy over there dead in his tracks," Sean announced, referring to a couple that was seated at a table behind Louise. Sean was clapping his hands, shaking his head up and down, and belly laughing. "I've never had a gay experience," Sean said, after he stopped laughing. He paused for ten seconds and then added: "Yeah, the closest thing to gay for me was a blow job from another guy. And that was pretty damn goo…" he said, busting up laughing before he could finish his punch line. The whole table roared with laughter. Debbie didn't even bother giving him a what-was-that-shit look.

The waitress delivered their meals, and they continued their conversation over breakfast. Malcolm took a bite of his French toast and caught himself unconsciously staring at Louise's boobs. She was the kind of girl who he'd like to fuck once and never call on again, leaving her in doubt about whether she was any good or not. He was thinking how he'd like to be suckling her when she said something about guys supposedly being able to give the best blowjobs. His hard-on disappeared and it felt like his dick wanted to crawl up into his abdomen. The whole table seemed to lose its festive energy, but the lull was short-lived.

"Hey Stu, how's the sausage?" Sean asked, grinning bigger than shit. Stu had eaten his pancakes, but for some reason had pushed his sausage links aside.

"Fuck you!" Stu said, as he flipped Sean off.

Thanks to Sean, they were all back to belly laughing again. The old couple sitting at the table behind Louise finally moved inside to escape the fodder.

"So Malcolm, what do you do?" Louise asked, as she flipped her long blond hair over her shoulder.

"Not much," he answered, not wanting to explain himself.

"He's a writer," Sarina answered. "Tell her, Malcolm. I don't want them to think I've got boring friends," Sarina added.

"Alright then, I guess I'm a writer," he conceded. He hated having to take on an identity, but it beat leaving them to think he might be an undercover drug agent. Maybe he should have been an agent. He'd done a pretty fancy job of slipping into the local scene and in a damn short amount of time.

"What have you written that I might have read?" Louise asked.

"I haven't published anything. I've actually just finished a book, and I'm currently working on a second," he answered. "I quit selling tractors after eighteen years and moved here. Ten months later, bored out of my mind, I sat down one evening and started writing. Five months later I finished a book," he explained. "For the time being I've decided to write and have fun instead of chasing money or fame."

"Where you from?" Sean asked.

"Central Valley."

"Where in the Central Valley?"

"Hour or so south of Sacramento."

"Well, welcome," Sean said, "I used to live in Sacramento."

"You know what it's like then," Malcolm said.

"I was only a kid when we moved here. All I can really remember was it being hotter than hell and burning my bare feet on the sidewalks," Sean smiled and nodded. "Oh, yeah, and running through the sprinklers, too."

"Funny thing is that I left there eighteen months ago, but I brought it all with me. I'm just beginning to realize that it was okay to leave it all behind; that it's alright to relax and live my life here now."

"I see it all the time," Debbie said. "People will come to the resort to let down, then they go all crazy when their masseuse is behind schedule and they have to wait fifteen minutes."

"Then they can't even relax and enjoy what they're really there for. It's tough when you've been living that life for so long. Like I said, it's taken me a year and a half just to begin to realize that it's okay."

"Like I said, welcome." Sean repeated, smiling and nodding his head again.

After breakfast, the crew all went back to Sarina's cabin. One of them had scored a chunk of hash and Sarina had invited them over to her place for an after breakfast delight. Malcolm sat out on the deck while the others sat inside and smoked out. It was a great breakfast and good company. Eating was something Malcolm had in common with all of them, but smoking wasn't. When he was their age he was doing exactly the same thing, so he couldn't condemn them. He just wasn't there anymore.

A half hour later the breakfast club set off on their own for the day and Sarina changed for work. Malcolm spent the afternoon out on the deck with his head in the PowerBook. Maya was in and out of the cabin occasionally meowing for his attention. Sarina had a break at four, but she had to return to do a banquet at six. The four-twenty crew arrived at four-fifteen. Sarina and Laine were the first to show up.

Daniel, a skinny black man, who had dreadlocks that rose

out of and dangled over the open top of a forest green sun-visor was the next person who forgot to latch the gate on his way to the deck. People not latching the gate drove Sheila mad because the deer came in and helped themselves to her garden. Cliff, the maintenance man, walked in with Sadie a few steps behind her master. Cliff was wearing the identical green visor that Daniel sported, minus the dreadlocks. Both visors had Carmel-by-the-Sea embroidered onto them.

Gina was next; she walked through the gate and started doing a funky dance on the stepping-stones on her way up onto the deck. There was something new about Gina. She had a small turquoise blue heart tattooed where a necklace would normally hang. Two kids showed up, too. One of them was an eighteen-year-old; his fourteen-year-old brother tagged along. They were proud to report that the younger one had been smoking weed since he was ten.

Malcolm left a little before six that evening, allowing enough time and space to avoid the five o'clock traffic jam on Highway 1 and Rio Road. He'd grown tired of the whole scene, wasn't connecting with anyone and was beginning to feel an environmental high just from hanging around all the stoned souls.

As much as Malcolm dreamed of living in Big Sur, he couldn't. Well, he could, but he couldn't surround himself with people who were loaded all of the time. He liked them and saw the value in their humanity, but he just couldn't connect with them very often. It was like walking around in another country unable to speak the language. He wasn't in love with Sarina; it had all been a contact high, just another illusion.

Big Sur had an ego, too. The locals and their identities were all tied to an old myth that they were trying to preserve by recreating what had already been created. They were living the lives of the dead. They were trying to live out an old legend and missing out on creating their own. Sarina had helped Malcolm; she'd led him back to a part of himself that he'd lost long ago. He might have quit drinking and drugging when he was twenty-five, but fifteen years later he was still trying to get himself pieced back together.

Malcolm stopped at the intersection of Highway 1 and Rio

Road, waiting for the light to turn green so he could make the turn towards the studio. The image of Mrs. Shams and her head bobbing around on her shoulder came to him. He could see her holding her right index finger up while she was giving him one of her priceless lectures. It amazed him that the old girl thought she knew what he needed. When the light turned green, he began to laugh out loud as he made the turn.

When Malcolm was drunk and stoned, his parents never tried to force-feed him any of their advice. They knew that if they tried, he'd just pull a Starbucks on them. The Mockingbird was an arrogant old thing, but behind the arrogance was a lonely old lady longing for communion.

So what did that make Malcolm, thinking he knew what was best for Sarina? Who was he to say what she needed? Who was he to say what anyone needed? He'd only experienced life through his own being; believing that things had to be a certain way was distorted and prejudiced. Right then, all of life seemed an illusion.

Chapter 29

Malcolm took his morning walk through Mission Trails, showered, and then drove to the Pink House for a coffee. Sometime during the day he needed to sign up for school. It was the last day for the automated phone-registration. On his way out the door, he had taken along the course catalog and intended to register from his cellular phone while sipping coffee on the Pink House front porch and watching the irregular regulars.

Jenny was just leaving the Pink House on her way to the office when Malcolm arrived. After greeting her, he volunteered to keep an eye on Diana. The porch seat was open, so he tied Diana up to save his seat and went inside to get his coffee. A few minutes later he settled into the prized seat. Diana was stretched out between the steps and the front door. She was capturing the attention of the patrons and copping a feel from the dog lovers as they came and went.

Malcolm paged through the course catalog, strategically trying to schedule his classes around what he believed to be the most productive time to bump into women. School and writing were important, but he did have his priorities.

Laura, one of Jenny's friends, came up the steps as Diana rolled over on her back, all four legs dangling in the air.

Laura bent down to tickle Diana's belly. "I bet her mama doesn't roll over for you that easily," she teased, smiling at her own humor as she stood up after petting Diana.

"You got that right," Malcolm answered, wishing that he was rolling Laura over right there on the porch.

"We get like that after awhile," Laura said, pointing her finger at Malcolm as if he was to blame for her general mistrust of men. She smiled and then walked inside to place her order.

Laura was the shadow who showed up late that one night at the beach for Ellen's birthday party a few months earlier. She was a petite dark-blondish-redhead, who taught yoga and cut hair. She had one hot little body on her, but after seeing her alone a few times, she finally surfaced with some goofy looking dude, so Malcolm threw in the towel along with any hopes of bagging her. Well, not completely, but his attention turned to one who appeared to give a greater return on time invested. With hindsight, he now knew that how something appeared might be deceiving. Who knows, he might have already bedded Laura if he hadn't spent the last several months chasing something that didn't want to be caught.

Luke, the local who had introduced Malcolm to Waylen, stepped up onto the porch while Malcolm paged through the course catalog.

"Morning, Malcolm," Luke said, as he extended his hand.

"Hey, Luke, good to see you," he said, setting the catalog down and shaking his hand. "What's going on with you?"

"Not much. Just stopped in for a bite," Luke answered in a peaceful tone, nodding his head and smiling. "How about yourself?"

"Trying to sign up for school. It's fucking me up, though. It's like I might have to get a job, and I'm also thinking about moving." Malcolm was a mess. He didn't want to over commit himself, but he also didn't want to spend the rest of his life chasing a degree at night school. It was just another one of the paradoxes that froze him and kept him in stasis.

"Sounds like maybe it's not that important. Like maybe you have some other things going on that need more of your attention," Luke suggested in a wise tone. He looked and sounded so peaceful when he spoke.

"Okay, two night classes, that's what I'm taking," Malcolm announced, becoming clear. "Thanks, I'm glad you came through," he said smiling. "That way I can still adapt to any changes that the rest of my life might present."

"Glad I could help," Luke answered with a smile. "I'm going in to order some lunch," he added. It's amazing how people can just appear, say a few words, then disappear, leaving another with a whole new perspective. Luke had helped Malcolm listen to himself.

Malcolm phoned and got through to the college computer on his first attempt. Ten minutes later he'd registered for the semester and paid for it with a credit card. Diana was still lying on the porch and rolled over on her back again when Laura walked out. She knelt down to tickle Diana's tummy.

"See you later," Laura said, as she descended the steps.

"I gave up on her mother rolling over a long time ago, anyway," Malcolm said in a loud voice to make sure Laura knew that he was addressing her as she stepped from the bottom step onto the sidewalk.

"Problem is, there's not much to pick from in this little town," she shouted back without turning around, en route to her car that was parked in the public parking lot.

"Who says you have to limit yourself to this little town?" he hollered, as she stepped onto the sidewalk across the street.

He was hoping to test Laura's loyalty to Jenny, and to her boyfriend. Waylen had mentioned that she was really unhappy with her current love. It actually hadn't only come from Waylen; he'd heard it from Jenny, too. That's when, once again, Malcolm asked himself: *What the hell am I hanging around this village for anyway, this fucking miniature world? Messing with this goddamn physical therapist...*

Around noon, Diana and Malcolm took off on a stroll around town and returned an hour later to find Jenny sitting on the porch waiting for them. She had started this cleanse thing where you take all these vitamins or supplements of some kind and eventually you shit out the linings of your guts until all you've got left is who knows what? She was eating fruit and vegetables, and drinking powders added to water or juice. Malcolm was eating everything she wasn't supposed to be eating.

So this cleanse thing had thrown a kink in their already fragile relationship, or whatever they had going. All they'd really had in common were meals, and Jenny's not eating had ended their lunch affairs. Ever since she started her new age diet, their sharing time together had gone to the shitter, along with everything else.

Malcolm let go of Diana's leash and she ran up the stairs and jumped up onto Jenny's lap.

"Would you like a tea?" Malcolm asked.

She nodded a silent yes.

"Lemon grass and peppermint?" he asked, knowing that she wasn't allowing herself the luxury of green or black teas because of the caffeine.

"I think I just want lemon grass," she answered, appearing

to be in one of her trance-like states.

"Okay," he answered, wanting to add a shot of something unhealthy to her potion; the temptation subsiding by the time he placed her order.

He returned a few minutes later with a mug full of her lemon grass brew. He also brought the honey, to save himself a second trip. They didn't say much, just sat next to each other in silence.

"I've come to the conclusion that I can only hang around people who don't have to talk all of the time," she said, breaking the silence.

"Hmm," Malcolm grunted, thinking about all the time at lunch and dinner he'd wasted with her in conversation about some boring drama that life had offered them. *Had I kept my mouth shut, we'd have probably been doing it this whole time,* he thought to himself.

It was quiet for a while, but then the silence began to get to Malcolm. He started telling her about how, after reading his book, Mrs. Shams had taken it upon herself to critique his grammar in the middle of their conversations. He also told her about how the ol' Mockingbird had informed him that he lacked confidence and fell far short in the world of academics.

"Maybe she's right," Jenny responded, stoically sipping her potion.

"All her critiques might be true, but who in the hell invited her to be the messenger? I know she's saying out loud what I am usually thinking about myself. I'm sure that's what pisses me off so bad, but the old gal doesn't know how close she is to getting put back in her place."

"Are you sure this isn't a few months worth of stuff that has been building up? Maybe you should be careful," Jenny suggested.

Great, now he had another feminine thinking that she knew what was best for him. One thing was certain: Jenny had yet to shit away her opinion. "More like a few weeks," he answered. The shadow of his inner critic seemed to follow wherever Malcolm went, taking voice in people like the Mockingbird and Diana's Master.

Jenny had to go home to get whatever it was that she was

eating for her special diet, so she relieved Malcolm of his dog-sitting duties. He was getting tired of the Pink House scene and decided to leave. He drove past Tillie's and spotted Sheila's car parked in front of the restaurant and stopped.

Sheila was inside visiting with Travis and Lisa. Sheila and Travis were sitting at the counter, Lisa standing on the opposite side. Lisa looked up when Malcolm walked through the door. Sheila and Travis turned to follow her smile. All three of them greeted Malcolm. He took an empty seat to the right of Travis. Sheila was on Travis's left and she kept on talking to Lisa. Travis shifted his attention to Malcolm.

"What's going on Jiminy?" Malcolm teased.

"Good things," he answered, smiling his great big happy-to-be-alive smile.

"Well, fill me in then," Malcolm encouraged.

"I met this woman from New Orleans at the Gallery last week."

"New Orleans, huh?"

"Yeah, she's doing a photo exhibit at the Henry Miller library," he explained. By the look in Travis's eye, he was still hot on her.

"She still around?"

"She left yesterday, but I'm going to see her," he said, clapping his hands and then rubbing them together.

"Cool. When?"

"Well, I'm going to Europe in a couple of months, and I've decided to stop in New Orleans on my way home."

"Sounds like a good time. So where you been hanging?"

"Big Sur mostly. I ran into Sarina a couple of days ago. I had to clear up some things with her about something I said the night we were all hanging out on her deck."

"What's going on with Sarina?" Malcolm asked innocently. He'd forgotten that he'd mentioned to Sarina how much he disliked Travis stepping on her that evening when all of them were out on the deck.

"Oh, she took something I said wrong. I had said something about the music that I had written when I was in my twenties not being as good as the stuff that I'm doing in my thirties, and she thought that I was knocking her stuff."

"Huh," Malcolm grunted, thinking how he'd stirred that one up real good.

Travis soon left to meet his band members for a rehearsal. Lisa was busy seating a few patrons who had walked in for a late lunch.

"So what's up Malcolm?" Sheila asked in her normal delightfully positive tone.

"Not much. Spotted your car out front, so I stopped."

"Yeah, I had to come to town to run errands. I called you, but your machine answered. I figured you were already out and about."

"You figured right again," Malcolm smiled. "You eat lunch yet?"

"Nope."

"How about some Sushi?"

"Okay, but I've got to stop off at the travel agent first."

"Where?"

"On Lighthouse. Oh yeah, there's a great sushi place about a block from there."

"You planning a trip?"

"Yeah, Sarina and I are going to Europe in a few months."

"Cool. Come on, I'll drive."

After lunch, Sheila asked Malcolm to stop off at the Rite-Aid drug store. He waited in the Tahoe while she ran inside. Fifteen minutes later she climbed back into the Chevy.

"Get everything you needed?" he asked, more to be friendly than to be nosey.

"Yeah, now Sarina and I have enough tampons to last for the next month."

"That's nice to know. Speaking of women, have you found one for me yet?" he asked, teasing seriously. "Oh, yeah, and not one of those old crones you're always trying to dump off onto me," he added, with a grin.

"You're just like my friend Bob. All you guys want are these young mistresses."

"Damn it Sheila! Don't go putting me in Bob's league," Malcolm shouted. "He's fifteen years older than me."

"Okay, okay. Settle down."

"I hate that when you try to make me older than I am.

He might want a mistress, but I'm still young enough to have one. Hell, look at your man. He's only two years younger than I am."

Chapter 30

When Malcolm had accompanied Mrs. Shams to the last potluck, Kerri, the daughter of long-time friends of Mrs. Shams, had volunteered to take the ol' Bird kayaking in Elkhorn Slough. Kerri had asked Malcolm if he'd like to accompany them, and he accepted her invitation. He didn't know why he accepted it, but he did. It was a lot like getting married; he didn't know why he had done that either. He'd mostly accepted Kerri's invitation because he didn't think she'd actually hold him to it; wrong again. Mrs. Shams had caught Malcolm taking the trash out one afternoon and informed him that Kerri had phoned to confirm the safari.

Kerri arrived a little after nine that morning and they all piled into Malcolm's Tahoe for the ride to Moss Landing. Kerri was a curly-headed brunette with blue eyes and a few freckles. She was tall and athletic, not the type of woman to wear make-up, and she was by no means frail. A tube of Chap Stick was the closest thing to lipstick Kerri would ever get. She had done a humanitarian stint in South America and spoke Spanish fluently. She had a habit of starting a sentence in English and finishing it in Spanish. It was hard to tell if it was a nervous habit or if she was just showing off.

Kerri was a high school English teacher. She had summers off with the exception of a part-time job at a local business on Cannery Row. Kerri was into kayaking and Mrs. Shams had previously expressed interest in exploring the Elkhorn Slough, an inland tributary that emptied out into Moss Landing, about twenty minutes north of Monterey.

So, they drove to Moss Landing where they rented a couple of kayaks, and, after a short lesson of how to recover from an unlikely spill, they began paddling from Moss Landing toward the slough. Kerri and Mrs. Shams shared a tandem kayak, and Malcolm paddled along in a single-seater. He was a little uncomfortable. The seat wouldn't go back far enough to allow him to straighten his legs, so he was having a difficult time with the oars.

"You doing alright over there?" Kerri asked, looking back to check on Malcolm. He was about twenty feet behind them, still trying to get the feel of things. Kerri was sitting in the rear of the boat. Mrs. Shams was in the front seat. Most of what Malcolm could see of Mrs. Shams was the back of her white head bobbing around on top of a life jacket.

"I wish this seat would go back some more. My knees are hitting the oars," Malcolm said, paddling up next to them.

"You mean the oars are hitting your knees," Kerri corrected.

"Oh this is just great. Now I've got two of you trying to tell me how to talk," he announced boldly. Kerri just looked at Malcolm awkwardly. Mrs. Shams's head danced around on her shoulders without turning around to say a thing. Malcolm imagined the ol' Bird to be wearing a righteous grin and holding up her index finger, chalking one up for Kerri.

They continued paddling back toward the slough. Malcolm soon mastered the kayak in spite of his knees hitting the oars. They paddled under the Highway 1 bridge. The Moss Landing Power Plant cooling towers rose above them to the south. They continued on the water eastward until they were far enough from the highway and the power plant for the noise to diminish considerably.

The first otter popped up less than ten feet in front of Malcolm. It appeared that they had scared the crap out of each other, Malcolm and the otter that is. The otter had a shellfish of some sort squeezed between its front paws. He popped up out of the water, looked at Malcolm, hissed, and dove back under. The pelicans were something else, too. Flocks of hundreds gracefully flew over their heads. There were several other species of waterfowl, and quite a few small beaches that were covered with seals. It wasn't an outing he'd have chosen to do on his own, but Malcolm was happy to be there.

They paddled a few miles back into the slough and wandered off into a smaller tributary, following it around as it narrowed, hoping that it would eventually lead them to a larger body of water. It didn't, so eventually they had to backtrack. It was a lot of extra work, but while they were making their way out of the mistake, less than fifty feet above, a huge flock of pelicans soared over the threesome. There was no way of counting them, but there had to be at least five hundred birds. They were silent with the exception of the whispering noise their wings made. It was quite a spectacle, but even more surprising than anything else was that not one of them got bombed.

They were on the water for well over three hours, and according to the map, they'd covered in excess of six miles that afternoon. It was a lot of work paddling, but well worth the effort. Mrs. Shams ended up getting her ass a little soggy, so Malcolm gave her a spare pair of his sweatpants to change into before their drive home. He checked his voice mail while the Mockingbird shed her soggy drawers. Gerald had called. He was on his way over to Pebble Beach for a few days and wanted Malcolm to join him for dinner that evening.

Malcolm returned the call and they confirmed dinner. Gerald said he'd make a reservation when he got into town and that he'd call after he had settled in. Mrs. Shams returned with her wet britches in hand. They were starving and decided on lunch at Phil's right there in Moss Landing. Over the years Phil's had developed from a small fish market into a thriving restaurant.

Kerri ordered a seafood pasta dish, Malcolm had fish and chips, and Mrs. Shams had half of a seafood quesadilla. Mrs. Shams and Malcolm ordered a Coke, but Kerri stuck to water. It took him awhile, but Malcolm finally caught on why Kerri was constantly offering to go after his refills. She was courteously using his cup to gulp her fill of soda at the fountain. He should have known that there was a self-rewarding motive behind her act of generosity.

"Pasta isn't a wise idea for a first date," Kerri announced. She was in no way shy. She was actually clownish and couldn't stand silence. When she'd asked a question, she expected an immediate answer. Malcolm bugged the shit out of her that way. He hated having to answer anything in haste, or at least when someone wanted him to anyway.

"Why is Pasta a bad dish for a first date?" he asked, finally giving in to the attention she sought. Mrs. Shams looked at Kerri and shook her head. You could tell that Mrs. Shams would have liked to have an on-and-off switch for Kerri.

"Well, it's messy. That's why."

"So," Malcolm said, shrugging his shoulders. Holding her tongue, Mrs. Shams continued to shake her head and smile.

"So, it's hard to make a good first impression if you have spaghetti sauce dripping down the front of you," Kerri reasoned.

"Hell, I say order what you damn well please. If you want pasta, get pasta. If that's all it takes to run someone off, let 'em run," Malcolm answered.

"Oh, I see. You probably like watching a woman eat pasta," Kerri said with a big smile.

Mrs. Shams started making some judgmental comment about something, and Malcolm looked over at Kerri. She had her lips puckered, sucking up a long strand of linguini, and winking at him. Malcolm just shook his head and laughed. Whatever Mrs. Shams said had been lost.

Kerri was quiet on the drive back to Carmel. She lay down in the back seat, while Malcolm drove and Mrs. Shams talked. He pulled into the driveway and within a few minutes they had said their goodbyes. Mrs. Shams went into her house, Malcolm walked to his studio, and Kerri left in her Nissan Pathfinder.

Malcolm showered and lay around for another hour. Gerald called at five-thirty and said he had made dinner reservations at Mondo's for seven-thirty. Malcolm told him he'd come to pick him up a little before seven. Mondo's was in Carmel and Gerald lived in Pebble Beach, so it was out of his way to go after Gerald, but Malcolm knew he liked to have a few pops with dinner and didn't want him getting hauled in on his way home.

Ready for his drive to Gerald's, Malcolm opened the door to the back seat of the Tahoe to put in his sweater. There was a folded note card that had been torn off of a things-to-do checklist that he kept in the pocket behind the driver's seat. He'd bought the notepad one day having had a glimmer of ambition, figuring that a to-do list would get him back on the track of once again living a productive life.

He picked up the note assuming that it had a phone number or something else that he had jotted down while driving one day. He unfolded the card to find a message:

Thanks for lunch! Hope your shoulders don't hurt you too much tomorrow. So, now, what are you really like? See ya--Kerri.

Well, now he knew what Kerri was up to when she was feigning sleep in the back seat on their ride home. He shook his head and laughed to himself. Mrs. Shams had already become disillusioned with him. He considered what she'd do once she found out that he'd slept with her good friends' daughter. His inclination was to pursue the matter just for the sake of having one up on the ol' Mockingbird. Then he thought about how much money he was saving on rent and knew what he wasn't, or *who* he wasn't going to do. Women were easier to come by than a good deal on an apartment in Carmel, or so he wanted to believe.

He arrived at Gerald's place a little before seven so they could catch up. Most of their friendship was banter over the telephone, so it was nice for them to see each other. Malcolm walked in and Gerald was sitting at the counter, sipping white wine and watching the democratic convention on television. Gerald poured Malcolm a seven-up, and they went into the living room to visit.

"What's going on with the book?"

"I'm in the middle of writing it," Malcolm answered, setting his glass down in a coaster on the coffee table.

"I mean with the first book," Gerald asked just to be making conversation, but something else was bothering him.

"Nothing's happening. Decided to let her breathe for awhile," Malcolm answered. "I'm focusing on this other book for now."

Gerald asked a few more questions, but was having a hell of a time listening to Malcolm's responses. They bounced around a bit from topic to topic, never really saying much. Gerald asked about the twenty-four year old in Big Sur, wanting to know if Malcolm was getting any of that action. Malcolm lied and told him yes. Then he handed Gerald the note he'd just found from Kerri.

"Sounds like that one's all yours for the picking," Gerald said, handing the note back to Malcolm as a big grin grew on his face. "What's she like?"

"A little muscular. You know, the athletic type."

"What, hundred and twenty pounds or so?" he asked, muting the television.

"Probably a hundred and forty."

"She is a little muscular then," Gerald said, finally seeming able to settle in on their conversation. Whatever had been eating at Gerald was taking a break.

"She reminds me of an old girlfriend who gave really great blow jobs," Malcolm said, grinning and raising his eyebrows.

Gerald grinned. "They say that the only thing better than a good blow job is a piece of ass," Gerald answered, as he glanced at the television, lost to his inner drama once again.

"That all depends," Malcolm replied, contemplating on how much he loved lying back and being pleasured, especially from a woman whose heart was into pleasuring.

"Come on, Slick, let's go have dinner," Gerald teased, before he swigged the last of his wine.

* * * * *

The Batmobile was double parked in front of Mondo's and people were swarming around it taking photos. A local man owned the vehicle and occasionally took it for a ride around Carmel. Traffic was backed up in both directions. A hotheaded guy in a black Jeep started honking and impatiently started to drive through the crowd. Booing and hissing, the people parted like the red sea for the hothead and then fell back around the celebrity automobile.

Mondo's was packed as usual, but Gerald was a regular and they were seated within a few minutes. Malcolm ordered aglio olio linguine with oyster mushrooms and crushed red pepper. Gerald had some other pasta dish that looked a lot like spaghetti but had some other fancy name. Salad and bread was served and, before you knew it, they were back on the bullshit trail.

Gerald had had it out with his wife on his way out of the house.

"She's been sitting around for the last three months waiting for her dog to die; she won't put it down. Christ, the fucking dog's sixteen years old," he said, before taking a gulp of his wine.

Malcolm dipped a slice of bread into the olive oil and balsamic vinegar and took a bite without replying. Gerald didn't want to be at home with his wife anyway, especially since he had a hot thirty-eight-year-old mistress who was breathing life back into him.

"I've had a hell of a week, man. One of my key people quit me and now I'm finding out that he's been siphoning away my clients for the last several months to start up his own practice. To top it off, he quit when the only other guy who knows what's going on around the place is off vacationing in Europe," Gerald complained with a tired-as-hell look.

"So you've been manning the fort?" Malcolm asked just to let him know that he was listening.

"I've had it all, and now I'm having trouble with my son and my stepdaughter. For twenty years I haven't had any type of relationship with my son because his lunatic mother fucked him up and turned him against me. Then, when she couldn't handle him anymore, she finally calls me to take over."

"Sounds about right," Malcolm answered. "How old are your kids?"

"The boy's forty-one. My stepdaughter's forty-three, and her husband just got fired. He's got one hell of an attitude problem. Sounds like you know who's going to be supporting another family all over again."

Malcolm listened.

"Then last week my son's wife booted his ass out and then he goes and gets himself arrested. He was climbing a telephone pole and got popped for illegally hooking up cable service, and to top that, he works for the phone company but was off duty and didn't have his truck or tools with him. Hell, I hope he doesn't go to jail over this one."

"That's an easy one," Malcolm told him.

"What do you mean?"

"Just turn the whole thing around," Malcolm answered, like it was no big deal.

"How?"

"He was climbing up there to check things out. You know, his friend was having phone troubles and he was just helping out. It was all in the line of duty."

"Yeah, but he was off duty."

"Like I said, turn it around. He was just helping a friend out. Fuck, you're the lawyer, handle it."

"You might have something there. Then my wife throws this shit at me that I'm an enabler, saying that I should have left him in jail," Gerald said, with his head resting in the palm of his right hand while he swished his wine glass around in little circles with his left.

"Oh, yeah, that enabler shit," Malcolm answered, shaking his head.

"He's my boy. I've got to help him out. I just hope he isn't lying to me."

"Even if he is, he still needs you."

"Yeah, but that's when she starts preaching this enabler shit."

"That's what's wrong with those fucking shrinks! They preach this enabler shit, telling you what you should and shouldn't do. How do they fucking know what you're supposed to do?" Malcolm asked, remembering that Gerald mentioned that his wife had seen a psychotherapist at one stage in her life. Gerald said that she was always accusing him of having affairs and he got tired of it and told her to get some help. "That pisses me off. He's your son, and he needs your help. They can call it enabling or whatever the hell else they want to call it, but it's nobody's goddamn business but your own," Malcolm answered, adamant about his theory of the whole therapy scene just shifting a person from one fucked up belief system to another and still leaving them to look outside of themselves for answers. "We live in an age when people seldom if ever learn to think and act on their own," Malcolm added in a disgusted tone.

"Their mother's a fucking lunatic. She's got him all fucked up. Then my wife throws that shit up in my face about how I'd have never helped my stepdaughter if she were in a jam like that."

"Ah horseshit!" Malcolm answered, wanting to slam his fist into the table but refraining. It was one of Gerald's favorite restaurants, and he didn't want to make a scene. Gerald wasn't a taker. He'd treated his stepdaughter as if she were his own.

"I've done nothing but give to that girl. Hell, I've given more to her than my own boy… you know, when a woman decides to attack, they lose everything and go right for the jugular. All the fucking rules they want you to live by go right out the window," he complained as the waiter served their main entree. "So what are you going to do with the book?" Gerald asked, wanting to shift the attention away from himself.

"Hell, I don't know. Let it sit, I guess. I'm going to write two more and then see what happens."

"You remember that one book I talked about proofing for a buddy of mine?" Gerald asked.

"Oh, yeah."

"It's getting published."

"Great," Malcolm answered, a little jealous, but more put off with the twinge of pressure he was putting on himself about becoming a success story.

"Yeah, I think a buddy of mine put up the money though," Gerald added, making Malcolm feel a little superior having not had to resort to the support of an outside investor. "Man, I really had it out with my wife before I left. I'm sorry to keep talking about it, but…" he hesitated, flashing back on his day.

"Fuck, Gerald, I don't mind hearing about it," Malcolm said, encouraging him. It had been some time since the old boy got a load off of his chest. "I got one question though."

"What's that?"

"Why do you call your son, your boy?" Malcolm asked, hoping to get him to realize that they were adults and their problems didn't have to be his alone to carry.

"You're right. I should be calling him my son."

"Well, he's a grown man, isn't he?"

"I mean, I thought that I was simplifying my life. But, hell, I've got more fucking problems now than I've ever had."

"Gerald, you're living. You're lucky you got problems."

"That's why I have this thing going on the side," he explained as the expression on his face became lighter. "I can't stand being at home. She just mopes around that fucking dog all day long. I just can't stand being around her, I'm telling you. She's driving me away," he said, trying to convince himself.

Malcolm was beginning to wonder if these life crisis things hit everyone or if they just struck certain people like Gerald and himself. Perhaps the midlife crisis thing was just an excuse for people who hadn't allowed themselves the other smaller crises that life had previously offered. One thing was certain: Malcolm's entire life had the makings of one crisis after another, and Gerald's life had been the same. Crisis is the wrong word, though; it was more like an adventure.

"Now I'm getting pissed!"

"About what?" Gerald asked.

"About that fucking dog. I mean, life's passing her by," Malcolm answered, thinking about how his ex-wife's animals had impacted his life and thinking about how Jenny's pup got all her attention. Attention that could have been redirected towards Malcolm, making sure he was getting some proper loving.

"She's got nothing that gives meaning to her life. She's unhappy and when I get home it all comes out on me."

"Maybe you need to take care of a little business at home, Gerald," Malcolm teased with a grin.

"She thinks I lost my drive. Told her that I can't get it up."

"Oh, that's just great. You can't get it up, but you're pouring it to Gail twice a week and then some."

"She told me to get some Viagra, but I told her that the drive just isn't there."

"Hey, Gerald, what are you gonna do when that flippin' dog does die?"

"What do you mean?"

"I mean, you better get her a puppy."

"She doesn't want one."

"Who cares what she wants. Get her one anyway," Malcolm answered, with a serious look. "I mean, it's a puppy or when her dog does die, the fuck-fest with your little honey might just come to a screeching halt."

"I'll get her daughter to do it when the other mutt dies."

"Don't wait that long. Get her one tomorrow," Malcolm said, trying to hold back his laughter, but he couldn't and Gerald soon joined in.

"Guess I am making their problems mine."

"Do you still want to be married?"

"No, but I'm not going through all that again. Can't do it to the family, but it sure is hell to be at home with her."

"When *are* you home?"

"Well, that's just it, not much, but when I am..."

"Why don't you just keep doing what you're doing? Hell, you're hardly ever home anyway. You're either here or at the boat."

"It's other people's problems that are dragging me down."

"Those problems aren't shit. I mean, who cares? You're living your life. Just keep doing it. The problems will take care of themselves. Besides, what's the worst that could happen?"

"We'd have to separate property. I don't really care about that anyway... hey, did I tell you about the Diebenkorn painting I bought for a hundred and seventy five thousand?"

"No."

"Fucker appraised for two and a half million."

"Where do you have this thing?"

"At my home."

"So she knows about it then?" Malcolm joked.

"Yeah, shit," he shook his head and laughed. Gerald didn't give a shit about the money. It was about living and that is exactly what he was doing.

"Gerald," Malcolm said in a serious tone.

"Yeah?"

"Get her the fucking puppy; tomorrow!"

Chapter 31

Malcolm's first stop was for treatment at Jenny's, moist hot packs followed by some ultrasound. He had hoped that she might decide to do some deep tissue massage on his low back, but that might have been too close to his genitals. He was getting ready to leave after his treatment, but she caught him in the doorway and asked him to come into her office.

"I got a call about the cabin out in Cachagua," she whispered. They stood nose to nose, just a few inches apart, in kissing territory. "I'm having second thoughts about renting it now. I was wondering if you'd go with me to check it out." She wanted a weekend retreat. Cachagua was about seven or eight miles east of the Carmel Valley Village. Exactly in the area she'd been looking.

"Just let me know when you wanna go," Malcolm answered. He wasn't all that hot about going out there, because Jenny wouldn't heed his advice on the place anyway, but at the same time he'd never been to Cachagua and was a bit curious.

A friend of Jenny's who had rented the cabin for several years had given her two months notice and had told the landlord about Jenny. So, when the landlord phoned Jenny to see if she was interested, it was almost a done deal. Jenny had made the required deposit to secure the cabin shortly after speaking to the owner. But now it was time for her to fully commit to her fantasy.

After helping to ease some of Jenny's anticipatory anxiety about actually realizing her dreamed up desire, Malcolm walked over to the Pink House for Coffee. He was sitting out on the bench when Danette's orange BMW pulled into the parking lot across the street.

"Hey brother! What's going on?" Waylen asked, as he stepped up onto the porch and slapped Malcolm five.

"Still driving the beamer, huh," Malcolm joked.

"Yeah, I know," he answered a little sheepishly. "She just can't live without me. She's gonna move in with me."

"Right on. Congratulations," Malcolm encouraged, not

wanting to rub Waylen's nose in the Danette mess. He was going to do what he was going to do, regardless of what Malcolm or anyone else might have to say about it. It was best just to shut up and be his friend.

"Got some nook' this morning, brother," he said, all proud of himself. He was still high on the sex, his eyes all glossed over. "Check that boodie out," he said, as a young curly headed blonde in her early twenties walked by on the sidewalk below. "I love boodie," he said, reaching out with his hand where the blonde had just past, grabbing air with his fingertips like he was copping a feel. "I got nookie this morning so watch out for me today, baby!" he yelled, clapping his hands and doing a dance with his eyebrows. "Hey, I got to go. I've got a client coming in. You gonna be around later?"

"I'll be here from two to three. Got to bring my landlord back for a massage. I'll be hanging here waiting for her," Malcolm lied. Hell, Waylen didn't even get a coffee, just stopped to tell Malcolm that he'd gotten laid and left. Malcolm really planned to be at the Pink House from three to four, or so he thought. He was a little jealous, and didn't want to hear anymore about Waylen getting nook'. He wouldn't have traded places with Waylen but was still a little jealous. It was more the fact that Waylen had a woman who was actually willing to entertain him, physically that was.

Malcolm drove home, and, after checking his e-mail, phoned Mrs. Shams to confirm the time of her appointment. He thought it was for three that afternoon, but she informed him that it was at two. It was a good thing he had called. He phoned Jenny's voice mail and left a message saying that he'd be hanging out at the Pink House from two to three if she wanted to join him for tea.

His phone rang as soon as he hung up. It was a shrink that he'd had a brief romance with earlier in the year, before the Kate thing had taken off. It was brief because she had tried to fix him. She was a girlfriend of his high school sweetheart who had phoned out of the blue over the holidays. Up until their brief fling, it had been over fifteen years since Malcolm had spoken with this woman. In those fifteen years, she had gone to school and ended up with a master's degree in psychology.

When Malcolm first started seeing her, she tried to tell him that he was full of anger and needed to get rid of it. Having decided that she was nuts, Malcolm told her that he liked his anger and instead got rid of her. Anyway, he told the shrink he was on his way out and that he'd call her back.

His cellular phone rang right after he hung up with his old love. It was another ex-girlfriend. They had been lovers for close to six years, had both divorced at the same time and wanted nothing more from each other than good hot sex. Or that's the way Malcolm saw it, but the woman was secretly in love. She just never told him because she knew he'd run. Malcolm had made it clear that they'd never be more than lovers and she went along with the façade, hoping that he'd come around later. Nearly six years had passed when she met a man who really cared for her and didn't mind her being the mother of two young girls, so Malcolm gracefully withdrew from her life with the exception of receiving an occasional phone call from her every six months or so just to say hello.

Mrs. Shams baited Malcolm into conversation on their drive to Pacific Grove. Holding her right index finger up, she'd interrupt him mid-sentence to correct his improper grammar. He had a habit of ending a sentence with "at."

He got the Mockingbird to the masseuse five minutes before two and it was a damn good thing. If the old broad had interrupted him one more time, he'd have probably backhanded her right out of the passenger side window. He locked up the Tahoe as Mrs. Shams hobbled across the street for her massage. It was a warm sunny day, so once inside the Pink House he ordered a black currant iced tea.

He sat outside alone, planning to finish reading Hawking's *A Brief History in Time*. Between pages, he checked out the young twenty-something blonde who was paging through a Martha Stewart homemaking book. He thought about how much he'd like to have her making his home. Thirty minutes later, the blonde left, and Malcolm was actually able to concentrate and finish the Hawking's read.

Jenny showed up with Diana at just before three. She sat at the same table the blonde had just vacated ten minutes earlier but in the seat on the opposite side. Malcolm was sitting on a bench a few feet away from her.

"How's it going?" he asked, as Diana jumped up onto the bench and lay down next to him.

"Okay. How about you?"

"Pretty good. I got two phone calls from old girlfriends this afternoon. That was kind of weird."

Jenny didn't respond. Diana rested her chin on Malcolm's thigh.

"One was the shrink."

"The shrink?" Jenny asked, as if she didn't know who he was talking about.

"Yeah, I told you about her. She was the one who told me I had a lot of anger I needed to get rid of, and I told her I liked my anger, that she was fucking nuts and got rid of her instead," Malcolm answered and laughed. He loved telling people that story.

"Oh yeah, I remember now," she said, laughing just like she had the first time he'd told her the story.

"Yeah, and then a woman who was my lover for almost six years phoned," he said, still smiling over the shrink story.

"I don't think you told me about her," she said in a curious tone.

"I quit seeing her a little over a year ago," he explained, throwing Jenny another curve ball. He had told her about a few other lovers he'd had since his divorce, but none that lasted as long as this love, actually nowhere near this long.

"It was just a year ago that you quit seeing each other?" she asked, calculating how this past lover fit in with all the short-lived romances since his divorce.

"Yeah, she met a guy who really liked her, so I encouraged her to move on."

"After having a relationship for six years?" she asked with a disbelieving look on her face.

"Yeah, she had two kids, and I wasn't going to marry her. It was really just a sex thing," Malcolm explained. If he hadn't confused her up to that point in their relationship, he'd certainly done so now.

Still disoriented from her massage, Mrs. Shams joined them after ordering a tea and pastry. She sat on the same seat that the young blonde homemaker had been warming. Malcolm's earlier fib to Waylen about the time he'd be back to the Pink House failed him, and Waylen showed up just as Mrs. Shams sat down. Being locals, Waylen and Jenny knew each other, so Malcolm introduced them to Mrs. Shams.

This is going to be great, Malcolm thought to himself. On different occasions, he had badmouthed all of them to one another. He'd complained to Jenny that Mrs. Shams was a nosey old broad who loved to give him advice. He'd told a little of his relationship with Jenny to Mrs. Shams, and Mrs. Shams had come to the conclusion that Jenny was just dragging him around. Jenny thought that Waylen was a testosterone-troubled man who was constantly led around by his pecker. Waylen thought that Jenny was a royal pain in the ass who was only worried about herself, because Malcolm had told him that she wasn't giving it up, and because Waylen liked to think that everyone else's relationships were extensions of his and Danette's. His view of women was a constant; they were all users.

Malcolm had also told Mrs. Shams how Jenny had said that he'd have to shave off his beard if he ever expected her to kiss him, and how, after he did shave it, she still wouldn't kiss him. To top it off, he had told Mrs. Shams the parting shot: "To hell with her! I grew it back." Mrs. Shams thought that that was about the funniest thing she had ever heard. What was even funnier was that he'd shaved it off again, but it wasn't for Jenny that time. He had shaved it off because it damn well pleased him to do so. Anyway, Malcolm was sitting there clean-shaven and was quite certain that Mrs. Shams now believed that he was finally getting a bit of action from Jenny.

So, all four of them had a nice little afternoon tea party. Malcolm had one hell of a fun time watching the group dynamics. What they said to each other was entertaining, but what they weren't saying was of even greater interest. It was fun watching their pretentious smiles and gestures that hid the intimacies that Malcolm enjoyed.

Mrs. Shams was speaking to Malcolm about something of little importance when Waylen started questioning Jenny about some guy she had dated in the past. He was still feeling pretty cocky after having been laid that morning.

"So Jenny, whatever happened with Lonny?" Waylen asked, trying to prod a reaction.

"He decided to quit seeing me. He was actually seeing someone else, but I was still trying to be friends with him. He freaked out and told me not to call him anymore because he just couldn't handle it," Jenny explained.

It surprised the hell out of Malcolm that Jenny was even responding to Waylen's inquisition. Malcolm expected that Jenny would've ignored Waylen, just like he was ignoring Mrs. Shams, who was still trying to carry on a conversation. She had been talking the whole time that Jenny and Waylen had been going at it, but Waylen and Jenny's exchange was too damned good for Malcolm to miss. He had just shaken his head and repeated a few of Mrs. Shams's words so that the Mockingbird thought he was listening to her song. He wasn't so damn interested in Jenny's old flame as much as he was interested in the dual between the testosterone-riddled and the testosterone-repulsed.

Mrs. Shams finally realized that Malcolm was more interested in listening than talking and quieted down. Waylen and Jenny continued their banter while Diana sniffed around for the stray crumbs of someone else's afternoon delight. Malcolm soon grew tired of the local gossip and suggested to Mrs. Shams that they leave. They said goodbye to Diana and the two opposites.

"I'll bet those two don't last for another two minutes," Malcolm said to Mrs. Shams, as he climbed into his seat behind the wheel.

"Why do you say that?" she asked.

"Because she thinks all men are pigs, and she thinks he's the biggest pig in town," Malcolm answered.

"Why does she think all men are pigs?" Mrs. Shams asked, as Malcolm pulled out of the parking lot and waved to Waylen, Jenny and Diana as they drove off.

"Jenny thinks that all of us men are just full of testosterone and that all we want is sex. She thinks that's all men want."

"Honestly!" Mrs. Shams said, with her head starting to do that wiggly dance on her shoulders.

"She's more afraid of us than anything," Malcolm claimed.

"That's interesting. She's afraid of men and you're afraid of women. You make a good pair."

Malcolm didn't respond. She had a point, but he didn't feel like defending himself. He also didn't feel like listening to any more of the old gal's advice, afraid that she might actually come up with a valid critique. As far as Malcolm was concerned, the ol' Mockingbird should have had a dear-kiss-my-ass-column for people who really gave a damn about what she had to say. They drove in silence for a while, as much silence as the ol' Bird would allow.

"She really thinks the world of that dog, doesn't she?" Mrs. Shams asked, after they had driven quietly for about five minutes.

"You got that right. I could never be with her, anyway. She's more interested in that goddamn dog of hers than she is any man, or human for that matter."

Mrs. Shams didn't respond. She had a knack of knowing just what to say to get Malcolm going.

"My ex-wife was a lot like Jenny, and I'm here to tell you that they treat their goddamn dogs like humans and their humans like dogs," he said in a pissed off tone, reminiscing on his failed marriage, or whatever it had been. During the remainder of the drive home they talked about dogs, and Malcolm thought about a few of the bitches he'd encountered over the years.

* * * * *

Later that afternoon, Malcolm took off on a drive with no destination, and then remembered that Gerald was in town, lone-wolfing it. He stopped by so that Gerald could have a drink for them both. Gerald started a pot of coffee when Malcolm arrived and then showed him some of the new pieces of art he'd acquired over the past few months. The house was filled with paintings. Most of them Malcolm remembered, but Gerald did have a few new pieces in the living room. He gave Malcolm a brief history of the new work before walking back into the kitchen to pour coffee.

"Is that new?" Malcolm asked, pointing to a painting that covered most of the narrow north wall of the kitchen.

"You haven't seen that?" he asked, as he reached in the

cupboard for mugs.

"No, I sure haven't," Malcolm answered, trying to make something out of the huge abstract. It was an oil on canvas, three feet wide and four feet in length.

"Some crazy old bitch did that," Gerald said, setting the cups down next to the coffee pot. Malcolm was surprised that Gerald was going to have coffee. He normally would have poured himself a drink.

"What do you mean by crazy?" Malcolm asked, wanting to compare his own definition of insanity to Gerald's. The piece was mostly full of dark colors with some deep reds dominating the lower quarter of the painting.

"I don't know. The guy I bought it from just said that she was crazy," Gerald answered, as he poured the coffees. "Actually, he said she was a mean old bitch."

They took their mugs into the living room and sat down. There were a few art books on the shelf in the corner of the room. Malcolm went over and picked one up.

"I think there might be a picture of a Diebenkorn painting in this book," Gerald said, moving from his chair and sitting next to Malcolm on the couch to help him find what he was referring to.

"Is it an abstract?"

"No, well, he did some abstract work but mostly figurative," Gerald answered, taking the book from Malcolm to find an example.

Malcolm looked around the room while Gerald paged through the book. He thought about the woman who Gerald called a crazy old bitch and then about how crazy had turned into mean.

"Here it is," he said, handing Malcolm the book and then pointing to the Diebenkorn landscape. It had nice colors but was boring. Malcolm looked at it for a minute and then turned the page.

"Who in the hell did this?" Malcolm asked excitedly. There was a figurative study of an attractive woman lying on her bed with a young boy rising over her, up on his knees and holding a knife in his raised hand as if he was going to come down and stab the woman. The woman was just lying there, appearing to be content and unalarmed.

"Oh, that's by a guy who lives in London. Hassel Smith, he's ninety-six-years-old or something like that. I could probably get that painting. My collector buddy owes me one. Actually he owes me eleven grand, and I think he has this piece."

"Is that how much it would cost you?"

"I'd probably have to come up with another four. It has some really good colors, doesn't it?"

"Buy it Gerald," Malcolm said, wishing he had the resources to buy it for himself. "Don't fuck around and let it get away from you either," Malcolm added.

"You think so?" he asked, somewhat surprised with Malcolm's strong reaction to the painting.

"If I had the money, I would. I wouldn't give it a second thought if I was working. Look, I don't know a damn thing about art, but I damn sure know what I see here."

"And what's that?"

"It's archetypal, Gerald. It's the boy slaying his mother. I'll bet money that this was the turning point in this artist's career," Malcolm explained.

"What do you mean?"

"I mean he's painted what your own boy's up against right now. Trying to slay his own inner mother, that's what's really running him still. That's what he's doing in this painting. Psychologically he's slaying his own inner mother complex so that he can rescue his own inner feminine counterpart. I'll bet his art changed forever after he painted this piece."

"Alright, I'll call my buddy tomorrow and tell him that my friend Malcolm says that I need to take a closer look at this piece. But, tell me why you think this painting might have had such an influence on his art."

"The painting is a symbolic slaying of the dragon and rescuing of the princess."

"Where in the hell do you see that here?" he asked, looking as if he had missed something.

"He's painted the battle that was being waged within him; a battle against his own inner mother."

"Well, where in the hell is this princess?"

"He already has her inside of him. She's a part of him that's been held captive for years."

"She?"

"Yeah, the inner feminine part of a man's soul, like feelings, intuition, anything that's non-patriarchal. By slaying his mother complex, he rescued his own inner feminine; he could then nurture her and allow her to blossom. I'd be damn interested to see this Hassel Smith's work once this huge psychological shift took place."

"Okay, I'll check into it if you say so," Gerald said, more to get Malcolm to shut up than anything else.

"I'm telling you Gerald, if that painting's still available you can probably make yourself a damn good chunk of change."

Chapter 32

After returning from Gerald's the previous evening, Malcolm phoned Jenny and asked her to consider joining him for a movie the following day. He just asked her to think about it, knowing that she was incapable of making a decision on the spot. She'd been that way ever since he'd met her, but the whole damn cleanse thing that included, but wasn't limited to, taking herbs every so often between meals and all the other bullshit had caused her already narcissistic existence to escalate to an even higher plane of self-centeredness.

Anyway, the call was to plant the seed in hopes that it would eventually sprout into a date. Malcolm figured that the advance notice might provide the opportunity to schedule her eating and shitting habits around a two-hour trip to the theater.

Kerri the kayaker had called around nine to see if he'd like to meet for coffee; the answering machine took the message. Malcolm never returned Kerri's call, deciding to save it as an excuse to call later if the Jenny thing didn't work out.

He headed to the Pink House, figuring that the odds of bumping into Jenny were above average. While standing in line for his cup of joe, he spotted her sitting in the back room talking to a girlfriend. By the time he'd creamed and sugared his coffee, she was preparing to leave, gathering up her goods and stuffing them into her daily organizer.

"Oh, hi Malcolm," Jenny said, as if she just realized that he was there.

"Good morning," he replied, looking right into her eyes.

"I still can't make up my mind about renting that other place," she announced, appearing to be almost distraught.

He looked at her and giggled without answering. He knew what it was like to be divided and unable to make a decision. For his entire life, up to the age of thirty-seven, he'd been able to make on-the-spot, snap-decisions that had huge impacts on his own, as well as other people's lives. More often than not they proved to be successful, but at thirty-seven something had shifted. He could hardly make a decision about much of anything, and if he did, he'd often end up changing it ten minutes later.

"Where's Diana?" Malcolm asked.

"Oh, she's at the beach with one of my friends."

"That's nice."

"I have to go to the bathroom," Jenny announced, as if she'd just had an epiphany.

Malcolm had brought along a book for cover. He put it on the counter behind the espresso machine, and then sat on the barstool. He was about to tell her she could leave her stuff and he'd watch over it, but she had already decided to do so without his invitation, setting her organizer down on top of his book.

The organizer was another thing about Jenny that at times made Malcolm laugh, and at other times drove him crazy. Organization was just another one of society's impositions to make all of time commercially productive. The organizational industry flourished by appealing to people with chaotic personalities.

These businesses thrived simply by promising to bring people order and contentment just by purchasing organizational tools like day planners and palm pilots. These tools were just alternatives to people using their own minds and intuitions. Using organizers precluded having to think for one's self. Just fill in a time slot and let the book be the final say, robbing one of the freedom and flexibility to adapt to what life offered in the moment.

Jenny came walking back up to the counter to find Malcolm reading. "I just don't know what to do," she announced, as he closed the book.

"I do," he answered. "Go to the show with me and let your mind rest. You'll probably walk out of the theater and be real clear about what you need to do."

She just sighed. "Then I have to pick a show, and I don't have the reviews to help me make a decision about what I'd like to see."

"Who cares what we see," he answered. "Let's just go and see what's playing without making it a big deal."

Jenny pulled a newspaper from the rack that was below the cream and sugar and sat down beside Malcolm to study the movie reviews.

"I'm going to sit outside at the perch," he told her and left. Besides Jenny, the noise from the espresso machine, as well as other distractions inside the old Victorian home, were irritating Malcolm.

Jenny walked up to the perch a minute or so later. "I need the other paper to decide," she informed. "And I want to go garage sale-ing for awhile."

"Okay, have fun," he said, hugging her and off she went. She had tight jeans on and Malcolm was able to catch a good shot of her ass as she waddled off on her mission. She was a scattered mess.

"I'll call you after a while," she said, after having crossed the street. "Do you have your cellular phone with you?"

Malcolm smiled and nodded. "I'll be here for a couple of hours reading." And reading is what he did for the next few hours. Reading and watching the stray feminine latte drinkers ascend and descend the steps of the old Victorian.

There was a demon-possessed dog inside a car parked in front of the Pink House who ravenously barked at people when they walked by. After the dog scared the living shit out of about the third person who walked past, a really hot-looking blonde woman with a southern accent decided it was reason enough to make conversation about the out-of-control canine. She said something to Malcolm about how the dog would only bark at certain people. He'd seen this woman on several different occasions, but this was her first invitation for the two of them to interact. Right then Jenny drove up. Malcolm smiled and said something to acknowledge the blonde, but before he knew it, Jenny was sitting next to him with Diana, and his encounter with the blonde fizzled back to the same silence he'd shared with her on their previous sits out on the patio.

"Go garage sale-ing?"

"Yeah, and I didn't think…" she said, as she opened up a different newspaper to the movie reviews.

"You know, the woman who writes these reviews was in class with me last semester. She told me she hardly ever watches the films. Just uses other people's opinions to write her critique," Malcolm said, and knew that he had slipped up as soon as he opened his mouth. She was looking for someone to tell her what she should see, and he'd robbed her of the very thing that was helping her to make a decision. "Why don't you just let me pick a movie," he suggested as she shuffled through the paper.

"What?"

"Why don't you quit worrying? Let me choose a movie and you just relax. Let me take care of you for a while. You don't have to worry about a thing."

"Why would I do that?" she asked, staring at Malcolm with an absurd look. It was hard to tell if she was being comical or serious. "I'm hungry, and I can't think right now," she added.

"Why don't you eat something?" he suggested, fed up with the whole fast thing. He couldn't figure out what in the world she was trying to shit away and then came to the conclusion that it must have been a metaphoric turd that she couldn't quite void.

"I have to take my herbs first and then wait for another hour before I can eat."

"Well, fuck! It seems to me that if you're hungry, you should eat."

"I have to go. I can't go to the show today. I have to go eat," she said, rising from the stool and pulling her crept up Levis down from her thighs.

* * * * *

Jenny phoned later that evening to tell Malcolm she had decided to rent the cabin in Cachagua. She thanked him for trying to settle her mind by offering to take her to the movies. After a short visit, he said goodnight, and headed to Tillie Gort's for dinner.

A dark haired fellow in his early forties came in and sat at the counter. His hair was cut short and he had a mustache. He was in excellent physical shape, looked as if he might have been a contractor or in construction. He ordered dinner and requested a glass of water with lemon. Then he went outside with his cellular phone to make a call and returned a few minutes later. He appeared to be of the nervous sort.

He made a comment to Chloe about how he'd been to the

Big Sur Jade festival and had come back to Monterey around four-thirty that afternoon.

"What was the traffic like?" Malcolm asked, curious if he got stuck in the jam that often backed up for miles south of Rio Road on Highway 1 at that time of the day.

"It wasn't bad," he answered in an uninviting tone.

Malcolm decided to keep to himself and respect the guy's privacy. Chloe kept walking by the counter trying to get things in order so that she could close at a reasonable hour. They made small talk about school whenever she passed by Malcolm. The cook set the guy's food up in the window and Lena, the other waitress, served him.

"Are you the husband of the woman who runs this place?" the guy finally asked Malcolm, noticing all the attention he was getting from Chloe.

"I'm not anybody's husband," Malcolm answered. "I was married once, but she didn't even call me her husband. She called me a hell of a lot of other things but husband wasn't one of them," Malcolm explained, swiveling his stool a little to the right so that he was looking at the man.

"Yeah, I've been a husband once, too," he said, in a more receptive tone. "I lived with her for eighteen years. Then I had to go and marry her. Three years later and that was it."

"Funny how that piece of paper can foul up a nice relationship, isn't it?" Malcolm asked, pouring more tea into his cup from the teapot.

"Man, you're not kiddin'," answered the stranger as he filled his tortilla with whatever he had ordered. "I lived with her for eighteen years; then married her," He repeated. "Funny thing is, I really didn't even want to marry her. Three years later, everything went to hell. I was stupid. She was the mother of my kids, though."

"It's that whole belief about what a husband and a wife are supposed to be that fucks it up."

"Hell, as soon as I married her she quit doing my laundry."

"That sounds about right," Malcolm laughed. "I always took my laundry out to have done until we got married. My ex did it for about half a year and then I was doing it myself. The laundry lasted longer than the sex though. It was cheaper to divorce her and to hire my laundry out again. I get laid a lot more now, too."

"Yeah, no shit. Well, I went out and got tied up with another one," he said, turning to see if Chloe or Lena were around. "And the sex was hotter than hell," he whispered after he saw that they were alone.

"Oh, yeah," Malcolm laughed, thinking about how he'd been hooked that way a time or two.

"I fell in love with her. She moved in with me, and I even asked her to marry me. But she moved out. She's drinking, and I'm an alcoholic. I mean, I don't drink anymore, but I could tell that she was."

"Huh," Malcolm grunted, just to acknowledge that he was listening. "How old is she?"

"Forty, but she's never been married. She had this dope dealer come and help her move out. I think she's fooling around with him. I went to her apartment one day when she wasn't expecting me. I rang the doorbell, but nobody answered. I looked in the window, and found him hiding, crouched down on the side of the couch."

"What does she do?" Malcolm asked, hoping she wasn't someone who he'd been pursuing.

"She's a nurse; works at some convalescent home."

"Shit! She's probably thieving meds," Malcolm said. With his mother being a nurse, he was familiar with the stories of nurses and doctors who were addicts and stole medication from the hospitals.

"She was on probation for something," he said, naively.

"If she's on probation, it was probably for stealing meds, and if she's not stealing the shit now, you can bet she's drinking and getting stuff from somewhere else," Malcolm reassured him. "Why you fucking around with her, anyway?" he asked.

He looked at Malcolm as if he'd just been slapped in the face.

"Look, I know this is none of my business, but she sounds like fucking poison to me."

"Yeah, but I fell in love with her. I mean the sex is so good. I was so in love with her that I couldn't see the signs."

"Yeah, and then you feel like a fool afterwards for not seeing what everyone else could see."

"I should have known. You know, in the whole six months she never called me by my name. She called me weirdo or pervert. Stuff like that. It was like she was teasing, but now I can see how I wasn't really a person to her."

"Your mind's working on you, man," Malcolm said. It was, too. He felt damn bad for this guy. He was the voice of humanity wanting to love blindly and see only the light side of the human condition. Hell, Malcolm wanted to believe in that, too, but he was finally coming to terms with how people treated each other to their faces, even behind the pretense of respect, meant very little. Yes, respect was important, but when denial was running so deep, as it was with this man, she could have been pissing in his ear and he'd have called it love.

"I just wish that I could quit thinking about her. I was fine most of the day until I drove back into town."

"Yeah, and then you smelled that perfume."

"I didn't go see her."

"I mean your thinking about her was like drinking for you, man."

"I'm obsessed. You're right: it's an addiction."

"You just might have to be alone for a while. I mean, it might hurt like hell, but you might have to be alone for a while and move through this so you can come out with a new way of seeing things."

"Yeah, I think you're right."

"I mean, until you can get past this shit, you won't be open to let something good come into your life."

"Yeah, and women can tell. It's like you have *desperate* tattooed on your forehead."

"I know. It comes and goes."

"When I was married I had all kinds of women hitting on me. I guess they thought I was safe or something. You know, they could have a little fling without getting attached," he explained.

"Hey, I like that idea. Think I'll have a wedding ring made," Malcolm teased.

"Hell, yeah," he smiled. "You can probably pick one up real cheap somewhere," he added.

"My buddy's a jeweler. He's probably got a band from some divorced guy who traded it in to buy his new bride a diamond," Malcolm laughed.

"From now on, I think I'll just use this gal for sex," he said, hopping back onto the merry-go-round that was whirling around in his head. "You know, without being attached."

"Good luck. Whenever I've been like you are over a woman, there was no way in hell I could go back to her just for sex. Believe me, I've tried. It fucking hurts!"

"Yeah, you're right. Sounds like you know about this stuff."

"It's fucking poison man, and you don't need that shit."

"How did you figure all this stuff out?"

"I haven't got anything figured out, but I've been on this ride a couple of times."

"Yeah, and if I don't get off, I'll end up in jail for stalking her."

"You dreamed her up," Malcolm said, testing his reaction, wanting to tell the guy that he was already in jail.

"What do you mean?"

"I mean you dreamed her up to teach you something. If you don't figure it out, you'll dream up another one and go through it all over again. I'm telling you, it's like a fucking drink."

"I got you, man. My negative shit brought her into my life."

"That's right," Malcolm answered, impressed that he was understood. He understood in words or concept anyway. "So, now, how do you step off that merry-go-round, out of that old dream?"

"I don't know, man. What do you do?"

"Fuck, I don't know. That's why I'm asking you," Malcolm answered.

Occasionally, Malcolm had mastered stepping back and taking an objective view of himself and the dramas that captured him, but his humanity had a way of drawing him back into life's illusions. Besides, he didn't know if he really wanted to escape them completely; it was the very sort of thing that spiced up life. But this man was really suffering, and Malcolm's answers wouldn't work for him. Like Malcolm, he had to find his own way.

"I've just got to step back and be alone for a while. I have to go through this shit I guess," the stranger answered. "Hell, they're only feelings," he added.

"Yeah, but that doesn't make it any easier," Malcolm said, knowing that some suffering lay ahead for this man.

He might have dreamed this woman into his life, but, for some reason, Malcolm had dreamed him into his life. He reminded Malcolm where he'd once been. For years Malcolm had recycled his obsession with Lauren, the woman he fell in love with after his divorce. As much as he hated to admit it, in some ways, it was also how he related to Jenny. Neither Lauren nor Jenny were druggies or sex addicts, but they both had a way of getting Malcolm to hop onto that merry-go-round in his head and ride it for days, if not years at a time. Lauren had had him on it for years, but with Jenny he was going to pull the brass ring early.

"My name's Max," he said, extending his hand to Malcolm.

"I'm Malcolm," he said, standing up and shaking Max's hand.

"Maybe next time I run into you, I won't be so screwed up, man."

"Just remember one thing. That shit's fucking poison," Malcolm whispered, as he walked behind Max towards the register.

"Do you know what resentment is?" Max asked, as Chloe rang Malcolm up.

"No, what?"

"You drinking poison and waiting for someone else to die."

Chapter 33

Sheila phoned. She and Andy had split up and she was on a downer, so Malcolm threw a bag together and headed for Big Sur. He stopped to see if Sarina was at the shop. He parked behind the building and snuck in through the back door. No one was inside, so Malcolm walked through the shop and found Sarina twenty feet in front of the entrance with her back to him, talking to her ex. She was oozing with attitude. Her arms were flying around like a fired up Italian woman. Sarina's ex spotted him first and she followed his gaze around to find Malcolm standing behind her in the entrance of the shop. She looked at him with an odd look, as if he had magically materialized on the threshold of her doorway.

"Where'd you come from?" Sarina asked.

"Travis said he ran into you the other day," Malcolm said, leaving his arrival a mystery.

"Yeah, I confronted him about that being under thirty crap."

"How'd that go?"

"He just made up some excuse saying I took it the wrong way."

"Well, I'm glad you got that all cleared up."

"Well, I wouldn't exactly say that it's cleared up. I don't think he really heard me, but I didn't feel like talking to him about it anymore," Sarina said, as she went inside to answer the phone.

Malcolm walked over to a wooden bench that was just outside the shop. Travis made it sound like it had all been resolved, but with Sarina it was more like she just didn't want to argue anymore because he wasn't going to get it anyway.

While he sat on the bench soaking up the sun, two of Sarina's girlfriends, Louise and Angie, showed up. He made small talk with the two girls while Sarina closed up shop. Then the girls all pranced off to a kitty cat party: a 'She' kitty cat party where Tomcats weren't allowed.

Malcolm drove to the girls' cabin. He made himself

comfortable and read a few chapters from L. Powy's *Love and Death*. He was having a hard time getting into the book so he walked up to Nepenthe and sat at the bar to have a fake beer. Sarina's step-grandmother was the hostess for the evening. Malcolm always looked forward to seeing Laine in costume; she was wearing a black and white zebra outfit.

He sat at the bar for a couple of hours. A pair of dykes came and sat next to him. Malcolm tried to make small talk with one of them, but she wasn't open, so he ignored her for the rest of his stay.

Sheila was real bitchy, probably ragging on top of the breakup. Things just weren't flowing very well for her that night. She had big tables with big parties and crying babies. After things had slowed down, Malcolm went and sat outside for Sheila to wait on him. He ordered the smoked trout appetizer, a salad with vinaigrette and blue cheese, and a baked potato. Sheila surprised him with a scoop of chocolate ice cream for desert.

Things had slowed down considerably. Sheila had been phased out for the evening and had gone inside to finish the last of her duties. Sarina came bouncing up the steps and spotted Malcolm sitting at the table.

"Dude, I'm so excited, but I've got to catch my breath," she said, panting and holding her hands to her heart.

Malcolm didn't respond, because he wasn't sure if he should. Sarina stood for a minute trying to catch up to herself and then sat down across the table from Malcolm.

"I got a call from this guy in New York. He wants me to come out for an audition," she announced, still out of breath.

"How'd he hear about you?"

"He was out here a few months ago for the Big Sur poetry slam. That's where we met."

"All the way from New York for a poetry slam in Big Sur?" Malcolm questioned.

"He didn't come out here for that, but yeah, that's how I met him. He heard me doing my thing and he came up after the slam," she explained. Sarina was good. Malcolm recalled the night out on the deck of her cabin when Travis had shown up. She had certainly hooked Malcolm with her hip-hop stuff. He was no expert but knew she had talent, perhaps even enough to escape from her environment. Big Sur was beautiful, and so were the people who lived there, but it was time for Sarina to leave her childhood home to gain some perspective.

"Anyway, he called and wants to fly me out to New York. Said he'll pay for the ticket."

"When are you going?"

"He wants me there in a couple of weeks. Then, if things work out, he wants me back again the following month for another shoot."

"Congratulations," Malcolm said, genuinely happy for her.

"You're the first one to hear about this," she said excitedly, but another part of her was still cautious or nervous. She looked around as if to see if anyone else had been listening. "You really are the first person I've told," she repeated, after having confirmed their privacy. "I mean, I just saw you sitting here. I spotted you right away and you're the perfect listener."

Malcolm didn't respond with any words. He appreciated her compliment, but doubted her sincerity at the same time. He doubted anyone's compliments, considered most to be subtle manipulative attempts, hooks for his ego to hang a hat on.

"Problem is that it interferes with the Europe trip Sheila and I planned. I can still go, but now I'll have to cut it short. Sheila's gonna be pissed. She says that her friends always flake out on her like this," she explained, her excited caution beginning to make sense.

"Sheila might be bummed, but she'll understand. She knows how important this is for you," Malcolm reassured, certain Sheila would want Sarina to realize her dream. "Besides, this might be your big chance. You've got to go for it," he said, before taking a drink of water.

"I know, but I just don't know how to break it to her," Sarina said nervously, as she stood up. "I'll be back, and don't say anything to Sheila."

Malcolm nodded his head to let her know that he'd leave the drama to the two of them. Sarina went inside the restaurant, and Laine walked out with a salad and a plate of grilled fish and sat down next to Malcolm.

"Do zebras eat meat?" she asked, with a growing smile.

"Only fish," he answered, and started belly laughing.

"What's so funny?" Sarina asked, as she came back to the table.

"Oh, nothing," Malcolm answered, not wanting to explain. She was too damn nervous to hear him anyway.

Sheila came out with a salad and set it down on their table. "How was dinner?" she asked.

"Who? Me?" Sarina asked in a panicky tone.

"Yeah you. Who else?" Sheila asked.

"It was okay," Sarina answered. "We had cheese and stuff. I almost invited Malcolm to join us, but…"

"But I'm a *he*, and it was a *she* gathering," Malcolm interrupted, to save her the need to explain.

"I'm going for a glass of wine. Anyone else want something?" Sheila asked, as she scooted her chair back to stand up.

"I'd like some more water," Malcolm said, just before Sheila left to go inside. Laine pulled out a pack of cigarettes. Knowing that Sheila didn't like smoke, she moved to a table behind them where Debbie sat waiting for Sean to be phased.

"This is great, you get to watch me squirm," Sarina laughed nervously.

"Yeah, like you freaked out when she asked how dinner was. 'Who? Me?'" Malcolm teased.

"It wouldn't be so bad, but we just talked about how her friends always make plans and then back out," Sarina said, nervously shifting in her seat as Sheila came back with a glass of wine and a pitcher of water.

"Sheila, I got the call. I'm going to New York."

"He called?" Sheila asked in a surprised tone. "That's great Sarina!"

"Yeah, he said he was going to book my flight."

"When are you going?" Sheila asked, as a short chubby woman and two young girls walked out of the restaurant.

The chubby gal spotted Laine, and her excitement interrupted the drama that was unfolding at Malcolm's table. The fat lady started singing, thrilled to have spotted the zebra. Sheila and Sarina stopped their discussion, their attention shifting to Laine and Chubs.

"We're headed back to camp," the woman announced.

"Well, have a nice evening," Laine said, in a cordial hostess tone. "I hope you enjoyed your dinner," she added.

"Oh, it was wonderful, as always," Chubs rattled manically. "We're staying at site twenty-five. It's one of our favorites!"

It would be hell hanging around Chubs when she slid into a depression, Malcolm thought to himself.

"What's your favorite campsite?" Chubs asked Laine.

"I really like forty-nine and twenty-five," Laine answered, faking a smile.

"What about sixty-nine? Have you tried that one?" the woman asked innocently.

"I think she's been there a few times," Sheila reactively quipped. Malcolm's table burst into a laughter that they all tried to suppress, hoping that the woman hadn't actually heard Sheila's remark.

"So now, when are you going to New York?" Sheila asked Sarina, shifting away from the campsite conversation.

"Probably within the next couple of weeks," Sarina answered in a less than excited tone.

"That's great! Aren't you excited?" Sheila asked, sensing Sarina's hesitation.

"Oh, yeah, if things work out, he said he wants me back the following month," Sarina continued with her confession.

"What about Europe?" Sheila asked.

"Well, he wants me there at the end of the month, so I think Europe will still work."

"Well, I don't see how that's going to work. I mean, I understand how important this is. You have to do it, but..."

"Yeah, but I'm still going to Europe with you like we planned. I just might have to cut the trip by a couple of weeks and fly back to New York."

"And leave me in Europe by myself?" Sheila asked, Laine still captured in the campsite number sixty-nine reverie.

"Either that, or you could come with me to New York."

"I don't know about that," Sheila answered in a disappointed tone. "We'll talk about it later."

"I'm still going to Europe with you Sheila. I'm not going to flake out on you. I'll just have to cut it short by a week or ten days," Sarina explained.

"Let's see what happens. We can talk later," Sheila answered, holding back her anger and disappointment.

The fat lady finally finished her song and left. Laine looked over to Malcolm's table with her tongue sticking out of her mouth and her eyes rolled cross-eyed. "What the fuck do I look like, the camp director or something?" she asked, before lighting up a smoke.

After she finished her cigarette, Laine came over to Malcolm's table. She was leaving and wanted Sarina to walk her to the parking lot. Some guy had supposedly been stalking Laine, probably one of the locals with a zebra fetish. Actually, it was probably more of an excuse to go back to the cabin to get high.

"Yeah, I'll walk with you," Sarina volunteered. "That way I can leave Sheila here with Malcolm so she can talk shit about me."

Malcolm sat with Sheila for a while after the Zebra and the Panther had left. They talked about the Europe thing for a bit and then he told her about his encounter a few days earlier at the Pink House with Mrs. Shams, Jenny and Waylen.

"Anything new on the Jenny front?"

"I'm not getting laid, if that's what you're asking."

"Good. She's not right for you anyway. What about Kate?"

"Who knows?"

Sheila was right. Jenny wasn't the right one for Malcolm. He was beginning to wonder if the right one even existed. Sheila was getting restless and was ready to move, so they walked down to the cabin. The lights were on.

"Maybe you could go to Europe later," Malcolm suggested, as they walked through the gate.

"I'm so fucking pissed I don't even want to talk about it right now."

"But really, you could just reschedule the trip."

"No. No. Really, you don't understand. I don't even want to talk about it right now. My life was already shitty enough without this."

Malcolm shut up as they walked up to the cabin door. Sarina and Laine were both inside. Once again, they were badmouthing Laine's husband, Sarina's Grandfather. They had actually been talking about the discussion Sarina and Sheila had just had up at the restaurant, but had shifted over to grandpa bashing when Malcolm and Sheila walked in.

Sheila switched back to her upbeat positive tone to hide what she was really feeling. Malcolm sat down and breathed in the dopey smoke remnants. Sheila went to the toilet.

"You guys want me to model my new outfits?" Sheila asked when she stepped out of the bathroom. She'd been shopping the day before, which was what she usually did when she was down.

"Sure," Sarina answered in a stoned tone.

While Malcolm sat with the other women awaiting Sheila's impending show, Laine handed him a lingerie magazine filled with women modeling thong underwear. She pointed out one specific model with beaded tassels hanging from her backside, while Sarina spouted off about her New York deal.

Sheila walked out with her first outfit. Nice tight pants and a backless top; the backless top being the in-thing to have.

"When are they coming out with a frontless top?" Malcolm quipped.

"Very funny," Sheila said on her way to change into another outfit. She was having fun but was still pissed.

There sat Malcolm, once again in the middle of another feminine powwow. "Maybe we shouldn't be doing all of this girl stuff around Malcolm," Laine said, with a great big smile.

"You know, I grew up in a family of four boys, then I sold tractors for the last eighteen years and all I had for company was a bunch dirt farmers," Malcolm answered, without getting a response. "But, for the last year and a half I've been mostly hanging around women, and I love it. You wouldn't believe the shit I've been learning. Well, maybe you would," he laughed, the women looking at him as if he was nuts, or so he thought.

"You know you love all this woman shit," Sheila teased.

"So," he said with raised eyebrows.

"It's cool. There's nothing wrong with it," Sheila said, settling into the couch next to Sarina.

"I just wish you'd quit comparing me to your friend Bob who's always after the young chicks."

"Well, you are."

"Yeah, but he's fifteen years older than me. It pisses me off that you put me in his league."

"Oh, get over it," Sheila teased.

"You whore," Sarina said to Laine, responding to something that had been said while Malcolm was carrying on with Sheila.

Laine laughed.

"I just wanted to say that because no one else can get away with calling their grandmother a whore," Sarina proudly announced, her shoulders alternately dancing up and down, wiggling her head and grinning.

Laine soon left, and Malcolm retired to the Tahoe. Making his bed, his thoughts went to what he'd said about hanging around with mostly women for the last year. Something had changed since he had started befriending women; he wasn't getting laid nearly as often as before, and he just didn't get it. It wasn't that he didn't have women in his past life, but it had been different. In the past, he'd never just hang out with a woman for the sake of hanging out; he'd hang out hoping...

He crawled into his sleeping bag and looked out of the window towards the cabin. He could see Sheila's silhouette through her bedroom window. It looked as if she might be reading. She was lying on her stomach moving around restlessly, probably cramping, upset about her breakup with Andy, and pissed that her European trip had been shammed. Overhead, a star fell.

Chapter 34

"Did I tell you about the time he showed up with his toes painted green?"

"Maybe," Malcolm answered. She had told him the story several times before, but he was unable to recall the details, just as he was unable to remember most of the particulars she felt compelled to bore him with time and time again.

"Yeah, he came by to pay his alimony wearing Birkenstocks and his toes were painted green. I just looked at him and wondered why had I ever married this idiot?"

"Uh," Malcolm grunted. Anything more than a grunt was an invitation for her to ask just another one of her infinitely thoughtless questions that spewed from her like shit out of the ass-end of a well-fed dairy cow. Most of her unanswerable queries seemed simply the need to have her doubts validated.

"That's when I realized I never really knew him. Should I turn here?" she asked, as they approached Malcolm's street.

He didn't answer, and she turned anyway. She knew where she was. She was half a block from his studio, and Malcolm was half a block from saying good-bye to the inquisition he'd been suffering ever since she'd arrived.

Shortly after her arrival on the previous day, they had a mid-afternoon lunch and then returned to his place. She'd come to town to buy a new purse at one of the local shops in Carmel. Knowing that she seldom made it over this way, Malcolm suggested she continue shopping and they could meet up later, but she decided to return with him to the studio. She was the friend of a friend who divorced about a year after Malcolm had. They'd hung out for a while, and ended up in bed a few times. That was until she started whining and trying to make Malcolm into something or someone he had no intention of becoming: a manipulated, emasculated, puppet-of-a-man who dangled from her strings.

So, they came back to Malcolm's place after lunch and lay around for a few hours while she asked questions often left unanswered. She was on the couch, and he was lying on the bed. It amazed Malcolm how she'd ask him some flippant, meaningless question, for which he had no answer, and before he had time to respond, she'd fire off another. The questions seemed like target-less shots randomly fired from a machine gun into the night, to keep a predator, real or imagined, at bay.

It wasn't her fault; Elena was Elena. She just didn't fit into Malcolm's world that weekend. He'd spent the entire previous week around people, having volunteered to man the booth at a farm machinery trade show in the Valley for a friend. Every night that week, after working the show, Malcolm had dinner with old colleagues and business constituents and then stayed the night with his parents, enjoying their company as well. Someone he saw at the show must have run into Elena and said something about seeing Malcolm, because she phoned out of the blue saying that she was coming to Carmel for the weekend.

Malcolm hadn't heard from Elena since that last Christmas holiday when he had returned home and run into her at an open house that an old client of his threw every year. She spotted him sitting in the corner of the kitchen where he was catching up with some old friends. She whispered something to her date, and left the guy standing alone and walked over to give Malcolm a hug, and a hard-on.

"You're looking hot!" Malcolm whispered into her ear as they embraced, her date watching them from a distance.

"Thanks, you're looking pretty good yourself," she whispered back. "If I remember right, you've got a birthday coming up."

"Quite a good memory."

"Some things are hard to forget. Have plans?"

"Yeah, I'm having dinner with a friend that evening," Malcolm answered, testing her reaction. He had dinner plans with Kate, a beautiful young woman whose pants he'd dreamed of invading for the past couple of years. Unfortunately, at the time, his dream had yet to be realized.

"Well, how about lunch then?"

"Sure, that'll work," he answered, thinking about having his birthday cake and eating it, too.

And it all came to pass: they met for lunch, and Malcolm ended up rolling out of her bed at six-thirty that evening. He hurried over to his youngest brother's apartment to shower off the remnants of their meal. He was only half-an-hour late picking up his lovely dream-puff, Kate, who, needless to say, took him out for dinner, but at that time, left the physical act of their love-making to the ethereal realms of Malcolm's imagination.

Thanks to Elena, the resurrection of his erection came to pass. Malcolm turned a year older that day, got his brains fucked out, what little he had, by Elena for lunch, and then, that evening, basked in the delight of who he was wishing would pop out of his birthday cake and be his happily-ever-after. It all worked out just fine, almost as if he'd planned the whole thing, with the exception of having his way with Kate, but eventually, that dream came true, too.

That was a few months before Kate and Malcolm really took off. He certainly didn't have a problem with the blood flow to his pelvis. It was more like, what's the use of it all? For years Malcolm had women running out of his ears; getting laid had become like eating the same meal at the same restaurant day after day, week after week, month after month, and year after year. It had become tasteless and left him feeling empty.

At one time in his life, he had met a woman who he believed he'd never grow tired of, but, for some reason, he left her, and, in reflection, it was just another over-the-rainbow lie he was singing to himself. Several years later Malcolm met another woman who provoked similar feelings of something deeper and beyond the physical. At long last, he thought he'd found his pot of gold; but their encounter was short-lived. This time, she ran, and once again he found himself chasing echoes. Now he was stuck in this purgatory, waiting and wondering what was to become of him and Kate.

For a man who had left that old life behind and moved into what consisted mostly of reclusive solitude, a week full of eighteen-hour days, communing with friends and clients and very little sleep had taken its toll. It had all been necessary, but Malcolm was approaching the meltdown stage. Anyway, that's how Elena came back into the picture, and now she had come to buy a purse and pay Malcolm a visit. And Kate… well, she was back east nursing a grieving mother, or so she claimed.

Between the barrages of machine gun fire, Elena managed to slip from the safety of the couch where she'd taken refuge and joined Malcolm on the bed. He rubbed her back and neck for a while and then told her to roll over so that he could do her front side, but she developed a timely bellyache and excused herself to the bathroom, defining her visit as non-conjugal. When Elena came out of the bathroom she sat on the couch, and began to talk about herself and a girlfriend, about all the different men they'd been dating.

"Did I tell you about that one guy I dated who had E.D.?"

"E.D.?" Malcolm asked.

"Erectile dysfunction," she translated, as if she was an expert in the field. "He was mushy anyway."

"Mushy?"

"Yeah, you know, too emotional."

"No, I don't know," Malcolm answered, glancing over to see the expression on Elena's face. He was confused, because it seemed that most of the pissing and moaning she'd done around him over the years had been all about men who were emotionally unavailable and unable to commit.

"He was so needy. One time he told me that his lips were dry, hinting for me to give him a kiss. I told him, look, if you want to kiss me, kiss me, but don't come off with this my lips are dry crap," she rattled on in a self-righteous tone, staring up towards the ceiling with a wrinkled up forehead full of disdain for the guy.

"What were you hanging out with that queer fucker for, anyway?" Malcolm asked.

"I'm a queer fucker magnet," she answered, without giving it two seconds thought.

Malcolm didn't respond but wondered what that made him, not that he really cared. Well, he cared, but not so much how she viewed him; he was more concerned about relieving his hard-on.

The first year after leaving his run-of-the-mill but productive life behind and moving to the Peninsula, several of his loves came a-calling. It was a novelty, having a man to visit in Carmel, but the novelty soon wore off, as they were more interested in having a guy who was available to them for more than a weekend full of frolicking and fine dining at Carmel-by-the-Sea.

Anyway, it was the following morning. Malcolm and Elena had gone out for breakfast. She had just dropped him off at the studio before driving home alone with her new handbag and her old bellyache. So, after a week filled with a life out of his past, Malcolm was finally able to sit with himself in solitude. Well, he thought he was alone, but there was also 'Her', his magical other, the wife he'd been wedded to since birth, the woman who had faithfully borne the brunt of his infidelities for the past forty years.

* * * * *

He had promised to help Jenny move a few things out to her cabin that afternoon. When he was in the Central Valley, he had picked up a kitchen table from his storage to lend Jenny, and they had made plans to take the loaner and a few of her things out to her cabin around noon. He'd been driving around with the table in the back of the Tahoe for a few days and was feeling cramped; he wanted to get it unloaded. The Cabin was twenty miles east of his studio, but for some reason he knew it was going to turn into an all day affair.

Jenny called about an hour after Elena had left and said she'd be at Malcolm's place around noon. She phoned at noon to say she was running late and that she'd meet him down at a café close to the Barnyard shopping center in an hour. Malcolm decided to go down for coffee while he waited for her. She phoned his mobile at two and said she was just then leaving her house. Malcolm told her that was fine, but he didn't want to get stuck in five o'clock traffic on the way back from delivering her goods. He'd been patient with Jenny, but his patience was growing thin. She showed up an hour later.

"I'm sorry Malcolm. I'm lost. I just can't get it together today."

"You might be lost, but you're a great big pain in the ass, too."

"Are you just now figuring that out?"

"Hell, no! You've been a pain since I met you."

"Oh, you're getting comfortable."

"Yeah, guess so," he answered.

"You ought to try being me sometime," she said, confirming Malcolm's newfound courage to tell her how it was. "It's not all that much fun," she added.

"Believe me, I know."

"I just wish I could quit living this way."

"Good luck," Malcolm answered, looking at what appeared to be a confused little girl. "But I've come to the conclusion that life's just one great big paradox and our suffering is due to a belief in the illusion that we can escape it," he added.

A thought fleetingly crossed his mind that he could possibly fall in love with Jenny. He hadn't, but he was entertaining the possibility. He was hoping that she liked sex, but so far, she had only confirmed the opposite. *There's nothing worse than falling in love with a woman who doesn't like to get nasty,* he thought to himself, hoping that his suspicions about Jenny would prove him wrong.

They transferred Jenny's goods from her car to the Tahoe, and after Malcolm ordered a few things to go from the café's deli, the two started on their drive towards Carmel Valley. Diana sat up on the armrest where she usually liked to ride.

Thirty minutes later they arrived at Jenny's new hideaway. The room had been re-carpeted and thoroughly cleaned. They unloaded the small stuff first and then finished with the kitchen table and chairs. The cabin had barn doors similar to the one's Sarina had at her shop, so it was easy to get the table inside.

"What do you think?" Jenny asked.

"I'm jealous," he answered, but more jealous about the fact that she wasn't sharing herself with him than about her new retreat. It was a great little cabin, set on a hillside, the perfect place for a guy like Malcolm to recluse, write, and… His idea of an ideal situation would have been renting the place, living in it all week long, and Jenny coming to stay with him on weekends. Malcolm was good at dreaming up ideal situations.

The landlord came over and pointed out a few things to Jenny. After she left, Jenny drank one of her magical herb potions and Malcolm ate a late lunch. Actually, it was more of an early dinner than a late lunch, as it was approaching five.

They hung out for a while to let the traffic on Highway 1 and Carmel Valley road clear. At six that evening, they started their trek back towards the mouth of the Valley.

"Thanks for all your help, Malcolm," Jenny said, as they pulled up next to her car.

"No problem," he answered, hoping for an invitation to do something with her that evening. It was weird. She always returned his phone calls, but when it actually came to making plans to be together, she was seldom available. It was like she wanted him in her life, but on her terms and often at a distance. She wanted him around, but she couldn't quite let him in once he arrived. "Are you making another run to the cabin tonight?" he asked.

"No, not tonight, I have to get a few things together. I'll probably go back tomorrow sometime."

"Okay. Well, it was really nice to see you today," Malcolm said, swinging his right knee around onto the seat to face her. "You really seemed to be all here today, even if you do feel lost."

"Really?"

"Yeah," he answered, smiling and petting Diana who was perched up on the armrest that separated the two.

Chapter 35

Tillie Gort's was packed. Lisa handed Malcolm a menu as he sat down at a table in the back room.

"I don't need a menu."

"Well, you're getting it anyway, because I can't take your order right now," Lisa said in a matter of fact tone, then smiled before excusing herself to take an awaiting party's order.

She returned a few minutes later with a glass of water and silverware, ready to take his dinner order.

"I'm waiting for Sheila. I'm meeting her here after class," he explained.

"So you don't want to order right now?"

"No, I'll wait for Sheila," he said, as she closed the order book. He reached for the water, and as he tried to pick it up, his finger caught the edge of the glass and it spilled all over the table and his lap.

"I'm sorry," Lisa apologized, as if she had spilt the water, then hurried off to get a towel.

What Malcolm teasingly was about to tell her before she ran off, was that he'd been secretly in love with her the whole time that he'd been coming into Tillie's, and that he could no longer keep it to himself, and that he spilled the water because of being so shook up over her.

"You're spilling things, and I haven't even told you the news yet. I'm getting married!" Lisa announced when she returned to dry the table.

"Congratulations! I knew there was a reason I was all shook up," he said, easing out of what little embarrassment he was suffering. While Lisa dried the table, Malcolm used a napkin to sop up the water from the thigh of his right pant leg. "Sorry Lisa, I've been in a trance for the last few days."

"That's not a problem," she reassured him, as she finished the chore.

Lisa walked off as the busboy walked up with a new glass of water and a couple of new place settings. Malcolm reached for his glass, this time with some awareness. Then he decided to get a note pad out of the Tahoe. On the way out, he passed the register to let Lisa know that he wasn't flaking on her and that he'd be right back.

When Malcolm returned, he spotted Gene, the bartender from Peppers, perched in a seat at the counter. He had his laptop computer out and was showing off some pictures he'd downloaded from the Internet. Malcolm walked up behind him and caught the image of some naked contortionist who had bent over backwards and appeared to have his head up his ass. Sensing that someone was approaching from behind, Gene quickly closed the file as if he was a young boy about to get caught at the magazine rack googling over a Playboy centerfold.

"Open that back up," Malcolm said, poking him in the back with the edge of his notebook.

"Ouch!" he yelped. Gene loved drama. He had acted in some of the local plays around town, lived his whole life as if he was on stage.

"Hurry up. Open it," Malcolm demanded, as if he had a gun in Geno's back.

"Ouch!" he yelped, as the two guys he'd been showing his photo gallery to looked on. "Okay, okay," Gene, conceded as he opened up the file.

It was a picture of an old, sick looking cat that had been completely shaved of its fur with the exception of its head. Gene's audience got a big kick out of it, but it was really boring. The picture was nothing more than odd, but it was just like Gene to have such a thing in his bag of tricks, and it was just like Gene to be flattering some stranger with such an oddity. Gene was pre-med. A few months earlier, he had taken Chloe to his anatomy lab, reached into this bucket, and pulled out a human head by the hair trying to impress her.

The next picture Gene flashed had two naked women who appeared to be doing it dog style, a necktie hanging loosely around the neck of the woman in the backside position, as if she was a man who had just returned home after a long day at the office. That was enough for Malcolm. He returned to his table.

As Lisa walked by to deliver an order, she noticed Malcolm's note pad. "Are you taking notes?" she asked, as she returned to the kitchen from the dining room.

He smiled. He'd taken the table in the far corner of the back dining room. Tillie's was busy and noisy and that particular table seemed to be the most removed and quietest place in the restaurant.

"I suppose that I've finally made it into one of your books. Lisa's finally getting married," she said excitedly, as she whisked by to deliver another order.

A few minutes later, Geno got up to go to the restroom and discovered Malcolm sitting alone with two place settings.

"Are there two of you sitting here?" Gene asked, curious of who might be joining Malcolm.

"Have a little respect for the lady will ya," Malcolm said, acting as if someone was actually sitting with him and avoiding a direct answer in order to aggravate Geno's curious nature. It bugged Gene not to be in the know. He was competitive, the type who thought he had a shot at every woman who crossed his path, especially if they were with another man; probably some sort of psychological complex about a young boy dethroning the king.

"Come on now, who is she?" Gene asked, as he returned from the restroom.

"Sheila."

"Sheila, huh," he said raising his eyebrows. "You know, I think I'm going to have to beat up her boyfriend."

"Which one?" Malcolm asked, really throwing him a curve.

"She has more than one?"

"No, but she broke up with the guy she'd been seeing for a while and now she's seeing someone else."

"Well, you're a stud. You should be taking care of that stuff anyway," he said, beginning to make his way back to the front dining room where his laptop and audience awaited him.

"Go for it, we're just friends," Malcolm answered, knowing that Gene didn't believe him, even if he was telling the truth. Malcolm didn't believe that he stood a chance either, or at least didn't want to believe he did.

He was still taking notes when Sheila arrived a little after nine. She walked right past Gene who was tucked away in the corner seat at the counter still enthralled with the images he had down loaded from the web.

"Hi buddy," Sheila said, having walked up to Malcolm's table, instinctively knowing where he'd be sitting.

"Hi Sheila," he answered, standing up to give her a hug.

"I'm still not used to you without your beard. You look so different."

Malcolm didn't respond to her beard comment. After hugging her, he sat back down. "Gene's at the counter," he announced, knowing that she'd be happy to see him, giving Malcolm a chance to finish his notes.

"Oh, good," Sheila said, in an understanding tone. Malcolm could treat Sheila like his men friends, didn't have to stop everything he was doing and get all goo-goo gaa-gaa over her just because she'd arrived. Had they become lovers, he'd have been a little bit more attentive to her, but that wasn't the case, not yet anyway.

He finished with the notes as Lisa walked past with someone's order stacked on her wrists and hands. She suddenly realized that she had walked right by the table she was supposed to be serving and was headed towards the bathroom. Realizing her mistake, Lisa looked up to find Malcolm looking on.

"That's going in the book, though," he said with a big grin. They both started laughing, and she smoothly did a right-about-face with the order.

Malcolm looked over to the counter to check on Sheila and noticed that Travis had wandered in. Sheila had mentioned in an earlier phone call that he might be joining them.

"Lisa, I'm going to move us into the other room so there's room for Travis," Malcolm announced, as she walked away from her delivery. He picked up the menus and Sheila's purse and went into the front dining room. After choosing a table and setting the menus and purse down, Malcolm turned to greet Travis.

The three of them were seated within a few minutes. Lisa came over to remind them that they'd be closing in forty-five minutes and suggested that they get their order in as soon as possible. She was politely giving them a push, which, for Sheila, only made things worse. Sheila was hyper, hungry and had just finished a boring three-hour speech class where she had to contain all of her boiling energy.

So, there they sat, Sheila, Travis, and Malcolm, with Gene sitting behind them at the counter staring at his online downloads and listening in to almost every word that floated up from the threesome's table. A young woman, Travis's friend, walked in to place a to-go order and spotted him. She came over to the table and Travis introduced her to Sheila and Malcolm. She was a real beauty, had just come from visiting her grandmother who was hospitalized after recently suffering a stroke.

Fifteen minutes had passed by the time Travis's lovely young lady friend had finished her visit, and they still hadn't ordered, so Malcolm called out to Lisa, suggesting that if she wanted them out of there at a reasonable hour she might consider writing up their ticket. They finally ordered and then caught up on each other's lives.

"How are you doing Travis?" Sheila asked.

"I'm stressing," Travis answered, shuffling in his seat.

"Why, what's going on?" Sheila asked.

"I've got to wear a tie," Travis announced despondently, disgust oozing from his face.

"Oh, you got the job!" Sheila said in an excited tone, as Malcolm mourned for Travis. For as long as he'd known Travis, he'd been the antithesis of anything that had to do with the confines of the traditional work world. Travis was an artist, a musician, and lived his life dancing to the rhythm of his own tune. Up until that time, his previous employment had consisted of waiting tables at Tillie's or working at the Coast Gallery. Jiminy, too, was falling prey to the machine of conventional duty.

Travis had been hired on at one of the upscale resorts in Carmel to work banquets. Other than money, there was nothing that could have motivated such a compromise. Jiminy was sure to shit-can the machine just as soon as he could see his way through his concession. Travis wasn't doing it for money even if he had taken the job to make a quick buck. He was wearing the tie so that he could afford to make music, nothing less.

"Just don't tighten that goddamn thing too tight," Malcolm

teased.

"Don't worry!" he said in an excited tone as if someone had just poked him in the ribs.

"How was your weekend, Malcolm?" Sheila asked.

"I had an old girlfriend come to town for an overnight visit."

"Was it any good?" Sheila asked.

"Sheila, you know you don't want to hear about it!"

"She does, but she doesn't," Travis teased.

"She always shuts me down right when I start to tell her the good stuff," Malcolm complained with a grin, before going on to tell the story about how one time he was lying around out of breath having just finished getting it on with this woman - it was Elena, but Malcolm didn't reveal her identity - when she cuddled up to him and asked if he wanted to know if she ever got pregnant or if he just wanted her to take care of it without his consent.

"Well, there's always that possibility when you're fooling around," Travis said.

"Yeah, but goddamn, couldn't she at least have left me in my orgasmic trance for another ten seconds before dropping that fucking H-bomb. I mean, that was like taking it all away after she'd given it up to me. I was lying there still high on life when she had to go and whisper that I love you into my ear. She's fucked, I'm telling you. That's how it is with her, though. I'm always on guard, waiting for the other shoe to drop, never knowing what she's gonna come with next."

"She doesn't think you guys are an item does she?" Sheila asked.

"No, she knows where she stands with me, but I still don't trust her. I know how a person can say one thing, but something else inside of them expects something different, even if they don't know it."

"You *are* using protection aren't you?" Sheila asked, cocking her head to the side with a don't-be-stupid look.

"Yeah, I'm using protection and she says she's on the pill, but we didn't even do it this time. She had a bellyache."

"So don't worry then," Sheila said, in a relieved tone.

"What's her name?" Gene asked, craning around from his

stool at the counter.

"Her," Malcolm answered, not surprised that Geno had been silently participating in their conversation. He was only worried that Malcolm might have been fishing in his pond, and Malcolm liked it, knowing a thirty-year-old considered him competition.

"*We* don't even know her name," Travis added.

"Don't worry. She's not a local girl," Malcolm answered, with a smug grin, leaving things a mystery. "How about you Sheila? How was your weekend?"

"I'm sore," she said, smiling a proud yet embarrassed smile.

Sheila had been getting it regularly from some guy she worked with. She never went into the details, but she did like to brag about how sore she was and how she loved getting it in all these positions that always left her back aching.

"Well, what else is new?" Malcolm asked to change the subject.

"Been fighting with Sarina. She's moving out," Sheila answered. She didn't have Andy to fight with anymore and was having too much fun with her new love, so Sarina was the logical person for Sheila to be battling.

Chapter 36

Kate phoned Sunday morning. Several months had passed since her father's death, but nothing had changed with the exception of her mother being prescribed medication for depression.

"Maybe she needs to see a professional," Malcolm suggested.

"You mean like a psychiatrist?" Kate asked in a defensive tone.

"Well, yeah, I mean if she's taking antidepressants…"

"She doesn't need a shrink. She needs time," she interrupted.

"I'm sure she does need time, but if she's taking an antidepressant…"

"Well, anyway, she'll be fine," Kate interrupted again. "Listen, I need to go right now. We're going shopping. I'll call you later…"

Malcolm drove to Turner and Cassi's early that afternoon, but they weren't home, so he drove back to the studio. Mrs. Shams was off with friends, as was often the case on Sunday afternoons, so he was on leave from her self-righteous criticisms. He read for a while and, early that evening, drove down to Big Sur. Sheila was working the night shift. After parking at the cabin, he walked up for an appetizer. The place was so busy that he could hardly make small talk with Sheila. Shortly after eating, he returned to the cabin.

Sarina had met some new guy who was a singer and had gone to watch his band play a gig. Malcolm passed time with Maya. Sheila came in around eleven.

"Still fighting with Sarina?" Malcolm asked, already knowing the answer, but wanting the details of their drama.

"We don't even talk anymore," she said and went on to give him the blow-by-blow details of their escalating feud. He listened for a while, then grew bored with the whole thing. Deciding to call it a night, he retired to the sanctuary of the Tahoe.

The following morning, Sheila was out watering her garden with one of those soaker-type spray wands.

"Morning," he said, walking through the gate.

"Good morning, Malcolm," Sheila said in a cheery tone. She was wearing a straw hat and a T-shirt that was just long enough to cover her panties.

"Wanna get coffee?" he said, closing the gate and walking towards her.

"Let's go to the bakery," she suggested. "I'm almost finished watering," she added, as Malcolm pulled the end of the watering wand to his face, taking a swig of water so that he could brush his teeth.

He nodded an okay. When he'd finished brushing, he went back to Sheila, pulled the end of the wand to his face and soaked his head in the process. After shaking the excess water from his hair like a dog that had just been bathed, he combed it back with a brush he'd slipped into the pocket of his shorts.

After coffee, Sheila wanted to drive down the coast a few miles to see if she could spot a new friend of hers who had started working at Nepenthe. She was a surfer, and Sheila figured they'd find her at one of the turnouts along Highway 1 where she'd park and hike down to the beach. Sheila was right; her friend was parked at a turnout known to the locals as Foolers. She had just started to unload her surfboard from the top of her van. After spotting Sheila in the Tahoe, she leaned the board against her van and came over to the passenger's side window.

"Hey Sasha! How's it going?"

"Good, how 'bout you? What are you doing?"

"Came to find you. I'm driving into town to go shopping. Thought you might like to come along."

"Oh, that's nice of you," Sasha said, as she glanced over at Malcolm.

"Oh, I'm sorry. Sasha, this is Malcolm."

"Hello," Malcolm said, not wanting to interrupt their conversation.

"How do you two know each other?" Sasha asked.

Sheila and Malcolm looked at each other, waiting for the other to answer.

"We met at Tillie's. What? About a year ago?" Sheila asked, looking to Malcolm.

"Yeah, that's about when our love affair began," he said.

"He wishes," Sheila snapped back.

"When are you going to town?" Sasha asked.

"I don't know, maybe in an hour or so," Sheila answered.

"Well, then I'll just strap my board down and head to your place..."

On their way back to the cabin, Malcolm quizzed Sheila about Sasha. She was a beautiful woman, in her late twenties or early thirties. She had blonde hair that was pulled back into pigtails. Sasha's hair was a little darker than Sarina's, but it was her natural color. She had hazel eyes and a long, lean, hard body that she kept by surfing and hiking. Her topside was exceptional, as was her bottom half.

"What's Sasha's story?" he asked.

"Oh, she's new around here and the locals are kind of givin' her a hard time," Sheila answered. It was just like Sheila to be siding with the underdog; that was one of the qualities that Malcolm liked most about her.

"Where's she from?"

"Up north somewhere; Oregon, I think," Sheila answered. She knew, but she didn't want Malcolm snooping around Sasha.

"I see," he answered, without asking another question.

"She's messed up, too. She's been married twice. I think she's still married, but her husband doesn't want to be married anymore. She's bi-sexual, too," Sheila added.

"Cool. I think I just turned lesbian," Malcolm teased.

"Shut up!" Sheila said, back handing his right shoulder.

"What?" he asked, turning down the drive that led to the cabin.

Sasha was right behind them. Malcolm grabbed his shaving kit and some clean clothes from the Tahoe and followed the girls into the cabin. They made small talk for a few minutes. Sasha wanted to know where Malcolm was from, and he gave her a few brief answers before excusing himself to shower.

When he came out of the bathroom, there was music playing but no one in the house. He rolled his dirty clothes up in his towel, picked up the shaving kit and walked out to put his things in the Tahoe. He found both girls lying belly-down on a blanket in the front yard, calves and feet swinging in the air as if in cadence to a soft melody.

Sheila was wearing a pair of thong panties and a bra. Sasha was buck-ass naked with the exception of her green Columbian outdoorsman hat and a pair of sunglasses with yellow lenses. Malcolm casually walked behind the two sunbathers to the Tahoe to stow his gear, still having an excuse for his presence. Returning to the cabin, he took in all of Sasha that he could.

Once back inside, he walked around in circles; he didn't know what else to do. All he could see was Sasha's long lean legs running up into her finely sculptured ass and those blonde tail feathers floating out from the hind side of her honey jar. Sasha's hair color was natural, that for certain was no longer a mystery. He wasn't quite sure what to make of this particular dream. *Are they fucking with me, or are they fucking with me?* Malcolm asked himself.

Malcolm had nothing in the cabin that he needed to get and no valid reason for sticking around, so he decided to say goodbye and make his way back into town. When he walked outside, they were still lying belly-down beside each other in the same position.

"Well, girls, I'm gonna hit it," he said, standing over them from behind, wearing his dark shades, admiring Sasha's pigtails.

"Okay, Malcolm. Well, it was nice to see you," Sheila said, as she stood up slightly self-conscious.

"Great to see you, too," Malcolm said, hugging her.

"It was nice to meet you, Malcolm," Sasha said, craning her head around and looking at him through her yellow lenses and smiling. "I hope you don't mind me not getting up?" she added.

"Oh, please, not on my behalf," Malcolm answered politely. There was no need for both of them getting up, and it was going to be quite some time before Malcolm went back down. What a way to start the day, or even the week.

He drove from Big Sur to Pacific Grove for his late morning appointment with Jenny. He never heard from Jenny over the weekend. They seldom ever did much together anyway, but now that she had her cabin, they didn't do anything at all. Beside the time he helped her move things, she never did invite him out to her retreat. He was seeing her on a professional level more than anything else, but Malcolm was interested in her as a woman, not as a physical therapist. Somehow, her volunteering to treat him was a way to keep him around, but at a distance. As long as he was a patient, she could keep him at bay.

He was Jenny's last patient before lunch, so he invited her to join him at the Pink House for coffee. Diana and Malcolm went ahead and ordered while Jenny straightened things up around her office. He tied the dog up at the perch and went inside to order his coffee and Jenny's tea. When he walked outside, Jenny was sitting up at the perch waiting for him.

"Are you still jealous about my cabin?" she asked. "I mean, you'll probably end up with it anyway," she added. She thought it suited Malcolm and when she grew tired of it, he'd take over.

"Yeah, I'm still jealous," Malcolm confirmed. "But I don't want it."

"It's just not big enough," she said.

"I thought about you this morning when I was driving and imagined you in a bigger place."

"Well, I can see myself living out there all of the time, but I'll definitely have to have more space. Sure you're not interested in it?"

"Nope," Malcolm answered with no hesitation. "I've got other plans, but I can't tell you them because I'd scare the shit out of you."

"What are you going to do, buy a Harley?" she joked.

"Nope, I want a bigger place, too, and I want to live in it with you."

"Ughhh," she said, as she wrinkled up her nose and smiled a disgusted gross look. It was hard to tell if her reaction was of terror or if she was trying to hide her joy of entertaining the possibility of actually coming together in this manner.

"I'm going to be living with a woman real soon," Malcolm announced. "It may not happen for you, but it is going to happen for me," he added, to take back some of the vulnerability that he'd had just hung out for her to gnaw on.

"You know, your right about living out there with someone though," she said. "I mean, it's so remote and all."

"Well, I'm opening myself up to it, and I can tell that it's going to happen for me. All this chaos that's spinning around in me is beginning to come together, and I'm ready to have a relationship with a woman."

"I thought you said you just got out of a relationship."

"I didn't just get out of a relationship," he said.

"What about that woman who was your lover for five years?" she asked, trying to gain a little more insight into the mystery.

"That ended more than a year ago, and it wasn't really a relationship; it was just sex," he answered carelessly. "Well, I guess it wasn't just sex, but it was," he added, trying to reclaim some of his feigned saintliness, and at the same time reducing the whole thing back into just another confusing paradox.

Jenny didn't respond. She was having one hell of a time trying to figure out Malcolm, and so was he. She'd read his book and must have figured out that he usually had more than one woman working. She knew about his marriage and about him falling in love with Lauren while divorcing, but now she was trying to figure out how this five year old love, or rather sex affair fit into the grand scheme of things.

"I'm ready to have a different kind of relationship with a woman," Malcolm said, in response to her silence, knowing that he'd shaken her up a bit. Right then one of Jenny's friends walked up and rescued Malcolm from the topic of their discussion. Shortly after her friend left, Jenny left to go home and eat something she had previously prepared for her special diet; at least that was her excuse.

Needless to say, he was fed up with Jenny and ready to shit-can the whole mess. So what if he had spooked her off? If she ran, it would open him to have what he wanted with another woman. If she didn't run, things were damn sure going to take a different turn in their celibate liaison; then maybe he'd run. He was tired of that same old song, tired of her leading their dance. Did she have him all figured out; was she really just snookering him, waltzing him right into her web? Or was she just as lost as Malcolm was?

* * * * *

He took a nap in the afternoon, and then wrote until eight

that evening, until his stomach started to growl. His mind bounced back and forth while trying to settle on a restaurant. He finally decided on the Bully III for a French dip. The Bully was a local pub in downtown Carmel where many of the local business people had lunch and dinner. They specialized in Prime Rib and other meaty menu selections. Malcolm chose the Bully in honor of Jenny's vegetarianism.

He sat at the bar and had a fine supper. About the only thing he had a hard time stomaching was the drunk sitting a few seats to his right. The guy was harassing the bartender. The place was crowded. There were more kids than he'd ever witnessed in a pub, more crying kids anyway, and apparently the parents didn't find it necessary to take their wailing toddlers out for a breath of fresh air.

Malcolm ignored the drunk as he continued to torture the help. Unfortunately, the lost soul had the uncanny ability to sense disdain and rejection, and it made him crave attention all the more. In no time, he had Malcolm sucked into his drunken drama. The guy was drinking tequila and beer, and claiming he ran a hotel down the road. He told Malcolm how he'd been working for this one resort that had been bought out. He ended up getting fired and then going back to work for his old boss who owned several properties in Carmel. He said he was a local who had lived on the Peninsula his entire life.

"Can you see the brunette back in the corner?" the drunk asked.

"Yeah," Malcolm answered, looking over at a blonde sitting at a table on the opposite side of the bar."

"Not that one," he said, noticing where Malcolm's eyes had taken him. "It's that brunette in the back. There," he added, pointing at the brunette. "See, over here. Get up and come over here," he motioned.

"I can see her," Malcolm assured him, still trying to figure out what was so great about the brunette when there was a beautiful blonde who was twice as hot.

"How's that blonde?" he asked, as Malcolm took another bit of French dip.

Malcolm just nodded with a mouth full.

"So that's your type, huh?"

Malcolm smiled without engaging him, but it didn't matter. He could have sat silent all night and the drunk would have kept on rambling. He didn't need anyone to answer him, just a body to aim his words at.

"I got a son," he said. "The wife and I are split up."

Malcolm nodded, and took a swig of water.

"We talk almost everyday on the phone, though," he explained, and then took another swig of beer. He still wore a wedding band. "We just split up a few months ago. She's up in Washington. I'm going there next weekend to see my son."

"You still love her?"

"Oh, yeah, but I can't stand her daughter."

"She's not your daughter?" Malcolm asked, almost sure of the answer he was about to get, but knowing that the question would most likely light a fire.

"No, the daughter was one of those premarital things," he said, turning to gawk at a young brunette waitress who was taking an order from a table behind them. "I had her sign a contract," he added, turning his attention back Malcolm's way.

"Who'd you have sign a contract?" Malcolm asked, looking straight ahead toward the blonde across the bar.

"The daughter. She's twelve-years-old, and she is one great big pain in the ass. She started fucking up real bad last year."

"How?"

"At school. You know, her grades and all," he said, hoping Malcolm would side with him. "That's why the wife and me are split up, because of her daughter."

"So, why are they in Washington?"

"That's where my in-laws are. She's living with her parents. We still talk almost every day. You should see the phone bill; it's crazy."

Malcolm didn't answer. He wasn't sure how to respond. He was still trying to read between the lines. If he loved her and she loved him, why weren't they together working things out?

"So, I'm flying up there next weekend, to see my little boy. It's killing me!"

"So she won," Malcolm said, having turned to look the drunk in the eyes.

"Oh yeah, she always wanted us to split up," he answered

very quickly, catching on to Malcolm's hint. Malcolm halfway believed the guy to be grateful for his stepdaughter's rebellion. It was almost like the drunk had set the stage for this breakup long ago.

"Why don't you go get 'em and bring 'em back home?" Malcolm asked, testing his reaction.

"I can't live with that girl. No way. I told her mother to keep her the hell away from me. She won't even talk to me when I call."

"Your wife?"

"No, my stepdaughter."

No shit, Malcolm thought to himself.

The drunk motioned to a brunette waitress he'd been drooling over for most the night. She walked over to check on him. He whispered something into her ear and she walked away.

"I just wanted to smell her," he said, smiling as if he'd really pulled something off. "I love women. I used to knock them around a little bit, you know, just a little bit, but now I just love them," he said, nodding with his arms crossed, rocking back and forth on the barstool.

"I bet you do," Malcolm answered with a grin, understanding all the more why his wife had taken the kids and moved to Washington. She was probably running for their lives.

The drunk rambled on for a while longer, showing Malcolm a picture of his little boy and complaining of how badly he missed his child. He continued badgering the help as they tried to tend to business. Malcolm settled up with the bartender, and slipped away while the drunk was sniffing one of the waitresses.

Chapter 37

He had another appointment with Jenny a few days later. On his drive to Pacific Grove, the whole thing about her calling him a slut and a pervert a few months earlier kept popping back into Malcolm's mind. He recalled being married and having his parents over for dinner. They had ordered takeout Chinese and brought it back to Malcolm's place. They were all sitting down at the dinner table enjoying their meal, having a nice conversation about something, when, from out of nowhere, right there with Malcolm's parents, Shelly blurted out: "All you ever think about is your dick anyway!"

Malcolm was beginning to see some sort of theme developing. There was a parallel with Shelly telling him that all he ever thought about was his dick, and Jenny calling him a slut and a pervert. He didn't have it all put together, but something was brewing.

Early for his appointment, he stopped for coffee at the Pink House. After paying for his drink, he turned to pick up the cream and sugar and found a little boy about three years old who had found the oil and vinegar bottles and held them upside down, dumping the contents onto the floor. Malcolm smiled at the boy without saying a thing to his mother. He wasn't going to rain on the kid's parade, but his mother caught on to the boy's scheme while Malcolm was still doctoring his coffee.

Malcolm left and sat at the perch to sip his brew. A while later, the boy and his mother came outside. She put him into a stroller and looked around as if she was lost.

"Excuse me. Do you have the time," the mother asked, looking up to Malcolm from the sidewalk below the perch.

"Yeah, I sure do," Malcolm answered, looking up to the town clock. "It's ten-fifty."

"Oh, thank you," she said, having followed his gaze toward the tower.

"Your little boy is really cool," Malcolm said, as he looked to the child.

"Thank you."

"Has he got any older brothers?"

"Yes, two of them," the mother confirmed.

"I'm from a family of four boys."

"Oh, so you could spot all that boy energy," the mother said, beaming a smile.

"*Oh* yeah, and believe me, he's really cool."

The mom smiled and nodded a thank you. "Have a good day," she said, as she began to push the stroller down the sidewalk.

Malcolm smiled. He was almost forty years old and had skated around having a child because of the responsibility that went along with the commitment, but at that moment, he felt ready for such a calling.

A few minutes later, Malcolm went over to Jenny's office. Lying face down on the table as Jenny worked on him, he fell into the fantasy of having a child with her. He actually felt giddy and began to giggle. "What's wrong?" she asked.

"Nothing, guess I'm just a little ticklish this morning," he answered, as the image of the little boy he'd just encountered at the Pink House flashed to him. Then it hit and his giddiness turned into a bellyache. He wondered if Jenny would view the little boy as a pervert, too. Or, what if they actually did end up having a child together, a little boy, would he also be a pervert? Malcolm took in some deep breaths; he didn't like what he was feeling.

Jenny stood over Malcolm. He was still lying face down. She started brushing something off her like a spider or something and then he realized that it was probably a dog hair. He flashed to Shelly and all of her animals. Anger began to resurface in Malcolm. He never did fit into her world. He was beginning to realize why Jenny had come into his life. Jenny reached down and picked up a dog's hair that she had brushed off onto his back. He had the makings of another mess on his hands just like he'd had with Shelly and hadn't even recognized it. He was actually entertaining the possibility of having a child with a woman who on some underlying level had a grave disdain for men; quite possibly the same disdain for men that his ex-wife harbored.

* * * * *

At two that afternoon, Malcolm went for a French dip at the Bully and ended up with a plateful of baby back ribs, mashed potatoes and steamed vegetables. It was the special, and for two bucks more than a French dip, he got a salad, to boot.

He sat at a corner table so that he didn't have the distraction of anyone's annoying voice creeping over his shoulder, like with the drunk on his previous visit. He had just finished his salad when he looked up to find three people approaching the empty table in front of him.

It was a couple in their mid to late fifties, each carrying a bed pillow and another woman in her thirties who appeared to be, what in this day and age we call, mentally challenged. When the threesome walked into the dining room, all the other background noise came to a screeching halt, almost as if they were in a theatre and the movie was starting.

The man sat alone on the opposite side of the table facing his wife and their guest. The young woman took the outside seat with her back to Malcolm. The wife, after taking off her coat in a theatrical like production, placed the two bed pillows down on the wooden chair nearest to the window and sat her injured ass onto the stack of pads.

Having settled in at the table, the couple started discussing their drink order without their guest saying a peep. One of the waiters walked by, and the wife asked if Angel was working, because they wanted to be certain that Angel waited on them. Angel ended up being the woman who was waiting on Malcolm. A few minutes passed and Angel floated over to greet her patrons and sprinkle on a little make-'em-feel-special dust. After an exchange of some small talk, she took their drink orders.

"I'll have a vodka tonic," said the husband.

"What kind of vodka do you want?" his wife asked, the waitress waiting patiently as if she was used to their routine.

"What do you mean what kind of Vodka? Whatever they're pouring back there," he answered in a short tone.

"Don't you want a Stoli?" the wife asked. "He'll have a Stoli," the wife told the waitress before the man could answer.

Malcolm couldn't hear what the girl ordered. Actually, he

probably could have if he'd been paying attention, but he'd become lost in his reaction to how the husband and wife were interacting. A ringing cellular phone drew him out of his trance.

"Oh, that's my phone ringing. It's in my coat pocket," the wife said, expecting her husband to retrieve the phone from her jacket that was lying on the empty chair next to him. He fished around in her pockets as the cellular continued to ring. He finally came across the trophy he'd been jigging for and handed his catch across the table.

"Oh, it must be yours," the wife announced after the attempt to answer the call on her phone failed.

Without saying a thing, the husband reached inside his coat pocket and pulled out a ringing cellular phone.

"Hello," he answered in an elevated tone. People are something else with a cellular call. A ringing phone in public isn't enough to announce their self-importance; they have to shout their business out loud so that the entire county can recognize their pomposity.

"Shhhh, lower," the wife said, motioning with her hand in a pushing down fashion.

The husband dropped his volume a couple of notches and continued his phone call. It was about some business concerning a property tax bill. The waitress delivered their drink order, and while the husband talked on the phone, the wife explained to Angel how her husband had to have this medical device installed for his heart condition. He snored so badly at night that they were afraid his heart would stop or that he would have a heart attack. Angel courteously assured the wife that she'd return to take their order as soon as the husband was off the phone.

"Yeah, we can meet you tomorrow," the husband told the caller. "No, she's never out of bed before noon," he continued, looking over to his wife. "One o'clock sounds good. How 'bout at the Crossroads? I'll buy lunch."

"At the Rio Grill," the wife interrupted, as if she knew who the caller was and what the call was all about.

"Yeah, okay, she said the Rio Grill at one, and we really appreciate everything you're doing for us."

When he hung up, the young woman who was their guest

actually picked up her drink, smiled, and said: "Cheers," as the threesome raised their glasses in a toast. Angel soon returned to take their order.

"You aren't having anything to eat, are you?" the wife asked the husband, as if she were monitoring his caloric intake.

Malcolm wanted to tell her to leave the guy alone and let him think for himself, but fortunately, in his disgust, he drifted off for a minute, and then returned to himself while the wife was ordering. She couldn't remember the side dishes that came with the entrées, so Angel had to repeat the options, in spite of the wife being a regular for who knew how many years. This only increased Malcolm's suspicion of her being high on some sort of pain medication.

"Do you do your own laundry?" the wife asked the guest.

The woman mumbled an answer that couldn't be made out.

"Well, you are twenty-seven years old. It seems like you should be doing your own laundry."

The young woman again mumbled something in response to the wife's inquisition.

The waitress brought Malcolm's check and then walked away. While reviewing his bill, he overheard the husband say something to the wife and then things started to heat up.

"There you go again. You know you're just trying to make me feel bad. He always does this," the wife said, turning to their guest.

"No I don't," the husband defended.

"Yes he does," again the wife said looking at their guest for support.

"No I…" the husband started to defend, but was interrupted by Angel.

"I'm sorry, but we're out of the rib special."

"Well, I don't know if anything else sounds good," the wife answered, reacting as if her childhood religion had just been jerked away from her.

"Pot roast is our other special," the waitress answered, hoping to reel the wife out of her despair.

"It's just like ribs without the bones," the husband chimed in. He'd been waiting for his chance to tell her what to do.

"Okay, I'll try the pot roast," she replied, not giving it any more thought.

Their salads showed up shortly after the order dilemma had been remedied. Malcolm signed the credit card receipt, and sat in silence while the rabbits munched away at their greens. He tucked the receipt into his wallet and took another swig of water. On his way out of the Bully, he decided to stop in the bathroom to wash off the remnants of that last order of ribs he'd cheated the old gal out of.

* * * * *

That evening Malcolm went to yoga. It had been close to a year since he'd last attended a class, but for some reason he felt as if he should go. A woman was there he'd met when he first moved to Carmel. She had moved away not long after their initial introduction. There was something about her that moved him. He remembered talking with her and how she had looked at him when they conversed; her blue eyes seemed to penetrate him. Her gaze wasn't intimidating; it actually had the opposite effect: it was one of warmth. She didn't seem to be afraid of Malcolm. Quite the opposite: she seemed capable of meeting and receiving him in a way that he'd experienced only a few times in his life.

After class, they walked up to each other and embraced. They didn't know each other all that well, but they hugged anyway. It was like they'd been lifelong friends.

"I'm Malcolm. I remember seeing you here before."

"I'm Allia," she said, with her eyes gazing into Malcolm's as if she were looking for something.

"You know what. I really like you a lot," Malcolm confessed, as she continued her gaze. "I remember how attracted to you I was the first time I ever saw you," he said, fearing he'd spook her.

"Thank you," she said, continuing to smile while looking deep into his eyes. She didn't budge, didn't look away.

"I wondered whatever happened to you."

"I moved to South Carolina."

"South Carolina?" he asked, surprised and disappointed.

"Yeah, I've been studying yoga there. I'm actually just here visiting for a week."

"If I give you my e-mail address will you stay in touch and let me know how you're doing?"

"Of course," she answered, her eyes and smile beaming; it was almost as if she glowed.

"I hope I'm not being too forward with you," Malcolm said, after realizing how honest he'd been with her. He normally wasn't that forthcoming because he feared that it was a turn-off to women.

"No, I like that. I like honesty," Allia answered, as she continued to receive him. He felt worshiped.

He wrote his e-mail address on the back of a card and handed it to Allia. "I'm serious; I really want to stay connected."

"I'll be in touch," she reassured.

They hugged again and then went their separate ways.

He drove home and took a hot shower. Allia had met him right were he was, eye-to-eye and heart-to-heart. Malcolm felt warm inside thinking about her.

He soaped up, rinsed, and then turned the hot water up and let it stream down his neck and back. "Wow, and I wasn't even a pervert," he sang out loud. She liked his forwardness, honored that about him. He started belly laughing as the water poured off his back. He softened, the muscles in his chest relaxed and his heart felt as if it was opening.

Chapter 38

Jenny and Malcolm continued to grow more distant after she'd rented the cabin. He saw her during the week for physical therapy but otherwise seldom heard from her. He had e-mailed her a few times to ask if she'd like to take a walk or a hike and she'd respond with: "A walk would be nice," or she didn't respond at all.

He'd grown tired of her unavailability and decided to call her but had misplaced her phone number. Instead he e-mailed her saying that he'd lost the cabin phone number and was frustrated with their lack of communication. She didn't respond, so he just showed up Monday morning for his next appointment.

"Did you get my e-mail?" Malcolm asked, as he approached the table in the treatment room.

"Uh huh," she confirmed in a distant tone, nodding.

"I would really like to go for a walk with you," he said, sitting down on the edge of the table facing her.

"We will," she said, standing over and looking down on him.

"I miss talking to you. I was hoping we could get together and catch up on things."

"And I've been busy doing my own thing. You poor little baby," Jenny answered sarcastically, shaking her head and making a pouting face.

"Yeah, and it's your fault. So stop it," Malcolm said, shaking his right index finger at her and laughing to make light of the situation, the whole time holding back his rage. He rolled over on the table so that the pain in his ass could go to work on the pain in his ass.

* * * * *

Malcolm drove down to Big Sur that afternoon. He parked in front of the cabin, but no one was home, so he walked up the hill to the restaurant. Sarina was busy waiting on tables.

Sasha was the hostess. Malcolm spotted her standing at the entrance of the restaurant behind the podium with the phone and reservation book.

"Hey Sasha," he said, as he approached the podium.

"Hey, I know you! Malcolm, right?"

"You got it," he said, happy that she remembered his name. *Guess I didn't have to be lying out naked sunning myself to have made an impression on her,* Malcolm thought to himself. If he had, she might well have ignored him. "Have you seen Sheila around?"

"She had a couple of days off and left with Shane yesterday. She'll probably be back later today or tomorrow sometime."

"Well, if you see her, will you have her call me?"

"Sure, where?"

"She can reach me on my mobile," he answered, handing her his card. Sheila knew Malcolm's mobile number by heart, but he wanted Sasha to have it, too.

"Oh, I didn't know you had a cellular phone."

"Now you do," he answered, with a friendly smile. "Thanks a lot, Sasha. I'll see you around, huh?" he suggested, as a party walked up to the podium.

"Okay, take care, Malcolm. I'll tell Sheila to call if I see her."

Malcolm walked down to the cabin, and sat out on the deck. When Sarina got off work, she came down to pick up a load of boxes. She was in the process of moving out. She was no longer staying at the cabin but hadn't completely moved all of her goods.

Around seven that evening, Malcolm drove down to the deli to pick up a few things for dinner. Then he drove back and ate out on the deck. A few hours later, he retired to the Tahoe for the evening. The following morning before driving to the bakery for coffee, he showered and left a note for Sheila to phone. He had just taken his first sip of the French roast when she called.

"Hey Malcolm, sorry I missed you."

"Hi Sheila, I drove down yesterday but couldn't find you."

"Shane and I drove down the coast."

"Yeah, that's what Sasha said."

"Where are you now?"

"Having a coffee at the bakery."

"Have you had lunch?" Sheila asked.

"Not yet."

"Okay, I'll see you in a few minutes."

Ten minutes later Sheila walked into the bakery and came to give Malcolm a hug.

"Can I get you a coffee or something?" he asked, before sitting back down.

"No, I wanna go somewhere else," she said in an unsettled tone.

"Where?"

"I don't know, but I have to leave for town soon, to study for a test I have tonight."

"Why don't we just walk over to the deli and get a sandwich?" Malcolm suggested.

"Sounds alright," she answered, looking around, seeming distracted. Sheila had a lot of nervous energy and was having a hard time hiding her discontentment.

Malcolm pitched his paper coffee cup into the trashcan as he walked out of the bakery and followed Sheila's lead. The deli was only a few minutes walk from the bakery.

"What time did you get back?" Malcolm asked, as they made their way to lunch.

"Last night, but I stayed at Shane's," Sheila answered, a few steps in front of Malcolm.

"I stayed in front of your place last night. I must have just missed you this morning. Sasha say I was looking for you?"

"No, I found your note."

"Oh yeah, forgot I left the note. I saw Sasha yesterday. Asked her to have you call me when you got back."

"No, haven't seen her yet."

"Oh, hey, what was that *I wish* shit about when you introduced me to her the other day?" Malcolm boldly asked, as they approached the deli.

Sheila walked inside without answering. They ordered sandwiches and Sheila picked out a bag of chips for them to share while Malcolm took a couple bottles of iced tea out of the cooler. After paying, they went outside, sat on a brick planter box and ate lunch.

"So, anyway, what was that *I wish* thing you said about me to Sasha?"

"I don't know," Sheila answered with a shrug before taking a swig of tea.

"Well, you've said it three or four times since I've known you. It kind of bothers me, and I'm wondering what it's about."

"I don't know. I just said it."

"Well, if you think I'm hanging around hoping that I get to fuck you one of these days, you're wrong."

"I don't think that at all or we wouldn't even be hanging out together. You're like family to me, Malcolm."

"I just wanted to be clear on things. Why'd you say it then?"

"I guess it was my ego," Sheila answered.

"Well, it felt like getting kicked in the nuts right there in front of Sasha. I mean, hell, I'm still a man even if we aren't doing it."

A friend of Sheila's walked up and interrupted their discussion. Sheila introduced Malcolm to the fellow, an old friend of her mother's. They visited for a bit and then the man was on his way.

"Well, Malcolm, I better go. I need to get to town to study for this test," Sheila said, in a friendly tone, almost as if they hadn't even had the discussion before her old family friend showed up.

"Okay, well, good luck."

"Thanks. I'll need it. You gonna stick around? You can hang out on the deck at the cabin," she offered.

"Yeah, I think I will," he answered, as she hugged him goodbye.

"Okay, I'll probably see you tonight then, right?"

"Yeah, probably."

In some ways, Sheila was holding Malcolm back, or he was letting her hold him back. She wasn't interested in being his lover in the physical sense, but she damn sure didn't want him taking a lover elsewhere. It was fine for her to have another, but she didn't want Malcolm running off with another woman. She feared losing the spiritual kinship they shared.

* * * * *

That night, Sheila drove in around eleven-thirty. Shane pulled in right behind her. Malcolm had already retired to the Tahoe. About fifteen minutes after they arrived, a light went on upstairs. From where Malcolm was parked, and by the way he was laying on his mattress, he could see up into her loft through a small window. The next time he glanced, the curtain had been closed, but the light was still on. He could see a silhouette of what looked like the two of them getting it on. He got angry, real angry. He didn't want her, but he was angry that she was holding him back, or he thought she was anyway, angry about her kicking him in the nuts in front of Sasha. His relationship with her felt demeaning and emasculating. "She's up in the loft getting laid by another man, and I'm fucking out here jacking off in the Tahoe…"

Chapter 39

Malcolm woke the next morning and went straight to the watering wand to slick back his hair. Shane came out and they visited for a bit, then he went inside to make a phone call. Sheila walked out onto the patio as Malcolm brushed his teeth.

"Could you hear me last night?" Sheila asked. "I thought maybe you heard me screaming. Shane was reading and he knocked over the lamp and broke a light bulb. There was broken glass all over the bed. I was trying to sleep. I threw a fit - I was so pissed off. It took forever to clean up."

* * * * *

Shane and Sheila went to the beach later that morning. They had plans to meet a couple that had just come back to Big Sur after traveling in South America. They invited Malcolm to join them, but he chose the bakery instead. They told Malcolm they'd probably see him there later.

After hanging out for an hour or so, reading and sipping coffee, Malcolm decided to have breakfast. He was eating when Shane and Sheila arrived on scene.

"What's up Malcolm?" Sheila asked, as the couple stood at the counter waiting to order.

"Having some breakfast. Think I'm gonna hike the loop at Julia Pfeiffer Burns Park," Malcolm answered from across the room. "Feel like I need to get some exercise," he added, thinking that a good workout might help dissipate some of the rage that boiled within him.

"That sounds like a good thing," Sheila answered, as Shane tried for Sheila's attention so they could order.

Malcolm watched them at the counter as they decided on breakfast. Sheila was in a jovial mood and made some reference to the help about how she'd been having good sex lately. Shane gave her a sharp look and then said something about not having to advertise things like that. They finally ordered and went outside to eat on the patio. Malcolm stayed inside and read.

After breakfast, the two walked back inside to pay their bill.

"Hey, Sheila. Think one of the girls might want to go for a hike?"

"I don't know, maybe," she said, in a cheerful tone but with a look of betrayal.

"How about Sasha?" Malcolm asked. "She's into hiking, isn't she?"

"Yeah, she is," Shane was quick to answer, rooting for Malcolm.

"Yeah, Sasha might want to go," Sheila answered reluctantly. "You could ask her."

"Well, if you see her, tell her I'm looking for a hiking partner," Malcolm said, putting Sheila in a spot to redeem her previous kick to his nuts.

"Okay," Sheila answered.

"But you better be careful Malcolm," Shane suggested.

"Why's that?"

"Sheila might get jealous."

Without words, Sheila turned to Shane and gave him a you-bastard look.

"It'll be alright Sheila," Malcolm said, as she turned her look to him. "Really, it'll be fine. I'm not going anywhere. I won't leave you. I promise," Malcolm reassured, as she shifted her betrayed look back-and-forth between the two men.

* * * * *

He hiked alone that afternoon and then returned to Sheila's cabin to take a shower before going up to Nepenthe for dinner. Sheila greeted him when he came in and then showed him to an empty table on the patio in her section. He ordered and then walked through the restaurant to the bathroom.

"Hey Malcolm," Shane said, waiting at the counter for an order. "Someone wanting to take a hike was looking for you earlier today," he added, holding his hands in front of his chest to emulate a big set of knockers.

"Who was looking for him?" asked Joan, a nosey waitress who was listening in on their conversation.

"Was I talking to you?" Shane snapped, putting her in her place.

"Boy you two *are* in love," Malcolm teased, grinning about the Sasha thing and continuing his walk towards the restroom.

"It's one of those love hate things," Joan answered.

Sheila was perturbed. She acted nice, but she was annoyed with Malcolm, and the prissy little girl came out of her when she waited on him. She wasn't as attentive as she usually was. She slid his order down in front of him and some of the food fell off of the plate. Later, when she returned to fill his water glass, she held the pitcher up high, and then splattering all over the place, let the water freefall into the glass until it overflowed. Malcolm ignored her pissiness, but immediately after dinner, he settled his bill, went down to the cabin, and retired to the Tahoe before her shift ended.

Chapter 40

The following morning, Malcolm walked into the yard to brush his teeth. No one seemed to be moving about the cabin, so he slicked back his hair and started off for the bakery.

"Hey, aren't you going to say goodbye?" Sheila hollered, as he walked out of the yard.

"I didn't want to walk in on you guys," he answered, as she stepped from the deck and followed him out to the Tahoe. It appeared that she had just woken up.

"I'm alone."

"Well, I didn't know that."

"You could have knocked."

"I'm just going down to the bakery. It's no big deal," he answered.

"Well, have a good day," Sheila said, before giving him a kiss on the cheek.

"I'll be around."

"I'm working lunch. Maybe we can have dinner tonight?" she suggested.

"Yeah, that might work. I'll see you later. I'll probably go for another hike."

"I'm off at four."

"I'll be back around five-thirty or six, but I'll probably see you before I go," he answered.

"Yeah, stop by before you hike."

Malcolm hung out at the bakery for a few hours, had a late breakfast and eventually returned to Nepenthe around two that afternoon. Sheila brought him an iced tea, and he sat out on the cement steps on the front patio. Sasha was the hostess. When Sasha walked out to help deliver an order for one of the waitresses, Malcolm caught her looking his way. She was trying not to be obvious, but she wasn't good at hiding it. I'm not saying that she wanted him, but he did catch her looking his way.

"So, how's it going?" Sheila asked, as she walked up to the steps, taking a quick break.

"Good, how 'bout you?"

"It's been busy. You go on a hike?"

"Not yet. I was going to see if Sasha wanted to come along."

"She already hiked eight miles this morning."

"Well, guess that saves me having to ask her," Malcolm answered, a little bummed, but relieved of having to risk her rejection.

"She might still want to go. I mean, you can ask her."

"Another time, maybe."

"Okay, well, I have to get back to work. Are we on for dinner?"

"Yeah, I'll be back around six. I'll come to your place to shower. Then we can leave from there."

Malcolm sat out on the steps for a while. Sean walked up and sat down next to him. He was looking a little bummed. He and Debbie had had a falling out and she had already taken up with some other dude.

"Hey, Sean, how's it going?" Malcolm asked.

"I've had better days."

"What happened?"

"Oh, it's a long one," he answered.

"I got time."

"Had to pay seven hundred fifty dollars bail for an old drunk-driving ticket from eight years ago. I had two classes to go at the DUI School, and then the DMV sent me my license back, so I quit going. I got pulled over, and the cop ran my number through the computer and ticketed me for driving with a suspended license. So, I had to go to court, and I can't drive, right?"

"Yeah," Malcolm answered.

"So I took the bus to Salinas and got there twenty minutes late. That's why I got fined. Actually, it wasn't a fine; it was bail. They set a new court date and I had to pay bail, and if I don't show up on time next week, I lose it, and to top it off, my fucking rent's due today. I could have done the time but had a bag of weed in my pocket and didn't want to get busted for that, too. I know it's my fault, but it's still fucked."

Malcolm bragged about getting hauled in drunk a few times

and about getting away from the law on plenty of occasions back in the good old days, just to find some common ground with Sean. He liked Sean. He seemed to have problems, but Malcolm liked the man anyway. He was just out there, didn't seem to have much, if anything, to hide.

"So if you don't drive, how you get to work?"

"Shit man, I walk."

"How far?"

"Four miles."

"Everyday?"

"Everyday."

* * * * *

He didn't return from the hike until around seven. Sheila wasn't at the cabin, so he showered, assuming that she'd soon show up. He had finished showering and was shaving when he heard someone walk in.

"Malcolm, are you in the shower?"

"No, I'm shaving," he answered, the bathroom doors swinging open.

"I've got to pee so bad," Sasha announced, as she dropped her drawers. Malcolm continued to shave away without once striking a nick as Sasha sat less than two feet behind him relieving herself.

"Have you seen Sheila?"

"Yeah, she went down the coast to look for you," Sasha answered, as she pulled up her drawers. "I'm a little drunk," she added, trying to button up.

"Where've you been?"

"Up at the restaurant; I stayed and had a few drinks when I got off. I haven't been this tipsy in a long time," she said, walking into the great room. "You know, I'm gonna run up to my van and change. If Sheila gets back before I do, don't leave without me."

Ten minutes later, Sheila drove up to the cabin, and five minutes after that, Sasha came stumbling down the hill wearing a black top, a pair of reptile skin print pants that were safety pinned in the back, and black high heels that she called come-fuck-me shoes.

Sheila phoned Deetjen's to reserve a table for dinner, but they were booked for the night. Malcolm offered to drive into town, so he folded up the mattress and pulled the backseat up so that Sasha would have a place to sit. He didn't want her rolling around on his bed and puking all over the place. She wasn't sloppy drunk, but she was well beyond a little tipsy.

"Oh, do you mind if we swing by my van so I can let Jezebel out to pee," Sasha asked, as they crested the top of the hill near the restaurant. "My van's right over there," she said, pointing to the employee parking area.

"Who's Jezebel?" Malcolm asked, as they drove toward the van.

"My Pug. She's a reformed slut, just like me. She was worn out breeding stock. I rescued her before the breeders put her down."

"Cool," Malcolm answered, as Sasha got out to tend to her dog's needs. Jezebel didn't have to pee, though. Hell, she was just there a few minutes earlier.

It was eight before they finally pulled onto Highway 1 and headed north. A few minutes into the drive, Sasha started philosophizing on how screwed up society was for women.

"I mean, I totally love myself, and I'm beyond all that crap. But, the thing that society has put off onto women about their weight really stinks. Isn't that right Sheila?" Sasha asked.

"Well…"

"I mean look at the media, the TV, and the magazines. I have a friend with an eating disorder who was in therapy for seven years, but she's never lost her obsessive compulsive behavior," Sasha interrupted before Sheila could respond.

"I like being obsessive compulsive," Malcolm announced.

"Yeah, but she can't get over it," Sasha answered.

"Yes you can, but you have to change the images," Malcolm argued.

"I don't believe that. I mean, after seven years of therapy she's still the same."

"Yeah, she doesn't believe it either; that's why she hasn't changed. She doesn't believe she can. Just like you don't believe she can. She doesn't want to change."

"The problem is that women can't be seen for what lies beyond their beauty. Sheila knows. We've talked about this before. Isn't that right Sheila?"

"Well..."

"People are just so black and white in America," Sasha interrupted. "Like Sean and how he only sees women as objects."

"You're both beautiful women, so fucking deal with it!" Malcolm yelled. "What the fuck, you want to be hit with the ugly stick or something?"

Malcolm wondered what Sasha would have been pissing and moaning about if she was fat and ugly. If Sasha wasn't being seen for who she was, it was because somehow she didn't believe in herself, or it was because she was hanging around people who were incapable of seeing beyond her beauty.

Sasha dominated the conversation for most of the drive to Carmel. Malcolm argued with her occasionally, even though he knew better than to argue with a drunk. He was glad she was drunk though, gave him a nice snapshot of what she was really all about. The image he had of her lovely little tail feathers was beginning to molt.

They decided to have dinner at the Rio Grill. Once seated, the topic shifted to Sheila's jealousy of Sasha flirting with Shane.

"Sheila, it just tears my heart apart that you don't trust me," Sasha said, in a drunk, serious tone. "I mean, my best friend Ginger is away at college on the east coast. Her boyfriend lives up in northern California, and I sleep with him, completely naked, at least once a month and she knows it. We aren't doing anything, but if we were, Ginger wouldn't care. She'd rather me be fucking him than some other woman who she doesn't even know."

"Well, that might be alright for your friend..." Sheila said, before being interrupted by Miss Freelove.

"We talk all the time on the phone and joke about it. Ginger's not jealous one bit," Sasha said.

"Well, I am, and if it gets in the way, you can count on me saying something about it. I mean, after all, he's my man."

"Sheila, you don't need to worry about anything happening

between me and Sean… I mean Shane. I mean, I think he's cute and all, but I'm much more interested in fucking you!" Miss Freelove boldly announced.

"How would that work?" Sheila asked, in a caught off guard, confused tone.

"Well, if you really want to know, I can show you," Sasha answered confidently.

Sheila didn't respond, and then Sasha started harping on her about trust, contradicting what she had just said about wanting Sheila's instant trust. She started preaching about how trust was earned, or at least developed over time.

Malcolm had been listening to everything without offering an opinion, although he was certainly forming one.

"Oh, my goodness, I think I've been talking too much," Sasha suddenly announced, realizing that she'd been rambling since they'd left Big Sur. "So, Malcolm, you don't have a girlfriend; what are your issues?" Sasha asked, two seconds after she realized that she'd been rambling.

"Issues?" he asked.

"Yeah, issues. You know, I mean, everyone has issues."

"I don't know, what are my issues?" he asked. As opinionated as she was, he figured she already had his issues all figured out.

"I don't know either. I was hoping that you could tell me," Sasha answered.

"Well, Sasha, first of all, I'm not gonna blab out a bunch of stuff just to satisfy a complete stranger's curiosity. I mean, hell, I don't even know you, not that I'm opposed to getting to know you. Maybe we could hang out some, then we might really learn some things about each other and not even have to talk about our *issues*."

Sasha listened and Sheila looked on.

"And the whole concept of *issues* bugs the hell out of me, too. The word is so damn limiting. Issues are just another way of labeling a person, and then they end up trying to escape the identity that someone else has pasted on them. It's part of that whole psychobabble mentality that claims to enhance life but really destroys it."

Sasha didn't want any part of Malcolm, and he was finished arguing with a drunk. Actually, she wasn't even the type of woman he'd pick to argue with sober.

"Sheila, it just really hurts me to the core that you don't trust me," Sasha suggested, shifting back to the same crap she was on before she got onto her soapbox of preaching the need for trust to be earned.

"So Sasha, where are your parents?" Malcolm asked, jerking her away from her attack on Sheila, and hopefully into the inner world of her own *issues*.

"They're in Canada."

"Is that where you're from?"

"Yes, but my parents moved to Canada from eastern Europe years ago," she answered.

"Do you get along with your parents?"

"Oh, yes my parents love me. They are always begging me to come home so they can take care of me, but it's just too heavy around there. My brother's a mental case, a real mess. That's why they want me to come home so badly," Sasha reasoned.

"Yeah, so they can have a *normal* child around to brag about," Malcolm said, thinking: *you dizzy bitch*.

"Exactly!" Sasha answered.

They had dessert before leaving the Rio Grill a little before eleven. Sasha asked to stop off at that bank around the corner so she could make a deposit into the teller machine.

"Do either of you have piercings?" Sasha asked, as they drove toward the bank. Sheila and Malcolm just looked at each other in amazement.

"You know, I didn't know much about my pussy until I got my clit pierced. Did you know that the place that they pierce a woman's clit is called the hood?"

"It seems like that would hurt," Sheila said.

"It wasn't any worse than having my nipples pierced. I'll show it to you sometime, Sheila," Sasha volunteered.

Then she started in on how she'd had the best sex in her life two weeks earlier, but they never really did it all the way, and then she started complaining about how the guy didn't like her piercings. Then she bounced back to wanting to be with Sheila, only to switch to how the whole sex thing had to be mind, body, and soul combined, and how American society had influenced and screwed up so many people. Malcolm wanted to ask her why the hell she was in California if she felt so strongly about the American influence.

He had a blast watching as she tried to balance her drunk-ass-opinionated-self on her come-fuck-me high heels while trying to navigate through the bank's automated computer system. Malcolm's father had phoned and left a message on his cellular while they were at dinner, so he returned the call when Sheila went to help Sasha make her deposit.

"Hey dad, how's it going?"

"Oh, pretty good. You up in the mountains?" he asked.

"Actually, I'm in Carmel with two girls, one drunker than a skunk and the other cold sober."

He laughed without responding to Malcolm's comment, which probably meant that his mother was close by. "Well, we're leaving for the Sierras in the morning, and we thought that if you were up that way you could join us."

"I'm not sure when I'll be back that way. I'm kind of chasing this hot young thing over in Big Sur right now, so it looks like I might be over this way for a while."

He laughed again without using words to respond.

"Mom and Justice are going with me, and I just wanted to let you know in case you were around," his father answered. Justice was Malcolm's nephew, so his father's response confirmed his mother was most likely listening to their conversation.

After getting Sasha back in the truck, she started babbling about wanting to go dancing. Malcolm ignored her and started the drive back to Big Sur. Sheila promised to take her dancing the following week. Then Sasha lay over on the seat and fell asleep for the rest of the drive back to Big Sur. Sheila used Malcolm's mobile to phone Shane at work, trying to catch him before he left. She wanted him to meet her at her house, but the phoned dropped the call before she could speak to him.

"It's a mess."

"What?"

"You know," Sheila said, turning to the back seat to check on Sasha.

"Oh, yeah, I got you."

"I hate being jealous."

"Maybe it's right to feel jealous."

"Not the way I feel jealous."

"Fuck it! You're jealous. Accept it."

"It just makes me feel so awful inside."

"Trying not to feel jealous makes you feel awful inside," Malcolm said, extending his right hand to her. Sheila took his hand in hers, and he squeezed it. "I'll always be here for you Sheila. That's a done deal; so don't even question it. Find something else to worry about," he added. "Something worth worrying about, and I mean it."

When they arrived back at Nepenthe, they drove right to Sasha's van to dump her off. Shane and Sean were just getting off work and walking to Shane's truck that was parked near Sasha's van. Sheila spotted Shane, and jumped out to catch him before he left. Sasha got out at the same time, staggered to Sean and started hanging on him. They were all standing about twenty feet in front of the Tahoe. Malcolm did a three-point turn and then pulled up next to them.

"Hey Sean, looks like you recovered from earlier," Malcolm said, watching as he steadied Sasha.

"It's all a front. No one recovers that quickly from a day like today."

"You need a ride?"

"Sure."

"Where do you live?"

"Down by Pfeiffer Beach."

"Hop in."

Malcolm wished everyone pleasant dreams as Sean climbed into the Tahoe for the ride home.

"It'll get better soon, Sean."

"It's always darkest before the dawn. Hell, it can't get much worse," Sean answered, as they pulled out onto Highway 1.

"Hell, before you know it, some little honey'll be knocking on your door wanting to work you over. If you're lucky, it might even be Sasha."

"Isn't she a work of art?"

"And then some. She's drunker than fuck tonight. Maybe you missed your chance."

"I could pick up the phone and have a woman over here like that," Sean said, snapping his fingers. "Hell, I don't need a woman. I need to dry out for a month."

"Maybe you need Sasha."

"If that girl comes around me, she's going to get a fucking like she's never had before. Hell, if she comes around, she better plan on staying for a few days."

Malcolm turned off the paved road onto a dirt trail and followed it up the hill to Sean's home.

"Wanna come in and smoke a bowler?"

"No thanks man. I gave that up when I quit the booze."

"Man, you really are a puritan, aren't you?"

"Believe me, I'd love to smoke a bowler with you, but I can't. I used to wake up trembling, Sean. It took three ten-milligram valiums just to get the shakes to stop, not to mention all the booze and smoke to get me through the rest of the day. For me, it's life or death."

"I hear you man. I may just have to go do the time and get cleaned out myself before this is all over."

"It's not all that bad."

"Yeah, I guess there's still women," he said, looking at Malcolm with a glimmer of hope in his eyes.

Chapter 41

More than a week had passed since Malcolm and Jenny last spoke. He was having a hard time swallowing her "poor baby" remark. She'd phoned once when he was gone and left a message. He purposely returned the call to her home in town over the weekend when she was hiding away at the cabin because he wasn't ready to talk with her.

Malcolm no longer wanted to be treated by Jenny. His original intention was being with her as a woman and that was the only way he was willing to meet her in the future. He didn't like the idea of being the patient and her playing doctor, and he didn't like her way of belittling him and keeping him at arms length. He no longer trusted her to work on his body because he didn't believe that she could actually see him for the man or the person he really was. If she couldn't clearly see him, how could she help facilitate a healing?

Jenny finally caught Malcolm at home. She phoned and wanted to meet for coffee the following day. They made plans to meet at the same café where he'd waited for her the day he had helped her move things to Cachagua. She had an appointment to get her hair cut at noon, so she suggested that they meet at ten-thirty.

Malcolm arrived at the café the next morning a little before ten-thirty. He waited for an hour, but Jenny never showed up. He finally got pissed but at the same time concerned, so he left, and on the drive home phoned her from his mobile just to make sure she hadn't been in a wreck. She answered and told him that she'd just called and left a message at his studio. Jenny had overslept and had to cut him short, saying she had to rush to make it to her hair appointment and would call later.

She phoned his mobile at one-thirty that afternoon and suggested they meet for lunch at the café where they were to have met earlier. Malcolm was around the corner at a coffee shop studying, so it only took him a few minutes to get to the café. Jenny and Diana showed up half-an-hour later. They ordered lunch and sat down at a table outside where Diana could join them.

"So, why haven't you been coming for your treatments?"

"Doesn't feel right," Malcolm answered, feeling righteously justified in the position he'd taken with her. He'd been waiting for the question.

"What do you mean?"

"Something doesn't feel right. I just don't feel like you see me."

"What does that have to do with your back?"

"Well, I mean, like the last time I was there I wanted to take a walk with you, and you just looked at me and said: 'Oh you poor baby.'"

"And?"

"It felt a lot like when you jokingly called me a pervert."

"I thought we cleared that up?"

"I thought we did too, but something just doesn't feel right. So, how do you see me?"

"What do you mean?"

"I mean, how do you see me? Do you see me as a poor baby or a man?"

"I see you how I've always seen you," she answered with a confused look, but not answering his question.

"Well, I'm beginning to wonder."

"What's there to wonder about?"

"I want to be seen for the man I am, not some poor, helpless baby. I don't see how we can have a relationship until you can really see me."

"So what are you saying?"

"I'm saying that when I invited you to dinner that first time, my intention was to come together with you as man and woman. I've been trying to talk to you about this for while, but you just won't make yourself available to me except at your office, and I don't feel that I can speak freely with you there. Becoming your patient was not my original intention and it doesn't feel right to meet you on a professional basis unless we can also meet person to person as equals. It's as if you can label me as someone who is wounded and in need of help, then you can reduce me down to something that you can control, just like the pervert and poor baby thing."

"Oh, now I know why I haven't wanted to be around you. You've created this whole drama in your mind," Jenny said, shaking her head. "This is obviously your stuff, not mine!" she added, holding up her hands in an attempt to shield against what Malcolm had to say. "I'm really uncomfortable with this. I really feel like leaving right now."

Malcolm didn't respond. The thing about him being responsible for the drama had thrown him and caused more confusion. She fidgeted in her chair.

"So what about your back?" she asked, still unable to hear what Malcolm was trying to say.

"What about it?" he asked, throwing it back into her lap.

"Well, you know how important that is to me."

"I'm more interested in exploring the possibility of having a relationship with you."

"What's the difference in having a relationship and exploring a relationship?"

"I want a man-woman relationship with you, not a doctor-patient relationship."

"We are, but I've been busy doing my own thing lately. Sometimes I go for months not talking to my friends."

"Well, I'm not interested in anything like that."

"So, since I'm not always available, you don't want to be my friend now."

"No, I want to hang out with you. If I didn't I wouldn't be here right now."

"Are you saying you want to have sex with me then?"

Malcolm didn't answer. He wanted to sleep with her, or thought he did, but that wasn't his only agenda.

"What are you trying to say?" she prodded.

Malcolm didn't answer because he was trying to choose his words, not wanting to add more confusion into their discussion.

"Are you saying that you want me to be your girlfriend?" Jenny asked in an impatient tone that was growing more impatient.

"No, I'm..." Malcolm hesitated, still looking for the right words.

"Are you saying that you want us to be exclusive?"

He still couldn't answer her. She wasn't giving him a chance.

"I don't get it. Are you saying that you want to have sex?" she asked again. She was firing off one question after another without allowing his answers to form. He was trying to answer according to what he felt, but she wasn't giving him enough space to access his true feelings. "Is this about sex?" she asked again.

"Yes, but no," Malcolm answered.

"I've already told you that I have no sex drive right now, and that I don't want that type of relationship. My body doesn't want it."

"This isn't about sex. I mean, yeah, that would be nice if it happened, but I'm not just talking about sleeping with you."

"Well, then what do you mean?" she asked disgustedly. "You know, I'm really uncomfortable with all of this right now… I want to leave, but I…"

"I mean, it doesn't even have to be sex. I'd just like to cuddle up with you and watch a movie once in a while."

"I don't feel like doing that. I told you that already. You want that, and you're imagining it with me."

"I'm not imagining it. I want it."

"I don't. I don't want any type of conventional relationship."

"Alright, fair enough," Malcolm said, disappointed, but relieved at the same time from gaining some clarity.

"I've already told you this," she said in a very defensive tone.

"The last time we talked about this, you said that you didn't feel right about it, that it might change and it might not change for you, but since neither of us were seeing anyone else there was no need to act on anything."

"Oh, I see what's going on here. We took that two different ways. I'm just living in the present. If it happens, it happens, but I'm not planning on anything. It's not like I'm willing to accept a waiting period and then we'll have sex or anything like that."

"Okay, so you don't care if I start seeing someone else?"

She didn't answer.

"Because I want to be with a woman who wants to be my lover."

"No, I think you *should* be open to that," she finally answered, but her tone had changed. She wasn't so defensive.

"Okay, fine. That's all I need to know. You know, I really like you Jenny. I just don't want to be known as the asshole who dumped you for another woman a few months down the road."

"Why? Did you meet someone?" she asked in a distant tone. It was almost as if she was just catching on to what he'd said about seeing someone else.

"No, I haven't been open to it because of the confusion between us," Malcolm answered. He wondered why she had asked the question in the first place if she wasn't really interested in a sexual relationship with him. Jenny's "Why? Did you meet someone?" was another one of her subtle hooks that he had swallowed in the past. It was her way to keep him dangling. She couldn't have him, but she wasn't willing to let him go either.

"I really like you too, Malcolm. But having a relationship like that just doesn't feel right for me. I mean, whoever gets you will really be lucky."

"Thank you," Malcolm answered, feeling relieved. "I'm finally getting clear on all this."

"Is that it?" she asked, fidgeting around in her seat.

"I think so. Can we just sit here without saying anything for a few minutes just to make sure we're finished?"

She nodded an okay. They sat for a few minutes while Malcolm petted Diana. Then they went their separate ways. He felt relieved, felt the freedom to go on with his life. He also felt that he could now get away with screwing one of her friends without catching too much hell over it. But, something else hadn't been resolved.

They had cleared the air on defining the personal type of relationship they were to have, but she had side stepped something else. Even in this setting, Malcolm didn't feel accepted in the process of their coming together. Her discomfort and defensiveness had not allowed them to get to the core issue at hand. He didn't feel respected by Jenny, didn't feel honored and it had nothing to do with sex or having her receive him in any physical way.

His masculinity had not been acknowledged or honored; the same masculinity that she'd been trying to poke holes into with her poisonous words: 'slut', 'pervert' and 'poor baby'. They were not words you called a man who you respected and held in esteem. They were words that she had used unconsciously; they were flippant and thoughtless. Much of what consciously came out of Jenny was from her heart. But the words: 'slut', 'pervert' and 'poor baby' came from a dark, unconscious place within her. These words were poisonous darts, hidden in reactive flippant jokes, aimed at the core part of his manhood, his very being.

Malcolm had held up a mirror for Jenny to see something that she didn't want to see. She couldn't stand to see that side of herself; she had unconsciously shifted it to sex and side stepped the core issue. It didn't appear that she'd be ready to explore that part of their relationship anytime soon. Instead of saying, "exploring the possibility of a relationship," he should have said, "exploring the possibility of *continuing* the relationship," because that's what he'd really meant.

His first clue should have been her remark about Diana being kinder than most people. His second sign should have been her aversion to men, especially the testosterone-riddled men she despised and liked to joke about, men like Malcolm. Maybe he'd been a little more successful in hiding his hard-on than all those other distasteful males who roamed the world with the sole purpose of trying to slip the wiener to dear little Miss Jenny.

Part of Malcolm's problem was that after unsuccessfully working on her for the first few months, sleeping with her had become more of a challenge than a desire. He'd learned something, though. He'd learned another reason why he'd married Shelly. It was the same reason he'd become involved with Jenny. Neither of them could fully receive and celebrate him. They couldn't celebrate the man, the physical man, he was. It was almost like he was addicted to this sort of abuse, this type of woman. Yes, it seemed that Malcolm was addicted to such a dream.

Their disdain for his masculinity, his sexuality and celebrating his humanity, was perhaps also his own disdain.

Somehow, he had dreamed them both into his life, to reflect an inner drama that was relentlessly waged between the masculine and feminine images within his soul. In other words, a subtle voice within constantly judged and found countless faults with his physical existence, his humanity. Deep down inside, unconsciously, Malcolm was still run by the puritanical belief of the flesh being sin.

The disdain he carried for himself was secretly whispering, trying to get him to pull the trigger. It was amazing that he hadn't wrecked a car or flown the Bonanza into a mountainside. It was miraculous that he'd actually survived this first half of his life. He owed both Shelly and Jenny a thank you. They'd helped him to see deeper into what his drinking and drugging had been all about: a slow attempt at suicide. It was becoming clearer to Malcolm how much his spirit longed to be separated from his physical body. It seemed that this was the greatest cause of his existential suffering.

Chapter 42

It had been awhile since Malcolm had paid Turner a visit. He drove over unannounced, knocked on the front door and, a minute or so later, Carson peeped through the blinds and announced Malcolm's arrival to the whole household, but ran away without opening the door. It was Turner who came to let Malcolm in.

"Hey, new carpet, huh?" Malcolm asked, noticing the smell as soon as he stepped into the living room.

"Yeah, come on in," Turner said quietly, holding his right index finger to his lips and then motioning for Malcolm to follow him. "Cassi's upstairs sleeping, and I don't want Carson to wake her," he said, wanting Malcolm to be quiet, so Carson would stay quiet as well.

Malcolm followed Turner into the kitchen where he resumed his domestic chore of loading the dishwasher. They talked about a few things, but Carson kept interrupting, wanting to be the center of attention. Turner kept telling him to quit yelling because he was going to wake his mother and his younger siblings. Carson would whisper for a couple of minutes and then shift back to full volume. Turner gave up.

"Well, I'm sterile," Turner announced, as he closed the dishwasher.

"When'd you do it?"

"Yesterday," he answered, as he wiped down the counter.

"Doesn't seem to have slowed you down any," Malcolm commented, intrigued with his agility. "Are you icing 'em?"

"Was earlier."

"Well, you better take it easy. Lewis was running around the next day like you are, and about two days afterwards he could hardly move."

"Come on," Turner said, leading Malcolm across the new carpet into the living room.

"Man this stuff is really nice," Malcolm said. "You bought a good pad this time."

"Really makes a difference doesn't it." Turner said, as he sat down on the couch. The discovery channel was on, and Carson crawled up between Turner and Malcolm.

"Look at this," Turner said, pulling down his sweats and showing Malcolm the hole in his sack right below the base of his penis.

"Holy shit!"

Carson started belly laughing. Malcolm was uncertain if it was in response to his "holy shit," his father baring his balls, or the discovery channel. Carson looked up the stairway, and Malcolm followed his gaze. Cassi was walking downstairs carrying their new baby girl, Mallory Catherine. Connor, their two-year-old, followed, whining and tugging on Cassi's pant leg.

"Somebody must be moving in next door," Cassi said, sounding half asleep as she looked out the window to the home across the street, continuing down the stairs. "Must be Shana," she added.

"Who's Shana," Malcolm asked without missing a beat. He stood and walked to the window. A U-haul van had backed into the neighbor's driveway.

"You haven't met Shana, Patti's older sister?" Cassi asked smiling. For years, Cassi had been tolerating Malcolm's inclination for younger women. She kind of liked it, especially with her being so much younger than Turner.

"I sure haven't," Malcolm answered. Shana and Patti's parents were neighbors of Turner and Cassi. "She doesn't have a half bad bottom half," Malcolm announced, watching Shana making tracks toward her mother's front door. "Actually, her top half's looking pretty damn good, too. Hell, she's all hotty! She single?"

"Last I heard, she was having troubles with her guy," Cassi answered, standing and rocking Mallory in place. The baby was restless and her mother's motion seemed to sooth her. "She was a nanny down in San Diego, but looks like she's not anymore," Cassi said, with her magic smile.

"Keep an eye on that for me will you, Cassi?"

"Sure thing," she answered, pacifying Malcolm while she continued to rock her infant.

"Hey, Turner, if I didn't have a bad back, and you didn't

have a hole in your sack, we could run over there and help unload that U-haul," Malcolm announced, as he sat down between Turner and Carson. Malcolm looked up to find Cassi grinning and shaking her head. She'd given up on changing Malcolm's behavior around her kids. If the truth were known, she'd probably given up on Turner and herself toning it down as well.

"I'm surprised he did it," Cassi said.

"She'd have another," said Turner, as he continued his gaze into the television.

"I told him not to do it," Cassi said, still looking out the window while rocking Mallory in her arms.

Cassi finally got Mallory Catherine quieted down and laid her in the bassinet. Connor had shifted out of his sleepy funk and was running around throwing a ball to anyone who would throw it back to him. Carson was restless. Cassi knew that the boys needed to get outside to move around, so she took them out to play and left Turner and Malcolm to watch over Mallory.

Turner and Malcolm could finally talk man-talk, but as soon as they started, Mallory began to cry. Turner got up to attend to her and brought her back to join them. Malcolm started telling him about a few of the deals he had going on with the women, pissing and moaning about how he wasn't getting laid. The more Malcolm talked, the whinier Mallory got.

Malcolm watched Turner trying to comfort his newborn and wondered what it would be like to have fathered a daughter. He started to talk about the Jenny drama he'd dreamed up to take the place of Kate's absence, and Mallory began to fuss again. Turner held her to his chest and lightly patted her back. Malcolm decided to shut up. Turner didn't want to hear about Malcolm's problems with the feminine, and neither did Mallory Catherine.

www.malcolmclay.com

Also by Mel Mathews:

LeRoi

SamSara

Fisher King Books can be purchased online at:

www.fisherkingpress.com

or by calling:

1-800-228-9316

LeRoi

ISBN 0-9776076-0-7

The most intriguing thing about Malcolm Clay was his battered MG. And now, with a cough of black smoke, even that had quit. Fortunately, the car had breath enough to limp up to the only two buildings in town: the garage and the diner across the street. Neither looked to have much reason to exist. No one was around. Maybe the mechanic was in the café getting a coffee. Maybe he'd had a heart attack from one strip of bacon too many. Maybe the place was an abandoned set left over from a bad remake of *Our Town*. "I've died," Malcolm thought, "and purgatory is the back road to Pumpkinpatch." There was nothing to do but wait since his cell phone had lost a signal about the same time the car had given up the ghost. He slumped back into the seat of the MG, then stood back up. "Well," he said to himself as he headed towards the diner, "if I'm in hell, I might as well find a bag of marshmallows, a pack of hot dogs and a wire coat hanger."

LeRoi is a story about blame and fear. Come along on the ride as Malcolm Clay stumbles upon what has secretly been running his life.

"This is a story of a man who is not afraid to be who he really is. Its authenticity and vulnerability made me laugh, cry, and wonder if I also have the courage to live an authentic life. A good read that is painfully sweet, honest and hopeful..." -- Sharon E. Martin - Atlanta, GA --

"I've read few novels written by men that have such keen insight into the struggle for truth and intimacy. To admit one's frailties is unusual. Malcolm Clay manages to do that in the most unusual of places, which is revealing in itself. One need not go on a trek to India or elsewhere to discover one's Self. Sometimes our greatest teachers are working the tiller at a diner..." -- Dana Lucas --

Fisher King Books can be purchased online at:

www.fisherkingpress.com

or by calling:

1-800-228-9316

SamSara

ISBN 0-9776076-2-3

After settling his bill, Malcolm returned to the sanctuary to say goodbye.

"Well, Niamh, I probably won't be seeing you again."

"So, this is it, huh, Malcolm?"

"This is it," he answered, as she came out from behind the bar.

"It's good to know you Niamh," he said, reaching for her hand. Instead, she kissed his cheek.

"Say, Niamh, how do I get out of here and to the closest Dart station?" he asked, a bit set back by her gesture.

"Ah, Malcolm, that's an easy one," she answered, almost as if she had anticipated this very question. "When you walk out the front door of Samsara here, you'll go left down Dawson Street until you've reach Trinity College, then follow the wall around to your right and stay on that path. It'll wind a bit, but stay on that path and eventually you'll see the bridge where the train crosses. It'll take you about ten minutes."

"Okay, Niamh, sounds easy, and I can always ask for help if I get lost."

"Listen to me, Malcolm," Niamh commanded in a firm, direct tone. "Just do exactly as I say: follow the path and you'll have no problems."

"Okay, I'll trust you Niamh," he answered, and trust her is what he was about to do.

* * * * *

In **SamSara**, it seems that Malcolm Clay has finally broken away from the chains that once bound him, or has he? He's certainly on the path as he wrestles with those old ghosts from his past. But it just might be the kiss from an angel that sets him free.

Cover Image:

The Sacrificial Man, a faceless man who has lost an identity, or better yet, all the identities that he once believed defined his masculine nature and his very existence. His entire life, up to this point, has been spent searching outside of himself in the ephemeral world, all vain attempts at an inner reconciliation.

Like Demeter, this man's inner consort, his soul, in raging grief, digs Her heels in and says: "No more! You give me back what is dearest to my heart, you give me back the raped and ravished feminine, and only then will I put an end to the scorching of this dry barren wasteland."

Menopause Man is about the transformation of a primitive man, concerned only with himself, his insatiable desires. This is a story about the rebirth of a man's inner reality, but not without his ego clutching, clinging to those old dead idols whom he once served and who once served him.

This story is about learning to see with the heart, learning that all that has been searched for over the years can only be found by seeing with the heart, not by falling prey to a various sundry of conventional dogmas that time and time again have failed him and left him lost, wandering about in those old barren deserts of dashed dreams.

Menopause Man is a story about the subordination of a primitive man's ego and all the futile battles that are waged in an attempt to sustain his illusion of domination, as he slowly acquiesces to the feminine, as he reluctantly learns to bow to the Goddess, to the essence of his soul that is embedded at the very core of his being.